P9-CCV-011

Shadow Dance

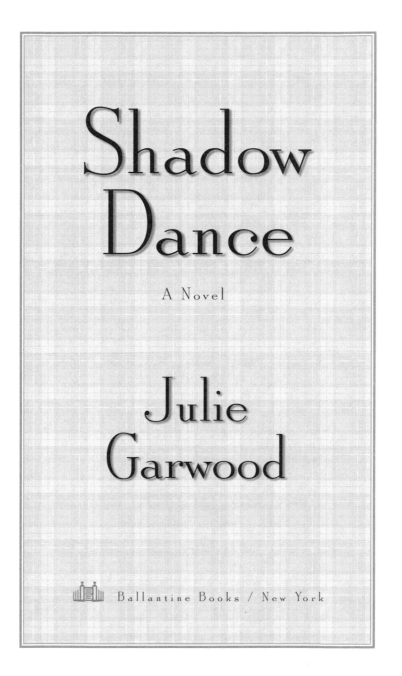

Shadow Dance

A Novel

Julie Garwood

Ballantine Books / New York

Copyright © 2007 by Julie Garwood

Published in the United States by Ballantine Books, an imprint of The Random House
Publishing Group, a division of Random House, Inc., New York.

BALLANTINE and colophon are registered trademarks of Random House, Inc.

ISBN 978-0-345-45386-0

Library of Congress Cataloging-in-Publication Data
Garwood, Julie.
Shadow dance / Julie Garwood.
p.   cm.
ISBN-13: 978-0-345-45386-0 (hardcover : acid-free paper)
ISBN-10: 0-345-45386-7 (hardcover : acid-free paper)
ISBN-13: 978-0-345-45387-7 (pbk. : acid-free paper)
ISBN-10: 0-345-45387-5 (pbk. : acid-free paper)
I. Title.

PS3557.A8427S53 2007
813'.54—dc22   2006035243

Printed in the United States of America on acid-free paper

www.ballantinebooks.com

1   3   5   7   9   8   6   4   2

First Edition

Book design by Susan Turner

Shadow Dance

Chapter One

THIS WEDDING WAS NO SMALL AFFAIR. THERE WERE SEVEN bridesmaids, seven groomsmen, three ushers, two altar boys, three lectors, and enough firepower inside the church to wipe out half the congregation. All but two of the groomsmen were armed.

The federal agents weren't happy about the crowd, but they knew it would be pointless to complain. The father of the groom, Judge Buchanan, wasn't about to miss such an auspicious occasion, no matter how many death threats he received. The judge was in the midst of hearing a racketeering case back in Boston, and the federal agents assigned to protect him would continue their detail until the trial was over and a decision had been rendered.

The church was packed to capacity. The Buchanans were such a large family that some of the groom's relatives and friends spilled over to the bride's side. Most had traveled to the little town of Silver Springs, South Carolina, from Boston, but there were several Buchanan cousins who had come all the way from Inverness, Scotland, to celebrate the marriage of Dylan Buchanan and Kate MacKenna.

The bride and groom were deliriously happy, and their wedding was a joyous occasion, but it never would have happened if it weren't for Dylan's sister, Jordan. Kate and Jordan were best friends and had been roommates in college. The first time Jordan took Kate to her family's home on Nathan's Bay, all the siblings had gathered to celebrate their father's birthday. Jordan certainly had no intention of matchmaking, and she definitely wasn't aware at the time that there had been a spark between Kate and her brother Dylan, so years later when the spark ignited into a flame and the two became engaged, no one was more surprised—or thrilled—than she.

Every last detail of the happy event had been meticulously planned. Like Kate, Jordan was a great organizer, and so she was given the responsibility of dressing up the church for the occasion. Admittedly, Jordan had gotten a little carried away. She'd put flowers everywhere, both inside and outside the church. Raspberry pink roses and creamy white magnolias lined the stone walkway, their lovely scent greeting guests as they arrived. Pink and white roses delicately intertwined with baby's breath in large wreaths with wide, lace-trimmed satin ribbons hung down on each side of the old weathered double doors. Jordan had actually considered giving the doors a fresh coat of paint but at the last minute had come to her senses and left them alone.

Kate had also asked Jordan to take care of the music, and Jordan had gone a little overboard on that assignment too. She'd started out with the notion of hiring a pianist and a singer for the ceremony and ended up with an orchestra. There were violins, a piano, a flute, and two trumpets. Seated in the balcony, the musicians played Mozart to entertain the gathering celebrants. When the groomsmen lined up in front of the altar, the music was to stop; the trumpets would then sound, the crowd would rise to their feet, and the pomp and splendor would begin.

The bride and bridesmaids waited in a dressing room just off the vestibule. The time had come. The trumpets should now be playing to begin the ceremony, but they were silent. Kate sent Jordan to find out what the delay was.

Mozart's lovely notes covered the noise of the door squeaking as Jordan peeked inside the church. She spotted one of the federal agents standing in an alcove on the left side of the church and tried not to think about the reason he was there. The bodyguards weren't really necessary, she thought, considering all the law enforcement professionals in her family. Of her six brothers, two were FBI agents, one was a federal attorney, one was a Navy SEAL in training, one was a cop, and the youngest, Zachary, was in college and hadn't yet decided which side of the law looked more appealing to him. Also standing at the altar would be Noah Clayborne, a close friend of the family and yet another FBI agent.

The agents assigned to her father didn't care how many others there were. Their job was clearly defined, and they wouldn't be distracted by the celebration. Jordan finally decided that they were a comfort, not a hindrance, and she should focus on the wedding and stop worrying.

She spotted one of her brothers slowly making his way toward the back of the church. It was Alec, Dylan's best man. She smiled as she watched him approach. Alec had gone all out for the wedding. He worked undercover, but he'd cut his hair for the occasion, an impressive consideration on his part to be sure. His job usually required that he dress and look like a deranged serial killer. Jordan had barely recognized him when he arrived at the rehearsal the night before. Now Alec stopped to speak to one of the bodyguards. She waved to get his attention and motioned for him to step out to the vestibule.

As the door closed behind him, she asked in a whisper, "Why aren't we starting? It's time."

"Dylan sent me back to tell Kate that we'll start in a couple of minutes," he answered.

Alec's collar was partially inverted, and she reached up to fix it. "Your collar's folded over," she said before he could ask. "Quit squirming."

When she had finished with the collar and straightened his tie, she stepped back. Alec cleaned up nice, she thought. The funny thing was, Regan, his wife, loved him however he looked. Love did weird things to people, Jordan decided.

"Is Kate worried that Dylan will take off?" Alec asked with a glint in his eye that told her he was joking. They were only a couple of minutes late now.

"Not really," Jordan answered. "She left five minutes ago."

He shook his head. "Not funny," he said, grinning. "I've got to get back."

"Wait. You still haven't explained why we're waiting. Is something wrong?"

"Stop worrying. Nothing's wrong." He was about to go back inside but suddenly stopped. "Jordan?"

"Yes?"

"You look nice."

It would have been a lovely compliment from a brother who never gave compliments if Alec himself hadn't looked so surprised by his observation.

She was about to return the favor when the outer church doors flew open, and Noah Clayborne came rushing inside tying his tie.

The man never failed to make a strong impression. Women loved him, and Jordan had to admit she could understand his appeal. Tall, athletic, outgoing, handsome—he was a man's man and a woman's fantasy. His sandy blond hair was always slightly in need of a trim, and his piercing blue eyes sparkled with mischief whenever he gave one of his devilish grins.

"Am I late?" he asked.

"No, it's good," Alec said. "Okay, Jordan, we can start now."

"Where have you been?" she asked Noah, exasperated.

Rather than answering, he gave her a quick once-over, smiled, and followed Alec inside. Jordan felt like throwing her hands up. He'd been with a woman, she decided. The man was incorrigible.

She should have been peeved, but instead she laughed. To be that free, that uninhibited . . . Jordan couldn't imagine what that would feel like. But Noah certainly knew the feeling.

Jordan hurried back to the waiting room, pushed the door open, and said, "It's time."

Kate motioned for Jordan to come to her. "What was the hold-up?" she asked.

"Noah. He just got here. If I had to guess, I'd say he was with a woman."

"That's not a guess," Kate whispered. "It's a given. I had no idea what a playboy he was until I saw it for myself. He disappeared from the rehearsal dinner last night with three of my bridesmaids, and all three looked like they hadn't slept when they got to the church this morning."

Jordan crossed her arms as she looked around the room, trying to decide which of the bridesmaids had disappeared with Noah. "Shame on him," she remarked.

"Oh, it wasn't all his fault," Kate replied. "They went willingly."

Kate's aunt Nora announced that they weren't going anywhere until they heard the trumpets, and then she began to line everyone up.

Kate motioned Jordan closer. "I need to ask a favor. It's kind of a tough one."

Difficult or not, it didn't matter. Kate had been there through thick and thin for Jordan, and Jordan would do anything she could to help her.

"You name it. I'll do it," she said.

"Would you please make Noah behave?"

Okay, maybe not *anything*. Jordan took a breath and whispered, "You're asking the impossible. Trying to control him is laughable. It would be easier to teach a bear to use a computer. Give me that assignment, and I promise I'll give it my all. But Noah? Come on, Kate . . ."

"Actually, it's just Isabel I'm concerned about. Did you see the way she glued herself to his side at the rehearsal?"

"Is that why you paired me with him in the wedding? To keep your little sister away from him?"

"No," she said. "But after seeing Isabel in action last night, I'm glad I did. I can't blame her. Noah's adorable. Aside from Dylan, of course, I think he's one of the sexiest men I've ever met. He oozes charisma, doesn't he?"

Jordan nodded. "Oh, yes."

"I don't want Isabel to become another NCG," she said. "And I don't want any more of my wedding party to disappear suddenly."

"What is an NCG?" she asked.

Kate grinned. "A Noah Clayborne Groupie."

Jordan burst into laughter.

"You're the only person I know who seems to be immune to his charms. He treats you like a sister."

Aunt Nora clapped her hands. "Okay, everyone. It's time to go."

Kate grabbed Jordan's arm. "I'm not budging until you promise."

"Oh, all right. I'll do it."

The trumpets sounded again. Since Jordan was to be the first to walk down the aisle, she was nervous and clutched her bouquet to her waist with both hands. She'd always been known as the family klutz, but she was determined not to trip over her own feet today. She would pay attention and concentrate on putting one foot in front of the other.

She waited in the center of the doorway until she heard Aunt Nora whisper, "Go."

She took a deep breath and started walking. The aisle seemed a mile long. Standing in front of the altar, Noah waited. When she was halfway there, he came toward her, looking amazing in his tuxedo. She relaxed. No one was paying her any attention. Every eye—at least every female eye—was on Noah.

She concentrated on his smile and took hold of his arm. For a brief second she looked into his eyes and saw the mischievous glimmer.

Oh, Lord, she had her work cut out for her.

Chapter Two

THE CEREMONY WAS BEAUTIFUL. TEARS ROLLED DOWN JORDAN'S cheeks when her brother and her best friend exchanged vows. She thought no one had noticed her red eyes, but when she took hold of Noah's arm while walking out of the church, he leaned down to her and whispered, "Crybaby."

Of course he'd noticed. He never missed anything.

After additional photos were taken, the attendants were separated, and Jordan ended up riding to the reception with the bride and groom. She could have been riding on the hood of the car, for all they noticed. They only had eyes for each other.

Kate and Dylan had entered the country club ahead of everyone else, and Jordan stood outside on the steps waiting for the rest of the wedding party to come up the circle drive to join her.

It was a beautiful evening, but there was a slight chill in the air, which was unusual for this time of year in South Carolina. The ballroom's French doors were opened to the side terrace. Tables had already been prepared with long white linen tablecloths topped with candles and centerpieces of roses and hydrangeas. Jordan knew the reception was going to be fabulous, the food exceptional—she'd gotten to taste some of Kate's selections—and the band superb. Jordan didn't plan on doing much dancing, though. It had been a long day, and she was running out of steam. A cool breeze swept across the veranda and made her shiver. She rubbed her bare arms to ward off the chill. She loved the pale pink strapless gown she was wearing, but it definitely wasn't designed to keep a body warm.

The cold wasn't the only thing bothering her. Her contact lenses were driving her crazy. Fortunately, she'd tucked her glasses into Noah's tuxedo jacket along with her lens case and lipstick. Too bad she hadn't thought to shove a cardigan in there.

She heard laughter and turned just in time to see Kate's younger sister, Isabel, take hold of Noah's arm and lean into his side. Oh, brother, here we go.

Isabel was a blond, blue-eyed beauty, but then so was Noah. Isabel's coloring was quite similar to his, and though he towered over her, they could have been related. Now that's a creepy thought, Jordan decided, since Isabel was blatantly flirting with him. She was such an innocent. Noah wasn't. Kate's sister was a very young nineteen, and from the way she was staring up at Noah with such adoration in her eyes, it was apparent she was already under his spell. To his credit, Noah wasn't encouraging her. In fact, he wasn't paying much attention to her at all. Instead, he was intently listening to Zachary, the youngest Buchanan.

"Gotcha."

Jordan hadn't heard anyone approaching and flinched in reaction. Her brother Michael poked her in her side and was now standing beside her grinning like an idiot. When he was a child, he loved to sneak up on her and their sister, Sidney, and scare the bejesus out of them. He had lived for a good scream back then. She thought he'd outgrown the horrid behavior, but apparently he sometimes regressed when he was around her. Come to think of it, all of her older brothers regressed when they were around her.

"What are you doing out here?" Michael asked.

"Waiting."

"That much is obvious. Who or what are you waiting for?"

"The other bridesmaids, but mostly Isabel. I'm supposed to keep her away from Noah."

Michael turned and took in the scene at the bottom of the steps. Isabel was practically glued to Noah. He grinned. "How's that working out?"

"So far so good."

He laughed while watching Isabel. She'd finally managed to get Noah's full attention. Her face was flushed.

"What we have here is a three-way," Michael surmised.

"Excuse me?"

"Look at them," he said. "Isabel's all starry-eyed over Noah; Zachary's all starry-eyed over Isabel; and from the scary look on that woman over there watching Noah like a cougar waiting for dinner, I'd have to say she's a mite more than starry-eyed." Michael shrugged as he added, "Actually it's a four-way."

"This is not a three-way, a four-way, or a ten-way," Jordan argued.

"I believe ten-ways would be called orgies. Ever heard of those?"

She was not about to let him bait her. Zachary had her full attention now. He was doing his best to get Isabel to notice him. Jordan wouldn't have been surprised if he'd started doing backflips.

"That's just sad," Jordan said, shaking her head.

"Zack?"

She nodded.

"I can't blame him," Michael said. "Isabel's got the whole package. The body, the face . . . without a doubt, she is—"

"Nineteen, Michael. She's nineteen."

"Yeah, I know. She's too young for Noah and me, and she thinks she's too old for Zachary."

A car carrying their parents pulled up to the entrance to the club. Jordan noticed that a bodyguard made sure he was directly behind the judge as they made their way toward the stairs. Another bodyguard rushed up the stairs ahead of him.

Michael nudged Jordan and said, "You don't need to be worrying about the bodyguards."

"You aren't worried?"

"Maybe a little. The thing is, the trial's gone on for so long now,
I've gotten used to our father with his shadows. It will all be over
in a couple of weeks after the sentencing." He nudged her again.
"Put all that out of your mind tonight, okay?"

"Yes, okay," she promised, even as she wondered how she was
going to do it.

"You should start celebrating," he said when she continued to
look worried. "You're footloose and fancy-free now that you've
sold your company and made all us stockholders rich. You can do
anything in the world you want."

"What if I don't know what I want?"

"You'll figure it out in time," he said. "You'll probably stay in
computers, don't you think?"

Jordan didn't know what she would do. She supposed she
would be wasting her degrees if she didn't continue working with
computers in some capacity. She was one of a very few women to
excel in computer innovation. She had started out with a large
corporation, but she'd ended up forming her own company, and
with her family's investment, she'd turned it into a huge success.
She had spent the last several years working nonstop. However,
when another company offered to buy her out at a phenomenal
price, she didn't hesitate to sell. She was restless and ready for a
change.

She shrugged. "Maybe I'll do some consulting work," she said.

"I know you've had a lot of offers," Michael said, "but take
some time, Jordan, before you jump into something else. Kick back
and relax. Have some fun."

Tonight was about Dylan and Kate, she reminded herself. She
could worry about her future tomorrow.

Noah was taking forever to walk up the stairs. He kept getting
waylaid by family and friends.

"Why don't you go inside?" Michael urged. "And stop worrying about Noah. He knows how young Isabel is. He's not going to do anything inappropriate."

Michael was right about Noah, but Jordan couldn't say the same for Isabel.

"Go and get her, will you? Bring her inside."

She didn't have to ask twice. Her brother was halfway across the veranda before the doorman had opened the door for her.

Jordan didn't have to be a watchdog after all. Noah was a perfect gentleman, just as Michael had predicted he would be. However, there were several rather persistent young women who couldn't keep their hands off him, and he certainly didn't seem to mind the attention. Since they were all over the age of twenty-one, Jordan figured they knew what they were doing.

Noah's virtuous behavior freed her from her responsibilities, and she actually began to enjoy herself. By nine o'clock she had had it with her contacts though. She found Noah, who still had her glasses and her lens case in his jacket pocket. He was on the dance floor with a platinum blonde swaying to the slow music. Jordan interrupted long enough to get her lens case and then headed for the ladies' room.

There was a commotion in the foyer. The strangest-looking man was arguing with the country club's security detail. They in turn were strongly urging him to leave, but he was having none of it. One of the federal agents had already patted him down to make certain he wasn't carrying a weapon.

"It's unheard of to treat a guest the way I'm being treated," he blustered. "I'm telling you Miss Isabel MacKenna will be happy to see me. I've misplaced my invitation, that's all, but I assure you I was invited."

He spotted Jordan walking toward him and gave her a bright smile. One of his front teeth crossed over the other and protruded just enough to make his upper lip catch whenever he spoke.

She didn't know whether she should interfere. He was acting so peculiar. He kept snapping his fingers and bobbing his head as though he were agreeing with someone, but no one was talking to him now. His clothing was bizarre too. Though it was the shank of the summer, the stranger wore a heavy wool tweed blazer with leather elbow patches. Needless to say, he was sweating profusely. His unruly beard was soaked through. There were streaks of gray in his beard, but she honestly couldn't judge how old he was. He was clutching an old leather folder to his chest, and there were papers sticking out every which way.

"May I be of assistance?" she asked.

"Are you with the MacKenna wedding party?"

"Yes, I am."

His smile widened as he tucked the thick folder under his arm and dug into his plaid wool vest pocket. He pulled out a wrinkled and stained card and handed it to her.

"I'm Professor Horace Athens MacKenna," he proudly announced. He waited until she had read his name on the card and then snatched it away from her and tucked it back in his vest pocket. He patted the pocket several times as he continued to smile at her.

The security detail had backed away but were warily watching him. No wonder—Professor MacKenna was a bit odd.

"I cannot tell you how thrilled I am to be here." He extended his hand and added, "This is a momentous occasion. A MacKenna marrying a Buchanan. It's stunning. Yes, stunning." He chuckled as he added, "I imagine our MacKenna ancestors are twisting and turning in their graves."

"I'm not a MacKenna," she said. "My name is Jordan Buchanan."

He didn't rip his hand away from hers, but he came close. His smile disappeared, and he seemed to recoil. "Buchanan? You're a Buchanan?"

"Yes, that's right."

"All right," he said. "All right then. It is a wedding of a MacKenna to a Buchanan. Of course I would be meeting Buchanans. Stands to reason, doesn't it?"

She was having trouble following. Professor MacKenna's accent was thick and most unusual, a combination of a Scottish brogue and a southern drawl.

"I'm sorry. Did you say the MacKenna ancestors would be turning in their graves?" she asked, certain she'd misunderstood.

"Yes, that's what I said, dearie."

Dearie? He was getting stranger by the second.

"I imagine the Buchanans would be doing a fair amount of tossing in their unholy graves too," he continued.

"And why would that be?"

"The feud, of course."

"The feud? I don't understand. What feud?"

He whipped out his handkerchief and wiped the sweat from his brow. "I'm getting ahead of myself. You must think I'm crazy."

Yes, that was exactly what she was thinking.

Fortunately, he didn't require a response to his statement. "I'm parched," he announced. He tilted his head toward the ballroom she had just exited. "I could use some refreshment."

"Yes, of course. Please, come with me."

He latched on to her arm and glanced suspiciously over his shoulder as they walked. "I'm a history professor at Franklin College in Texas. Have you heard of Franklin?"

"No," she admitted. "I haven't."

"It's a fine school. It's located just outside Austin. I teach medieval history, or at least I did until I came into some unexpected money and decided to take some time off. A sabbatical of sorts. You see," he continued, "about fifteen years ago I began researching my family history. It's been a most invigorating hobby for me. Did you know that there's bad blood between us?" He didn't wait for an answer. "Bad blood between the Buchanans and the MacKennas, I mean to say. This wedding should never have taken place if history tells us anything."

"Because of a feud?"

"That's right, dearie."

Okay, it was official, she decided. The man was wacko. She was suddenly thankful the agent had checked him for hidden weapons, and she was uneasy about taking him into the ballroom, especially if he was intent on making a scene. On the other hand, he did seem harmless, and he did know Isabel . . . at least he said he did.

"About Isabel," she began, determined to find out how the professor knew Kate's sister.

He was too caught up in his story to listen.

"The feud has been going on for centuries, and every time I think I've gotten to the root of it, lo and behold, I find another contradiction." He vigorously nodded several times and then darted another quick glance behind him as if fearful that someone would sneak up on him. "I'm proud to say I've tracked the feud all the way back to the thirteenth century," he boasted.

As soon as he paused to take a breath, Jordan suggested they find Isabel.

"I'm sure she'll be thrilled to see you," she said. Or appalled, she thought silently.

They continued along the corridor and entered the ballroom just as a waiter was passing by with a silver tray of champagne flutes. The professor took a glass, gulped the drink down, and hurriedly reached for another.

"My, that's refreshing. Is there food?" he asked bluntly.

"Yes, of course. Come, we'll find you a seat at one of the tables."

"Thank you," he said, but he didn't budge. "About Miss MacKenna . . ." His gaze circled the ballroom as he said, "I haven't actually met the woman. In fact, you'll have to point her out to me. I've been corresponding with her for some time now, but I have no idea what she looks like. I know that she's young and that she's in college," he added. He gave Jordan a sly look and said, "I imagine you're wondering how I found her in the first place, aren't you?"

Before she could answer, he shifted the fat folder from one arm to the other and motioned to a waiter to bring him another drink.

"I make it a habit to read every newspaper I can get my hands on. I like to keep current," he explained. "Of course, I read the major papers on the Internet. I read everything from political events to obituaries, and I do retain most of what I read," he boasted. "It's true. I never forget anything. It's how my brain works.

I've also been tracing my family history, and tied to my history is the ownership of Glen MacKenna. I found out through court records that Miss MacKenna will inherit the magnificent land in just a few years."

Jordan nodded. "I've heard that Isabel's great-uncle left her a sizable peace of land in Scotland."

"Not just any land, dearie, Glen MacKenna," he scolded. He sounded like a professor now, lecturing one of his students. "The land is tied to the feud, and the feud is tied to the land. The Buchanans and the MacKennas have been at war for centuries. I don't know what the exact origin of the dispute was, but it has something to do with a treasure that was stolen from the glen by the vile Buchanans, and I'm determined to find out what it was and when it was taken."

Jordan ignored the insult to her ancestors as she pulled out a chair for the professor at the nearest table. He dropped his folder down, and said, "Miss MacKenna has shown quite an interest in my research, so much so that I've invited her to come and see me. I couldn't possibly bring everything with me, you see. I've been doing this research for years."

He looked expectantly at her. She assumed he wanted some sort of response, and so she nodded and asked, "Where do you live, Professor?"

"In the middle of nowhere." He grinned after making the statement and explained. "Because of my financial situation . . . my inheritance," he corrected, "I've been able to move to a peaceful little town called Serenity deep in Texas. I spend my days reading and researching," he added. "I enjoy the solitude, and the town is really an oasis. It would be a charming spot to retire to, but I will probably go back to where I was born, Scotland."

"Oh? You're going home to Scotland?" Jordan scanned the room for Isabel.

"Yes, that's right. I want to visit all the places I've read about. I don't remember them." He pointed to the folder. "I've written down some of our history for Miss MacKenna to read. Most of the

heartache the MacKenna clan has had to endure has been the fault
of the Buchanan clan," he said, wagging his finger in her face. "You
might want to have a peek at my research too, but I'll warn you,
chasing these legends and trying to get to the bottom of things can
become an obsession. On the other hand, it is also a delightful distraction from the humdrum of everyday life. Why, it could even
become a passion."

Passion indeed. As a mathematician and a computer engineer,
Jordan dealt with facts and abstracts, not fantasy. She could design
any business plan and the computer software to go with it. She
loved solving puzzles. She couldn't think of anything that was
more of a waste of time than chasing down legends, but she wasn't
about to get into a lengthy discussion with the professor. She was
going to find Isabel as quickly as possible. After settling Professor
MacKenna at a table with a plate of food in front of him, she
started her search.

Isabel was outside and just about to sit down when Jordan
grabbed her.

"Come with me," she said. "Your friend Professor MacKenna
has arrived. You get to take care of him."

"He's here? He came here?" Isabel looked astonished.

"You didn't invite him?"

She shook her head. Then she changed her mind. "Wait. I
might have invited him, but not formally. I mean he wasn't on the
list. We've been communicating with each other, and I mentioned
where the wedding and reception were being held because he
wrote that he was touring the Carolinas and would be in this area
around this time. He actually showed up? What's he like?"

Jordan smiled. "He's difficult to describe. You'll just have to see
for yourself."

Isabel followed Jordan inside. "Did he tell you about the
treasure?"

"A little," she answered.

"What about the feud? Did he tell you about the Buchanans
and the MacKennas fighting all the time? The feud's been going on

for centuries. Since I'm inheriting Glen MacKenna, I want to know as much as possible about the history."

"You sound enthusiastic," Jordan said.

"I am. I've already decided I'm going to be a history major, and I'll minor in music. Did the professor bring any of his research with him? He wrote that he had boxes and boxes . . ."

"He has a folder with him."

"But what about the boxes?"

"I don't know. You'll have to ask him."

The professor showed better manners with Isabel. He stood and shook her hand.

"It's a great honor to meet the new owner of Glen MacKenna. When I get to Scotland I will be certain to tell my clansmen that I've met you, and that you're as bonny a lass as I thought you would be."

He turned to Jordan then and said, "I'll also be telling them about you."

It wasn't what he said but how he said it that pricked her curiosity.

"Me?"

"The Buchanans," he corrected. "You do know that Kate MacKenna married beneath her."

He'd raised her ire with that remark. "And why is that?" she asked.

"Why, the Buchanans are savages. That's why." He pointed to the folder and said, "In here is just a sample of some of the atrocities against the peace-loving MacKennas. You should read it and then you'll understand how fortunate your relative is to be married to a MacKenna."

"Professor, are you intentionally insulting Jordan?" Isabel asked, shocked.

"She's a Buchanan," he said. "I'm simply stating the facts."

"Just how accurate is your research?" Jordan folded her arms across her chest and frowned at the rude man.

"I'm a historian," he snapped. "I deal in facts. I'll grant you that some of the stories could be . . . legends . . . but there's quite a bit of research to make the stories credible."

"As a historian you believe you have proof that the MacKennas are all saints and the Buchanans are all sinners?"

"I know it sounds slanted, but the proof is indisputable. Read it," he challenged once again, "and you can only come to one conclusion."

"That the Buchanans are savages?"

"I'm afraid so," he said cheerfully. "They're thieves as well," he added. "They've chipped away at the MacKenna land until Glen MacKenna is barely half the size it used to be. And of course they stole the treasure too."

"The treasure that started the feud," Jordan said, letting her irritation show.

He gave her a sly grin and then dismissed her as he turned to Isabel. "I couldn't travel with all the boxes, and I'll have to put them in storage when I leave for Scotland. If you want to look through them, you'd best come to Texas within the next two weeks."

"You're leaving in two weeks? But I start school, and I . . ." She stopped, took a breath, and blurted, "I can miss the first week."

Jordan stopped her. "Isabel, you can't miss an entire week. You'll need to get your class schedule and your books . . . you can't go running off to Texas. Why can't the professor e-mail the research files to you?"

"Most of my research is handwritten, and I've only put a few dates and names on my computer. I could send those, and I will as soon as I get back home, but without my papers, none of it will make sense to you."

"What about mailing the boxes?" Jordan suggested.

"Oh, no, I could never do that," he said. "The expense . . ."

"We'll pay for shipping," Jordan offered.

"I don't trust the mail. Those boxes could get lost, and that's years of research. No, no, I won't risk it. You'll have to come to Texas, Isabel. Perhaps when I come back . . . although . . ."

"Yes?" Isabel asked, thinking he had come up with a solution.

"I might decide to stay in Scotland, depending on my finances, and if I do, my research materials will stay in storage until I'm ready to return for them. If you wish to read what I've accumulated, it's now or never," he asserted.

"Could you have someone photocopy the files?" Isabel asked.

"I have no one to do it for me, and I simply don't have the time. I'm getting ready for my trip. You'll have to make the copies yourself when you come."

Isabel let out a huge sigh of frustration, and Jordan, seeing how important this was to her, felt sympathy for her dilemma. As irritated as she was that the professor had created a biased record against her ancestors, she was sorry that Isabel wouldn't get to learn more about the history of her land.

"I might decide to do a little research on my own," Jordan said as she stood to leave Isabel and the professor to finish their discussion.

The obnoxious man had gotten under her skin, and she was determined to dig up a few facts to prove him wrong. The Buchanans were all savages? What kind of a history professor would make such a blanket statement? Just how credible was he? Was he really a history professor? Jordan was definitely going to check him out.

"Perhaps I'll prove the Buchanans were the saints," she asserted.

"That's hardly possible, dearie. My research is impeccable."

She glanced over her shoulder as she walked away. "We'll see."

Chapter Three

Iᴛ ᴡᴀs ᴀꜰᴛᴇʀ ᴛᴇɴ ʙᴇꜰᴏʀᴇ Jᴏʀᴅᴀɴ ꜰɪɴᴀʟʟʏ ʜᴀᴅ ᴀ ᴄʜᴀɴᴄᴇ ᴛᴏ remove her contacts. She walked back to the ballroom and stood near the entrance trying to spot Noah in the crowd on the dance floor. He still had her glasses in his pocket.

Professor MacKenna had left the reception an hour before, and Isabel had apologized profusely for his rude behavior. Jordan told her not to worry, that she hadn't been offended, and she left Isabel fretting about the boxes of research. Jordan thought about offering to help her out but changed her mind. Even though she was, as Michael reminded her, fancy-free these days and was curious to read some of his likely bogus research, doing so meant she would have to suffer more of the professor's company. No, thank you. Nothing was worth spending even one hour with that man.

"What's got you frowning?"

Her brother Nick asked the question as he sauntered over to her.

"I'm not frowning. I'm squinting. Noah has my glasses. Do you see him?"

"Yeah. He's right in front of you."

She focused in, spotted him, and then did frown. "Look at those silly women panting all over your partner. It's disgusting."

"You think?"

"I think," she replied. "Promise me something."

"Yes?"

"If I ever act like that, you'll shoot me."

"Be happy to," Nick promised before laughing at her.

Noah had excused himself from his fan club and walked over to join them.

"What's so funny?"

"Jordan wants me to shoot her."

Noah glanced down at her, and for a second or two she had his full, undivided attention.

"I'll do it," he offered

There was a little too much glee in his voice to suit her. She had just decided to walk away from the two of them when she spotted Dan Robbins heading her way. At least she thought it was Dan. He was too blurry to be sure. She'd had one dance with Dan earlier in the evening, and no matter what music was playing, whether it was a waltz, a tango, or hip-hop, Dan bounced to his own tune in something that resembled a spasmodic version of a polka. Jordan changed her mind and stayed put. She moved a little closer to Noah and smiled at him. The ploy seemed to work. Dan hesitated and then turned away.

"Don't you want to know why she wants me to shoot her?" Nick asked.

"I already know why," Noah said. "She's bored."

She slipped her hand into his pocket, found her glasses, and put them on.

"I am not bored."

"Yes, you are," Noah said.

He was looking over her head when he spoke to her. She suspected he did it on purpose just to irritate her.

"He's right," Nick said. "You have to be bored. All you had was your company, and since you sold everything . . ."

"Your point?"

Nick shrugged. "You've got to be bored."

"Just because I don't like the same things you two do doesn't mean I'm bored or unhappy. I have a wonderful social life and—"

Noah cut her off. "Dead people have a better social life."

Nick agreed. "You really don't have much fun, do you?"

"Of course I do. I enjoy reading and . . ."

They were both grinning at her. They were obnoxious clowns, and she was about to tell them so when Nick said, "You do like a good book. What was it you were reading a couple of days ago?"

"I don't remember. I read lots of books."

"I do," Noah said, his voice gratingly cheerful. "Nick and Dylan and I had just gotten back from fishing, and you were sitting on the deck reading the complete works of Stephen Hawking."

"It was riveting."

They had a good laugh over her defensive comment. "Stop making fun of me and go away. Both of you."

Her timing could have been better. As soon as she told them to leave, she spotted Dan approaching her again. She grabbed hold of Noah's arm. She was sure he knew what she was doing and why— he'd have to be blind not to notice Dan strolling toward them— but he didn't say anything about it.

"Your sister lives in a box," said Noah.

Nick agreed. "Jordan, when was the last time you did anything just for fun?"

"I do lots of things for fun."

"Let me qualify that question. When did you do anything fun that didn't involve computers or computer chips or software?"

She opened her mouth to answer and then closed it. She couldn't think of anything, but surely that was only because she was under pressure.

"Have you ever done anything impractical?" Noah asked.

"Where's the logic in that?" she asked.

Noah turned to Nick. "Is she serious?"

"Afraid so," Nick answered. "Before my sister would ever consider doing anything on the spur of the moment, she would have to first analyze all the data, then figure the statistical probabilities of success . . ."

The two men were having a fine time tormenting her and would have continued if their employer, Dr. Peter Morganstern, hadn't joined them. He carried a plate with two pieces of wedding cake.

Morganstern had become a good friend of the family and wouldn't have missed the wedding for anything in the world. Jordan liked and admired him. He was a brilliant forensic psychiatrist who ran a highly specialized unit within the FBI. They called it the lost-and-found department. Her brother Nick and Noah were part of Morganstern's program. Among their responsibilities was finding lost and exploited children, and Jordan believed they were a substantial reason for the program's success.

"You three seem to be enjoying yourselves."

"How do you stand working with them?" Jordan asked.

"There are moments when I question my sanity. Especially with this one," he said, tilting his head toward Noah.

"Sir, I'm sorry you and your wife got stuck at the same table with our aunt Iris," Nick said. "Did she find out you were a doctor?"

"I'm afraid so, yes."

"Iris is an obsessive hypochondriac," he explained to Noah.

"What are the odds the doctor would get stuck sitting next to her?" Noah asked.

Everyone turned toward Morganstern's table where Aunt Iris sat.

"One chance in one hundred seventy-nine thousand seven hundred," Jordan answered before she could stop herself.

The men turned back to look at her.

Astonished, the doctor asked, "Is that an exact number or a guess?"

"An exact number based on six hundred guests," she said. "I never guess."

"Does she do this kind of stuff all the time?" Noah wondered aloud.

"Pretty much," Nick answered.

"Just because I have a mind for math—"

"But with no common sense," Nick finished.

"I could certainly use you on my team," Morganstern said. "If you ever consider a change in careers, come work for me."

"No," Nick said emphatically.

"Absolutely not," Noah said at the same time.

The doctor turned his head toward Jordan and gave her a conspiratorial wink. "I wouldn't put her in the field right away. Like you two, she would need extensive training." He looked as though he was pondering the possibility for a second or two, and then said, "I've got a good feeling about Jordan. I believe she'd be an asset to the unit."

"Sir, isn't there a rule against two members of the same family working together?"

"I don't have that rule," Morganstern said. "I wouldn't make her go through the academy. I'd train her myself."

Noah looked appalled. "Sir, it still isn't a good idea," he insisted while Nick vigorously nodded agreement.

Exasperated, Jordan turned to Noah and said, "Listen, Mister Buttinsky. This isn't your decision. It's mine."

The doctor seemed fascinated by Noah's reaction to his proposal.

"Would I get to carry a gun?" she asked.

"A gun is out of the question," Nick said.

"You're too uncoordinated and you're blind as a bat," Noah interjected. "You'd shoot yourself," he predicted.

She smiled at Morganstern. "It was lovely talking to you. Now, if you'll excuse me, I'd like to get away from these two cretins."

Noah grabbed her arm. "Come on. Dance with me."

Since he was already dragging her toward the dance floor, she felt it would be pointless to argue. The bride had coaxed her sister into singing. Isabel had the most wonderful voice, and when she began to sing Kate's favorite ballad, a hush fell over the crowd. Young and old, they were all mesmerized by her.

Noah pulled Jordan into his arms and held her tight against him. She had to admit it wasn't completely unpleasant. She did like the feel of his hard body pressed against hers. She liked his scent too. Whatever he was wearing was ruggedly sexy.

He was looking over the top of her head when he asked, "You wouldn't really consider working for the doctor, would you?"

He actually sounded a little worried. She couldn't resist provoking him just a little. "Only if I get to work with you."

He smiled as he shook his head. "Not gonna happen. And you can't really be serious, right?"

"Right," she agreed. "I wouldn't consider working for Doctor Morganstern. Happy now?"

"I'm always happy."

She rolled her eyes. Oh, brother. The ego. "By the way," she said, "Doctor Morganstern wasn't serious. He was teasing to get a rise out of you and Nick. It worked too. You did get riled."

"The doctor never teases, and I never get riled."

"Okay, even if he wasn't teasing, I still wouldn't consider working for him."

He flashed a smile, and for a fleeting second she forgot how irritating he could be.

"I didn't think you would be interested."

Annoyed, she asked, "Then why are we having this conversation? If you knew the answer, why did you ask?"

"Just making sure. That's all."

They swayed to the music for a good half a minute, and she was actually feeling relaxed when he ruined it.

"You'd be terrible at it, by the way."

"It?"

"The job."

"How would you know if I'd be good or bad?"

"You live in a comfort zone. That's how I know."

"I'll bite. What's a comfort zone?"

"It's where you live. You never step outside your safe environment, your comfort zone," he explained. "You stay in the shadows."

Before she could object, he said, "I'll bet you've never done any-thing in your entire life that was spontaneous, or taken any risks."

"I've taken plenty of risks in the past year alone."

"Yeah? Name one."

"I sold my company."

"That was a calculated decision and you netted a huge profit," he countered. "What else?"

"I've been doing a lot of running. I thought I'd try for the Boston Marathon next year," she offered.

"It's a regimen, requires discipline. Plus, you do it to stay fit," he argued.

He wasn't looking over her head now. He was staring into her eyes, and he was making her extremely uncomfortable. For the life of her, she couldn't think of a single spontaneous action or risk she'd ever taken. Everything she did was well thought out and planned down to the last detail. Was her life really that boring? Was *she* that boring?

"Having trouble coming up with one?"

"There's nothing wrong with being careful." Great, now she sounded like a ninety-year-old.

He looked like he was about to laugh. "You're right," he said. "Nothing wrong with being careful."

Embarrassed because she had only just realized how dull she was, and guessing that he had already figured that out about her as well, she hurriedly changed the subject to get the focus off of her-self. She blurted out the first thought that came into her mind.

"Isabel has a great voice, doesn't she? I could listen to her all night. Did you know she's been hounded by agents wanting to make her a star? She's not interested though. She's only a freshman, but she's already decided she wants to be a history major, then get her master's and teach. Interesting, don't you think? She's giving up fame and fortune. I think that's amazing, don't you?"

Noah gave her a piercing smile that went right through her, but he looked puzzled as well. No wonder. She was babbling like a toddler. She knew she should stop talking, but she couldn't seem to make herself close her mouth. Thanks to his scrutiny she had a bad, bad case of nerves.

For the love of God, Isabel, wind it up. Enough already.

"And did you know that in a few years Isabel is going to inherit land in Scotland? It's called Glen MacKenna," she rushed on. "She invited the strangest little man to the wedding and the reception. I just met him, and he has all the information he's collected in boxes in Texas. He's a professor, you see, and he's done quite a lot of research on a feud that he says has existed for centuries between the Buchanans and the MacKennas. According to the professor, Dylan and Kate should never have gotten married. There's a legend about a treasure too. It's fascinating, really it is."

She finally had to pause to take a breath or she'd pass out.

He stopped dancing for a few seconds and then asked, "Do I make you nervous?"

Duh.

"When you stare at me you do. I'd appreciate it if you would go back to being rude and stare over my head when you speak to me. That *is* why you do it, isn't it? To be rude?"

His face lit up. "And to irritate you."

"It works. You do irritate me."

Would Isabel never finish the song? She was taking forever. Jordan smiled nonchalantly at the couples gliding by as she wished for the dance to end. It would be rude to just walk away, wouldn't it?

Noah nudged her chin up with his index finger and looked squarely at her. "May I make a suggestion?" he asked.

"Sure," she said. "Suggest away."

"You ought to think about getting into the game."

She sighed. "What game would that be?"

"Life."

Apparently he wasn't through giving her suggestions on ways to improve her dull existence.

"Do you know the difference between you and me?" he asked.

"I can think of more than a thousand differences."

"I eat the dessert."

"And what's that supposed to mean?" she asked.

"Only that life's too short. Sometimes you just have to eat dessert first."

She knew where this was going. "I get it. I watch life while you live it. I know you think I should do something spontaneous instead of always planning everything out, but for your information, I'm already doing something spontaneous."

"Yeah?" he asked, and the challenge was there in his voice. "What's that?"

"Spontaneous," she stalled.

"And what would that be?"

She knew he didn't believe her. Come hell or high water, she was determined to do something spontaneous, even if it killed her. The satisfaction of wiping that arrogant know-it-all grin off his face would be worth any sacrifice, even if it wasn't logical.

"I'm going to Texas," she said, enforcing her decision with a nod.

"What for?" he asked.

"Why am I going to Texas?" She didn't have the faintest idea at first, but fortunately, she was a quick thinker. Before he could say another word, she answered her own question.

"I'm going on a treasure hunt."

Chapter Four

PAUL NEWTON PRUITT LOVED WOMEN. HE LOVED EVERYTHING about them: their soft, smooth skin; their feminine scent; the luxurious feel of their silky hair brushing over his chest; the erotic sounds they made when he touched them. He loved their infectious laughter, their stimulating screams of delight.

He didn't discriminate. The color of their hair or the color of their eyes or their skin—he loved them all. Tall, short, thin, fat. It didn't matter. They were all wonderful, and to him, each one was so very unique.

Admittedly, he had a special fondness for the way some of them smiled at him. It was a smile he couldn't possibly describe. He only knew that one glance his way and his heart raced. The lure was that powerful. He simply couldn't resist, couldn't say no. Beguiling and enticing. That certain smile never failed to captivate him.

Before he'd had to shape up and change his behavior in order to survive, he'd been quite the ladies' man. And that wasn't his ego talking. It was just the way it was. He'd been irresistible back then.

But things were different now.

In his old life, if he grew bored, he would say his good-bye with expensive gifts so there wouldn't be any ill feelings toward him. He could not bear to think that even one of his women would ever hate him. Only when he knew for certain that he had pleased them could he move on to the next lovely, sometimes enchanting, woman. And there was always another one.

Until Marie. He had fallen in love with her, and his life had changed forever. The life he knew was gone. Paul Newton Pruitt was gone. A new name. A new identity. A new life. No one would ever find him.

Chapter Five

SHE HAD TO BE OUT OF HER EVER-LOVING MIND. A TREASURE hunt? What had she been thinking? Apparently she'd been more interested in proving to Noah Clayborne that she wasn't a complete bore than in using common sense.

Jordan knew she had no one to blame but herself for her present circumstances, but she still wanted to blame Noah, simply because doing so made her feel better.

She leaned against her dilapidated rental car on the side of the beat-up, two-lane highway in the middle of nowhere, Texas, while impatiently waiting for the engine to cool down so she could pour more water into the coolant reservoir. Thank goodness she'd stopped awhile back on the interstate to pick up a couple of bottles of drinking water for the rest of her trip. She was fairly certain the radiator had a leak, but she'd need to keep the engine running long enough to get to the next town to have a mechanic look at it. It was at least a hundred-ten in the shade, and of course the car's air conditioner had bit the dust about an hour ago, along with the super-duper satellite system the rental agency had thrown in as a consolation prize for messing up her reservation and knowingly dumping a lemon on her.

Sweat trickled down between her breasts; the bottoms of her sandals were melting into the pavement, and the sunscreen she'd lathered on her face and arms was giving up the fight. Jordan had dark auburn hair but a redhead's complexion, and it didn't take much sun for her to burn and freckle. She supposed she had a choice. She could either sit in the car and die of dehydration while she waited for the engine to cool down, or she could stay outside and be slowly cremated.

Okay. She was being a little overdramatic. That's what the heat will do to you, she thought.

Fortunately, she had her cell phone with her. She never left home without it. Unfortunately, since she was temporarily stranded in the middle of the vast flatland, she couldn't get a signal.

Serenity, Texas, was fifty or sixty miles away. She hadn't been able to find out much about the town, only knew that it was so small the name warranted only the smallest typeface on a map of Texas. The professor had called Serenity a charming oasis. But when she'd met him he'd been wearing a heavy wool, tweed blazer in the summer heat. What did he know about charming?

She had checked the professor out before leaving Boston, and although he was strange and eccentric, he was the real deal. The man was multidegreed and certified to teach. An assistant in the Franklin College administration building, a woman named Lorraine, had raved about his teaching abilities. According to her, the professor made history come to life. His classes were always the first to fill up, she said.

Jordan found that nearly impossible to believe. "Really?"

"Oh my, yes. The students don't mind his accent, and they must be hanging on every word because no one ever fails his classes."

Ah, now Jordan understood. An easy grade.

The woman also mentioned that he'd taken early retirement, but she hoped he would reconsider and come back.

"Good teachers are so hard to come by," she had remarked. "And on the salaries they're paid, most can't afford to retire at such an early age. Why, Professor MacKenna is barely in his forties."

Lorraine obviously didn't mind divulging personal information about a past faculty member, and she hadn't even asked Jordan why she was so interested. Granted, Jordan had lied and told the woman she was a distant relative, but Lorraine hadn't required any verification.

She was a talker, no doubt about that. "I'll bet you thought he was much older, didn't you?"

"Yes, I did."

"I did too," she said. "I could look up his birthday for you if you'd like."

Good heavens, she was accommodating. "That won't be necessary," Jordan answered. "You said he officially retired? I thought he'd taken a sabbatical."

"No, he retired," she insisted. "We'd be thrilled to have him back. I doubt he will ever teach again though. He received such a nice inheritance," she continued. "He told me he had no inkling that he was getting it, that the money was quite a surprise. He made the decision then and there to buy some land far away from the hustle and bustle of the city. He was doing research into his family's history, and he wanted a place where he could work in peace and quiet."

Looking around her now, Jordan imagined the professor had found his peace and quiet. There wasn't a soul in sight, and she had a feeling that Serenity was just as stark as the surrounding landscape.

A half hour passed, the engine cooled, and she got back on the road. Since there wasn't any air-conditioning, she kept the windows down, and the blistering hot air felt like blasts from a furnace on her face. The terrain was as flat as one of her soufflés, but once she drove around a yawning bend and saw the fences on either side of the road, the area seemed less desolate. At least there were signs of habitation. A rusted barbed-wire fence that looked like it had been constructed about a century ago enclosed empty pastures. Since she didn't see a single crop growing, she assumed the fences were for horses and cattle.

The miles rolled by, but the scenery didn't change much. Finally, she drove up a couple of gentle slopes, and then the road curved. Around a sharp bend she spotted a tower off in the distance. A sign on the side of the road announced that Serenity was just a mile away. As she made the turn, she picked up her cell phone and saw that she had a signal. The road dipped and then topped a hill. There, spread out before her, was the west side of Serenity.

It looked like a place too tired to die.

The speed limit dropped to thirty miles per hour. She passed several small homes. A rusted pickup truck sat on blocks in the front yard of one house. The tires were missing. Another house had a discarded washing machine in a side yard. What little grass there was among the weeds was untended and burned out. A block farther on she passed an abandoned gas station with one pump still standing. Vines grew up the side of the vacant building, and she could only guess what sort of critters could be living in it.

"What am I doing here? I never should have sold my company," Jordan whispered.

Pride. That's what got her into this ridiculous adventure. She didn't want Noah Clayborne mocking her. "Comfort zone," she muttered. "What's wrong with wanting to be in my comfort zone?"

She thought about driving on through Serenity to the next big city, returning the rental car with a few choice words, and getting on the first flight to Boston, but she couldn't do that. She'd promised Isabel that she would meet the professor and then call and tell her what she'd learned.

Admittedly, Jordan was a little curious about her own ancestors as well. She certainly didn't believe that all of her Buchanan ancestors were savages, and she wanted to prove it. She also wanted to know what caused the feud between the Buchanans and the MacKennas in the first place. And what about the treasure? Did the professor even know what the treasure was?

Jordan drove on and reached the main street. The houses looked lived-in, but the lawns were parched and brown, and the shades were drawn.

Serenity was as inviting as purgatory.

The red light on her dashboard began to flash, indicating the engine was overheating again. She found a small convenience store a couple of blocks away and pulled in. It was so hot she felt like her back was glued to the seat. She parked in the shade, turned the motor off so it would cool down, then pulled out the notepad with the professor's phone number and dialed.

On the fourth ring, his voice mail picked up. She left her name and number and was putting her phone back in her purse when it rang. The professor must have been screening his calls.

"Miss Buchanan? Professor MacKenna here. I have to hurry. When do you want to meet? How about dinner? Yes, dinner. Meet me at The Branding Iron. It's off Third Street. Just head west and you'll run into it. There's a nice motel right across the street. You could check in, refresh yourself, and meet me at six. Don't be late."

He hung up before she could say a word. He'd sounded nervous, worried maybe. She shook her head. There was something about him that made her uneasy. She wasn't sure if it was simply because he was such a nervous man, always looking over his shoulder as though he expected someone to pounce on him, or if it was something else that bothered her, something she couldn't quite define. No matter the reason, her philosophy was simple: better be safe than sorry, and so she would only meet him in a public place.

An air-conditioned public place, she qualified. She was hot and sweaty and trying hard not to be miserable. Think positive, she told herself. After she peeled off her clothes and took a nice shower, she'd feel much better.

She still wished she could keep on driving so she could get back to Boston sooner, but that was out of the question. The car she was driving had a high probability of breaking down on the road, and just picturing herself stranded in the middle of the night made her shudder. No, that was definitely out of the question. Besides, she'd promised Isabel, and she couldn't go back on her word. And so she would meet Professor Weirdo, talk to him about his research over dinner, get photocopies of his research, and leave Serenity first thing in the morning.

Good, she was already feeling better. She was determined now, and she had a plan.

"Oh, no," she whispered.

The plan crashed and burned when she pulled into the motel parking lot and got a good look at the hellhole Professor MacKenna had recommended. She was pretty sure Norman Bates ran the place.

The driveway was a gravel pit all the way up to each of the units. There were eight in all, slapped up against one another like warehouse boxes. The white paint was chipped, and the single window in each of the rooms was coated with grime. She couldn't even begin to imagine how awful the rooms must be. Bedbugs would run from this place. They had higher standards.

But she could handle it for one night. Right?

"Wrong," she said aloud.

Surely she could find something better, a place where she wouldn't have to be afraid to take a shower.

Jordan didn't consider herself pampered or a snob. She didn't care if the motel was a bit run-down, but she wanted it to be clean and safe. And this place didn't measure up to either one of her basic standards. Since she had no intention of spending the night, she didn't need to see the rooms.

Jordan put the car in park and leaned out the window to get a good look at the restaurant across the street. She made the mistake of resting her arm on the hot edge of the window. She flinched and jerked her arm back inside the car.

The Branding Iron reminded her of a train because the building was long and narrow with a barrel-shaped roof. On the side of the road was a billboard with a purple neon horseshoe. She presumed it was meant to look like a branding iron.

Now that she had her bearings and knew where the restaurant was, she pulled out of the lot and drove on. She was almost certain that the car rental agency didn't have a branch in Serenity, which meant that she was stuck with this lemon until she drove to a larger city, the closest being over a hundred miles away. Jordan decided that once she checked into a motel for the night, she'd notify the rental company, then she'd find a mechanic to patch up the radiator, and she would be sure to buy a dozen gallons of water before she headed out of town. Just thinking about driving into the middle of nowhere with a malfunctioning car made her nervous. Mechanic first, she told herself. Then decision time. She might leave the car here and take whatever form of public transportation was available. Surely there were buses or trains or something.

She soon came to a wood-plank bridge with a sign announcing that she was crossing Parson's Creek. The creek didn't have a drop of water in it, and as she clattered across, she read a warning posted on the railing that the bridge was impassable during high water. Not much of a concern today, she thought. The creek was as dried up as the town appeared to be.

On the other side of the bridge, a wooden sign painted forest green with bold white letters greeted her: WELCOME TO SERENITY, GRADY COUNTY, TEXAS. POPULATION 1,968. In smaller, hand-painted letters were the words, "New home of the Grady County High School Bulldogs."

The farther east she drove, the larger the homes became. She pulled to a stop at a corner, heard children laughing and shouting, and turned toward the sound. On her left was a neighborhood swimming pool. Finally, she thought. She didn't feel like she was in a graveyard anymore. There were people and noise. Women were sunbathing while their children played in the pool, and the lifeguard, baking under the sweltering sun, sat on his perch half asleep.

The transformation after crossing the bridge from one county to another was astonishing. On this side of town, people watered their lawns. The area was clean, the houses well kept, the streets and sidewalks new. There were actual signs of commerce with shops open on either side of the main thoroughfare. On the left, a beauty shop, a hardware store, and an insurance office, and on the right, a bar and an antiques shop. At the end of the block, Jaffee's Bistro had tables and chairs set outside under a green-and-white awning, but Jordan couldn't imagine anyone wanting to sit outside in this heat.

The sign on the door said "Open." Her priorities immediately shifted. Air-conditioning sounded like heaven at the moment, and so did a nice cold drink. She'd find a mechanic and a motel later.

She parked the car, grabbed her purse and her satchel with her laptop, and went inside. The blast of cold air made her knees weak. It was blissful.

A woman sitting at one of the tables rolling silverware into napkins looked up at the sound of the door opening.

"Lunch hour's over and dinner isn't being served yet. I can do you up a nice tall glass of iced tea if you'd like."

"Yes, thank you. That would be lovely," Jordan replied.

The ladies' room was around a corner. After she washed her hands and face and ran a comb through her hair, she felt human again.

There were ten or twelve tables with checkered cloths and matching cushions on the chairs. She chose a table in the corner. She could see out the window, but the sun wasn't in her face.

The waitress returned a minute later with a frosty glass of iced tea, and Jordan asked her if she could borrow a phone book.

"What are you looking for, honey?" the waitress asked. "Maybe I can help."

"I need to find a mechanic," she explained. "And a clean motel."

"That's easy enough. There are only two mechanics in town, and one of them is closed until next week. The other one is Lloyd's

Garage, and that's just a couple of blocks from here. He's kind of difficult to deal with, but he'll get the job done. I'll get you the phone book, and you can look up his number."

While she waited, Jordan pulled out her laptop and set it up on the table. She'd made some notes the night before and a list of questions to ask the professor, and she thought she'd look them over again.

The waitress brought her a thin phone book open to the page with the listing for Lloyd's Garage.

"I went ahead and called my friend Amelia Ann," she said. "She runs the Home Away from Home Motel, and she's getting a room ready for you right now."

"That's very nice of you," Jordan said.

"It's a lovely place. Amelia Ann's husband died several years ago and didn't leave her anything, not one dime of life insurance, so Amelia Ann and her daughter, Candy, moved into the motel and started managing it. They've made it real homey. I think you'll like it."

Jordan called the number for the garage on her cell phone and was curtly informed that no one could look at her car until tomorrow. The mechanic told her to bring it in first thing in the morning. "Figures," Jordan said with a sigh as she flipped her phone shut.

"Are you just passing through Serenity, or did you get lost?" the woman asked. "If you don't mind me asking," she hurriedly added.

"I don't mind you asking. I'm meeting someone here."

"Oh, honey. It isn't a man, is it? You didn't follow a man here, did you? Tell me you didn't. That's what I did. I followed him all the way from San Antonio. It didn't work out though, not for long anyway, and he up and moved on." She shook her head and made a tsking sound. "Now I'm stuck here until I can earn enough money to move back home. My name's Angela, by the way."

Jordan introduced herself and shook the woman's hand. "It's nice to meet you, and no, I didn't follow a man here. I *am* meeting a man for dinner, but it's business. He's bringing me some papers and information."

"Nothing romantic then?"

She pictured the professor and almost shuddered. "No."

"Where are you from?"

"Boston."

"Really? You don't have that accent, at least not much."

Jordan wasn't sure if the comment was good or bad, but Angela was smiling. She had a lovely smile and seemed to have a sweet disposition. In her younger days she'd been a sun worshipper, Jordan guessed, because she had deep creases in her face, and her skin looked a bit like dried leather.

"How long have you lived in Serenity?"

"Close to eighteen years."

Jordan blinked. The woman had been saving for eighteen years and still didn't have enough to move back home?

"Where are you going to meet this businessman for dinner?" Angela asked. "You don't have to tell me. I'm just curious is all."

"We're having dinner at The Branding Iron. Have you ever been there?"

"Oh, yes," she said. "But it's not as good as the food here, and it's located in a bad part of town. The restaurant's a local landmark, so it stays open, and they do a real good business on weekends. It's not safe after dark. Your businessman must be a local, or maybe a local told him about the place. No one outside of Serenity would even know to suggest The Branding Iron."

"His name is MacKenna," she said. "He's a history professor, and he has some research papers for me."

"I haven't met him," Angela said. "Of course, I don't know everyone in town, but I'll bet he's new to the area." Angela turned to leave. "You go ahead and enjoy your tea, and I'll leave you alone. Everyone thinks I talk too much."

Jordan knew the waitress was waiting for her to disagree. "I don't think you do."

Angela turned back, a big smile on her face. "I don't think I do either. I'm just friendly, that's all. Too bad you can't have dinner here. Jaffee's making his special shrimp dish."

"I think the professor suggested the restaurant because it's right across the street from a motel he recommended."

Angela's eyebrows lifted. "The Lux? He suggested The Lux?"

Jordan smiled. "Is that what the motel's called?"

She nodded. "There used to be a big old sign that lit up. The word 'luxury' flashed off and on all night. Only the first three letters still light up, and that's why folks call it The Lux. They do a good business at night . . . all night as a matter of fact." Her voice dropped to a whisper as she added, "The creep that runs the place charges by the hour. Get my drift?"

She must have thought that Jordan didn't understand because she hurriedly explained, "It's a whore place is what it is."

"Yes," Jordan said, nodding so the waitress wouldn't feel the need to explain what a whore was.

Angela thrust her hip out and leaned against the table. She kept her voice low. "It's also a firetrap if you ask me." She darted a quick look to her left and then her right to make sure no one had crept into the empty restaurant to eavesdrop, then said, "It should have been torn down years ago, but J.D. Dickey runs the place, and no one dares mess with him. I think he runs some of the whores too, if you ask me. J.D. is a real scary one, all right. He's got a mean streak a mile wide."

Angela was a wealth of information and wasn't the least bit shy about telling everything she knew. Jordan was fascinated. She almost envied Angela's openness and friendly candor. Jordan was the complete opposite. She kept things bottled up. Bet Angela can sleep at night, she thought. Jordan hadn't had a good night's sleep in over a year. Her mind was always racing, and there were nights when she paced the floor of her apartment while she worried about one problem or another. In the morning light, none of those worries seemed all that important, but in the middle of the night, they became monumental.

"Why hasn't the fire department or the police closed the motel? If it's a fire hazard . . ." Jordan wondered aloud.

"Oh, yes, it is."

"And prostitution is illegal in Texas . . ."

"Yes, it is," she agreed again before Jordan could continue. "But that doesn't matter much. You don't understand how things are around here. What we have is a different county on each side of Parson's Creek, and they're run as different as night and day. Right this minute you're sitting in Grady County, but the sheriff in charge of Jessup County is one of those folks who thinks he can turn a blind eye to what's going on. You get my drift? Live and let live. That's his motto. If you ask me, he's afraid to go up against J.D., and you know why? I'll tell you why. The sheriff of Jessup County is J.D.'s brother. That's right. His brother. Isn't that something?"

Jordan nodded. "What about you? Are you afraid of this man?"

"Honey, anyone with a lick of sense would know to be afraid."

Chapter Six

J.D. DICKEY WAS THE TOWN BULLY. HE HAD A NATURAL TALENT: he didn't have to work hard at all to get people to hate him. Building his reputation as a badass was a job he thoroughly enjoyed, and he knew for a certainty that he'd accomplished his goal when he strolled down the main street of Serenity and people hurried out of his way. Their expressions said it all. They were afraid of him, and in J.D.'s mind, fear meant power. His power.

J.D.'s full name was Julius Delbert Dickey Jr. He didn't much care for the name though, thought it was too girly-sounding for the tough-as-iron image he was going after, and so, while he was still in high school, he began to train the residents of his hometown to call him by his initials. Those few who resisted were subjected to his special, though unsophisticated, form of behavior modification. He beat the daylights out of them.

There were two Dickey brothers, and both of them grew up in Serenity. J.D. was firstborn. Randall Cleatus Dickey came along two years later.

The Dickey boys hadn't seen their father in over ten years. A federal prison in Kansas was providing the Senior's room and board for twenty-five to life for an armed robbery that, as he explained to the sentencing judge, had just gone bad. Looking back, he told the judge, he realized he probably shouldn't have shot that nosy guard after all. The man was only doing his job.

The boys' mother, Sela, stayed around until J.D. and Randy graduated from high school. Then she decided she had had enough of motherhood. Tired and worn as thin as a broomstick trying to keep her rambunctious sons out of trouble, and failing miserably at the job, she packed her clothes and snuck out of town in the middle of the night. The boys figured she wouldn't be coming back anytime soon because she took with her all of her large cans of Extra Super Hold Aqua Net hairspray. Their mother's hair grooming products were her only luxury, and she always kept at least five or six cans on hand.

They didn't miss her or her chronic complaining about having to do without, and since J.D. was pretty much running things anyway, life didn't change much after she left. They had been dirt poor growing up, and they were still dirt poor, but J.D. was determined to change that. He had big plans, but his plans required money. Lots of money. He wanted to own a ranch. He had his eye on a nice little piece of land located just thirty miles west of town. The land was small by most Texans' measure at just over five hundred acres, but J.D. figured that once he was firmly established as a gentleman rancher, he'd be able to gobble up all the land around him. The ranch he meant to have was prime land with several good watering holes for the cattle he was going to buy as soon as he figured out a good way to get his hands on some money. There was a nice fishing lake too, and brother Randy loved to fish.

Yes sir, he was going to become a cowboy. He felt like he was already halfway there. He owned the boots and the hat, and he'd worked on a ranch two full summers in a row while he was in high school. The pay stunk. The experience was invaluable.

J.D.'s dream was put on hold for five years with good behavior. He'd killed a man in a bar fight and got five years for manslaughter. There were extenuating circumstances. According to witnesses, the stranger had started the fight and had gotten in some pretty good cuts with his switchblade before J.D. knocked him out. He hadn't set out to take the man's life, but he punched him hard, and as bad luck would have it, the stranger struck his head on his way down.

J.D. boasted to his brother that he would have gotten more time behind bars if he hadn't given each one of the jurors the evil eye as he was leaving the courtroom.

Randy's take on the incident was different. In fact, his brother's incarceration opened his eyes, and he saw for the first time that the real power was on the side of the law. So, while J.D. was serving his sentence, Randy was changing into a law-abiding citizen, and within a few short years he managed to influence enough people to get himself elected sheriff of Jessup County.

J.D. couldn't have been happier for his brother. Randy's new title and his new status in the community were achievements to celebrate. After all, having a sheriff in the family could come in real handy.

Chapter Seven

JORDAN CHECKED INTO THE HOME AWAY FROM HOME MOTEL and was given a spacious room in the back of the courtyard. The door had solid double locks. The room was square shaped and clean. A king-sized bed faced the door and a desk and two chairs sat against the wall facing the window. No laptop hook-up or Internet access, she noticed, but she could do without for one night.

Angela's friend, Amelia Ann, made her feel like an honored guest. She brought her extra little soaps and fluffy towels fresh out of her dryer.

After Jordan unpacked, she stripped out of her clothes and took a nice, cool shower. She washed and dried her hair, put on a skirt and blouse, and had just enough time to head back to The Branding Iron. She couldn't remember the last time she'd eaten dinner at six, but since she hadn't had anything to eat since break-fast, she was actually hungry.

Dinner was unforgettable . . . but not in a good way. As it turned out, Professor MacKenna was quite an appetite suppressant.

Though it was just six o'clock, the parking lot of The Branding Iron was full. A waitress met her at the door and showed her to a booth tucked way in the back dining room.

"We have better tables, but the guy you're meeting wanted privacy. I'll show you where he is. Stay away from the fish tonight. It smells funny," she whispered as she led the way. "I'll be serving you," she added with a smile.

Professor MacKenna didn't stand when Jordan reached the table, didn't even bother to nod as she took her seat across from him. His mouth was stuffed with bread, and he should have waited until after he had swallowed to speak to her, but he didn't. He talked around a wad of bread the size of a golf ball that was half in and half out of his mouth.

"You're late," he said, his voice garbled by food.

Since it was only a few minutes past the hour, she didn't feel the need to apologize or respond to his ridiculous criticism. She picked up a linen napkin, unfolded it, and placed it in her lap. His napkin was still on the table, she noticed. Jordan tried desperately not to look at his mouth while he chewed. Had he not been so vulgar, he would have been comical.

The urge to bolt almost overtook her. What in God's name was she doing here? Hadn't she been perfectly happy and content before the conversation she'd had with Noah at the wedding reception? Now look at her. Having dinner with Professor Uncouth. Lovely, she thought. What a lovely adventure.

Okay, new plan, she told herself. Get through this dinner as quickly and as painlessly as possible, get the research papers, and leave.

"I've already ordered my dinner," he said. "Have a look over the menu and pick something."

She opened her menu, ordered the first item that caught her eye, a spicy chicken dish, and sparkling water. The waitress brought her her drink, gave her a sympathetic look with a meaningful glance toward the professor, and hurried to another table, pretending not to notice that he was waving an empty breadbasket at her.

Jordan waited until his mouth was empty before speaking. "As a history professor," she began, "surely you know the Buchanan clan couldn't be all bad. Over the centuries I'm sure there . . ." She stopped talking when he vigorously shook his head. Then she asked, "You really believe they were all horrible men?"

"I do. They were despicable."

"Give me an example of something despicable the Buchanans did to the sainted MacKennas," she challenged.

His behavior and his attitude changed the second he started talking about his research. Thankfully, he wasn't chewing when he began his history lesson . . . his one-sided, slanted history lesson.

"In 1784 the magnificent Laird Ross MacKenna sent his only daughter, Freya, to the clan Mitchell. She was pledged to marry the Laird Mitchell's oldest son, who everyone knew would become laird just as soon as his esteemed father passed on. According to my documents, there was a terrible attack en route to the Mitchell holding."

"The Buchanans attacked?" Jordan asked.

He shook his head. "No, not the Buchanans. It was the clan Mac-Donald who attacked. The Laird MacDonald was against the alliance between the MacKennas and the Mitchells because he believed it would make them too powerful. The ambush occurred on the bank of the great loch, and in the skirmish, the fair lass, Freya, fell in."

He waited for her to acknowledge what he'd told her, and so she nodded. "Did she drown?" she asked, wondering how he would pin her death on the Buchanans.

"No, and it was written that she could swim, but the rain began, and the loch was stirred into a frenzy. Suddenly there was a great shout, and one of the MacKennas looked across the loch just in time to see a Buchanan warrior pull Freya out of the water. The lass was still alive, for her arms were flailing."

"Then that is a good story about the Buchanans," she pointed out. "You've just told me that a Buchanan warrior saved the woman's life."

The professor's eyebrows lowered. "The lass Freya was never heard of or seen again."

"What happened to her?"

"The Buchanan took her. That's what happened. He saw her, he wanted her, and he took her."

She thought the professor expected her to be shocked, and she knew he wouldn't appreciate her laughter. "Was there only one witness to this . . . kidnapping?"

"One reliable witness."

"A MacKenna."

"Yes."

"Then you must agree that the story might have been exaggerated so that the Buchanans would be held responsible." Before he could argue with her conclusion, she asked, "Can you give me another example . . . with documented proof?"

"I'll be happy to," he said.

Unfortunately, his salad arrived, and he began his story while digging into his plate. Jordan looked down at the table so she wouldn't have to watch.

He stabbed at his lettuce as he said, "Look in your history books, and you'll read that in 1691, King William III ordered all the clan chiefs to sign a loyalty oath by January 1, 1692.

"The MacKennas were the most honored and respected clan in all of Scotland. William MacKenna, as head of the MacKenna clan, headed for Inverary in November with a band of clansmen to sign it. On the way he was met by a messenger who told him that the king was making changes to the oath and that they were to return home until they received word. When they arrived back at their holding, they discovered their livestock had been scattered, and many of their buildings had been set afire. By the time they were able to establish order again, the deadline had come and gone.

"It was then that they learned that the messenger had been a liar and not from the king at all. The loyalty oath had not been postponed."

He gave her another one of his glowering glares. Uh-oh. She knew where this story was heading.

"And?" she prodded. "What happened then?"

"I'll tell you what happened." He dropped his fork and leaned forward. "King William was furious with the MacKennas for disobeying his order. As punishment he made the MacKennas pay a heavy toll and relinquish a good portion of their land. Worse, they fell out of favor with the monarchy for decades to come." Nodding, he picked up his fork and stabbed a tomato wedge. "There's no doubt who sent the messenger and who wreaked havoc on the MacKennas."

"Let me guess. The Buchanans?"

"That's right, dearie. The despicable Buchanans."

He'd raised his voice and nearly shouted "despicable Buchanans" at her. Other diners in the restaurant were watching and listening. Jordan didn't care if he wanted to make a scene. She'd keep up.

"Was there actual proof that the Buchanans sent the messenger or attacked the MacKenna lands?"

"There was no proof needed," he snapped.

"Without actual documented proof, this is all hearsay and fairy tale."

"The Buchanans were the only clan underhanded enough to want to discredit the revered MacKennas."

"So says a MacKenna. Did it ever occur to you that maybe the story's been reversed, and the Buchanans had at some point been attacked by the MacKennas?"

The wicked look on his face told her she'd punched all of his buttons. His fist hit the table. "I know my facts. Don't forget, the Buchanans started it all. It was they who stole the MacKenna treasure."

"Exactly what was this treasure?" Jordan asked. This was the subject that had piqued her interest in the first place.

"Something very valuable and that rightfully belonged to the MacKennas," he answered. Suddenly he sat upright in his chair and scowled. "That's what you're really after, isn't it? You think you'll discover the treasure . . . maybe even find it for yourself. Well, I can assure you the centuries have hidden it well, and if I haven't discovered it, you certainly won't be able to stumble upon it. All of the atrocities committed by the Buchanans over the generations have obscured the origin of the feud. It's likely that no one will ever find it."

She didn't know why she was letting him get her all riled up, but she was suddenly determined to defend her family name. "Do you know the difference between fact and fantasy, Professor?"

Their conversation became more heated. The two of them barely managed to keep their voices below a shout, even though Jordan did get a little carried away with a few choice names for his clan.

All conversation ceased as soon as dinner arrived. Jordan couldn't believe the huge hunk of nearly raw meat that was placed in front of the professor. Next to it was a giant baked potato fully loaded. Her little chicken dish looked like a child's portion in comparison. The professor's head went down, and he didn't come up for air again until he had devoured every bite. There wasn't a piece of gristle or fat left on his plate.

"Would you like more bread?" she asked calmly.

In answer he shoved the bread basket at her. She was able to get the waitress's attention and politely requested more. From the waitress's wary expression, Jordan assumed she'd witnessed the argument, and she smiled to assure the woman that all was well.

"You have a great passion for your work," Jordan complimented. She decided that if she didn't start humoring him, he might leave without letting her see his research, and the trip would be completely wasted.

"And you admire my dedication," he answered and then launched into another tale about the dastardly Buchanans. He stopped long enough to order dessert, and by the time it arrived, he'd worked his way back to the fourteenth century.

Everything in Texas was big, including food. She stared at the top of the professor's head as he devoted himself to inhaling every bite of the huge wedge of apple pie with two scoops of vanilla ice cream.

A waiter dropped a glass. The professor looked around and noticed how crowded the room was becoming. He seemed to shrivel up in the booth as he kept a close eye on who was coming and going.

"Is something wrong?" she asked.

"I don't like crowds."

He took a sip of his coffee and said, "I've stored some data on a flash drive. It's in one of the boxes for Isabel. Do you know what a flash drive is?"

Before she could answer, he said, "All Isabel has to do is slip the flash drive into her computer. It's like a disk, and it can store volumes of data."

His condescending tone irritated her to no end. "I'll make sure she gets it," she said.

He told her the price of the flash drive and said, "I assume you or Miss MacKenna will reimburse me."

"Yes, I will."

"Now?" He pulled a receipt from his pocket and stared expectantly at her, obviously wanting payment right this minute, and so she got the money from her billfold and handed it to him. He wasn't the trusting sort. He counted the money before tucking it into his wallet.

"As to my research . . . I have three large boxes. I've spoken at length with Isabel, and against my better judgment I have decided to let you take them to make photocopies for her. She has assured me that she takes full responsibility, and so I will rely on her integrity as a MacKenna. I'll know if anything is missing. I have a photographic memory. Once I've read something, it stays with me." He paused to tap his forehead. "I remember names and faces of people I met ten, twenty years ago. It's stored up here. The important and the unimportant."

"How long do I have to make the copies?" she asked, wanting to move the conversation along.

"I've been so busy getting ready for my trip. I'm leaving sooner than I originally planned. You'll have to stay in Serenity and make your copies here. It shouldn't take you more than two days at the most. Maybe three," he allowed.

"Is there a print shop in town with copy machines?"

"I don't believe so," he replied. "But there's a machine at the grocery store, and I'm sure there are others around town."

After two more cups of coffee, he requested the bill. As the time for their parting grew closer, every minute seemed to drag. When the check came, he pushed it toward her. At this point she wasn't surprised.

Her brother Zachary had always been able to gross her out. He was much better at it than any of her other brothers, but tonight the professor had usurped his title as the king of gross. Professor MacKenna wiped his mouth with his napkin, which had lain folded on the table throughout the meal, and scooted out of the booth.

"I want to get home before it gets dark."

It wouldn't be dark for at least another hour. "Do you live far from here?"

"No," he answered. "I'll meet you at the car and transfer the boxes. You'll take good care of them? Isabel spoke highly of you, and I'm trusting her."

"I'll take good care of them," she promised.

Ten minutes later the bill had been paid, the boxes had been transferred to her car, and Jordan was, for the time being, rid of the professor.

She felt liberated.

Chapter Eight

JORDAN WAS UP BRIGHT AND EARLY THE FOLLOWING MORNING. She drove the car over to Lloyd's Garage and was parked and waiting for him to open his doors.

She hoped to get the car patched up, then drive to the grocery store she was told had a copy machine. If all went well, she could get one box finished and maybe half of another. Two of the boxes were filled to the top, and, fortunately, the professor hadn't written on both sides of the paper because the pen he'd used on some of them had bled through.

The garage doors opened ten minutes after eight. After popping the hood and looking at the engine for about thirty seconds, the mechanic, a brute of a man about her age, leaned against the fender, crossed one ankle over the other, and gave her a slow and definitely creepy once-over while he wiped his hands on an oily rag.

He must have thought he'd missed something in his rude inspection because he gave her the once-over again, and then again. Honest to Pete, her car hadn't gotten this much attention.

She was going to have to put up with the jerk because he was the only mechanic in town until next Monday.

"I'm pretty certain the radiator has a leak," she said. "So what do you think? Can you patch it up?"

The mechanic had his name, Lloyd, printed on a strip of masking tape and stuck to his shirt pocket. The edges were curling up. He turned away, tossed the dirty rag on a nearby rack, and then turned around again.

"Can I patch it? Depends," he drawled. "It's egregious is what it is."

"It is?"

"You know . . . salivient."

Lloyd obviously liked to use big words whenever possible, even when those words didn't make sense. Salivient? Was that even a word?

"But you can fix it?"

"It's almost beyond repair, sweetie."

Sweetie? I don't think so. She silently counted to five in an attempt to keep her temper under control so she wouldn't blow up. It wouldn't do to alienate the man who could get her car running.

Good old Lloyd had worked his way down to her feet and was on his way back up when he said, "What we have here is a serious situation."

"We do?" Determined to get along no matter how irritating the man was, she nodded. "You said it was almost beyond repair?"

"That's right. Almost."

She crossed her arms and waited for him to finish another trip down her legs and back. He should have them memorized by now. "Would you care to explain?"

"Your radiator has a leak."

She felt like screaming. She'd already told him that.

"I could probably repair it temporarily, but I can't guarantee it would hold," Lloyd continued.

"How long will it take you to repair it?"

"Depends on what I find under the hood." He raised his eyebrows meaningfully, and when she didn't immediately react, he added, "You know what I mean?"

She knew exactly what he meant. Lloyd was a real degenerate. Her patience ended. "You've already looked under the hood," she snapped.

Her obvious anger didn't appear to faze him. He must be used to rejection, she decided. Either that or he'd stood outside in the sun too long and had fried his brain.

"Are you married, sweetie?"

"Am I what?"

"Married. Are you married? I need to know who to bill," he explained.

"Bill me."

"I'm just being hospitable. You don't need to snap at me."

"How long will the repair take?"

"A day . . . maybe two."

"Okay, then," she said pleasantly. "I'll be on my way."

He didn't understand until she walked around him and opened the car door.

"Wait a minute. You're leaving with a leak . . ."

"Yes, that's right."

He snorted. "You won't get far."

"I'll take my chances."

He thought she was bluffing until she started the engine and began to back out of the garage.

"I could maybe fix it by noon," he blurted.

"Maybe?"

"Okay, for sure by noon," he agreed. "And I won't charge you much."

She put the brakes on. "How much?"

"Sixty-five, maybe seventy, but no more than eighty. I don't take credit cards, and since you're from out of town, I won't take a check. You'll have to give me cash."

Lured by the promise that she could have her car back by noon, she agreed, and handed the keys over to Lloyd.

She walked back to the motel but stopped in the lobby to speak to Amelia Ann.

"I have several boxes of papers I need to photocopy," she said. "The grocery store near the Parson's Creek bridge has a copier, but it's quite a walk from here and I was wondering if there are any copy machines closer."

"Let me do some checking for you while you go have some breakfast. I think maybe I can find one for you."

The Home Away from Home Motel had a closet-sized coffee shop. Jordan was the only customer. She didn't have much of an appetite and ordered toast and orange juice.

Amelia Ann came looking for her. "I only had to make a couple of calls," she said. "And you're in luck. Charlene over at the Nelson Insurance Agency has a brand-spanking-new copy machine. The company put it in last week, and it's on trial, so they don't care how many papers you have to copy just as long as you pay for the paper you use. Steve Nelson carries the insurance on this motel, so he's not going to mind doing a favor."

"That's wonderful," Jordan said. "Thank you so much."

"I don't mind helping out when I can. Charlene said to tell you the machine has a feeder, so it will copy lickety-split."

The news just kept getting better. The insurance agency was only three short blocks away from the motel, and the copier was in a room all by itself, so Jordan wouldn't bother Charlene or her boss while she worked.

The copy machine was an absolute dream, and she made quick progress. She was interrupted only once when a client of the agency, Kyle Heffermint, stopped by to get some figures. While Charlene was gathering them for him, he spotted Jordan in the copy room and took it upon himself to act as the welcoming committee for the town of Serenity. He leaned against the wall and chatted as Jordan continued to feed pages into the machine. Kyle was a pleasant man, and she enjoyed hearing all about the history and politics of the community, even though his habits of repeating her name and punctuating his comments by raising one eyebrow were a bit annoying. After she declined his fourth offer to "show her around," Charlene came to the rescue and ushered him to the door.

Jordan had copied two full boxes before noon. Staggering under the weight, she carried the first and the second box of originals back to her motel room and then returned for the copies. She stuffed some of the pages in her tote bag with her laptop so she could start reading while she had lunch.

It was a quarter to twelve when she arrived at Lloyd's Garage to find the coolant reservoir and most of the engine lined up on a tarp.

Lloyd was sprawled out in a metal chair, fanning himself with a folded newspaper, but the second he spotted her in the doorway he tossed the paper aside and jumped to attention. He put his hands up as though to ward off a blow and blurted, "Now don't get yourself in a roar."

The radiator hose was draped over the coolant reservoir in the center of the tarp. She stared at it while she casually asked, "What is all this?"

"Parts . . . belongs inside your car. I ran into a few problems," he continued. He couldn't quite look her in the eye. "I was wanting to make sure it was a leak in the radiator and not something else, so I pulled the hose to check for a tear and there wasn't any, and then I decided to check the clamp, and it was okay, and then I decided I might as well check a couple of other things too. And what do you know . . . the leak turned out to be in the radiator after all, just like I suspected. Better safe than sorry, don't you think? And I'm not charging extra for the extra work. A thank-you will be fine. Oh, and one more thing," he added in another rush. "I'll get it fixed by tomorrow noon, like I promised."

She took a deep breath. "You promised it would be fixed by noon today." She was so furious she'd been played, her voice shook.

"No, you made an assumption."

"You promised noon today," she repeated forcefully.

"No, I never said today. That's where the assumption part

comes in. I just said noon. I didn't say noon today or noon tomorrow." And without pausing for breath, he asked, "Since you're going to have to stay in town another night and don't know a soul, how about having dinner with me?"

Lloyd apparently lived in another dimension.

"Put it all back. Put it all back now."

"What?"

"You heard me. I want you to put everything back where it belongs. Do it now, please."

Lloyd must not have liked the look in her eyes because he took a hasty step back. "I can't," he said. "I've got another job to finish first."

"Really? Then you weren't taking a nap when I walked in?"

"I wasn't napping. I was taking a break."

She knew it would be pointless to argue with him. "When will my car be ready?"

"Noon tomorrow," he said. "See what just happened here? I said noon tomorrow, so I can't get out of it. Once I say something, it's said."

She blinked. What in heaven's name was that supposed to mean? Maybe she hadn't heard him correctly. "Once you say something . . ."

"It's said," he repeated with a nod. "And that means I can't take it back."

"I would like you to put it in writing," she said. "Guarantee the time the car will be ready and the price," she added. "Then sign it."

"All right. I'll do it," he promised as he turned and went inside the shop. He came back out a minute later with a pad and a pen. He leaned against the car as he wrote and signed the guarantee. He even dated it without being asked.

"Satisfied?" he asked after he'd given her the paper and she'd read it.

She nodded. "I'll be back here at noon tomorrow. Don't disappoint me."

"What are you gonna do? Hurt me?"

"I might." She started to walk away.

"Hold on now."

"Yes?"

"You've got to eat sometime. What about having dinner with me?"

She attempted to be gracious as she declined his invitation. She even went so far as to thank him for inviting her. He seemed placated when she left him.

Her steps slowed as she walked over to Jaffee's Bistro. It was beastly hot. By the time she got there, she was dying from the heat and the humidity. How did the residents of Serenity stand it? The temperature on the thermometer outside the restaurant registered ninety-eight.

Angela was carrying a plate to one of the tables when Jordan walked in.

"Hey, Jordan."

"Hey, Angela." Good Lord, now she was beginning to sound like a local. The realization made her smile.

"You want your usual table? Let me just clear it for you."

The restaurant was nearly full, and all the customers watched her as she made her way to the corner table. They were obviously curious about outsiders.

"Are you in a hurry, or can you do with iced tea for a little bit?"

"I can wait, and tea would be great."

Angela brought the drink right away and then went back to helping the other customers while Jordan looked over the menu. When she had decided on a chicken salad, she put the menu down, opened her laptop and turned it on, and then spread out some of the research papers so she could start reading.

She made notes while she read so she could check the professor's research when she got back to Boston.

"Your fingers are flying over those keys," Angela said. "Am I interrupting your train of thought?"

"No, you're not," she said, glancing up from the screen.

"What were you doing?"

"I had been making notes, but just now I was merging my calendar with a spreadsheet. Nothing important," she added as she closed the laptop.

"So you must know a lot about computers . . . you know, how they work and all."

"Yes," she answered. "I work with computers."

"Jaffee's got to meet you. He's got a computer, but it won't work right. Maybe you could answer a couple of questions for him after you have your lunch."

"I'd be happy to help," she said.

The restaurant had emptied by the time she finished her salad. Angela came out from the kitchen with the owner. She made the introductions, and Jordan complimented him on the restaurant.

"It's a charming place," she said.

"It's named after me of course," he told her with a grin. "My first name's Vernon, but everyone likes to call me just plain Jaffee. I like it too," he admitted. "Where are you from, Jordan Buchanan?" Jaffee had a wonderful twang in his voice, like a guitar string being plucked.

"Boston," she replied. "What about you? Did you grow up in Serenity, or are you a transplant like Angela?"

"Transplant," he replied, flashing a smile. "From another tiny town you've probably never heard of. I did a spell in San Antonio. That's where I met my wife, Lily. She worked at the same restaurant, and you know . . . we kind of clicked. We've been married fourteen years, and we're still clicking. What's the weather like in Boston? Does it get as hot as it does here?"

The conversation about the heat lasted a good ten minutes. Jordan didn't know anyone, aside from a meteorologist, who was more interested in the weather than Jaffee.

"Mind if I sit with you a spell?" he asked as he pulled out a chair across from her and sat down. "Angela said you wouldn't mind answering some questions about computers."

"I don't mind at all," she said.

"Did you like your salad? City girls always like salads, don't they?"

She laughed. "This city girl does."

Jaffee was such a nice man, and he was definitely in the mood to chat.

"I had quite a crowd here for breakfast. Always do. I don't have half that many for lunch. Truth is, I barely break even in the summer months, even serving dinner, but come fall I do a real nice business. My wife has to come in and help out then. My chocolate cake is famous around here. I expect folks will come dribbling in later this afternoon for a slice or two. Don't you worry though. I already put back a slice for you."

She thought he was going to get up when he shifted in his chair. She reached for one of her folders so she could read another outrageous story about the saintly MacKennas and the demonic Buchanans.

Jaffee wasn't going anywhere. He was merely getting comfortable. "Chocolate cake is how I ended up owning this coffee shop."

She put the folder down and gave him her full attention. "How did that happen?"

"Trumbo Motors," he said. "Dave Trumbo to be exact. He owns a dealership in Bourbon, which is about forty miles from here. Anyway, Dave and his wife, Suzanne, were vacationing in San Antonio, and they had dinner in the restaurant where I was working. I'd made my chocolate cake, and boy oh boy, did he take to it. He had three slices before his wife made him stop." He laughed then. "He's got a real love for chocolate, but Suzanne won't let him have it very often. She worries about his cholesterol and such. Anyway," he continued, "Dave couldn't get that cake out of his mind, and he sure didn't want to have to drive all the way to San Antonio, which as you know is quite a trek from here. So what did he do? He made me an offer I couldn't refuse. First of all he told me about Serenity and how there wasn't a good restaurant to speak of, and then he told me he went to his good friend Eli Whitaker. Eli's a rich rancher who's always looking for a good investment. Dave convinced him to give me start-up money. Eli owns this building, but I don't have to pay rent until I start making a big enough profit. He's what we call a silent partner. He rarely looks at the books, and some months when I get my bank statement, I see there's been a deposit made into the account. He won't own up to it, but I know he or maybe Trumbo is putting the extra money in."

"They sound like good men," she said.

"Oh, they are," Jaffee replied. "Eli's a bit of a recluse. He comes in here a lot, but I don't think he's left Serenity since he settled here fifteen years ago. You just might get to meet him this afternoon. Dave's bringing him his new truck. Eli buys a new one every year."

Jordan thought Jaffee was about to get up, so she reached for the folder again.

"Dave's our best advertisement. The man loves his chocolate, and lots of folks come in because Dave told them how good the food is."

"Does Trumbo Motors have a good mechanic?"

"They sure do. More than one." Jaffee chuckled. "I heard Lloyd was giving you a hard time."

Her eyes widened. "You did? How did you hear that?"

"This is a small town, and people like to talk."

"And they've been talking about me?" She couldn't keep the surprise out of her voice.

"Oh my, yes. You're the talk of the town. Beautiful woman like you coming here, not putting on any airs at all, talking to ordinary folks."

She couldn't imagine whom he was talking about. She certainly didn't feel beautiful. And what ordinary folks had she talked to, and what did he mean by ordinary?

"You look flabbergasted," he said, grinning. "It's different here than Boston. We like to think we're more friendly, but the fact is we're nosy. You get used to it, everyone knowing everyone else's business. I'll tell you what, when Dave gets here with Eli's truck, he'll come in for cake, and I'll introduce you. I'll bet good money he already knows about your car situation."

"But you said he lives in another town . . ."

"He does," he said. "He lives in Bourbon, but everyone in Serenity buys their cars and trucks from him. He's got the best dealership around. I keep telling him he ought to go on television to advertise like those city fellas do, but he says no, he doesn't want his picture taken. He's camera shy I guess, and he likes dealing with the local folks. He's always coming over to Serenity. His wife gets her hair and nails done over here too, so she hears the latest news from the other ladies in the beauty shop."

Jaffee finally got around to his computer questions, and when Jordan explained what various commands were for, he seemed satisfied. He went back to the kitchen to start a sauce, but Jordan kept thinking about life in a small town. It would drive her nuts if everyone knew what everyone else was doing. Then she thought about her family, and she realized she already lived that life.

All six brothers were loving, sweet, and horribly intrusive. Maybe they had learned to interfere because of their jobs. Four were in law enforcement, though she probably shouldn't count Theo because he worked for the Justice Department, and unlike Nick and Dylan and Alec, Theo didn't carry a gun all the time. They were used to snooping into other people's lives—but then again, as far back as she could remember, they always made sure they knew what she and her sister were up to. They used to scare the heck out of her high school dates. She would complain to her father, but that never did any good, and she thought that secretly he was on her brothers' side.

Big families were just like small towns. No doubt about it. Just like the Highland clans she was reading about. According to the professor's research material, the Buchanans were always interfering. They seemed to know every little thing the MacKennas did, and every little thing made them mad as hornets. They never forgot a slight. Jordan couldn't imagine how they kept track of all the feuds going on.

Papers were spread out all over the table. She was trying to decipher some notes the professor had made in the margins. They didn't make sense—numbers, names, dollar signs, and other symbols randomly scribbled. Was that a crown? Some of the numbers could be dates. Had something important happened in 1284?

She heard Jaffee laughing and looked up just as he came out of the kitchen. A man followed carrying a dinner plate with a huge slice of chocolate cake. Had to be Dave Trumbo.

The big man strode toward her with an air of self-confidence. His face was hard, as though each feature had been carved in stone. His shoulders were broad, and from the way he was dressed in a crisp white shirt, striped tie, dark gray pants, and black loafers, she knew he took time and care with his appearance. Trumbo was what her mother would call dapper. He removed his designer sunglasses and chuckled over something Jaffee had said.

He had a winning smile and an easy way about him. He looked her right in the eye as he shook her hand and told her how nice it was to meet her. Oh, he was smooth all right. She didn't have to ask if he'd lived in Texas all his life. Dapper Dave had a slow Texas drawl. Noah was born in Texas and would occasionally slip into that drawl too, she remembered, especially when he was being flirtatious.

"Jaffee told me you were having some trouble with Lloyd, and I'm real sorry to hear it. If you want, I could have a talk with him. If he doesn't cooperate, I'll tell you what. I could have your car towed over to Bourbon and one of my mechanics could put it back together for you. It's a shame you can't just trade it in for a new car. I've got a deal on a brand-new Chevy Suburban no one could turn down."

"Her car's a rental, Dave," Jaffee reminded him.

He nodded. "I know it is. That's why I said it was a shame she couldn't trade it in. You ought to go after the people who rented you that vehicle. It's not right, doing business that way."

Jaffee told Dave that she was from Boston, and she answered several questions about her city. Dave hadn't been there yet, but wanted to take his family there for a vacation.

"Dave's got a boy and a girl," Jaffee interjected.

He nodded. "I sure do. It's why I have to work so hard. I best eat this cake in the kitchen in case my wife happens by. She's coming to town sometime this afternoon to get something or other done to her hair. She's perfect the way she is, but she likes to keep up she says with the latest styles she sees in the magazines. If she sees me eating this cake, she'll have a fit. She has me on a low-carb, low-fat, low-taste diet." He patted his stomach. "I am getting a little thick in the middle, but this cake is worth a couple of extra miles on the treadmill."

He didn't look thick, he looked trim and fit. He wouldn't stay that way though if he continued eating so much sugar. She spotted what she thought was the top of a chocolate bar wrapper sticking out of his shirt pocket. Dave did love his chocolate.

Jaffee turned to look out the front window. "Eli's parking his truck across the street," he said. "It looks brand-new."

"It's a year old this month," Dave said. "Which is why he's trading it in. Eli can afford any car he wants, and Lord knows, I've tried to get him to buy a luxury sedan, but he keeps on ordering the same pickup, just a new model, every year. He won't even choose a different color. Always black."

Jordan could see the rancher crossing the street. Eli Whitaker was a good-looking man—tall, dark, and admittedly handsome. She'd expected a rancher to be wearing cowboy boots and a Stetson, but he was dressed in jeans, a polo shirt, and tennis shoes.

He gave her a broad smile when Jaffee introduced her, and his hand felt warm when he shook hers. "It's a pleasure to meet you, Jordan," he said.

Jaffee quickly filled him in on the reason she was in town.

"Sorry to hear about your bad luck, but if there's a good place in the country to get stranded, I think you've picked the right one. You'll find the people around Serenity just about as hospitable as they come. You let me know if there's anything I can do to help."

"Thank you," Jordan said. "Everyone's been very helpful. My car should be ready tomorrow, and I'll be on my way again."

The three men stood at her table and continued to chat for a few more minutes, though they did most of the talking and she did most of the listening.

Finally Dave Trumbo said, "Well, it was a pleasure visiting with you, Jordan Buchanan, and next time you're in this area, you be sure to drop by Trumbo Motors. No one undersells me," he boasted. He threw his hand over Eli's shoulder and said, "You want a piece of cake, Eli? Let's go back to the kitchen and let this young lady get back to her homework."

Get back to her homework? Did he think she was in summer school?

"That's not homework, Dave," Jaffee said. "Those are stories she's reading about her relatives in Scotland. Stories from way back when. She came all this way to read these papers from some professor. Isn't that right, Jordan?"

"Yes, that's right. It's Professor MacKenna's research."

Dave peered over her shoulder at what she was reading. "You understand all that?" he asked.

Jordan laughed. "I'm trying. Sometimes it's not very clear," she answered.

"Looks like homework to me. I'll let you work in peace." He turned and, with his hand still on Eli's shoulder, headed toward the kitchen with Jaffee close behind.

Time got away from Jordan, and it was almost four o'clock when she gathered up her papers. Jaffee stood in the doorway watching her slip her laptop into her bag. He scratched the back of his neck and said, "Listen, about those commands . . ."

"Yes?"

"They're not working. We're kind of computer illiterate in Serenity, but we're trying to catch up with the rest of Texas and the world. All the young kids learn about computers over in the consolidated schools, but we're not quite there yet in Serenity. The town's beginning to grow and we just got our first high school built, so we're hoping to get some good teachers in here soon. Maybe they can even teach some of us old folks. I've got a nice big computer in the back, but it's not responding to any of the commands you gave me. I did something . . . I don't know what, and I ruined it."

She smiled. "Ruined it? Unless you took a sledgehammer to it, it's difficult to ruin a computer. I'll be happy to look at it."

"I'd sure appreciate it. I've put in several calls to computer technicians over in Bourbon, but they're dragging their feet getting here."

He'd been so nice to her, letting her hang out in his restaurant all day, it was the least she could do. She grabbed her bag and followed him into the kitchen. Jaffee's office was in a little nook by the back door. The computer was archaic by today's standards. There were cables running every which way. Most of them weren't necessary.

"What do you think?" Jaffee asked. "Can you save her and get her running again?"

"Her?"

"I sometimes call her Dora," he admitted sheepishly.

She didn't laugh. His face was turning red, and she knew it was embarrassing for him to admit he humanized the machine.

"Let me see what I can do." She figured she had plenty of time to get back to the insurance agency and finish copying the papers in the last box. There wasn't that much left to do, so if the agency closed, she could always finish in the morning.

Jaffee returned to his work in the kitchen, and she went to work rebuilding the computer. She removed every cable, tossed out two of them, and unscrambled and rerouted two others. Once that was done, it didn't take her any time at all to get the computer running. Next she tackled the programs someone had installed for him. They too were archaic. Jaffee was trying to run three different ones, and all of them were complicated. Had she had the time and the equipment, she would have written a new program for him. She would have had fun doing it too, and oh, God, what did that say about her? She swore then and there that if she ever named her computers and humanized them, she'd pack it in.

Since she couldn't install new software, she decided to try to simplify one of the existing programs.

The next time Jaffee checked on her he was thrilled to see the blue screen.

"You've got it working again. Oh, thank goodness. But what's all that gibberish you're typing?"

It would take too long to explain. "Dora and I are having a little chat. When I'm finished, the program will be easier for you to run."

After the last customer had left at eight-thirty, Jaffee closed the restaurant and sat down with her to go over the changes she'd made.

She spent an hour helping him familiarize himself with his computer. He made copious notes on Post-its and stuck them on his wall. She had already programmed in her e-mail address so he could write to her with questions if he got into a bind, but he asked that she also give him her cell phone number just in case he couldn't get the e-mail to work.

She thought she was finished, but he handed her a stack of e-mail addresses and begged her to put those in his address book. Eli Whitaker was at the top of the list. Dave Trumbo came next. She smiled when she read his e-mail address. DangerousDealer-Dave. She added it without comment and went on to the next one.

When everything was complete, Jaffee insisted on walking her back to the motel.

"I know it's not that far and we've got streetlights, but I'm going to walk with you just the same. I want to stretch my legs anyway."

It was still hot outside, but the temperature had dropped a little with the setting of the sun. When they reached the drive that led to the motel entrance, Jaffee wished her a good night and strolled on.

Jordan walked into the lobby thinking she could take a short-cut to her room. The lobby was packed with women.

Amelia Ann rushed forward to greet her at the door. "I'm so happy you could make it."

"I'm sorry?" Jordan responded.

Amelia Ann's daughter, Candy, sat at the front desk. She printed Jordan's name on a pink name tag and hurried over to stick it on her shoulder.

"We're happy you can join us," Amelia Ann bubbled.

"What am I joining?" Jordan asked, smiling at all the women staring at her.

"I'm giving Charlene a late-night bridal shower. You remember Charlene," she said in a whisper. "She let you photocopy your papers at the insurance agency where she works."

"Yes, of course." Jordan searched through the smiling faces for Charlene's. "It's so nice of you to invite me, but I don't want to intrude."

"Nonsense," Amelia Ann protested. "We'd love to have you."

Jordan lowered her voice. "But I don't have a gift."

"That's easy to fix," Amelia Ann said. "How about giving her a place setting of china? Charlene chose a real pretty pattern. Vera Wang."

"Yes, I'll be happy to—" Jordan began.

"Don't worry about a thing. I'll order it tomorrow, and I'll add it to your bill. Candy? Go wrap another gift card and write Jordan's name on it."

Jordan met all twenty-three women and was thankful that they were wearing name tags too. For the next hour, she watched the unwrapping of the gifts while she drank sweet punch and ate mints and white cake with thick, gooey icing.

By the time she returned to her room, Jordan was on a sugar high. Then she crashed.

She slept hard that night, returned all of her phone calls the next morning, and didn't leave the motel until after ten. Her plan was to walk over to the insurance agency to copy the rest of the papers, bring them back to the motel, and then run over to Lloyd's Garage and wait there for Lloyd to finish the repairs. And he would finish them, she decided, even if she had to stand behind him and prod him with a crowbar. One thing was certain: she wasn't going to put up with any more delays or surprises.

Her plan didn't work out. Charlene gave her the bad news. "They picked up the machine and hauled it off about an hour after Steve told the salesman he wasn't going to buy it. Did you have a lot more to copy?"

"A couple hundred pages," she answered

She thanked Charlene again and retraced her steps to the

motel. Okay, new plan. She'd get the car, check out the copy machine at the grocery store, and if that machine didn't have the capability of feeding the pages in, she'd look for another one.

Lloyd was pacing in front of the garage. The second he spotted
her he shouted, "It's ready. All ready to go. Early too. I told you I'd
fix it, and I did. Okay?"

He was a nervous twit. His hand trembled when he thrust the
itemized bill at her. He was obviously in a hurry to get rid of her,
for he didn't even count the money she gave him.

"Is something wrong?"

"No, no," he rushed out. "You can be on your way now." Without a backward glance, he hurried back into the garage.

She put her purse and her laptop on the passenger seat next to
her and started the engine. Everything seemed to be in working
order. Lloyd, she decided, ranked up there with Professor
MacKenna for weirdness. She was happy she didn't have to deal
with him any longer.

She drove directly to the grocery store and was elated to find a
modern copy machine with all the bells and whistles. She was back
in business. She thought she could have everything done in a couple of hours if she hurried. Then she'd call the professor and get his
boxes back to him.

Better safe than sorry, she reminded herself. To be prepared in
case the car acted up on the road again, she bought water and
planned to stop at a filling station to buy some antifreeze for the radiator if it sprang another leak.

She carried four gallons of water, two in each arm, out of the
store. The parking lot was deserted. No wonder. No one would
choose to go grocery shopping in the god-awful heat of the day.
Today was already a scorcher. She squinted against the sun bouncing off the cement. She felt like she was getting sunburned just
walking across the lot. She placed the containers on the ground
next to the trunk of the car. While she was digging through her
purse for the keys, she noticed a piece of clear plastic protruding
from the seam of the trunk and thought it was odd that she

hadn't noticed that before. She tried to pull it free, but it wouldn't budge.

She found the key, slid it into the lock, and the lid sprang upward as she stepped back. Jordan looked inside . . . and froze. Then she very gently lowered the lid.

"No," she whispered. "Couldn't be." She shook her head in denial. She was just seeing things, that was all. Her mind was playing tricks on her. It was all that sugar she'd eaten . . . and the heat. Yes, that was it. The heat. She'd had a terrible heat stroke and just didn't know it.

She opened the lid again. She felt as though her heart had just stopped beating. There, curled up like a tabby cat inside the biggest Ziploc bag she'd ever seen, was Professor MacKenna. His lifeless eyes were open, and he seemed to be staring at her. She was so stunned she couldn't breathe. She didn't know how long she stood there staring down at the man, two seconds, maybe three, but it seemed an eternity before her mind would let her body react.

Then she freaked. She dropped her purse, tripped over one of the gallons of water, and slammed the trunk lid closed. No matter how desperately she tried, she couldn't convince herself that she hadn't seen a dead body in her trunk.

What in God's name was he doing in there?

Okay, she was going to have to look again, but oh, Lord, she didn't want to. She took a deep breath, turned the key again, and mentally braced herself.

Oh, God, he was still there.

She left the key in the lock, ran to the side of the car, and all but dove through the window to get her cell phone from the front seat.

Who should she call? The Serenity Police Department? County or local? The sheriff? Or the FBI?

Jordan knew two things for certain. One, she was being set up, and two, she was in way over her head. She was a law-abiding citizen, damn it. She didn't carry dead bodies around in her trunk, and she, therefore, didn't have the faintest idea what to do with it.

She needed advice—and fast. The first person she wanted to

call was her father. He was a federal judge, so of course he would know what to do. But he was also a worrier, like most fathers were, and he had enough on his plate now with the explosive trial under way in Boston.

She decided to call Nick. He worked for the FBI, and he would tell her what to do.

The phone suddenly rang. The sound so startled her she let out a yelp and nearly threw the phone down.

"Yes?" She sounded as though she were being strangled.

Her sister was on the line. She didn't seem to notice the hysteria in Jordan's voice.

"You are not going to believe what I found. I wasn't even looking for a dress, but I ended up buying two of them. They were on sale, and I almost got one for you too, but I thought our tastes are so different you might not like it. Should I go back and buy it anyway? The sale won't last long, and I could always return it—"

"What? Oh, God, Sidney, what are you talking about? Never mind. Are you home?"

"Yes. Why?"

"Is anyone else home with you?"

"No," she answered. "Why? Jordan, is something wrong?"

She wondered how Sidney would react if she told her the truth. Yes, something's wrong. There's a dead body in the trunk of my car.

Jordan couldn't tell her. If Sidney did believe her, she'd only become upset, and there really wasn't anything she could do about it from Boston. Besides, as dear as her younger sister was, she could never keep a secret, and she'd immediately find their mother and father and tell them. Come to think of it, she'd tell anyone who'd listen.

"I'll explain later," she said. "I have to call Nick now."

"Wait. What about the dress? Do you want—"

Jordan disconnected the call without answering the question and quickly dialed Nick's cell phone.

Her brother didn't answer. His partner, Noah, did.

Dear God in heaven, she couldn't catch a break to save her life.

"Hi, Jordan. Nick can't talk right now. I'll have him call you back. You still in Texas?"

"Yes, but Noah—"

"Great state, isn't it?"

"I'm in trouble."

The panic in her voice came through the phone loud and clear. "What kind of trouble?" he asked quietly.

"There's a dead body in the trunk of my car."

He didn't miss a beat. "No kidding."

Could he have been more blasé? "He's in a Ziploc bag."

"Yeah?"

She didn't know why she'd felt the need to add that extra bit of information, but at the moment it seemed vitally important that he know about the plastic.

"And he's wearing blue-and-white-striped pajamas. No slippers though."

"Jordan, take a breath and calm down."

"Calm down? Did you hear what I just said? Did you catch the part about the dead body in the trunk of my car?"

"Yes, I heard what you said," he replied, his voice maddeningly unruffled. He sounded as though her news wasn't such a big deal, which of course was ridiculous, but even so, the fact that he was so calm helped her get a grip.

"Do you know who he is?"

"Professor MacKenna," she said. She took a deep breath and lowered her voice. "I met him at Dylan's wedding reception. I had dinner with him last night. No, that's not right. Two nights ago. I thought he was disgusting. He ate like a wild animal. It's horrible to talk about the dead like that, isn't it? Except he wasn't dead . . ."

She realized she was rambling and stopped in mid-sentence. A minivan pulled into the lot and parked near the front door. A middle-aged woman got out, squinted at Jordan, and then went inside.

"I've got to get out of here," she whispered. "I've got to get rid of him. Right? I mean it's pretty obvious I'm being set up for murder."

"Jordan, where are you now?"

"I'm in a grocery store parking lot in Serenity, Texas. It's so small it's barely on the map. It's about forty miles west of Bourbon, Texas. Maybe I could dump the body there. You know, find an isolated spot and—"

"You're not going to dump the body anywhere. Here's what you're going to do. You're going to call it in, and so will I," he explained. "I'm also going to get a couple of FBI agents over there within an hour, two tops. And Phoenix isn't that far away. Nick and I will get there real soon."

"I am being set up, aren't I? Oh, God, I hear sirens. They're coming for me, aren't they?"

"Jordan, hang up now and call it in before they get there. If you're arrested, you ask for a lawyer and don't say another word. Got that?"

The wailing of the siren indicated the police were just a couple of blocks away when the 911 operator answered Jordan's call. She quickly explained what the emergency was and then gave her name and location.

The operator was giving her instructions to stay where she was when a gray sedan came careening into the lot.

"The sheriff's car just pulled in."

"The sheriff?" The operator sounded surprised.

"Yes," Jordan said. "That's what's printed on the side of the car, and I'm sure you can hear the siren through the phone."

Jordan couldn't hear the operator's next question. The car screeched to a stop about twenty feet away, and a man jumped out of the passenger side of the front seat. He wasn't wearing a uniform.

He ran toward her, a chilling look on his face. She saw something flying at her and instinctively turned away trying to protect herself, but the blow caught her on her right cheek and she went down.

Chapter Nine

THE ARGUMENT WAS OVER JURISDICTION. JORDAN HEARD raised voices and opened her eyes just as a paramedic placed an ice pack on her cheek. She tried to push it away. She was dazed and disoriented.

"What happened?" she asked in a whisper as she struggled to sit up. The cement was burning her arm.

One of the paramedics, a young man dressed in a blue uniform, took hold of her arm to help her. Still feeling light-headed, she leaned against him.

"You got hit," he said. "That's what happened. When Barry and I pulled up, the Dickey brothers were here. We heard Sheriff Randy yelling at his brother, J.D., because J.D. jumped out of the car and lit into you. He stopped yelling at him, though, when he saw me sprinting across the lot. Now he and his brother are arguing with Serenity's chief of police."

"What are they arguing about?" she asked. Her head was pounding, and her jaw felt as though it had come unhinged.

"J.D. insists that you were resisting arrest and that he thought

he was helping his brother out when he hit you to restrain you so
Sheriff Randy could get his handcuffs on you."

Jordan grew more and more clearheaded by the second. "That's
not true."

"I know it isn't," he whispered so the Dickey brothers wouldn't
hear him. "Barry and I heard your 911 call, and we got here as quick
as we could, which really wasn't any time at all because our little
clinic is only three blocks away. We knew something had happened
to you. One second we could hear you talking as clear as a bell, and
the next second we hear what sounded like a half shout. You know
what I mean?"

"He knocked the phone out of my hand."

"He smashed it to bits is what he did. I'm afraid you're going
to have to buy yourself a new one. Right now they aren't arguing about your phone though. Sheriff Randy is saying that you
were in his county when you took off and headed over here.
You're in Grady County now," he explained. "Randy Dickey is
sheriff in Jessup County, and how he ended up sheriff is a mystery none of us can figure out. He must have made a lot of
promises. Anyway, Sheriff Randy's jurisdiction ends at the foot
of the bridge that crosses the creek. Once you get on that
bridge, you're in Grady County. We have a sheriff too, but he's
in Hawaii on vacation with his wife and kids, and we only see
him once in a blue moon because he lives way east in Grady's
county seat."

Barry, the other paramedic, had been listening to their conversation. He popped a toothpick into his mouth, parked it in the corner, and strolled over.

"The only reason Sheriff Randy comes around here is because
his brother lives in Serenity. He likes to go fishing with him. Del,
you ought to make her keep that ice pack on her cheek. It's already
swelling under her eye. I think we need to take her to the clinic
and get an X-ray."

"No, I'm okay. I don't need an X-ray."

"We can't make you go with us," Del said. "If you refuse treatment, there's nothing we can do, but if you start feeling sick to your stomach or dizzy, you tell us, okay?"

"Yes, I'll tell you."

"Could I ask you something?" Del asked. "What was it like finding a body in your car? It would have given me a heart attack. Barry and I figure you didn't have anything to do with the murder because, if you did, you sure wouldn't have called 911, would you?"

"You look like you're hurting," Barry said.

"I'm okay. I've just got a little headache, that's all, and I don't want to take anything that might dull my anger. I swear to heaven—"

"Now, now, it's not good to get all upset," Barry said. "Especially after taking such a hit."

Del motioned Barry closer. "If Maggie Haden could get away with it, she'd hand her over to Sheriff Randy and his brother in a heartbeat."

Barry agreed. "She wouldn't lose any sleep over it either," he whispered.

"Who's Maggie Haden?" Jordan asked. She was trying to see what was going on with the chief and the Dickey brothers, but the paramedics were blocking her.

"That's her there. She's the chief of police," Del answered. "The chief and Sheriff Randy have a history. You know what I'm talking about? Everyone in town knows he got her the job."

"She shouldn't have gotten the job," Barry grumbled. "She wasn't qualified. Just because she was on the police force over in Bourbon doesn't mean she should be the chief here in Serenity. But since nothing much ever happens here, I guess people don't care if she knows what she's doing or not." He shifted the toothpick to the other side of his mouth and squatted down in front of Jordan. "It's payback," he whispered. "She wanted the job, and Randy owed her since he got married to someone else and left her high and dry."

"How long has she been chief of police?" Jordan asked.

"About a year," Del said.

"More like two years," Barry offered.

"Don't let the way she looks color your judgment. She's a lot tougher than you'd think. She can be a real viper."

Jordan leaned around Del to get a look. The chief had brassy, bleached blond hair and wore enough makeup to work in a circus.

"Getting the job of chief of police is a big deal around here. Serenity is kind of behind the times. The police station only just got a computer, and all the 911 calls are routed through Bourbon."

"I'm feeling much better now," Jordan said. "And I'm tired of sitting on the ground and being a bystander. Please let me get up."

Barry lifted her but didn't let go of her. He insisted that she sit on the back bumper of the ambulance. "You lean on me if you feel dizzy."

Surprisingly, she wasn't at all dizzy, but her throbbing cheek reminded her that one of those brothers had punched her. Seething now, she was about to ask the paramedics which one was J.D. when Barry said, "Listen, if the chief does decide to hand you over, I'll say we're taking you to the clinic for an X-ray. I'm telling you right now, you don't want to go anywhere with those brothers."

"Okay," she agreed. "You're being very kind to me," she said. "I appreciate it. I know it looks suspicious. I'm a stranger in town . . ."

"And there's that body in your car," Del reminded her.

"Yes," she said. "But I am innocent. I didn't kill anyone, and I assure you no one was more surprised than I was when I opened that trunk."

"I'll bet. My name's Del, by the way. And he's Barry."

"My name's Jordan Buchanan and—"

"We know who you are. The chief already got your driver's license from your wallet," Barry said. "She read your name out loud. You don't remember? Del, maybe we should go ahead and get her head X-rayed."

She hadn't been aware that anyone had gone through her purse to get her identification. Had she been knocked unconscious?

Maybe she'd just been knocked senseless. That's what her mother used to ask her when she'd done something she didn't approve of. Did you get knocked senseless?

"I don't need an X-ray," she said for the second time. "And I didn't do anything wrong."

"Looking guilty and being guilty are two different things," Del said. He pulled the stethoscope from around his neck and handed it to Barry.

"I think you're going to be okay," Barry whispered as he folded the stethoscope and put it in the metal case before snapping it shut. "The chief knows that you weren't over in Jessup County, and she also knows you weren't involved in any car chase. There's a witness."

"And that witness is going to make it real hard for her to hand you over to the Dickeys."

"She still might," Del said.

"No, she can't," Barry argued. "Not with the witness. A woman coming out of the grocery store saw the whole thing. She also called 911, and she told the operator what she saw and how J.D. punched Miss Buchanan without any provocation. She said J.D. hopped out of the car like he had a swarm of wasps on his tail and grabbed her phone and punched her silly. Then he smashed her phone."

"Miss Buchanan better hope that J.D. doesn't get to the witness and scare the wits out of her so she'll change her story."

"It won't matter. Every emergency call is taped, so there's a record, and J.D. can't change what's already on the tape."

The two men were talking about Jordan as though she weren't even there. She was astonished that no one was doing anything about the body. She'd seen the chief of police glance into the trunk, but that was all. As far as Jordan knew, no one else had even looked. The paramedics certainly hadn't. No one seemed interested in finding out who the victim was. She wondered when they were going to get around to that question.

"You think we'll be taking the body to Bourbon?" Del asked.

"I'll bet so. We'll have to stick around until the crime scene people get here and the coroner releases the body."

Weary of being on the sidelines, Jordan thanked the paramedics once again, and then walked closer to the chief and waited for her to acknowledge her.

One of the Dickey brothers noticed Jordan's hands were free.

"Someone ought to put that suspect in handcuffs," he said. "Someone who ought to know her job by now," he added.

Jordan stepped forward. "Are you the one who hit me?"

He didn't look her in the eye when he answered her. "No one hit you," he snapped.

"For God's sake, Randy, look at her face. Someone sure as hell hit her," Maggie Haden yelled. "And there's a witness." Because the sheriff looked so surprised, she added with a nod, "Yes there is. A witness who saw your brother slap the cell phone out of this woman's hand and then hit her with his fist." Lowering her voice, she said, "So you can see nothing can be done or changed now. It's too late. There could be a potential lawsuit over this."

J.D. had been slouching against the hood of the sheriff's car and shouting his jabs at the police chief, but when he heard about a witness, he lunged forward.

"What witness? Who saw what? If I'm going to be accused of something I didn't do, I should get to know this witness's name."

"In good time, J.D.," the chief said.

"Chief Haden, I want to press charges," Jordan demanded.

"You be quiet," Haden snapped.

"I want you to arrest him," Jordan insisted.

The chief shook her head. "I don't care what you want. Now keep your mouth shut."

J.D. nodded his approval and then said, "Randy, doesn't it seem curious to you that the chief is ranting about a little rough treatment subduing a violent suspect, and that suspect murdered a man. You can't argue with that. The evidence is right there for anyone to see. The body ain't in my car or yours, Randy. It's in her car. And since when do we care about manhandling a murderer?"

The Dickey brothers were two of the most unattractive individuals Jordan had ever encountered. They were both built like used-up wrestlers who'd let their muscles go to flab. Their necks were thick, their shoulders round. J.D. was taller than his brother, but not much. Randy carried quite a paunch, and his face was elongated by a double chin. Both men had small eyes, but J.D.'s were set close like a ferret's.

The chief of police finally turned her attention to Jordan.

"My name is Chief Haden," she said. "And you are?"

Since she was holding Jordan's driver's license in her hand, the chief knew exactly who she was, but if she wanted to go through the formalities, Jordan wouldn't argue. She told her her name and gave her address.

"I want some questions answered right here and now. Do you know who the man in the trunk of this car is?" she asked. "The deceased. Do you know his name?"

"Yes," Jordan answered. "His name is Professor Horace Athens MacKenna."

"How do you know him?" she asked.

Jordan quickly explained where and how she'd met the professor and why she was in Serenity. Chief Haden didn't look like she believed a word Jordan was saying.

"You'll be coming with me to the police station," she said. "You've got a lot more explaining to do. We'll wait here until the coroner arrives, so don't give me any trouble or I'll cuff you right now."

Without a word, Sheriff Randy and his brother walked back to their car. J.D. had a disgusting smirk on his face.

"Chief Haden, may I ask you a question?" Jordan asked. She was still seething with anger, but she kept calm. Pleasant was too much to ask for.

"Make it quick." The chief's tone was snippy.

"How did the sheriff know there was a body in the trunk?"

"He said his brother got a tip on his cell phone. I can't say if he's telling the truth or not."

Sheriff Randy ignored the comment. His brother didn't. Whirling around, he shouted, "Did you just call me a liar?"

When the chief didn't answer, J.D. said, "Are you going to take the word of a murderer over a law-abiding citizen?"

"The FBI can check the sheriff's cell phone records and get a printout of all the calls both of the brothers received in the past twenty-four hours. That will be helpful, won't it, Chief Haden?" Jordan asked.

J.D. snorted. "Yeah, right. As if the FBI would go to that kind of trouble for a homicide in this nickel-ass town. They won't give you the time of day."

"I already called them, and they're on their way here," Jordan responded.

She'd certainly gotten everyone's attention with that statement.

"Why would you call the FBI?" the chief demanded.

"My brother Nick is an FBI agent. I talked to his partner and he assured me that he and Nick would be here shortly, but in the meantime, he's sending over a couple of agents from the area's district field office."

Sheriff Randy didn't seem to be fazed hearing the FBI was going to get involved. J.D., on the other hand, looked startled and angry.

"She's bluffing."

Sheriff Randy continued on to his car. "Hold on there," J.D. called out. "My brother has the right to question her."

"No, he doesn't," Jordan said.

J.D.'s eyes bored into her. She didn't flinch. She knew he was trying to frighten her, but she wasn't about to shrivel up or cower. Then he took a threatening step toward her. Bring it on, she thought. He'd caught her unaware with the first punch, but she wasn't about to let that happen again. This time she would be ready for him.

"Maggie, are you gonna let the FBI come in here and tell you what to do?" J.D. whined. "After all Randy and I have done for you? You wouldn't be such a hot shot chief of police if it weren't for—"

Haden cut him off. "Listen here," she said. "I'm not letting any-one tell me what to do. Randy?"

The sheriff turned back. "What, Maggie?"

"What are you doing all the way over here anyway? And how come you're out of uniform?"

"I was planning to take the day off," he said. "Can't you see the fishing poles in my car? I came over to go fishing with my brother."

"You always drive your pickup when you go fishing," she pointed out.

"I didn't today, did I?"

"No need to get snide with me. You ought to get on with fish-ing and let me do my job."

"But the FBI . . ." J.D. began.

Jordan deliberately interrupted. "I hope your police station is large enough to accommodate my family. I'm certain by now all of my brothers have heard and are on their way. And I've got a lot of brothers. Funny thing is, most of them are in law enforcement. Theo, my oldest brother," she said, her tone annoyingly cheerful, "he doesn't like to boast, but he's pretty high up in the Justice De-partment." She stared at J.D.'s ugly face as she added, "The United States Justice Department. Alec is working undercover for the FBI now, but he'll want to come here too. Oh, and then there's Dylan. He's a chief of police himself," she continued. "I imagine he'll want to have a little chat with Sheriff Randy and J.D. You see, none of them is going to believe that nonsense about a car chase, and like me, they're going to wonder who's lying and why."

"You bitch," J.D. snarled.

"Get in the car, J.D.," his brother said. "Maggie, I want to talk to you in private."

"You stay right where you are," the chief said to Jordan. "Boys, you keep a watch on her," she called out to the paramedics as she hurried toward the sheriff.

Jordan watched the two in conversation from where she stood. The chief got as close to the sheriff as she could and nodded several times, obviously agreeing to whatever he was telling her. Not good, Jordan thought. Not good at all.

A couple of minutes passed and then finally the Dickey brothers got in their car and took off.

Chief Haden looked disgusted. "I'm going to find out what's going on here. What'd you do to provoke the sheriff?"

"I didn't do anything," Jordan countered.

As though Jordan hadn't spoken, she continued, "You're going to tell me why the sheriff wanted to take you with him for questioning. What is it he knows about you?"

Before Jordan could tell her that she didn't have the faintest idea what was in either of the Dickey brothers' twisted minds and she wasn't about to start guessing, the coroner, wearing sunglasses and a Dallas Cowboys cap, pulled into the lot in a powder pink convertible.

Del took hold of Jordan's arm. "Come on back to the ambulance and wait with us."

Jordan went with the paramedic, but she kept her eye on Chief Haden, who was next to the rental car conversing with the coroner. When she was ready to leave, she shoved Jordan into the backseat of her squad car but didn't bother handcuffing her. They drove to the corner and stopped. Haden called her deputy and left a message with his wife to find him and tell him to report to the police station as soon as possible.

"Tell Joe I've got a murder investigation."

Jordan inwardly cringed over the glee she heard in the woman's voice. The chief gunned the engine and roared through town with her siren blasting away.

Chapter Ten

THE POLICE STATION WAS EXTREMELY SMALL. JORDAN THOUGHT it looked like an old western movie set. There were two desks with a waist-high wooden railing between them and a swinging gate to the inner sanctum with a tiny office the size of a toll booth at the back for the sheriff. A door on the left led to a hallway with a bathroom and a single jail cell.

There was only one other person in the station, a young woman sitting in front of a computer, crying. When the chief and Jordan walked in, she dabbed at her eyes with the cuff of her shirt-sleeve and lowered her head. Jordan heard the chief curse under her breath.

"Still having trouble, Carrie?"

"You know I hate this."

"Of course I know. You've done nothing but complain since you took this job."

"I didn't take this job," she muttered. "It was forced on me. And I haven't complained all that much."

"Don't argue with me in front of a suspect."

"Am I a suspect?" Jordan asked.

She expected the chief to tell her that of course she was a suspect. The body was in her car, after all. Then the chief would read her her rights, and she'd ask for an attorney.

None of that happened.

"Are you a suspect?" the chief repeated. She cocked her head and frowned as though she couldn't make up her mind. "I'll determine that after I question you."

Jordan thought she was kidding, but the look on her face indicated she was, in fact, serious. Did she think that Jordan would willingly answer all of her questions and incriminate herself so that she could be arrested? Surreal, she thought. This was simply surreal.

The cell was real enough. It was tucked around the corner from the front office.

The chief led Jordan into the tiny room and then stepped out and closed the door. "I'm locking you in here so I'll know you won't be running away while I go back to talk to the crime scene people. I'm taking the key too," Haden added, "just in case someone comes along and wants to let you out."

Jordan didn't say a word. She couldn't. She was speechless. She needed to calm down and collect her thoughts, so she sat on the cot and placed her hands on her knees, palms up, her back straight, her focus on the stone wall across from her. After a few minutes she closed her eyes and tried to remember some of her yoga exercises to gain what her instructor had told her was inner peace. Okay, so inner peace was out of the question, but if she could get her heartbeat to stop racing and her breathing to slow down, then maybe she would be able to stop freaking out inside.

Two full hours, and then some, passed before the chief came back to the station. She opened the cell and dragged a straight-back chair in with her. Jordan could hear the chief's assistant muttering in the other room, but she couldn't make out what she was saying.

"Is your assistant crying?" Jordan asked.

The chief stiffened. "Of course not. That wouldn't be professional."

They both heard a sob.

"My mistake," Jordan said.

"I'm going to be taping this interview," Haden announced as she produced a small recorder and laid it on the cot.

The chief of police was incredibly inept. Jordan wanted to ask her if she had ever investigated a homicide before, but that question would only make her angry, especially if Jordan pointed out that she hadn't been read her rights.

"I have questions to ask. Are you ready to give me some honest answers?" She didn't wait for Jordan to respond. "You can start by telling me how you could be driving a car and not know there was a dead body in it."

Her accusatory tone didn't sit well with Jordan. "I told you, I picked the car up at the garage and didn't look in the trunk until I was at the grocery store."

"And this friend of yours, this Professor MacKenna, he meets with you one day and is found murdered two days later—and you have no idea how that happened, right?"

"I think I should have an attorney present if you're going to continue with these questions," Jordan said politely.

Chief Haden pretended she hadn't heard her.

Two can play this game, Jordan decided, and she pretended she didn't understand a single question she was asked from that point on.

Eventually the chief stopped in frustration. "I thought we could have a friendly conversation," she said.

Jordan tilted her head and studied the woman. "You've locked me in a cell and you're taping every word I say. That doesn't seem very friendly to me."

"You listen here. You aren't going to be able to intimidate me like you did the Dickey brothers with your talk about the FBI and the Justice Department. You can get yourself an attorney when I say you can, and you might as well know that, because you aren't cooperating, you are now making yourself a suspect in this murder investigation."

She turned off the tape machine and finally got around to reading Jordan her rights. Then she dragged the chair out and slammed the cell door shut.

She poked her head around the corner an hour later and said, "Here's a phone book. You can look through it and pick out your own attorney. You can even get one from back east if that's what you want, but you're going to sit in this cell until you answer my questions. I don't care how long it takes." She handed the book through the bars and said, "Let me know when you want to make your call."

Could she be railroaded and charged with murder? If only Jordan had the approximate time the professor was killed, she would be able to figure out where she was and if anyone had seen her. She hoped he hadn't been murdered during the night because she couldn't prove she had stayed in her motel room. They could say that she jogged over to the professor's house, killed him, but then how did she get the professor's body into the trunk of her car, which was locked inside of Lloyd's Garage? What was her motive? Would they make one up?

This was going nowhere. She didn't have enough information to form any kind of a defense . . . or alibi. She didn't even know how the professor had been murdered. She'd been too stunned to take a good look at him all wrapped up like leftovers.

She was completely out of her element . . . or out of her comfort zone as Noah would say. This was really all his fault, she decided, because he'd pointed out to her how dull her life was. She'd been perfectly happy not knowing she was boring. Now she felt powerless. In order to survive, the body needed water and food, but Jordan needed a computer and a cell phone too. Without all of her tech gadgets she was lost.

Jordan hated feeling out of control. When she got out of here . . . if she got out . . . she'd take a couple of years and go to law school. She wouldn't feel so vulnerable if she knew the law, now, would she?

The chief interrupted her pity party. "Are you going to make the call to an attorney or not?"

"I've decided to wait for my brother."

The chief snorted. "Are you going to hold to that story? You're just stalling is all. You'll change your mind soon enough because you're not going to get anything to drink or eat until you start cooperating. I don't care how long it takes. I'll starve you to death if I have to," she threatened.

"Is that legal?" Jordan asked sweetly.

Haden had a real mean streak in her. She poked herself in the chest as she said, "I can do anything I want in this town. Understand? I'm not as soft as I look."

Jordan couldn't resist. "No one could ever think you looked soft."

She'd gotten a rise out of the chief. Her face colored. "I wonder how much sass you would have if I decided to turn you over to the Dickey brothers."

She pointed her finger at Jordan and was about to threaten something more when she was interrupted by Carrie.

"Maggie?"

"I told you to call me Chief Haden," she bellowed.

"Chief Haden?"

"What?"

"The FBI's here."

Chapter Eleven

"Where is she?" Nick asked.

"This is my investigation," Chief Haden said. "The FBI has no place here."

Nick and Noah had entered the police station expecting to deal with a competent law enforcement professional. They were mistaken. And neither of them was in the mood to put up with foolish territorial issues.

"He asked you a question," Noah barked. "Where is she?"

"Never you mind where she is," Haden countered. "Like I just told you, this is my investigation. You and your friend need to get out of my police station."

Nick had already told her that Jordan was his sister, and he'd shown her his identification and credentials. Now it was her turn. She damn well was going to answer his questions.

Chief Haden would have taken a step back to get away from his anger, but the railing was behind her, trapping her. She knew she had started out on the wrong foot, but she wasn't about to back down. The sooner the two of them realized who was in charge, the better.

The man who identified himself as Agent Nick Buchanan was intimidating and fierce, but he wasn't nearly as frightening to her as the agent who walked in with him. There was something in his piercing blue eyes that told her not to get in his way. She knew it wouldn't take much to get him to pounce, and she didn't want to be the one he pounced on. Her only option was to strike first.

Nick was about to lose his temper when the young woman sitting in front of a blank computer screen piped up, "Your sister is sitting in a cell just around the corner. She's doing okay, but wait until you see her." She was winding a strand of her long curly hair around one finger and smiling up at Noah when she shared the information.

"My sister is locked in a cell?" Nick asked.

"That's right," the chief answered after flashing a glare at her assistant.

"What are the charges?"

"I'm not willing to share that information just yet," she said. "And you're not going to be seeing your sister or speaking to her until I'm finished with her."

"Nick, did she just say, until she's finished with her?" Noah asked. He sounded amused.

Nick didn't take his gaze off the chief when he answered. "That's what she said."

The chief's lower lip jutted out, and her eyes narrowed. "You don't have any jurisdiction here."

"The chief thinks she can mess with the federal government," Noah remarked.

Haden was furious. The two agents were pressing in on her. She pushed through the swinging gate and stood alone near the doorway, blocking access to the cell.

The FBI agents were arrogant thugs, she thought, smartmouthing her. The two of them were so full of themselves and so cocky the way they tried to throw their weight around. But they didn't know who they were dealing with. The fact that a woman had risen to the position of chief of police in Serenity, Texas, should have been an indication to them that she wasn't a powder puff. Even though Serenity was a bit-of-nothing town, she had had to work hard screwing others, both figuratively and literally, to get where she was. Two muscle men carrying badges and guns had rattled her for a few minutes, but she was back in control now, and they weren't going to tell her what to do. Screw them. This was her town and her rules. She was the power here.

"I'll tell you what you can do. You can leave your phone number with my assistant, and when I've finished interrogating my suspect, I'll give you a call." She addressed Nick. "Now go on and get out of my police station and let me get back to work."

The suspect's brother smiled at her. She thought he might start laughing. The possibility didn't sit well.

"What are we gonna do about this situation?" Nick wanted to know.

Haden's bravado ended abruptly. Noah started walking toward her. She stepped out of his way. If she hadn't moved, he would have walked over her or through her. He didn't leave any doubt about that.

Noah glanced over his shoulder at Nick and grinned.

Nick conceded, "Yeah, yeah, you've still got it."

The "it" was spook tactics. Noah had always been able to freeze anyone, male or female, with one hard look. Nick, on the other hand, according to Noah, had still not perfected the art.

"You can get the key from her," Noah said.

"You listen here. I'm not letting that woman out until she starts cooperating." Haden's voice was loud and surly.

On the other side of the wall Jordan patiently waited for someone to come and get her. She knew that Nick and Noah had arrived because she could hear the chief of police arguing. When she saw Noah, her shoulders sagged with relief. She was so happy to see him.

He was appalled by the sight of her. "What happened to you? You look godawful."

"Thank you. It's lovely to see you too."

Noah ignored her sarcasm. Given the circumstances most women would have been a little upset, he thought, but Jordan wasn't like most. As miserable as she looked, she could still give him attitude. He had to admire her spunk.

He leaned against the steel bars and smiled at her. "You want out of here?"

Exasperated, she replied, "What do you think?"

"Tell you what. You tell me what happened to that pretty face of yours, and I'll let you out."

She gingerly touched her cheek and winced. "A fist ran into it," she said. "Is Nick still out there? I don't hear him."

"I can't imagine you could hear anything over that woman's screeching."

"How did you get here so quickly? I thought you were going to send some agents from the district."

"I was able to charter a small plane, so I didn't need to call them."

"Nick willingly got into a small plane? It takes a lot of coaxing to get him into a commercial jumbo jet. I can't imagine he'd fly in a small one."

"I didn't say willingly, did I? I had to do some pushing and shoving."

She was impressed. "Did he get sick?" she asked, smiling over the possibility. It was comical to see him turn green.

"Yeah, he did."

She laughed. "I'm so happy you're both here," she admitted.

He shrugged. "You should be."

His arrogance didn't bother her so much today. She heard the chief's raised voice again and asked, "What's going on out there?"

"Nothing much. Your brother's just having a little chat with the chief of police."

"Chief Haden's a real softie, isn't she?"

Noah laughed. "She's about as soft as a rattlesnake," he said. "She's trying to give my home state a bad name, but don't you worry about her. Nick can handle her."

Jordan stood and tried to brush the wrinkles out of her blouse.

"Do you think you could find the key and get me out of this cell?" she asked sweetly.

"Sure enough," he agreed. "Just as soon as you tell me whose fist ran into your face."

At that moment Haden stormed around the corner, a sour look on her face, the key in her hand. She unlocked the cell door, muttered something under her breath that Jordan pretended not to hear, and said, "It's been . . . suggested that we sit down and talk this out. You know . . . get to the bottom of this mystery."

Nick was standing in the doorway. Jordan's hair had fallen forward, partially covering her face, but when she brushed it back over her shoulder, he got a good look at her injury.

"What happened to you?" he demanded. "What son of a—"

"It's okay," she said quickly before he could finish his obscenity. "I'm fine, really."

His eyes blazed with anger as he addressed the chief. "Are you responsible for this?"

"Of course I'm not responsible," she snapped. "I wasn't even there when the alleged incident occurred."

"Alleged?" Noah spun around to confront Haden.

"Jordan, who hit you?" Nick asked.

The chief swung the door open as Nick posed the question. The woman wouldn't move out of Jordan's way, so Noah stepped forward, took hold of Jordan's arm, and pulled her toward him.

"Jordan, answer me," Nick demanded.

"His name is J.D. Dickey. I don't know what the J and the D stand for. His brother Randy is the sheriff of Jessup County. The two of them were together in Sheriff Randy's car. We're in Grady County now," she added.

"Why wasn't the guy who assaulted you arrested?"

"I tried to press charges."

"What do you mean, you tried?" Nick asked.

"I mean I tried. She wouldn't let me."

She'd rendered her brother and Noah speechless. They'd never encountered such incompetence.

They all filed into the outer office. Since there weren't enough chairs to go around or the space to put them in, they ended up standing in a cluster near the assistant's desk. Jordan noticed that Carrie was trying—without much success—to get Noah's attention.

Maggie Haden made her way around the group to her office and sat on the edge of her desk tapping her foot impatiently while she listened to the conversation.

"We'll get him in here," Noah promised.

"Where exactly were you arrested?" Nick asked.

"Three or four blocks from here."

"She was never arrested," Haden called out.

"Then why was I locked in a cell? Remember what you told me? You weren't going to give me anything to drink or eat until I answered your questions. You also said that you didn't care if I starved to death."

"I said no such thing."

Carrie had been quietly content to stare up at Noah until she heard what the chief said. Her head snapped up, and for a second she stopped twirling her hair.

"Yes, you did. I heard you," she said.

"I was bluffing," the chief said.

"Bluffing?" Noah questioned. "Don't we call that lying to a federal agent and obstructing justice, Nick?"

"That's what we call it," he agreed. "You want to arrest her or should I?"

"Now hold on." Haden's voice had risen an octave. "Your sister wouldn't cooperate. I had to lock her up."

"Jordan, is that true?" Nick asked.

"What do you think?"

"Just answer the question," he demanded impatiently.

Nick was behaving more like a big brother than an FBI agent now, but she was still too thankful and happy that he was there to be bothered by his high-handed attitude.

"I requested an attorney," she began, "and I also informed Chief Haden that I had called you. She then informed me that I wasn't a suspect but that she was going to interrogate me with her tape recorder on, and when I wouldn't answer her accusatory questions without an attorney, she changed her mind and decided I was a suspect after all."

Turning to the sour-faced woman, she said, "I can't remember. Was that before or after you threatened to hand me over to the Dickey brothers?"

All turned to stare at the chief, waiting for her explanation.

Haden's chest heaved as she took a deep breath. "I did not threaten any such thing."

"Yes, you did," Carrie volunteered. "You said—"

The chief cut her off with a scorching glare. "Put a cork in it, Carrie, and get back to that computer. You're on work release, not a vacation."

Carrie's face turned bright red. She lowered her head and stared at the keyboard. Jordan could see that she was embarrassed that Nick and Noah had heard what the chief said.

"I can't work the computer. The stupid thing's broken."

Jordan felt sorry for her and wondered which would be worse, working for the chief from hell or going back to prison to serve out the rest of her sentence.

Carrie sounded pitiful. "I don't know what to do."

As galling as it was to inadvertently help the chief of police, Jordan couldn't stop herself from helping Carrie. With a sigh, she reached around Carrie, hit two buttons, waited half a second, then hit a couple of keys, and the computer screen lit up.

Carrie looked like she had just witnessed a miracle. Wide-eyed, she stared at Jordan and whispered, "How did you do that?"

As Jordan explained, Nick argued with the chief about jurisdiction. The chief liked the word and used it as an answer no matter what question was asked.

"Has the coroner given you an approximate time of death for the victim?" he asked.

"This is my jurisdiction and therefore my case. You don't need to be butting your nose in."

"Why haven't you brought J.D. Dickey and his brother in?" he asked.

"What business do you have with the sheriff?"

"What business did he have in Grady County?"

"This is my jurisdiction," Haden huffed.

"When are you going to arrest J.D. Dickey?" he asked.

Haden's cell phone rang. She turned her back on the agents and stepped around her desk.

She covered her mouth. "I know who it is," she snapped under her breath. "You listen here. They're pressuring me to arrest you." Several seconds passed, and then Haden said, "For socking the woman. What'd you think they wanted me to arrest you for?"

"Doesn't she know we can hear every word she's saying?" Noah asked Nick.

"Apparently she doesn't."

Haden's voice had risen. "And I'm telling you my hands are tied here. I'm doing the best I can."

She disconnected the call and tossed the cell phone onto her desk. Nick waited until she turned around before he asked the obvious.

"Were you just talking to J.D. Dickey?"

"No, I wasn't."

"If you don't bring him in, we will."

"This is my jurisdiction."

Nick asked her again if the coroner had given an approximate time of death for Professor MacKenna.

"I already answered the question. This is my jurisdiction and my case." She folded her arms and began tapping her foot. "I want you to get out . . ."

"We are not going away," Noah interjected.

"What was the cause of death?" Nick asked.

"My jurisdiction," she repeated, dragging the word out.

And so it went. No matter what question was asked, jurisdiction was her answer.

Jordan felt as though she were watching a tennis match, her gaze bouncing back and forth between her brother and the chief.

Carrie touched her arm to get her attention. "How come I can't get the printer to print?"

Jordan leaned over the desk and said, "Your printer isn't hooked up to the computer." Her attention returned to the ongoing argument.

Carrie distracted her again. "Can you fix it?" she pleaded.

"Yes, okay."

"I found the manual for the computer," she whispered. She was keeping her eye on the chief now, making sure she wasn't listening. "But I haven't read it. I told her I had but . . . you know. I got busy doing other stuff. I guess I should read it, huh?"

"That's probably a good idea," Jordan said. She walked around the desk and began hooking up the cable while Carrie continued to whisper.

"Your brother's really good-looking, but he's got that wedding ring on. It is a wedding ring, isn't it?"

Jordan smiled. "Yes, it is."

"Is his wife alive? I mean, some guys keep on wearing their wedding rings for years after their wives die."

"Yes, his wife is alive, and yes, they're happily married. In fact, he and Laurant are expecting their second child in three months."

Carrie's voice dropped lower. "Jaffee's really nice-looking too. I mean, he's losing his hair and all, but that makes him kind of sexy. I was walking past his restaurant on my break yesterday, and he and his friends were standing there talking to you. That rich rancher . . . you know who I mean . . . his name's Whitaker . . . now, he's really hot. He's on the lean side, but I can tell he's got muscles, and I like muscles. I bet he works out, don't you think?"

Jordan didn't answer, but Carrie didn't seem to mind. "That one there though"— she nodded in Noah's direction—"he's got to be the sexiest man I've ever seen."

Was there any man Carrie didn't find appealing? Just how long had she been in prison? Jordan hoped the discussion had ended, but Carrie wasn't going to let it go.

"I mean . . . don't you think?"

"Yes, he is sexy," Jordan replied.

"That's what I thought."

Jordan happened to glance up at Noah and realized he'd been watching her. Had he heard the conversation? She hoped not.

The chief was drawn away by another phone call, and Jordan seized the opportunity.

"Nick, what happens now?"

"We're waiting for your attorney."

"Who is he?" she asked.

"I haven't met him, but he comes highly recommended."

"Doctor Morganstern called him," Noah told her.

Startled, she gasped and her hand went to her throat. "You told Doctor Morganstern about this? Why did you tell him?"

Dr. Morganstern was a brilliant man, and his opinion mattered to her. She didn't want him to think less of her, or to think that she was somehow responsible for this mess.

"What's the big deal?" Noah asked.

"You shouldn't have bothered the doctor. He's a busy man."

Nick shook his head. "We work for him, remember? We can't just take off without letting him know where we're going. We had to tell him what we were doing and why."

"Why does that bother you?" Noah asked.

"I just told you why. He's a very busy man," she said as she walked over to Noah and sat on the edge of the desk next to him. "It doesn't really matter to me. I just didn't want you to bother him. That's all."

He nudged her. "Yeah, it does bother you." He leaned over and whispered, "You didn't kill the guy, did you?"

"No, of course I didn't," she whispered back.

"Then you have nothing to worry about."

"Tell that to the chief."

"She isn't your problem any longer."

Before she could ask him to explain, Nick's cell phone rang. He glanced at the number and told Noah, "Chaddick's calling back."

He flipped the phone open and said, "What have you got?"

Jordan tapped Noah's arm. "Who's Chaddick?"

"An FBI agent making some calls for us and checking some things out. He'll come in on this if we need him."

"I appreciate it," Nick said into his phone. "Right. I'll meet you there. I'll give you a call when I'm leaving Serenity. You're going to set it up? That's great. Thanks again."

Jordan and Noah looked at him expectantly when he ended the call.

"Strangulation," Nick said without preamble.

"So it was up close and personal," Noah remarked.

"A crime of passion," Nick said. "Rope was used. Chaddick said some fibers were found imbedded in the skin."

"It takes a lot of strength to strangle someone. I doubt Jordan has that kind of strength. Even coming up behind him, even with the element of surprise—"

"I didn't strangle anyone."

"Didn't you notice his neck?" Nick asked. "Didn't you see any bruising or discoloration?"

"No, I didn't."

"Were you wearing your contacts? Could you see—"

"Yes, I was wearing my contacts. I could see just fine."

"Then how could you have missed—"

She cut him off. "Look," she said, her irritation growing, "I was too busy noticing he was wrapped up like a sandwich. Oh, God, I'll never eat anything from a Ziploc bag again."

"Jordan, get a grip," Nick said. "This isn't the time to get all emotional. I know this is upsetting—"

"Upsetting?" She pushed off the desk and took a step toward him. "The way I feel goes way past upset."

He put his hand up. "Calm down. I'm just trying to get as much information as possible before your attorney gets here. I wish your powers of observation—"

She took another step in his direction. "You know what I wish? I wish I'd called Theo."

Noah grabbed hold of Jordan's arm and pulled her back. "But you didn't call Theo. You called Nick. Take a deep breath, okay?"

He made her sit back on the desk. "What do you suggest we do about her?" he asked, motioning to the chief of police. The woman was pacing in her tiny office while she talked on the phone. "I think we should lock her up and throw away the key."

"Jordan?" Carrie whispered her name.

"Yes, Carrie?"

"You shouldn't get mad at your brother. I wish I had a brother who could have helped me when I got into trouble. I do have a brother," she explained earnestly. "He drove the getaway car. He didn't get away though. They caught him too."

Jordan didn't know what to say and so she simply nodded.

"Since you helped me with this stupid computer, I want to help you. Did you know that Maggie . . . I mean Chief Haden . . . used to live with Sheriff Randy Dickey? Everyone in town thought they would get married. She thought so too, but he married someone else. And you know what else I heard? Sheriff Randy had a connection through his new wife with one of the town council people, and he got them to give the chief of police job to Maggie so she'd have to move over here to Serenity. I also heard she was going to get fired from her old job anyway." She placed her hand to the side of her mouth as though to share a secret and spoke just above a whisper. "She was mean back then too, and she did a lot of favors for the Dickey brothers." She gave a wink and went on. "She let them get away with a lot of stuff. At least that's what I heard."

"What about her deputy? What's he like?"

"Oh, he's nothing like her. He should have gotten the job of chief of police. He has a lot more experience, and he's worked here longer. I heard he's looking for a job outside of Serenity."

"I don't doubt that. It would be pretty awful working for her."

"I could find him for you."

"You could?"

"I'm sure I could. Deputy Davis is kind of hardnosed about stuff, but he's honest, and as far as I know, the only person he's sleeping with is his wife. He treats me like a real person."

"Would you like Carrie to get on the phone and help you find the deputy?" Jordan asked Noah.

"That'd be real nice," Noah said, smiling at the young woman.

Carrie didn't move. She just sat there staring at Noah as though she was in a daze. Jordan tapped her on her shoulder.

"He said that would be nice."

"What?"

"It would be nice if you would find Deputy Davis."

"Oh . . . okay." Without looking, Carrie picked up the receiver on the other side of the desk and put it to her ear. The cord was too short to reach, so the phone came flying across, knocking a can of soda and a large stack of files to the floor.

"Shoot!" she cried as she jumped up and rounded the desk to clean up the mess. "I'm so stupid."

Noah leaned down to help her. "No, you're not. Accidents happen to everyone."

"Especially me," she said. She grabbed the Kleenex box off the desk and wiped up the spilled drink. "I'm so embarrassed. I must look like a lobster. I can feel my face turning red."

Noah straightened a pile of folders and handed them to her. "I think it's a very pretty face."

When he took her arm to help her stand up, the rosy blush on Carrie's cheeks turned a deep crimson. "Thank you," she said.

"Do you think you could find the list of town council members?" Nick asked her from across the room.

Carrie's attention swung to him. "I know I could. They're in my Rolodex. There's only three."

"Let's get them in here," Nick said to Noah. "They'll have to officially replace her."

"You're replacing Chief Haden?" Carrie asked.

The chief had just finished her call, and there was a smug look on her face until she heard a snippet of the conversation.

"No one's replacing me," she said as she stepped out of her office. Her frown was directed at Jordan. "I knew I was right about you. I just had an interesting talk with Lloyd. Remember him?" Chief Haden asked Jordan.

How could she forget? "Of course I remember him. He worked on my car."

"He says you threatened him."

Jordan was taken aback. "He what?"

"You heard me. He says you scared him."

"I did not threaten him."

"He says you did. He says you told him you were going to hurt him."

Uh-oh. Jordan remembered the conversation. "I might have—"

"No more," Noah said. "Jordan, I don't want you to say another word." Turning to Haden, he said, "Get Lloyd in here. Now."

"You're not telling me what to do." Chief Haden started walking toward Jordan, her hand resting on the gun at her hip.

When Noah blocked her, she raised her arm and jabbed her elbow into his chest.

"That's it," Noah said. He latched on to her arm and turned her toward the door that led to the cell. "Chief Haden, you have the right to remain silent . . ."

Haden's eyes became slits. "Don't you tell me my rights."

"I'm required to," he said. "This is an arrest."

Haden tried to pull away. She grabbed the handcuffs sitting on her desk. "This is outrageous." Her voice turned into a hiss. "You have no grounds." She swung the cuffs and struck Noah on the shoulder.

He grabbed the cuffs out of her hand, took the gun from her holster, and pushed her ahead of him. "Obstructing a criminal investigation and assaulting a federal agent . . . I think that's enough."

"I know people!" Haden yelled as he nudged her inside the cell.

"I'll bet you do," he agreed.

"Powerful people."

"Good for you." He slammed the door shut in her face. "You'll be staying here until arrangements can be made to transfer you to a federal facility for processing."

"This is bogus," she said.

"You'll be needing a lawyer. I'd get a good one if I were you."

It finally penetrated that he wasn't bluffing. "Now hold on here. Hold on now. Okay, okay, I'll cooperate."

Carrie watched wide-eyed. She wanted to stand up and cheer, but she knew the action might come back to bite her. Her parole officer had told her that her poor impulse control had gotten her into jail, and, if she wanted to change her life, she was going to have to learn to think before she acted. Besides, the chief would eventually get out of jail, wouldn't she?

As Noah walked past Nick, he said, "Nothing I hate worse than a crooked cop." He glanced out the window. A late-model sedan pulled up to the curb. A man emerged from the driver's seat carrying a briefcase in one hand and holding a cell phone to his ear with the other.

Noah turned to Jordan. "Your attorney's here."

Chapter Twelve

LOUIS MAXWELL GARCIA WAS THE EPITOME OF REFINEMENT. HE oozed confidence and charm. His smile was warm and somewhat sincere, and his manners were as polished as alabaster. Neither his designer suit nor his starched pinstriped shirt had a wrinkle anywhere.

After the introductions were made, the attorney insisted that they call him Max.

"Doctor Morganstern speaks highly of you," Nick said. "Isn't that right, Noah?"

Noah didn't say a word. He simply moved closer to Jordan and folded his arms across his chest. His expression was impassive. Slow to warm to anyone, Noah always was skeptical, and Max, vouched for or not, had yet to prove his capability.

"We appreciate you taking this on and getting here so quickly," Nick said.

Max's gaze was locked on Jordan. "I could never say no to Doctor Morganstern."

"Why is that?" Noah asked.

"He's done a lot of favors for me over the years," he said and then turned to Jordan. "Is there somewhere we could talk in private?"

Jordan thought about suggesting the chief's office but quickly changed her mind. The small room with the door closed would be too claustrophobic.

"There really isn't anyplace private here," she said. "We could sit outside on the bench, I suppose, if you don't mind the heat."

Max had a lovely smile. "That's not a problem for me. I'm used to the heat. Where's the chief of police?" he asked then. "I should talk to him first and find out what the charges are. It would be nice if we had his cooperation sharing information."

"Yeah, well, that's not gonna happen," Noah said.

"Chief Haden's a woman," Nick said. "And Noah's right. She's not going to cooperate."

"And why won't she?" he asked.

"She's locked in a cell around the corner," Nick explained.

Max asked the obvious. "And why is that?"

"I arrested her," Noah said.

Jordan thought Max didn't look the least surprised, but then as an attorney he was certainly adept at hiding his reactions.

"I see," Max said. "And what was the reason for her arrest?"

Nick explained, and when he was finished, Max scratched his jaw and asked, "Are there any other surprises you would like to mention?"

"Did Doctor Morganstern explain why I needed an attorney?" Jordan asked.

"Yes, he did. He told me you found a little something in your car trunk."

Carrie waved to get Jordan's attention. "I've got Deputy Davis on hold," she said. "Who wants to speak to him?"

"I will," Noah said as he walked around Carrie's desk and picked up the phone.

Max glanced into the hall that led to the jail cell. "I'm going to try to talk to the chief," he said.

"Why?" Nick asked.

"I want to find out what she has."

"You're wasting your time."

Noah's conversation with the deputy lasted less than a minute. After he had identified himself, Noah told the deputy that his boss was under arrest and he needed to get to the police station as quickly as possible.

Max's conversation with Haden lasted much longer, though it didn't start out well. Jordan winced over the woman's crude vocabulary, but within minutes Haden had stopped yelling, and she guessed that Max had somehow charmed her.

"What do you think?" Nick asked. "It's gotten real quiet in there."

"Maybe Max convinced her to be reasonable," Jordan suggested.

"It doesn't matter," Noah said. "He's wasting his time."

"He won't let her out, will he?" Carrie worriedly asked Jordan.

Max returned to the front office. "The chief of police doesn't think she wants to get an attorney's advice, and she agrees that it would be prudent to cooperate with the FBI. She's also agreed to let us step outside and have our conference, and when we're finished, we'll sit down with her."

Noah shook his head. "That's not gonna happen."

Max ignored Noah's remark. "And what do you think about letting the chief off the hook?" he asked Nick.

Nick glanced at Noah before answering. Jordan thought her brother was a bit amused by the question. Did Max expect him to override Noah?

"My partner just told you that's not gonna happen, and that means it's not gonna happen." Before Max could argue, Nick continued, "The deputy is on his way here. Jordan and you can talk to him."

Max looked directly at Noah and said, "Doctor Morganstern warned me about you two. He said you'd give me trouble."

Noah shrugged. "We don't make trouble, but when push comes to shove, we shove. We get the job done."

Max nodded and placed his hand on Jordan's shoulder. "Shall we step outside?"

Nick opened the door. "Jordan, now that your attorney's here, I'm going to drive to Bourbon and look at the body." Turning to Noah, he asked, "You've got this covered, right?"

"I've got it," Noah assured him.

Max picked up his briefcase and walked with Nick and Jordan outside. Noah followed and pulled the door closed behind him.

The stifling air took Jordan's breath away. She didn't think she could ever get used to this kind of heat.

After Nick had left, Max sat down on the bench next to her. He opened his briefcase, removed a notepad and pen, and was snapping the leather case shut when Noah began his interrogation.

"Where'd you go to law school?"

"Stanford. When I finished, I joined a law firm on the West Coast and worked there until four years ago."

"Why did you leave?"

"I wanted a change."

"Why?"

Max smiled. "I got tired of defending Silicon Valley boys who were stripping their dot-com companies. I decided to move back home and start over."

Max's answers were as rapid as the questions.

"I appreciate any help you can give me," Jordan said, interrupting Noah's interrogation.

"I'll do what I can," he answered warmly. He glanced up at Noah. "I'll need to speak to my client alone."

After scrutinizing the situation for a second, Noah turned to go back inside the police station. "Jordan, you need anything, you call me," he said.

"I will," she promised.

Unlike Noah, the attorney didn't grill her for answers. He simply asked her to take him through the events, beginning with the wedding she had attended and her first encounter with the professor.

Max listened intently and made notes as she went through her actions that morning. When she reached the part about J.D. Dickey's assault, Max raised an eyebrow.

"I told Chief Haden that I wanted to press charges," Jordan explained. "But she refused."

"Did she give you a reason why she wouldn't arrest him?"

Jordan shook her head and explained what she had heard about the relationship between Haden and the Dickey brothers.

"I'll definitely be speaking to Deputy Davis when he gets here," Max said. "I assure you that J.D. Dickey can be brought in on charges. You'll probably have to stay in Serenity a little longer than you planned . . ."

"I don't know," Jordan replied hesitantly. "I think I should just let it go, get out of town, and leave this whole nightmare behind me."

"I understand," Max said. He gave her a sympathetic look and touched her hand. "You just let me know, and we can see that Mr. Dickey pays for what he did to you."

Noah stood at the window watching the conversation between Jordan and Max outside. Jordan kept her eyes on her knees as she talked, and he could tell she was recalling the details of her day. Max Garcia wrote on his pad and cast a caring glance at her from time to time. "Lawyers," Noah mumbled with mild disgust.

Suddenly a car pulled up to the curb, and a man wearing blue jeans and a plaid shirt got out, walked over to Max and Jordan, and shook their hands.

Carrie looked through another window. "That's Joe," she said.

Joe Davis was a young man, but he already had deep worry lines in his forehead. He immediately spotted the gun when Noah walked out to join them.

"Are you the agent I spoke to on the phone?" Joe asked. "Clayborne, right?"

"That's right," Noah answered, stepping forward to take his hand. "I hope you're nothing like the chief, because if you are, we've got a big problem."

"No, sir, I'm nothing like her," Davis assured him. "This is one hell of a mess. I was out on a friend's ranch and my wife couldn't reach me until I got back. I've had three calls from three council members. The president will be over shortly."

"His reason for coming here?" Max asked.

"He wants to personally fire Chief Haden. They've been look-ing for a reason to get rid of her, and now with a false arrest and a failure to press charges I'd say they have grounds enough. They've all had to put up with complaints about her over the last year. In the past couple of months the complaints have escalated."

"You're the man in charge then," Noah said.

He nodded. "I told the council members I would take over until they can find a replacement."

Davis turned his attention to Max. "Is your client ready to talk to me?"

Jordan nodded. And the questions started all over again.

Chapter Thirteen

J.D. WAS IN A FRENZY. HE KNEW HE NEEDED TIME ALONE TO GET a handle on his temper before he did something else he would later regret. He drove down a dirt road on an isolated stretch of flat land outside of Serenity, his hands gripping the steering wheel, fishtailing around one curve and then another, damn near losing control of his truck as he sped on. Dust fanned out around the truck, and he could barely see where he was going because of the grime that covered the windshield. He almost drove into a gully but swerved to the right on two tires and bounced back onto the road. He slammed on the brakes then, jumped out of his pickup, and started kicking the door while he cursed his own stupidity.

He was in such a panic, it was hard to think straight. He knew he'd messed up, but he couldn't do anything about that. It was too late. Randy was as mad as a hornet at him but had promised he'd try to smooth things over.

Damage control. That's what it was all about at this point.

He knew what Cal would be saying to him right now if he

knew about this terrible situation. His cellmate in prison would tell him to take responsibility for his failure and then try to understand what went wrong. Learn from your mistakes. When a job goes bad, it's imperative to figure out what went sour before taking on another job. Any fool knew that. Yes, that's what Cal would say. He was such a wise man.

And what had J.D. learned? He'd learned that he'd gotten too damned greedy. He'd had a real sweet life with his new career until the professor came along and put all sorts of big ideas into his head.

He hadn't wanted the sweet life to go away, and he certainly didn't want to go back to prison and this time maybe get stuck with the needle for premeditated murder.

Luck just hadn't fallen his way, that was all. He'd gone back to Jordan Buchanan's room at the motel twice but couldn't get in. The first time, Amelia Ann had been inside running a vacuum. The second time, there had been a couple of electricians installing new lights outside the room's door.

He stopped kicking his new truck and fell back against the fender. Wiping the sweat and dirt off his forehead, he tried to concentrate. The bitch had messed everything up. No, that wasn't true. She'd complicated his life, but she hadn't ruined it. He could still fix things. He'd fix her too, he decided. Yeah, he'd fix her.

First things first. He had to finish the job, and that meant keeping Jordan Buchanan in town until he could figure out what she knew. What were the possibilities that she knew why the professor had to be silenced? Zero to none, J.D. figured.

Still, he had to be certain.

Chapter Fourteen

THE ORDEAL WAS FINALLY OVER, AND BY SEVEN-THIRTY THAT evening Jordan had been cleared of any and all charges. As soon as the new chief of police had been given the official time of death—with a three-hour window—and had checked Jordan's alibi, she was free to go.

Jordan had accounted for her every moment the evening before. She realized how fortunate she was that she had never been alone, only when she'd gone to bed for the night, but Professor MacKenna had been long departed by then.

The president of the town council insisted on firing Maggie Haden while she was still behind bars. He also insisted that Chief Davis not let the woman out until he had left the station.

Maggie didn't take the news of her termination well.

"You had to have known this was coming," Davis told her.

Her response was predictably vile, and as she was gathering up her personal possessions and throwing them into a cardboard box, she went into a tirade about sexual discrimination.

"People have complained to the council about me because I'm

a woman. You never could stand it that I got the job and you didn't. You've been needling the council to fire me."

"You aren't going to take any responsibility for your actions today?" he asked.

"I'm getting a lawyer, and I'm going to sue every one of you. You won't have a penny to piss on when I'm finished."

"Listen here. You shouldn't be making any kind of threats. It took a lot of fast-talking to convince Agent Clayborne to drop the assault charge. He could still change his mind."

"It was a trumped-up charge."

The box she'd filled was in the center of the desk. She looked down at the contents, then picked it up and hurled it against the wall.

"I don't need any of this junk."

"You need to leave here now." Davis tried to take hold of her arm.

She jerked away. "Don't get too comfortable sitting behind my desk. You won't be chief of police for long. My attorney will force the council to give me back my job. I'll be wearing my badge and gun before you know it. Then you'll be officially terminated. My first order of business will be to get rid of you."

Jordan had walked to the end of the sidewalk with Max to say good-bye, but she could still hear Haden's voice loud and clear. Max handed Jordan his business card with all of his phone numbers, including his private cell number. He told her to call him anytime, night or day, if there were any other problems.

"I suggest you leave Serenity as quickly as possible," he advised. "Whoever put the body in your car had a reason, Jordan. I wouldn't stay around here to find out why. Leave the investigation to the local police. If Chief Davis needs help, he knows he can ask Noah or your brother." He abruptly changed the subject. "I've got to get going, but I wanted to ask . . ."

"Yes?" she said, wondering why he was so hesitant.

"I'll be in Boston next month for a conference, and if you're free I'd love to take you to dinner."

Noah had already thanked the attorney and was waiting by the door for Jordan to say her good-bye. She was smiling at Max, but there was something else in her expression. Surprise, he thought. Curious, he decided to find out what Max was saying to her. His cell phone interrupted. He would have ignored it, but then he saw the number and changed his mind. Nick was on the line.

Jordan tucked Max's business card into her pocket and watched as he got into his car and drove away. She waved good-bye to him. For some reason the action bothered Noah. It seemed too . . . personal, too friendly. He wondered if Max had hit on her and decided that, yes, he definitely had. Jordan was a beautiful woman, and Noah had noticed that the attorney was noticing. That bothered him too. It wasn't professional behavior for her attorney to take such a personal interest in Jordan's physical assets. Oh sure, he'd done his share of noticing. But that was different.

The door behind Noah opened with a bang and Maggie Haden stormed out. She spotted Jordan at the end of the sidewalk and headed toward her.

Jordan turned around and saw blood in Haden's eyes, but she didn't back away or look for help. She could hold her own. She stood her ground and waited to see what the crazed woman would do. She was ready for anything.

She didn't get the opportunity to find out. One second Haden was flying toward Jordan, and the next second Jordan was staring at Noah's back. How he'd gotten in front of her so quickly was beyond her.

Haden was blaming her for everything but the heat. As a parting shot she yelled, "This isn't over."

"Yeah, it is," Noah asserted.

Jordan tapped Noah on the shoulder, but he didn't turn around until Haden was out of sight.

"Yes?"

"You didn't need to get in front of me. I can take care of myself."

He gave her the famous Noah Clayborne smile. "Is that right?"

He brushed the hair over her shoulder and gently patted the side of her face. "If you can take care of yourself, how come your cheek's swollen?"

He had her there. "It was a surprise attack," she said earnestly. "I wasn't ready."

Only after she gave her explanation did she realize how truly lame it sounded.

"I see. So when you're ready and it isn't a surprise, then you can take care of yourself? How much warning would you like to have?"

She didn't think the sarcastic remark required an answer. Besides, she couldn't come up with anything.

"Didn't your older brothers teach you how to defend yourself?"

"Of course they did. They taught Sidney and me all about gun safety and shooting and fighting, clean fighting and dirty fighting." She added, "And all sorts of other things we weren't at all interested in."

"Why weren't you interested?"

"Because we were girls, and we liked girly things."

"Is building a computer a girly thing to do?" he asked, smiling. "Nick told me you were always drawing and designing."

"I still did some girly things," she insisted. "But Sidney and I paid attention to our brothers' lessons too. Really."

He abruptly moved to another topic. "Are you hungry?"

"I'm starving," she said. "And I've found the most perfect restaurant to take you to for dinner. You'll love the food. Can we just take off though? Did Chief Davis—"

"He knows where you're staying tonight. We can leave."

The restaurant was just a couple of blocks away.

"My glasses are in my purse, and my purse is in my rental car," she said as they walked along. "Do you think that when Nick drives back, he could bring them?"

"Nick isn't coming back to Serenity."

"Why not?"

They crossed the street and turned south. "Doctor Morganstern called him and wants to meet with him in Boston. Nick doesn't know why."

"Do you have to go too?"

"No," he answered. "I've been ordered to stick with you."

She pushed into his side. "You don't need to sound so disgruntled. Am I such a pain then?"

Noah looked down at her. Ordinarily, he would have relished this situation, and even jumped at the opportunity to spend the night watching over a beautiful woman, but this was no ordinary situation, and Jordan was no ordinary woman.

"Am I?" she asked when he didn't respond. He shrugged in answer. "Why would Nick ask you—"

"Nick didn't ask me to stay," he said. "Morganstern ordered me to stay with you."

She tilted her head. "Why? I've been cleared of all charges. Yes, I know the professor was placed in my car, and I know what you're thinking . . ."

He grinned. "I don't think you do."

"What about my rental car? Do you know when it will be released?"

"No, I don't. An FBI agent from this district is driving another car here for us and picking up your things first in Bourbon," he said. "A friend of his is following and will take him back home. He'll call me when he gets here."

"What about the rental agency?"

"They'll have to figure out a way to get the car from Bourbon. It's no longer your problem."

"And why is that?"

"Nick had a little chat with the owner. As soon as he mentioned a lawsuit, the guy folded. Your brother's law degree comes in handy on occasion."

They reached Jaffee's restaurant. Noah pulled the door open for her. There were only two tables occupied, and both were by the front window.

"Hey, Jordan."

"Hey, Angela," she replied.

The waitress was carrying an empty tray back to the kitchen. "Your table's ready," she called out.

Noah followed her to the corner table. "You have your own table here?"

"Yes, I do."

He laughed.

"I'm not teasing. This is my usual table. And watch. She'll bring me my usual drink."

Noah chose the two chairs with backs against the wall. Jordan noticed and thought that taking such measures was second nature to him now. Noah, she believed, would never be caught unaware.

Angela hurried over to the table with a glass of iced tea and two glasses of iced water. Smiling at Noah, she asked, "Now, what can I get for you?"

"I'll have iced tea."

She left to get his drink but paused in the doorway. Her gaze was on Jordan when she tilted her head toward Noah and gave the thumbs-up.

"I guess she doesn't realize I can see her," Noah remarked. There was laughter in his voice.

"She means well."

Jaffee hurried out with menus. "Hey, Jordan," he called from across the room.

"Hey, Jaffee."

"Who's this?" he asked bluntly as he handed them their menus. Jordan introduced Noah. "You're FBI, aren't you?" Jaffee asked.

"Yes, that's right."

Jaffee nodded. "Is your brother going to be joining you?" he asked Jordan.

"You know about Nick?"

"Sure I do," he answered. "Did you forget what a small town this is?"

"Nick got called back to Boston."

"Are you her bodyguard?"

Jordan answered. "He's my friend."

"A friend with a gun?" Angela remarked as she joined the group.

Jordan took it all in stride when both Angela and Jaffee pulled out chairs and sat down.

"Start at the beginning, hon," Angela said. "Don't leave anything out."

"I'll bet you know more than I do," Jordan replied.

"Probably," she agreed. "But I want to hear you tell what happened. It must have been something finding what you did in your car."

"They ought to be able to eat their dinner in peace first," Jaffee said. "Then she can tell us what happened."

Angela nodded. She pushed the chair back and stood. "Deputy Joe Davis came in."

"He's Chief Davis now," Jaffee reminded her.

"That's right, he is. And it's about time too," she added with a nod. "Chief Davis came in here to check on your whereabouts, Jordan, and we told him you were here until almost ten, and then Jaffee walked you over to the motel."

"We told the truth," Jaffee said, shooting a look at Noah.

"We didn't have to lie," Angela said.

Noah nodded. "That's good to hear."

"You two go ahead and look over the menu. I've got a real nice pot roast if you're interested."

As soon as Angela and Jaffee returned to the kitchen, Noah said, "Joe Davis asked me to go with him to Professor MacKenna's house tomorrow morning. He's hoping I'll see something he missed."

"Could I go with you?" She sounded so eager.

"I don't see why not. I doubt Joe will mind. The detectives from Bourbon have already been through the place, but they didn't find anything significant. Tell me, what did you think of the professor?"

"I guess you want the truth."

"Yes, I want the truth."

"He was a disgusting, gross, opinionated bore."

He laughed. "Don't hold back on me."

"I'm not exaggerating," she insisted.

She then told him about the dinner she'd suffered through, stressing the professor's appalling table manners.

"I understand you were arguing with him?"

"Where did you hear that?"

"The waitress at the restaurant mentioned to Joe that you were shouting, and he mentioned it to me."

"I was not shouting. Oh, wait. Yes, I was. That is, I raised my voice. I didn't shout though. The professor was being horribly insulting to the Buchanans, and I felt it was my responsibility as a Buchanan to defend our good name."

"You think maybe you overreacted?"

"No, I don't. I'll read you a little of his research, and then you can make up your own mind. His slanted research," she thought to add.

Angela carried out their dinner, and they were left alone to enjoy their meal. Noah couldn't believe how great the food was. "Jaffee could make it anywhere," he said. "I wonder what keeps him in Serenity."

"Chocolate cake."

"Yeah?"

While they ate, she explained what Jaffee had told her. She also mentioned that Trumbo of Trumbo Motors and Whitaker, a wealthy rancher, had dropped by to say hey to Jaffee and have cake with her.

"'Hey'?" Noah repeated. "Sugar, how long have you been in Serenity?"

"Two days."

"Then what's with the 'hey'?"

"I'm blending in. I'm adapting to my environment," she said and added, "and I'm not your Sugar."

He shook his head and grinned. "You're all sass, aren't you?"

Angela removed their dishes, filled their glasses, and sat down at their table again. Not to be left out, Jaffee soon joined them.

"Dinner was wonderful," Jordan said, and when Noah didn't comment, she nudged him under the table.

He remembered his manners and gave sufficient praise, but he wasn't looking at Jaffee. He was watching the door. The restaurant was rapidly filling up with townspeople. Noah didn't like the crowd one little bit. He casually leaned back and shifted slightly closer to Jordan, and his hand moved closer to his weapon. He was ready for anything. A town meeting or a lynching.

Jordan noticed how tense he'd become and put her hand on his thigh.

"Hey, Jordan," a young woman called out.

She smiled. "Hey, Candy."

"Hey, Jordan."

"Hey, Charlene."

"Hey, Jordan."

"Hey, Amelia Ann."

And so it went. She acknowledged each person as he or she walked over to the table. Before long a crowd had gathered three deep.

"You remember Steve, don't you?" Charlene asked. "He's my boss at the insurance agency."

"I remember. It's nice to see you again, Steve."

"Jordan, I just love my china. Thank you so much," Charlene continued.

"You're welcome. I hope you enjoy it."

Noah nudged her. "China?" he whispered.

She smiled. "Vera Wang."

Jaffee turned a chair toward him and straddled it. "Okay, we've been patient long enough. We have to know what happened."

"We heard what happened. Everyone in town's talking about it," Angela said. "But we haven't heard it from you. What was it like seeing that corpse?"

"It was gross," Candy answered for Jordan.

Everyone began to ask questions at the same time. Noah found it interesting that Jordan didn't have to answer any of them. There were always one or two in the group who already knew the answer and were happy to supply it for her.

In the middle of the question-and-answer session Noah's phone rang. They all stopped talking so they could hear what he was saying.

After a few seconds he said, "Jordan, stay here. The FBI agent is out front with a car for us. I'll only be a minute."

Charlene waited until he had left the restaurant and then commented, "He's quite a handsome fellow, isn't he?"

"He's Jordan's friend," Angela announced.

"Her special friend?" Amelia Ann wanted to know.

The women looked expectantly at her. "Just a friend," Jordan assured them.

"You're staying the night, aren't you?" Amelia Ann said.

"Yes, I am."

"Is he going to be staying the night too?"

"Yes," she answered again.

Amelia Ann pushed forward. "In your room or somewhere else?" she asked in a whisper.

"Somewhere else."

"At my motel though, right?"

"I would assume so . . . if you have the room."

"I'll tell you what I can do," Amelia Ann said. "I'll help you out because I've got available rooms."

"How will you help me out?" she asked.

"I'll put him in the adjoining room."

Charlene winked at Jordan. "It's up to you to unlock the connecting door."

"Charlene!" Candy whispered, drawing the name out. "He could be seeing someone else . . . like serious."

How about ten someone elses, Jordan thought.

Charlene gave her a playful nudge with her elbow. "Too bad

Kyle Heffermint isn't here. He sure seemed interested this morning."

"If you women are through embarrassing Jordan with your silly talk about sleeping arrangements, I'd like to know what happened when Maggie Haden got canned." It was Charlene's fiancé, Keith, who asked the question.

Everyone speculated and recounted what they had heard. Then Keith said, "Your friend, the FBI agent, promised Joe Davis he'd stay over."

"Why did he promise that?" Charlene asked.

"Joe asked him to look at the dead man's house. Since he's experienced and all, Joe thought he might have some insight and suggestions, or maybe see something in that house that could help Joe find the killer."

Amelia Ann's hand went to her throat. "I don't believe anyone in Serenity is a killer. Whoever murdered that man had to be an outsider. We're too friendly here to want to kill anyone."

"As friendly as we are here, don't you think it's odd that none of us knew the MacKenna fella?" Jaffee asked.

"That's because he kept to himself," Keith said. "I heard he rented a house less than a mile from here."

Jaffee nodded. "He never came in here to eat, not once. He didn't even stop by for a slice of my cake."

"Jordan told me he used to be a teacher."

"Did you get all those research papers copied?" Jaffee asked Jordan.

"No," she answered. "I still have one more box."

"Now that the guy's dead you can just take those boxes with you, can't you?" Candy asked. "He's not going to want them."

Jordan shook her head. "The research material is now part of the investigation, and it's also part of Professor MacKenna's estate. I can't take the boxes with me."

"Maybe you could read the rest of the papers tonight," he suggested.

It was sweet of him to be concerned about her project, she thought. She doubted she would get much reading done tonight though. She was exhausted from her long, stressful day, and she knew that as soon as her head hit the pillow, she'd be fast asleep.

Noah walked back into the restaurant but was stopped by Steve Nelson and another man. Steve was doing most of the talking and looked quite earnest, and Jordan wondered if he was trying to sell Noah insurance. Every now and then Noah would nod. Soon a group had gathered around him, and the discussion became more animated. She could hear them bombarding Noah with questions and offering him their conjectures. He seemed to take it all in stride and patiently listened to each person's views. At one point, he glanced over at her and smiled. It was apparent that Serenity hadn't seen this much excitement in years. It was also apparent to her that Noah was being very accommodating. They wanted to talk, and he was willing to listen.

Chapter Fifteen

THE GOOD CITIZENS OF SERENITY CONTINUED THEIR DISCUSSION about the events that had suddenly rocked their small town, but after an hour, Noah excused himself and insisted that he and Jordan had to leave. The Texas night air was still muggy and hot when they stepped outside. Noah turned up the dial for the air-conditioning in the new car, and Jordan ooh'd and aah'd over the working feature.

She found her purse lying on the backseat and reached for it. She turned again to get her laptop, but it wasn't there. She looked on the floor behind her. Still no laptop.

"Oh no," she said.

"What's wrong?" Noah asked.

"My laptop's not here." She turned around and looked under the seat. "It was in my rental car this morning."

"Did you see anyone take it out at the grocery store?" he asked.

"No, when Chief Haden took me to the police station, she wouldn't let me take anything from my car."

"We'll make some calls tomorrow and find it," Noah assured her.

He parked the sedan in the back of the motel courtyard. They backtracked to the lobby where Amelia Ann was waiting with a key for Noah. He didn't comment when he saw that his room was next to Jordan's. He unlocked his door, went to the connecting door, unlocked it, and then followed Jordan into her room.

"You keep this unlocked and wide open," he said.

He waited until she agreed. "Okay, but no surprises," she teased. "You stay in your room, and I'll stay in mine."

He laughed as he walked into his room. "You don't have to worry about that."

Jordan was startled by how much his words hurt. Had he bothered to look at her, he would have seen it in her eyes. Fortunately, he hadn't bothered. Her reaction puzzled her. It didn't make any sense. She didn't want him to be attracted to her, did she?

No, of course she didn't. She was only having such weird, crazy thoughts because she was tired and stressed out. That's all there was to it.

She couldn't let it go. Noah had said she didn't have to worry. Why not? How come she didn't have to worry? What was wrong with her? The man allegedly had hit on nearly every woman he came into contact with, and not having to worry about him hitting on her could only mean he wasn't interested. So why wasn't he?

She walked into the bathroom, looked at herself in the mirror, and shrugged. Okay, she had to admit she wasn't a beauty queen, and she definitely wasn't looking her best tonight. Her eyes were bloodshot from wearing her contacts too long; her hair was hanging in her face, and there wasn't a spot of color in her complexion except for the big fat bruise under her eye.

Enough self-scrutiny, she decided. She couldn't do anything about her appearance anyway, at least not tonight. Besides, if she wanted to get any reading done at all, she'd better try to revive herself.

Removing her contacts and taking a long hot shower helped. She washed her hair but didn't take the time to blow it dry and curl it. It was still dripping wet when she combed it back over her shoulders. She put on a gray, cotton Jockey T-shirt and gray-and-white-striped boxer shorts. After she brushed her teeth, she slipped on her horn-rimmed glasses and once again looked in the mirror.

Great, now she looked like a commercial for psoriasis cream. She'd scrubbed her face so vigorously, her complexion was one big red blotch.

She laughed at herself. Oh, yes, she was a real sex goddess all right, but at least she wasn't sleepy any longer. Maybe she could get some reading done after all.

She went back into the bedroom, removed the bedspread, folded it, and tucked it in the corner by the nightstand. Then she pulled the sheet back, grabbed a batch of uncopied papers from the third and last box, and sat down in the middle of the king-sized bed to read.

She kept glancing into the connecting room, but Noah was nowhere in sight. Her bed was parallel to his, which meant that if she wanted to, she could watch him sleep. Concentrate on the research, she told herself and picked up the top paper.

There were scribbles in the margin again. And there was for a second time a number she had seen before: 1284. Something significant must have occurred that year to the Buchanans and the MacKennas. But what? Was that the start of the feud or when the treasure was stolen? What happened in 1284?

Her frustration mounted. If she had her laptop and had Internet access, she could start doing her own research right this minute. Because she didn't, she would have to wait until she was back in Boston.

She sighed. "Okay," she whispered as she began to read. "What have the Buchanans done this time?"

This story took place in 1673. Lady Elspet Buchanan, the only daughter of the ruthless Laird Euan Buchanan, was attending the annual festival near Finlay Ford. Quite by accident she met Allyone MacKenna, favored son of the just and honorable Laird Owen MacKenna. The Buchanans later accused Allyone of sneaking into their camp to bewitch the fair lady, but the MacKennas knew for a certainty that it was the woman Elspet who put an unholy spell on their laird's son.

Regardless, as luck would have it, it didn't take more than a couple of glances for Elspet to fall head over heels in love with Allyone. He was, after all, according to the descendants of the MacKenna clan, as handsome a warrior as ever there was.

Because he had been bewitched, Allyone loved Elspet as much as she loved him, but both knew they could never be together. Yet they could not stay apart. Elspet pleaded with Allyone to give up his family, his position, and his honor, and run away with her.

The night before they were to meet in the forest and sneak away together, the Laird Buchanan found out what his daughter was planning. Enraged, he locked her in the tower of his castle and called his warriors together to find and kill Allyone.

Terrified that her father knew where Allyone was going to be waiting for her, Elspet was determined to warn her lover, but as she was tearing down the slippery steps, she lost her footing and fell to her death.

It was written that she died whispering his name.

When Jordan read that poor Elspet had died calling out for her love, tears began to stream down her face. Perhaps it was because she was exhausted. It wasn't like her to become so emotional.

"What the hell?"

The sound of Noah's voice jarred her. She looked up and saw him standing in the doorway frowning at her. He'd obviously just gotten out of the shower. He had put on jeans but nothing else.

"What happened?" he demanded as he strode into her room pulling a white T-shirt over his head.

"Nothing happened." She rolled over and grabbed a box of tissues from the nightstand.

"Are you sick or something?"

She tried but couldn't make herself stop crying. She pulled a tissue out and wiped her cheeks. "I'm not sick."

"Then what the hell, Jordan?"

He threaded his fingers through his hair and stood there looking at her without moving for about fifteen seconds. Finally he sat down on the bed and pulled her into his side.

"Tell me," he insisted.

"It's just that . . ." She paused to pull another tissue from the box. "It was so . . ."

He thought he'd figured out the problem and leaned toward her. "It's okay, Sugar. I know you've had a rough time today. It must be catching up with you. Go ahead and cry. Let it all out. I know how bad it was."

She started to agree with him, paused, and said, "What? No, nothing has caught up with me. It was just so sad . . ."

"Sad? I wouldn't call what you went through sad. I'd call it grueling."

"No . . . the story . . ."

He was stroking her arm and distracting her. It suddenly occurred to her that he was trying to comfort her. And how adorable was that? And sweet and caring . . . and . . . uh-oh.

Oh, dear God, she was beginning to like him, and not in an acceptable isn't-he-a-nice-friend kind of way. Noah could be sensitive. She'd never taken the time to notice before. She remembered how kind he'd been to Carrie that afternoon at the police station. He'd made her feel important and pretty. Now, Jordan realized, he was trying to make her feel better and to not feel so alone.

"Do you think you're gonna stop crying anytime soon?"

She looked at him and smiled weakly. She was just inches away from his gorgeous eyes . . . his mouth . . .

She jerked back and hastily looked away. "I'm done," she announced. "See? No more tears."

"You're done? Then what's that watery stuff coming out of your eyes?"

She punched his shoulder. "Stop being nice to me. It freaks me out."

He laughed. "I gotta tell you, when I saw you crying at the wedding, I thought it was just an aberration, but now you're doing it again. You're different here," he concluded.

"How am I different?"

"Every time I've seen you on Nathan's Bay, your nose is in a book or a computer. You're always all business."

And no fun at all, she silently added for him.

"Well, maybe *you're* different here too," she countered.

"How's that?" he asked.

"I don't know. I guess you just seem a little . . . sweeter. Maybe it's because you're closer to home. You grew up in Texas, didn't you?"

"My family moved to Houston when I was eight years old. We lived in Montana before then."

"Your father was a lawman before he retired."

"That's right."

"And your grandfather and his father . . ."

"I come from a long line of lawmen," he said.

He began to stroke her arm again. It wasn't distracting now. It felt good.

"Nick told me you carry a compass with you that belonged to your great-great-grandfather."

"His name was Cole Clayborne, and he was a lawman in Montana. My father gave me his compass when I started working for Doctor Morganstern."

"So you'll never lose your way. That's what my mother told me."

"She did?"

"Know what else she told me about you?"

"What's that?"

"She said she's the only woman in the world who can tell you what to do."

He laughed. "She's right."

A knock on Noah's door interrupted them. He went into his room to answer it and found Amelia Ann standing there holding a bucket with several bottles of beer submerged in ice.

Amelia Ann hesitated for a second and then said, "Hey. Um . . . I know you've had a busy day . . . traveling and all . . . and . . . I thought you might be thirsty." She pushed the ice bucket at him.

Noah took it from her and gave her a warm smile. "That's awfully nice of you. Thank you."

"If you're hungry," she continued, "I could pop some corn or something."

"No, thank you. I really appreciate the beer though." He began to close the door. "Have a good night," he said.

Amelia Ann angled her head to peer around the door at him. "If there's anything else I can do . . . anything you need . . . you just call up to the front desk."

"I will. Thank you," he said as he closed the door.

When he returned to Jordan's room, he was twisting the cap off a beer bottle.

"The lady who runs the motel . . . what was her name . . . ?" he began.

"Amelia Ann?" Jordan supplied.

"Yes, Amelia Ann. She just brought us some beer. That was nice, wasn't it? Want one?" he offered.

"No, thanks," Jordan answered. "And I don't think it was 'us' she wanted to be nice to."

He took a swig from the bottle. "You still haven't told me why you were crying," he reminded her.

"It's foolish."

"Tell me anyway."

"I read this story the professor had transcribed, and it affected me. Would you like me to read it to you? Then you'll understand."

"Sure. Go ahead," Noah said as he sat on the bed.

She began to read in a clear, concise voice, but by the time she reached the end of the tragic story, her voice trembled, and the tears were back.

Noah was laughing at her. He couldn't help it. "You're just full of surprises," he said as he handed her the box of tissues. "I never would have guessed."

"Guessed what?"

"You're a romantic."

"There's nothing wrong with being a romantic."

Jordan returned to the research papers and read another ridiculous account about the barbaric, bloodthirsty Buchanans. This legend wasn't at all romantic but a detailed description of a gory battle which, according to Professor MacKenna, was started by the Buchanans.

"No surprise there," she mumbled to herself.

"Did you say something?"

"The man taught history, for heaven's sake. Medieval history. His class should have been called Fantasy because that's what he was teaching."

Noah smiled. When Jordan became passionate about something, her face lit up. How come he'd never seen this before?

"So what would you sign up for? Fantasy 101?" Noah asked.

"No, I'd call it Let's Make Up Stuff 101."

He laughed. "I'd take that class. Exams would be a snap. Is any of the research accurate?" he asked. He took a swallow of his beer and leaned back against the headboard.

"I don't know," she said. "The farther back in history, the crazier the legends become. But there's some mention over and over again about a treasure that was stolen."

"You know what they say."

Jordan reached for the bottle in his hand and took a drink. "What do they say?"

"There's always a thread of truth in every lie. Any guesses what the treasure was?"

She took another sip of his beer and handed it back before answering. "A jeweled crown is mentioned several times in different stories, but there's also a mention of a jeweled sword."

She took the bottle from him again, emptied it in one long gulp, and handed it back. Noah didn't say a word. He simply got up and brought two bottles back with him.

"Move over, Sugar," he said as he dropped down next to her.

She scooted out of his way. When he offered her a bottle, she shook her head.

"No, thank you. I'm not in the mood for beer tonight."

"Is that right?"

She stacked the papers to put them back in the box. "Even though the professor's research is grossly biased, he really believed there was a treasure. I'm sure he thought the Buchanans stole it from the MacKennas."

"Do you think there was a treasure?"

She was embarrassed to admit it. "I do," she said and then hastily added, "I've gotten caught up in all of this. Maybe I'm just being fanciful." She sat back and stretched her legs out. "Some of the stories though . . . they're fun to read because they're so . . . out there."

"Yeah? Tell me an out-there bedtime story."

He put his untouched bottle of beer on the nightstand next to the one he'd offered Jordan, then crossed one ankle over the other and closed his eyes.

"I'm ready, Sugar. Once upon a time . . . Read me something gory."

She filed through the papers until she found one especially bloody tale. It was quite graphic, which was probably why Noah enjoyed it so. When she was finished with that one, she told him about another battle.

"The legend describes two angels coming down to earth to escort a fallen warrior to heaven. This happened during a fierce battle. It was reported that all the warriors on both sides of the field saw the angels coming. Suddenly time stopped. Some of the warriors had swords raised, others were about to throw their lances or swing their maces, but they were all frozen in those stances. They watched transfixed as the warrior was lifted up into the sky."

"What happened then?"

She shrugged. "I suppose they thawed out and continued with the battle."

"I like these. Read another one," he coaxed.

"Do you want to hear something romantic or something gory?"

He didn't open his eyes when he replied, "Let me think about this. I'm in bed, and right next to me is a scantily clad woman who's in dire need of a little action . . ."

She poked his side. "I am not scantily clad. I'm wearing shorts and a T-shirt. There's nothing scanty about my clothing."

His eyes remained closed, but he was grinning now. "But I happen to know that you're not wearing anything underneath that T-shirt and shorts."

She quickly looked down at her chest. Nothing showed through the fabric, thank God. "Only you would think about that."

"Any man would."

"I don't believe that," she scoffed.

He laughed. "It's what we do."

She tried to pull up the sheet, but it was trapped under his legs. "Why don't you just not think about it."

He opened one eye. "Don't think about it?"

"Do you want to hear another story or not?"

"Huh."

She sighed. "Huh what?"

"You didn't argue with me about needing a little action."

He had her there. "I didn't feel it was necessary to respond to such an incorrect assumption. What story would you like to hear?"

He'd gotten her all riled up again. He didn't know why he got such a kick out of her indignation, but he did. "Am I rubbing you the wrong way, Sugar?"

She rolled her eyes. Oh, brother. "You're not rubbing me at all. I'm putting these papers away," she warned.

"Sorry. It's just that you're real easy—"

She interrupted. "That's what all the boys tell me," she joked.

"Yeah? But are you any good?"

Her eyes sparkled playfully. "What do *you* think?"

Noah didn't answer at first. He stared into her incredible blue eyes and lost his train of thought. Sexual banter had always come as second nature to him, but suddenly he had no reply. An image of

Jordan—sans T-shirt, sans shorts, making love—whizzed through his head and rendered him speechless.

He grabbed the beer bottles on the nightstand and headed for his room. His words were gruff when he finally answered her. "I think I'd better get out of here."

Chapter Sixteen

TWO PHONES RANG SIMULTANEOUSLY.

Jordan woke to the sounds coming from Noah's room. She rolled over in bed and opened her eyes a crack as she listened to Noah answer the ring that sounded like his cell phone. She heard him ask "Darlin'" to hold on a minute, and then he answered the other ring. He obviously didn't like whatever the caller was saying to him because his voice turned hard. Then he began to snap out orders. She heard him explain in his don't-mess-with-me tone that he expected results by noon.

A few minutes later he strolled through the door. "That was Joe Davis on the line . . ." he began.

"Before you tell me what he has to say, you might want to talk to Darlin' if she's still holding on."

"Ah, hell . . ." he said as he hurried back into his room.

She could hear him apologizing to the caller as he returned. He dropped down on Jordan's bed, grabbed the edge of her T-shirt when she tried to get up, and said, "Hold on. She's right here." He handed his cell phone to her. "Sidney wants to talk to you."

She didn't believe her sister was on the line until she said hello.

"How come you have Noah's phone number?" Jordan asked.

"I don't know. I've always known it. That isn't important now. Theo told me what happened. Did you know about the body when we talked before?"

"Before what? I don't remember," she said. "Does everyone know what happened?"

"Dylan and Kate don't know, but then they're on their honeymoon, so Alec didn't think we should bother them with any worries. Jordan, tell me, are you okay?"

"Yes," she assured her sister. "The police sorted it all out, and I'm coming home tomorrow. I'll tell you everything then. I promise. Sidney . . ." she began.

"Yes?"

"Do Mom and Dad know what happened?"

"Nick called and talked to both of them."

"He shouldn't have," she said. "They'll worry, and they both have enough to think about now, what with the trial and all."

"They would have found out. Zack would have let it slip."

"Who told Zack?"

There was a long pause, and then Sidney said, "I might have mentioned it to him."

Jordan didn't want to argue. She talked to her sister for a few more minutes to reassure her and ended the call. As she handed the cell phone to Noah, she said, "When I found that body, I should have called Dylan."

"Why? Because Nick told your family?"

She nodded. "Sidney insists they would have found out . . ."

"They would have."

"Maybe," she allowed.

After she had dressed and packed her things, she zipped her bag shut and went to the connecting door. Noah was snapping his gun holster closed.

"You were about to tell me what Chief Davis had to say," she said.

"Right. He told me Sheriff Randy has no idea where his brother is. He said he has people looking for him."

"Do you believe that story?"

"No," he answered. "The sheriff knows exactly where J.D. is. He probably wants to sit down with Chief Davis and work something out before J.D. comes in. That's my guess anyway."

"Would the sheriff of Grady County usually handle a murder investigation?"

"Yes, but Davis told me he's on vacation."

"Hawaii," she volunteered. "Why doesn't the FBI help the chief?"

"Davis seems to think he can handle this without the FBI's interference."

"What about Lloyd? Has Davis spoken to him yet?"

"No," he answered. "No one can find him. His garage was unlocked, but Davis says that's not unusual. A lot of people in this town don't lock their doors."

"I'll bet they do now. After all, one of their own was murdered."

"Except Professor MacKenna wasn't one of them. He didn't own the house. He rented it, and he kept to himself. Very antisocial. No one really knew him."

"I think Lloyd knows what happened. If he didn't kill the professor, I'll bet he knows who did. He was so nervous when I picked up the car. I think he knew the body was in the trunk."

"I'd say he's the primary suspect."

"He couldn't wait for me to leave," she said. "And that was peculiar because when I first drove the car in, he hit on me and kept trying to get me to go out with him. He tried to keep me in town."

"Did he continue to try to get you to go out with him after you threatened him?"

"I did not . . . oh, okay, I guess I did. But it was all so stupid. He asked me what I would do if my car wasn't ready when I came back the second time, and before I could answer, he asked me if I would hurt him. I believe I agreed that I would."

"I see."

"No, you don't see. Lloyd happens to be a very big man. I would have to stand on a chair to hit him."

"A chair, huh?"

She was irritated that he was making fun of her. "I went over all of this with Chief Davis, and I believe you were standing right there. Weren't you paying attention?"

"Lloyd will turn up," he predicted.

She nodded. "When do we meet Chief Davis at the professor's house?"

He checked the time. "In an hour."

"Would you mind if we stopped at the grocery store first? I'd like to photocopy the rest of the research papers. It shouldn't take long, I promise."

"All of those boxes need to go to Davis?" he said.

"Copies don't have to go to him. I'm going to ask Candy if she'll mail them to Boston for me."

Candy was working at the front desk and was all in favor of helping out and making some extra spending money. Jordan filled out a form with the necessary mailing information, told Candy she would bring her the boxes to be mailed, paid her in advance, and headed back to her room.

Noah was leaning against his door talking to Amelia Ann when she returned. Amelia Ann had brought him coffee and a basket of homemade cinnamon rolls. Jordan noticed that she had put on makeup. The blouse she wore was tucked into her slacks, and the top three buttons were undone. Ten to one she was wearing a push-up bra. Amelia Ann's nervous laughter followed her as Jordan walked into Noah's room, grabbed the car keys from the desk, and said, "I'm going to start loading these boxes in the car."

"I'm right behind you," he answered.

Sure you are, she thought to herself, just as soon as Amelia Ann finishes flirting.

She carried one box outside, rounded the corner of the building, and immediately noticed their car's right rear tire was riding low.

"Great," she whispered. The tire was either going flat or needed air, and the way her luck had been going, she'd wager it was flat. She dropped the box on the pavement, slipped the key into the trunk lock, and stepped back as the lid popped open.

She couldn't believe what she was seeing. She couldn't move. She shut her eyes, opened them, and nothing had changed.

"Oh, come on," she whispered.

She slammed the trunk lid down and ran as fast as she could back to Noah's room. His door was closed. She pounded on it with her fist.

He knew something was wrong the second he looked at her face. "Jordan? What's the matter?"

She grabbed his shirt and panted to get the words out. "There's a dead body in the trunk of our car."

Chapter Seventeen

LLOYD WAS FOLDED UP LIKE A CONTORTIONIST. ONE LEG WAS bent underneath him, and the other was pressed against the back of his head. He died with the most startled look on his face, not pained, just startled, like a big glassy-eyed carp on the end of a fishhook. Jordan didn't think she was going to be able to get his expression out of her head for a long, long time.

"You're right, Jordan. Lloyd was a big man." Noah stood in front of the open trunk, peering down at the body. He glanced over his shoulder to look at her.

She sat on a stone wall, waiting for him to finish his inspection of the body. She refused to look at poor Lloyd a second longer.

"He's not in a Ziploc bag," she commented weakly. She couldn't imagine why that was important to her, but at the moment it was.

"No, he isn't," Noah agreed.

Chief Joe Davis stood beside him. The two men were now on a first-name basis. Murder had a way of cutting through formalities.

Davis leaned into the trunk and then said, "So we agree? One blow, back of the head. Then he was stuffed into the trunk, right?"

Noah nodded. "Looks that way, Joe."

"The blow cracked his skull," Joe concluded. "Had to be someone strong. Someone real strong."

In unison the two men turned and looked at Jordan. Were they wondering if she were strong enough to kill Lloyd? She folded her arms and frowned at Noah. He'd better not be thinking such a crazy thought.

Joe looked at Lloyd again. "What's going on?" he asked in frustration. "Two bodies in what? Two days? Three?"

"Is this your first homicide?" Noah asked.

"Second if you count Professor MacKenna," he said. "Though I didn't see the body, the investigation is on my shoulders now. This is the second murder Serenity's ever had. We're a peaceful community. That is, we were until your girlfriend hit town and men started dropping like flies."

Noah let Joe's assumption that Jordan was his girlfriend slide. "You know she didn't do this. She didn't kill either one of them."

"Lloyd was my primary suspect. He had her car in his garage, so he had the opportunity."

"What about motive?" Noah asked.

Joe shook his head. "I hadn't figured that out yet. I'm gonna get some help. I've got two sheriff's deputies driving over, and they both have more experience."

"With homicides?"

He shrugged. "I don't know. I've also got detectives from Bourbon on their way too."

"Where's the coroner?" Noah asked as he checked the time. "We've been waiting for forty-five minutes now. And where are the lab techs?"

"Things move considerably slower in small towns, you know that. Everyone has to come in to Serenity from other places. They're all on their way," Joe assured him.

"You know I've got friends who can help."

Joe nodded. "I know, and if I need the FBI's help, I'll ask."

"What about Sheriff Randy?"

"I'll be meeting with him this afternoon. We were gonna meet this morning. He called last night," he explained. "But now that I've got to deal with this situation," he said, nodding to Lloyd, "I had to push his meeting back and the meeting you and I have at MacKenna's house."

"I want to go with you," Noah said.

Joe shook his head. "No. Randy knows me. He'll clam up about his brother around you."

"Where's his brother? And don't try to tell me I won't be talking to him."

"I don't know where J.D. is, but Randy will tell me. Then we'll decide what to do."

What was there to decide? J.D. had assaulted Jordan. He should be dragged into jail and locked up. Nothing much to decide about that.

"If you don't bring J.D. in, I will."

Joe cocked his head and frowned. "Is that a threat?"

Noah snapped. "Damn right it is."

Joe put his hands up in a conciliatory gesture. "Okay, okay. I hear you. But please, let me talk to Randy alone. I live in this town," he reminded him. "I've got to try to do this the right way, so let me take this one step at a time."

Unlike Joe, Noah didn't care or need to get along with anyone. He was about to tell him that he wasn't going to be patient and that, one way or another, he would be talking to both Dickey brothers, but Jordan drew his attention.

Jordan scooted off the wall and walked over to him. She brushed her hand down his arm, and said, "Joe, Noah and I would like to help any way we can. Isn't that right, Noah?" He glanced down at her. When he didn't respond, she leaned into his side and repeated, "Isn't that right?"

"Sure," Noah finally answered. This was one of the most absurd situations he'd ever encountered. There was a dead man in the trunk, an inexperienced and possibly inept policeman running the investigation, and a woman who was slowly driving him nuts and now wanted him to be nice.

"I guess you two will be staying on in Serenity a while longer," Joe stated. It wasn't a question.

"Yes, we will," Noah said. "So far Jordan's the only connection between the professor and Lloyd."

"I'll go tell Amelia Ann we'll need the rooms again tonight," Jordan offered.

Noah grabbed her hand and pulled her back. "You stay close to me."

"I'm going to—"

"She already knows," Noah said as he tilted his head toward the window behind the wall. Amelia Ann and Candy were both watching, wide-eyed. Fortunately, from their angle they couldn't see inside the trunk of the car.

Joe suggested they both go back into the motel. "You two don't have to wait with me. I'll call you as soon as I'm finished here and finished talking to Randy."

Noah put his arm around Jordan and headed inside.

"Noah?" Joe called.

"Yes?"

"You'll be needing another car."

"Looks that way." Noah felt Jordan's shoulders slump under his arm. "You okay, Sugar?" he asked.

"I'm fine," she answered with a sigh. "But I'm beginning to think this friendly little town isn't so friendly after all."

Chapter Eighteen

ALTHOUGH AGENTS CHADDICK AND STREET FROM THE FBI's regional office hadn't officially been assigned to the investigation, they were doing as much as they could to help Noah figure out what was going on.

The two men brought Noah and Jordan yet another car, a Toyota Camry. Jordan, who was beyond spooked at this point, insisted that one of them open the trunk and have a look inside before she got into the car. Agent Street had a rather warped sense of what was funny. He thought it was humorous that Nick's sister had found another body and laughingly called her a corpse magnet.

Chaddick handed Noah a large manila envelope. "Everything you asked for is in there," he said. "There are copies of MacKenna's bank statements for the past year, but I'll go back further if you want."

"MacKenna was into something all right," Street said. "For eight months he's only made cash deposits. Five thousand dollars every couple of weeks."

"And he drove all the way to Austin to make those deposits," Chaddick added. "He also purchased a new car eight months ago, and the mileage indicates he's done some serious driving since then. One of the assistants at the college where he taught told me the professor received an inheritance."

"Strange inheritance," Street said. "Cash every couple of weeks that can't be traced back to anyone."

"What about his phone records?" Noah asked.

"They're in the envelope too," Chaddick said. "In the six months that he lived in that house he only received a couple of telemarketing calls. No calls made out either, except for one very short call someone made a half hour before J.D. Dickey says he got a tip that there was a body in Jordan's car."

"Are you telling me someone called J.D. from inside MacKenna's house?"

"That's what I'm telling you."

"But I called the professor," Jordan interjected. "When I got to Serenity. He had given me his number. That call has to show somewhere."

"Then what about cell phone records?" Noah asked the agents.

Street answered. "We can't find any record of a cell phone listed in MacKenna's name. Jordan, if you'll give me the number you called, we'll check it out."

"We went ahead and had a couple of our people process MacKenna's car. I'm betting the only prints they find are his," Chaddick said. "Joe Davis is in way over his head, but he won't ask for help from us. You want us to push our way in? We could take over and get you two out of here."

Noah shook his head. "Not yet." He looked at Jordan and reevaluated. "I don't know. Maybe it would be a good idea to take her . . ."

Jordan knew where this was going and decided to nip it in the bud. "I'm staying here with you, Noah. Besides, I promised Chief Davis I'd stay another day. For all we know, he might decide to arrest me."

"He's not going to do that, and if I think—"

"This isn't negotiable," she said. "I'm not leaving." To emphasize her decision she tried to stare him down.

"She's a lot like her brother," Chaddick commented, smiling.

"She's a lot prettier," Noah said. After thanking the two men for their help and promising to stay in touch, Noah opened the car door for Jordan, then circled and slid into the driver's seat. "Let's go for a ride."

"I'd like that," she said. "If we have the time, I'd like to drive to Bourbon and buy a new cell phone."

"You can't get along without a phone for a few more days?"

"You don't understand. It's my PDA, my camera, my Rolodex, my global positioning system, and, most important, my personal computer. I can access the Internet and e-mail. I can also send pictures or text or video clips electronically."

"You know what else you can do? You can make phone calls."

She laughed. "That too. And after I purchase a phone, I'd like to stop by the police station and talk to the detectives and find out what happened to my laptop."

"Nick already talked to them. They said they never saw it."

"It didn't just dance away. It was in my rental car, on the seat next to me. Maggie Haden must have seen it too when she went through my purse to get my identification. I'll bet she took it. She did go back to the grocery store lot when she locked me in a cell. She could have taken it then."

"We'll keep looking, but for now we're meeting Joe Davis at MacKenna's house, remember?"

"After he talks to Sheriff Randy," she reminded him. "I'm surprised you didn't insist on being there when he talks to him."

"I'm more interested in his brother." He handed her a slip of paper. There were two addresses with directions from the motel.

"What's this?"

"I thought maybe we'd drive by J.D. Dickey's place. See if he's home."

"And if he is?"

Noah started the engine and put the gear in drive. "I'd like to stop in and say hey."

"Hey?"

"Just trying to fit in, Sugar."

"What's the other address?"

"Maggie Haden, your old friend."

"Why do you want to drive by her house?"

"I've got J.D.'s license plate number. He drives a red pickup truck. He could be with her. You did tell me that she has a history with both Dickey brothers."

Jordan flipped on the air conditioner. "And if he's there?"

"We'll see."

"Do you mind?" she asked as she lifted the envelope Chaddick had given to Noah. "I'd like to look at his bank statements."

"Go ahead. Add up all the cash deposits," he suggested.

"If it was five thousand dollars every two weeks for six months, that's sixty thousand dollars."

After she added all the deposits, the total was actually ninety thousand dollars. "The last two months the professor was alive, the deposits had increased in both amount and frequency. Where did the money come from?"

"That's the ninety-thousand-dollar question."

"What do you think he was into? You think maybe drugs? Or gambling? He didn't seem the type to get into either one of those vices."

"Exactly what type gambles? Was he the type of man to lie about getting an inheritance?"

"Point taken."

"Read me those directions to Dickey's house."

Jordan did as he asked, spotted Hampton Street, and said, "Turn right at the corner."

She then returned to speculating. "The professor told me that he had changed his plans and was leaving for Scotland earlier than he'd originally intended."

"Anything else?"

"He was jumpy at dinner when he noticed how crowded the restaurant had become. I thought he might be claustrophobic."

Noah slowed the car. "That's Dickey's place on the corner."

It was a ranch house, no larger or smaller than any of the other houses on the street, but certainly the nicest. It had recently been painted a dark gray, and the black shutters also had a fresh coat of paint. The roof was new, and the yard was surprisingly well tended. There was even a flower bed with blooming marigolds along the front of the shrubs.

"This can't be his house. It's so nice," Jordan said.

"This is the address Agent Street gave me. It's Dickey's house all right. I guess, when he isn't beating up women, he takes care of his lawn."

Dickey's truck wasn't parked in the gravel drive.

"You didn't expect to find him home, did you?" she asked.

"No, but I wanted to see where he lived. I'd sure like to look around inside."

"Me too," she whispered as though admitting such a thing would get her into trouble. "We can't even look in the windows because the blinds are down." She bit her lower lip. "I wonder if my laptop is in there."

She'd sounded so earnest, he tried not to laugh. "Sugar, you've got to let it go."

"My laptop? I don't think so. I want it back."

"You might have to get a new one."

He didn't understand. She'd programmed the laptop, changed out all the chips, added a ton of memory. Her life was in there.

"If you lost your gun, how would you feel if I told you to let it go and get a new one?"

Her laptop was obviously a sensitive subject. Noah let it drop.

"Give me directions to Haden's house," he said.

They only had to drive a couple of blocks. It was exactly as Jordan expected—stark and uninviting. The yard was a combination of dirt, gravel, and weeds. Like Dickey's house, Haden's didn't have a garage, and there were no cars or trucks in her driveway.

"I don't have any desire to look inside her house," he said. "She probably sleeps in a coffin."

"With my laptop."

"Jordan, you really need to ease up. The police are looking for it."

He was right. She *was* obsessing about it. "Maybe Haden packed up and left town."

"I doubt she'd leave. No, she won't give up that quickly. She had too much power to let it go without a fight."

"She must know she couldn't possibly get her job back," said Jordan.

"She's probably gone off somewhere to think up a strategy to force the council to make her chief again right now."

Noah turned the next corner and headed back toward the center of town. "Where do you want to eat?"

"There's only one place we can go. Jaffee's. There are other restaurants around, but if we eat anywhere else, he'll hear about it because they all talk to each other about everything."

"So what if he hears about it? What's the big deal?"

"His feelings will be hurt." She wasn't joking.

"Why do you care . . . ?"

"He's been so kind to me," she said, "and I like him. Besides, you enjoyed the food, didn't you?"

He nodded. "Yeah, okay. We'll go to Jaffee's."

He drove back to the motel and parked in the back lot. Jordan carried the envelope Chaddick had given them, as they made their way to the restaurant. When they passed Lloyd's Garage, she felt a shiver go down her spine.

"For a while there I thought Lloyd killed the professor and put him in my car, and that's why he was so nervous. I didn't know what his motive was, but I knew that eventually Chief Davis would find one. Now Lloyd's dead. Want to hear my new theory?"

He smiled. "Sure."

"Lloyd must have seen the murderer put the professor's body in the trunk of my car. Don't you think that's what happened?"

"Could be."

"You don't sound too enthusiastic, but I know what you're thinking. Why didn't the murderer kill Lloyd right away? Why did he wait? I think he didn't know that Lloyd had seen him, but if that's the case, how did he find out?"

Noah didn't have to answer any questions. Jordan was doing that all by herself. She'd pose the question, work it out in her mind, and come up with what she considered a plausible explanation.

Jaffee's place was nearly empty. There were just a few businessmen lingering over iced coffee as they discussed the news of the day. One of them was Kyle Heffermint, the man she had met at the insurance office.

"Do you know any of these men?" Noah asked as they walked past the front window.

"Just one," she answered. "Kyle Heffermint. He's what I'd call a name-dropper."

Noah didn't have much use for anyone whose claim to fame was that he knew someone famous. "I don't like name-droppers," he remarked as he opened the door for her.

The group stopped talking as Jordan and Noah walked past. She smiled at Kyle when he nodded to her, and continued to their table in the corner. Angela greeted them with her usual iced tea as the men continued to watch them. The waitress put her hand on her hip, glanced over her shoulder, and then looked at Jordan again.

"Don't mind them," said Angela. "They're just talking up the news of the day."

"Why are they staring at me?" Jordan asked.

"First of all," replied Angela "you're easy to look at, being so pretty, and second of all, you're the news of the day. We all heard about you finding Lloyd and all."

"I've brought a blight on Serenity."

"Well, I wouldn't say that. You just have a habit of finding dead people, that's all. It's kind of like that movie. You know the one where dead people talk to the kid? Except they don't talk to you. Either one of you in the mood for beef today? Jaffee's making beef burgers. He also made a big pot of beef stew."

Angela had just walked back into the kitchen to place their

hamburger orders when Kyle sauntered over. The light reflecting off his belt buckle, as big as a Cadillac grille, signaled his approach.

"Hey, Jordan."

"Hey, Kyle. It's nice to see you again."

"Who's your friend?"

Jordan introduced Kyle to Noah. He shook his hand and then turned back to her. "I understand you're going to be staying in town a little longer, Jordan. You think we might have dinner tonight?"

"I'm sorry, no. I have plans with Noah. Thank you for asking though."

This time he didn't press. "Jordan, I heard about what happened to you, and I have to tell you, Jordan, I don't know what I would do if I ever found a body in my car, and look at you. You've found two bodies. That's got to be some kind of a record, Jordan, don't you think?" he asked with a raised eyebrow.

While he talked to her, Noah put his arm around the back of her chair. Each time Kyle said her name, Noah gently tugged on a strand of her hair.

"Agent Clayborne, I might have some information for you. I happened to drive by Lloyd's Garage the other night, and noticed a light on in his office. I thought to myself that it was mighty odd seeing someone in the office so late, 'cause Lloyd never worked late."

"Did you see Lloyd?" Jordan asked.

"I saw a shadow of a man, Jordan, but I don't think it was Lloyd. I only saw him for a second or two. The shadow didn't seem to be as big or as wide as Lloyd." He raised both eyebrows as he asked, "Is that information helpful to you, Agent Clayborne?"

"Yes, it is," he said.

"Jordan, I really would love to see you again. There's this—"

Noah cut him off before he could say another word. "She has plans with me."

Jordan tried to soften Noah's curtness. "Thank you for asking."

As soon as Kyle walked away, she whispered, "You were rude to him. What came over you?"

"Jordan, nothing at all, Jordan."

She laughed. "I told you he was a name-dropper."

"He's got the hots for you," he said. He wasn't smiling. "In fact, it appears that half the men you've met since you've been in Serenity have the hots for you." Noah reached across her and brushed a strand of hair away from her face, his fingers gently touching her cheek.

Her breath caught in her throat. He had merely touched her, and she'd reacted. She'd always thought she was immune to his charm, but she was becoming worried that she wasn't.

"Me?" she answered incredulously. "I'm not the big attraction around here . . . you are. Carrie at the police station was all but standing on her head to get your attention. And what about Amelia Ann with her bottles of beer and her cinnamon rolls? She's definitely sweet on you."

"I know she is," he admitted with a grin, "but I think you are too."

She pulled back. "Oh brother. Not every woman drops to her knees in front of you."

Too late she realized exactly what she'd said. And she knew without a doubt he wouldn't let it go.

"Yeah?" he laughed. "It's a nice fantasy. You think you'd ever . . ."

"Never."

Jordan's cheeks turned bright pink. Her blush was lovely, he thought. He enjoyed embarrassing her because that's when she showed another side of herself, the side that was vulnerable and sweet and innocent. She was beautiful, no doubt about that, and every man in Serenity seemed to notice.

Why did that bother him? He wasn't the jealous sort. And he certainly had no reason to be jealous. Jordan was a good friend, that's all. So why did he get an uneasy feeling when he was with her? He didn't have an answer. How could he explain what he didn't understand? One thing he knew: he didn't like the idea of any man getting close to her.

Ah hell, he wanted her.

Chapter Nineteen

JORDAN LOOKED THROUGH THE PROFESSOR'S PHONE STATE-
ments while they ate lunch.

"I thought you were hungry," he said. "You've barely touched your food."

"This hamburger could feed a family of six. I ate as much as I wanted." She moved on to more important matters. "I called Professor MacKenna when I got into town. This isn't the same phone number I called. And I remember Isabel told me that she and the professor often talked about the MacKenna clan. Her phone number isn't here either."

"I'll bet he only used throwaways," said Noah. "Untraceable."

"Since he moved to Serenity the professor's life became untraceable."

She picked up a french fry and was about to take a bite, then changed her mind. She pointed it at Noah. "And why did he move to Serenity? What made him choose this little town? Because it was so isolated? Or because it was close to something illegal he was involved in? We know whatever he was doing was illegal. Who makes a total of ninety thousand dollars in cash deposits?"

He took the french fry and popped it into his mouth.

She thought about the various possibilities and said, "It's obvious that whoever killed those two men is determined to keep me here. Don't you agree?" Before he could answer, she said, "Why else would both bodies be put in my cars?"

He loved watching her face as she thought aloud. She was so animated and eager. Over the past couple of years Noah knew he'd become overly cynical, but in his line of work, it was only a matter of time before the calluses formed. He'd learned not to get too close and not to expect anything, but he still hadn't quite figured out how to leave the work at work.

"Do you know what we need?" she asked.

He nodded. "A suspect."

"Of course. Anyone come to mind?"

"J.D. Dickey's at the top of my list," said Noah.

"Because he knew the body was in my car."

"Yes," he said. "I had Street run his name, and J.D. did some hard time."

He told her what he'd learned about J.D. When he was finished, Noah said that if Joe Davis didn't locate J.D. and bring him in for questioning soon, Noah was taking it out of his hands.

"Does that mean you'll stay on in Serenity?"

"It means Agents Chaddick and Street will take over the investigation. This is their district," he thought to add. "And you and I will get out of here."

"Will you go back to work for Doctor Morganstern right away, or will you take a few days off and go home?"

"Nothing to go home to," he said. "I sold the ranch after my father died."

"Where do you call home?" she asked.

He smiled. "Here and there."

"Uh-oh," she said. "Here come the troops."

Jaffee and Angela were headed to their table. Jordan knew what they wanted, the gory details about finding Lloyd in the trunk. Fortunately, Noah was saved from having to answer a hundred questions because he got a call from Chief Davis.

"Gotta go," he said. He quickly paid the bill.

They were leaving the restaurant when Angela caught Jordan's attention and gave her the thumbs-up.

"She still hasn't figured out I can see her reflection in the window," Noah commented, laughing.

"Are we meeting Joe now?" Jordan hurried to catch up.

"He said he's twenty minutes away. That gives us enough time to get the boxes of research to MacKenna's house."

"Why there?"

"That's where Joe wants them. Probably because the police station is so small. No place to store them until he can go through them."

"I don't know what he expects to find," she said. "It's just historical research."

"He still needs to look through them."

"Would you mind if we made a quick stop at the grocery store on the way to the professor's house?"

He didn't object, and while he carried the first two boxes to the car, she stuffed the last two hundred and some pages she needed to copy into her tote bag and carried the empty third box.

She didn't have to wait in line at the store. As soon as she walked in, shoppers scurried to get away from her. They stood in clusters staring at her while they whispered. She heard one woman say, "She's the one."

Jordan plastered a smile on her face and continued on to the photocopy machine. There had been a line—one woman and two men had been waiting—but as soon as they saw her coming, they scattered. Jordan was mortified. Noah thought the attention she was receiving was quite funny. She didn't. After all, she hadn't done anything wrong. She made that comment to him once they were back in the car.

"People do tend to die around you," he pointed out.

"Just two." She sighed. "Oh, God, did you just hear what I said? Just two? I've become insensitive about the death of two men. What's happened to my compassion? I used to have some."

She finished separating the professor's papers from the copies and handed Noah the originals. "Would you please put these back in the empty box?"

"You're afraid to open the trunk, aren't you?"

"No, of course not. Just do it, please."

She really wasn't afraid, she told herself. She was just skittish. She didn't want to admit it though. She stuffed the copies into her tote, put it on the floor, and sat back.

She was suddenly weary and feeling out of sorts. "Nick should be back in Boston by now," she said when Noah got back into the car.

He started the engine before he answered. "I'm sure he'll call when he gets home."

"And when he does, you'll tell him about Lloyd?" she asked and then promptly answered the question. "Of course you will."

"You don't want me to?"

"I don't mind. I just don't want him to get on another plane and come back. I also know he'll tell the rest of the family, including my parents, and they have—"

"Enough to worry about," Noah finished for her. "Jordan, it's okay for them to be concerned about you every once in a while."

She didn't comment. Instead, she stared out the window at the desolate landscape. The yards on the street they drove down hadn't weathered the heat well. All the lawns had burned patches of brown weeds and dirt.

What had Jordan been looking for when she came to Serenity? Her brother and Noah had both challenged her to step outside her comfort zone, but she wouldn't have paid attention to any of their suggestions if she hadn't been so discontent in the first place.

Her life was so regimented, so organized . . . so mechanical. She knew what she wanted. The wow factor. The problem was, it didn't exist. At least not for her. She needed to get back home and stop thinking such crazy thoughts. Her life was mapped out for her. Structure. That's what she was used to and what she needed. Everything would be in perspective once she was in Boston again.

There was just one little problem.

Noah noticed her disheartened expression. "What's the matter?"

"I'm never going to get out of this town, am I?"

Chapter Twenty

PROFESSOR MACKENNA HAD LIVED ON A QUIET, DEAD-END street about a mile off Main Street. It was a dismal setting. There were no trees or shrubs or grass to soften the ugly tract houses, most of which were in dire need of repairs.

Chief Joe Davis was waiting for Noah and Jordan. The front of his shirt was soaked through. As Jordan and Noah walked to the front door, the chief pulled out a handkerchief and wiped the back of his neck.

"Were you waiting long?" Noah asked.

"No, just a couple of minutes, but damn it's hot. Pardon me, ma'am, for using a curse word in your presence." Joe unlocked the door. "I'll warn you, it's even hotter inside. MacKenna kept all of his windows closed and his shades down, and he never turned on the air conditioner far as I can tell. It's a window unit, but it wasn't plugged in." He held the door open and cautioned, "Watch your step. Someone really trashed the place."

Jordan fought the urge to gag as she entered the living room.

The smell of overcooked fish mixed with some kind of metallic odor permeated the air.

The entire house couldn't have been more than eight hundred square feet. There was little furniture. A gray plaid sofa, so dilapidated Jordan thought the professor must have found it on a curb somewhere, had been shoved against the wall facing a picture window that had been covered with a white flat sheet. A square oak coffee table sat in front of the sofa, and there was one small round table with a lamp and a torn shade. An old Philips television set was on a crate in the corner.

She couldn't tell if there was a rug in the living room or not. The floor was covered with newspapers, some yellow with age, and there were also ripped notebooks and shredded textbooks everywhere. Some piles of papers were a foot high.

They waded through the trash to get to the dining room around the corner. A large desk was its only piece of furniture. The professor had used a wooden folding chair, but someone had hurled it against the wall. It lay in fragments on the floor.

A power strip on the desk had five cell phone charge cords plugged into it. The cell phones were missing. Jordan nearly tripped over an extension cord. Noah grabbed her around the waist before she went headfirst into the desk.

"Whoa there," Joe said.

She nodded as she pulled away from Noah and walked toward the light-deprived kitchen. The smell was getting stronger, even fouler. There were dirty dishes in the sink, a feast for the roaches crawling over the counter, and trash overflowed from a shopping bag the professor had been using as a trash can near the back door. Garbage was decomposing in the sack.

Jordan backtracked through the living room and went down the hallway. There was a bathroom on one side—surprisingly clean, considering the condition of the rest of the house—and on the other side was a small bedroom. The drawers in the dresser had been ripped out and dumped on the floor. The double-bed mattress and box springs had also been overturned, both shredded with a knife.

Noah came up behind her, looked at the mess for about five seconds, turned around, and strode back into the dining room.

"Do you think whoever trashed the place found what he was looking for?" Jordan asked as she followed him.

"He? There could be more than one," Joe said.

"What's missing, Jordan?" Noah asked.

"Besides cleaning supplies? The professor's computer."

"That's right," said Noah.

"The cables are still here," Joe said. "See? On the floor behind the desk. And look at all those phone chargers. I'll bet the phones he was using were untraceable."

Jordan thought she saw something moving under one of the newspapers. A mouse maybe. She didn't freak. She wanted to, but she didn't. "I'll be outside . . . getting fresh air."

She didn't wait around for permission. Once she reached the sidewalk, she rubbed her arms and shivered over the thought that one of the insects might have gotten into her clothes.

Noah and Joe came outside ten minutes later. As Noah walked past her he whispered, "Mouse spooked you, didn't it, Sugar?"

Sometimes Jordan wished Noah wasn't quite so observant.

"Hey, Jordan, you want to open the trunk?" Noah called from behind the car.

"Not funny," she called back.

His grin suggested otherwise. After he opened it, he turned to Joe. "Are you sure you want to store the boxes here? They're going to be covered with bugs in no time."

"I'll seal them up tight," he said. "A couple of deputies will help me go through everything in the house including the boxes, page by page. I'm not sure what we're looking for, but hopefully something will stick out."

Jordan suddenly remembered. "Chief Davis, I have a flash drive the professor gave me to take home. Will you need that?"

"I'll need everything that will give us a clue to the professor," he answered. "I'll see that you get it back."

He picked up one of the boxes and started up the sidewalk. "I guess when we're finished with all this, I'll send it to a relative. That is, if I can find one," he added.

"He's part of the MacKenna clan," Jordan said, "but I can't imagine any of them would claim the professor. He was kind of a nutcase."

She immediately felt guilty talking about the dead that way, but she was only being honest.

Joe paused at the doorway. "Did you get a chance to read all of those papers?"

"No, I didn't. I read a few accounts from each of the boxes, but that's all."

Noah opened the car door for her and handed her the keys. "You go ahead and turn the air on. I'm gonna be a minute."

"You sound angry."

"Not angry, irritated. I've been real accommodating, and as you know, that's a stretch for me, but I pulled it off, didn't I?"

She didn't smile, but she wanted to. "Yes."

"I know Joe talked to Sheriff Randy Dickey, but he still hasn't said a word to me. That means he's made some kind of deal. So . . ."

"Uh-oh."

"I'm through being accommodating. Get in the car."

Joe came outside then. Noah headed toward him as he locked the front door.

"Did you forget to tell me what Randy Dickey had to say?" Noah asked.

"No, I didn't forget. I thought maybe we could talk about it over a beer later."

"Tell me now."

"You've got to understand. Up until the time his brother got paroled, Randy was doing a good job as sheriff. Folks were happy with him. But J.D.'s a hothead, and Randy would like to give him a second chance to redeem himself. I agreed with him."

"That's not your call."

"Yes, it is," Joe said. "Unless Jordan presses charges against J.D. for that hit she took, there's not a whole heck of a lot you or she can do. I'm not being contrary. I'm just telling you the way it is. And like I said before, I have to live in this town, and that means I've got to get along with people in authority. Sheriff Randy can make my life miserable. It doesn't matter that he's in another county. He'll still do it."

"Oh, yeah. He sounds like a real good sheriff."

"That's not what I mean. He just wants a favor, that's all."

"And if he doesn't get that favor, then he'll make your life—"

"Okay, okay," he said with his hands up. "I know what I said. But J.D.'s his brother," he repeated. "And he'll get bounced back to prison before you can snap your fingers if she presses charges, and Randy will be beholden to me if she doesn't."

"I thought you didn't want this job to be permanent."

Joe looked sheepish. "My wife says I shouldn't let my ego get in my way. I did get passed over before, but now I'm chief," he said, "and I could be talked into staying on if that's what the council wants."

"I want to talk to Randy."

"I mentioned that to him, and he's okay with it."

"He's okay with it?" Noah could feel his neck getting hot. "Where is he now?"

"The truth?"

"No, Joe, lie to me."

"Hey, no need to get your back up. Randy's out looking for his brother right now. Honest to God, he really doesn't know where J.D. is, and he told me he's worried sick that J.D. might do something foolish."

"J.D.'s way past the foolish stage."

"He's going to turn up, and when he does Randy will bring him over to have a sit-down and work this out."

"Work this out? J.D. is a suspect in a homicide investigation."

"But it's *my* homicide investigation," said Joe.

Noah ignored the statement. "The timetable hasn't changed, Joe. Randy has until tomorrow to bring J.D. in."

"And if I can't find him?"

"Then I will."

Chapter Twenty-one

FOR THE FIRST TIME IN HIS SORRY LIFE, J.D. WAS TRULY AFRAID. He'd dug himself into a hole so deep he didn't know if he was ever going to be able to climb out.

The problem was his employer. The man scared the hell out of him. All he had to do was look at him in a certain way, and J.D. felt his blood run cold. He'd seen that look back when he'd been in prison. Lifers with nothing to lose had that attitude. Kill or be killed. That's what the look meant.

Cal had taught him to steer clear of those men, and on too many occasions to count, he'd protected him from them. No one went up against Cal—no one in his right mind, anyway.

Cal couldn't protect him now. J.D. was completely on his own, and his boss was no different from the killers he'd hidden from in prison. The boss carried that same attitude all right, and he was more vicious than most. J.D. had watched him pick up the professor and throw him like a Frisbee into a wall. It wasn't so much his strength that scared J.D., it was the look in his eyes as he squeezed the life out of the man. J.D. knew that look would haunt his dreams for the rest of his life.

Greed had gotten the MacKenna man killed, and greed had made J.D. a willing accomplice to a murder. Now was too late for regrets. He was in that hole, and he could feel the dirt pouring in to bury him.

The boss had made J.D. get rid of the body and had ordered him to keep the woman in town until he could find out what she knew. J.D. could only think of one way to do that. He'd frame her for murder. His brother would keep her in jail then. That had been J.D.'s plan, anyway, but it all went south when the woman found the body while she was in the wrong county. He knew he'd overreacted when he saw the phone in her hand, but all he could think of was getting it away from her. No, that wasn't true. He hadn't been thinking. If he had been, he never would have hit her.

Like a fool, he thought Maggie would be able to fix things his way. She was the chief of police after all, and he knew she would do whatever he told her to do.

Bad luck followed bad luck, Cal used to say. J.D. understood what that meant now. Maggie couldn't fix anything after she got fired. Her power was gone. As if that wasn't enough bad luck, the Buchanan woman was connected to the FBI.

He had dreaded telling the boss about the woman's brother and the other FBI agent, who was sticking to her like bad perfume on a new jacket.

Fortunately for J.D., the boss already knew about the FBI. He told J.D. that it didn't matter how many FBI agents were in town, J.D. still had to keep her here until he could get her alone and interview her. The way he'd drawn out the word "interview" made J.D. wish he could run away. But it was too late for that. Much too late. The incident with Lloyd had seen to that.

It was no coincidence that J.D. had run into Lloyd as the mechanic was packing his car to get out of town. Maggie had tipped him off that Jordan Buchanan was telling everyone who would listen that Lloyd had acted mighty suspicious when she'd picked up the car. She'd even suggested Lloyd knew the body was in the trunk.

J.D. had only wanted to talk to Lloyd to find out what he'd seen, yesterday, but the second Lloyd spotted him, he ran inside and tried to barricade himself in his house.

"I just want to talk to you, Lloyd," J.D. had called out.

"Go away or I'll call the sheriff," Lloyd shouted. "I ain't fooling! I'll do it."

"Did you forget where you live?"

"What kind of question is that?"

"You live in Jessup County, you moron, and that means if you call the sheriff, you'll be calling my brother. And you know he'll do anything I ask him to," he lied.

Lloyd cursed.

"That's right," J.D. shouted. "You let me inside and we'll have us a talk. I'll wait real patient right here until you make up your mind. I'm not going to hurt you, Lloyd."

"You hurt that other man."

"No, I didn't. I swear I didn't. He was already dead when I found him. Someone . . . I'm not saying who, told me to put him in the woman's car. That's all I did."

"If I believe you, will you let me leave town?" Lloyd asked. "Just until this blows over and that FBI man leaves Serenity."

"That's exactly what I was hoping you would do. You know, leave town until the FBI gets out of here."

"So why do you need to come inside?"

"I don't," said J.D. "And I'll tell you what. If you want, you can call me and tell me where you're holed up, and if it isn't too far away, I'll send over one of my best girls to keep you company. She'd spend at least one whole night taking care of you. I can give—"

"Okay, I'll call you," Lloyd eagerly blurted.

J.D. knew Lloyd was watching him through the peephole, so he didn't smile. Convinced that he wouldn't call Chief Davis or the sheriff, he sauntered back to his pickup. Then he drove around the corner, turned off the motor, and waited for Lloyd to leave so he could tail him.

He hadn't killed him. He'd simply made a phone call and told the boss where Lloyd could be found. As far as J.D. was concerned, he had done nothing wrong. He'd just shared some information.

Chapter Twenty-two

CRIPPLE CREEK BAR AND GRILL HELD THE OFFICIAL COUNTY record for having the most animal heads hanging on its walls. A couple of stuffed rattlers even hung from the rafters. At one time there had been more, but the ceiling fans had played havoc with them, and the customers didn't appreciate chopped snake skin occasionally raining down on them while they drank at the bar.

Agent Street had given Noah directions to the bar, suggested he and Jordan ignore the décor, and promised the pizza at Cripple Creek was the best in the state. The chef, he explained, was a transplant from Chicago.

The façade resembled a large log cabin big enough to accommodate Paul Bunyan. The interior reminded Jordan of a ski resort. High, open ceilings with exposed beams and a balcony that overlooked the dance floor were all constructed from knotty pine. The air was heavy with the scent of pine air fresheners, and a band played twangy country-and-western songs from a small, raised platform tucked in the corner.

As though it were the most natural thing in the world to do, Noah took hold of Jordan's hand and pulled her along as he threaded his way through the crowd.

Agent Street stood by a booth near the back. Noah waited until Jordan slid into the booth before he sat next to her.

"What's in the folder, Agent Street?" Jordan asked.

"Please, call me Bryce," he insisted, and was about to answer her question when the waiter appeared to take their drink orders.

"You're off duty, right?" Bryce asked Noah.

"I haven't officially been on duty for a couple of days now. I'm just helping out a friend."

"You want a beer then?"

"Sure," he answered. "Jordan?"

"Diet cola would be nice."

As soon as the waiter walked away, Bryce said, "I've got a lot of information about the Dickey brothers. Randy's okay, but J.D. has had trouble with the law off and on for years. He's been in a lot of fights, but one bar fight landed him in prison."

Noah waited to hear something new. "What's interesting," Bryce continued, "is that J.D.'s former cellmate, a man named Calvin Mills, is still doing twenty to life for murder. Cal, as he's called, worked for a security company. He was really into all kinds of surveillance equipment, knew all the latest gadgets. Cal liked to drive by his house a couple of times a day to listen to his wife chatting it up on the phone."

"He didn't trust her," Jordan surmised.

"As it turned out, ole Cal had good reason not to," Bryce said. "He parked down the street one afternoon and listened to her pillow talk with a man she'd met at work. Cal later told the detectives he might have been able to forgive her the affair if she hadn't been making fun of his ... equipment." He shot Jordan a quick glance before continuing. "According to Cal, his wife called his manhood a cocktail wiener."

"That would do it all right," Noah drawled, leaning back. "So he killed her, did he?"

"He sure did," he said. "Fortunately for him, the judge was a man, so Cal didn't get as much time as he might have."

Noah nodded. "The judge was sympathetic."

Jordan couldn't tell if they were joking or serious. "The man killed his wife."

"Yeah, I know," Noah said, "but still, you just don't make fun of a man's equipment."

Bryce was in full agreement. It was only when Noah winked at her that she knew he was teasing.

The drinks arrived, and after they placed their order for a couple of specialty pizzas, Bryce continued. "Cal taught J.D. everything he knew about surveillance. He took a real interest in J.D. One of the guards said Cal thinks of himself as some sort of technological guru."

"Did you find out anything about J.D.'s finances?" Jordan asked.

"Yes, I did," Bryce said. "He made a lot of cash deposits over the last six months, but unlike MacKenna, J.D.'s deposits were never more than a thousand dollars at a time."

"Blackmail. That's what he was doing," Jordan said. "He was listening to people's conversations and then blackmailing them."

"That's my guess," Bryce agreed.

"I wish I could get inside his house," Noah said.

"Yeah, well, without a warrant you can't."

Bryce handed Noah his notes and said, "Here's everything I've got so far. If you need anything else, just let me know."

"Thanks," Noah said, "I appreciate your help."

"Glad to do it," Bryce replied. "It's nice to finally work with you. You and Nick Buchanan are practically legends in the agency. I've heard about some of your cases, and you've got quite a track record."

Noah's expression turned somber. "I wish it were better. They don't all work out the way we want."

Bryce nodded his agreement. "I know, but some do. I heard what you did with the Bains case in Dallas. It was all the talk for a while. I also heard recently that Jenna Bains is at SMU this year."

A smile creased the edges of Noah's eyes. "Yeah, she's doing great."

Jordan had been listening to the conversation with interest. "Who's Jenna Bains?" she asked.

Noah answered. "A kid who didn't deserve what she got."

Bryce saw Jordan's puzzled look at the vague answer Noah had given and said, "Jenna Bains was a kid whose parents died when she was young, and so she was sent to live with her only relative, an uncle, who just happened to be a crack dealer. Things got really bad at the uncle's house. He was strung out most of the time, and some thugs moved in and took over his operation. Jenna spent a couple of years with these scumbags. When they didn't have her locked up in a closet, they used her as their personal slave. Finally, the authorities got wind of the drug operation and moved in, but unfortunately, the leader of the gang was tipped off and got away before the raid. He took Jenna with him as a bargaining chip. That's when Noah and your brother were called in. The guy had Jenna for over two months and kept moving around, so it was hard to catch him, but they finally tracked him down at an abandoned apartment building. I heard, when they got there, Jenna was pretty beat up and unable to say much." He looked at Noah for verification.

Some of the anger that he had felt back then resurfaced, and Noah said, "She was scared out of her mind. She hung on to me for dear life, and all she could say was, 'Don't leave. Don't leave.' "

Bryce looked at Jordan again and continued. "When Jenna was released from the hospital, Social Services stepped in, but Noah found her a home with a great family."

"They were friends of mine," Noah explained. "I knew she'd be in good hands. I just didn't want to see her get caught up in the system after all she'd been through."

"Well, from what I've heard, someone anonymous has paid her college tuition. And the rumors say it's you."

Noah didn't respond to Bryce's comment. "Jenna's a great kid. She wants to become a teacher."

"That was a fine thing you did," Bryce said.

Noah dismissed the compliment with a shrug. "A lot of people would have done the same."

The conversation was interrupted by the arrival of the pizzas. Jordan could only eat one slice, but as Bryce and Noah devoured the rest, they continued talking about the Dickey brothers.

Jordan sat back against the wooden bench and listened, but she wasn't really hearing what the two men were saying. She was looking at Noah. She'd always known that he was dedicated to his work, and she had definitely seen the fun-loving side of him, but there obviously were things about him she didn't know.

Noah finished his beer and ordered a bottle of water. She watched as he crossed his arms and leaned his elbows on the table, listening intently to Bryce's suggestions about the investigation. He had the loveliest profile, she thought. And when he smiled . . .

Oh dear, she knew what was happening. Where was Kate when she needed her? On her honeymoon, of course. Kate could talk some sense into her, but she wasn't here, and Jordan suddenly realized she was in big trouble. She was becoming a Noah Clayborne groupie.

She wondered what it would feel like to be kissed by him. To be touched . . . to hold on to . . .

"Jordan, are you ready?"

The question jarred her. "Ready for what?"

"To leave," Noah said.

"Yes, of course. Bryce, it was a pleasure," Jordan said, smiling. "I know you're doing a lot of the legwork on your own time, and I want you to know how much I appreciate your help."

"You're very welcome, but you don't have to thank me. You're Nick's sister."

The three of them walked outside together. Bryce said goodbye at the door. "When's the deadline again?"

Noah answered. "Tomorrow, noon. If I haven't talked to both Dickey brothers by then, you take over."

"Sounds good to me."

Jordan was quiet on the ride back to the motel. A couple of times Noah glanced over at her and asked if she was okay.

"I'm fine," she replied.

She wasn't though. Inside, she was a colossal wreck. All Jordan could think about was Noah. She needed to get back on course. No more crazy thoughts about him. No more wondering what it would be like to sleep with him. Don't go there, she told herself. But the more she warned herself not to obsess, the more she thought about him.

Yoga. That's what she needed. When she got to the motel, she'd take a quick shower, put on her pajamas, then sit in the middle of the bed in the lotus position. She'd breathe deeply and clear her thoughts. And he would not intrude. She would be in charge of her thoughts, not him.

"What's wrong with you?" Noah asked.

"Why do you think something's wrong?"

He began to laugh. "You're glaring at me, Sugar."

She came up with a lame excuse and stared out the window the rest of the way to the motel.

She carried her tote bag into her room and stopped abruptly. The door into Noah's room was open. Noah's bed had been turned down, and there were chocolates on his pillow. Her bed hadn't been touched.

She shook her head and laughed. "I'm surprised Amelia Ann isn't in bed waiting for you."

He smiled as he walked into his room. "She's not my type."

She wanted to ask him what his type was but resisted; instead, she grabbed her pajamas and headed into her bathroom.

She actually felt better, and her thoughts were less jumbled by the time she finished showering and washing her hair. She even took time to dry it.

While she was removing the bedspread, she saw Noah on his phone. Every now and then, she heard him laugh. She thought he might be talking to Nick. She'd just gotten settled on her bed with her stack of photocopies when Noah strolled into her room.

"Nick wants you to call him on his cell phone. Wait a couple of minutes though. He had Morganstern on the other line." He handed her his phone. "I'm going to get in the shower. No matter what, do not open that door for anyone. Got it?"

"Yes."

He'd already gone into his bathroom before she remembered to ask him if he'd told Nick about Lloyd. Of course he had. Still, he might have left the news for her to impart. She didn't want Nick to come back to Serenity. If all went well, she'd be on her way back to Boston sometime tomorrow.

After she had organized the rest of her research copies, she dialed her brother. Nick picked up on the second ring.

He didn't waste time on a greeting, but answered with, "Found another one, huh?"

Chapter Twenty-three

JORDAN SAT IN THE MIDDLE OF THE BED, READING YET ANOTHER chilling account of a terrible battle between the Buchanans and the MacKennas. Each clan had called up its allies and had gone to war in hopes of annihilating the other. She was so caught up in the story she didn't notice Noah standing in the doorway watching.

Noah told himself to turn around and go back into his room, but he couldn't make himself move. She drew him to her, and she didn't realize it. He loved being near her, talking to her, listening to her crazy stories and theories, and he loved watching her smile. The most wondrous thing about her was her ability to make him laugh. No other woman made him feel the way she did.

She was damned pretty, he decided. Even when—like now— she was wearing glasses. He didn't know why they were such a turn-on to him, but they were. If she had them on when he ran into her on Nathan's Bay, he'd look over the top of her head so he wouldn't be distracted. Once Dr. Morganstern had noticed what he was doing and had commented on it. Now Noah wondered if the doctor had known Noah was attracted to Jordan before he did.

When had she stopped being his partner's kid sister and become the amazingly sexy woman he wanted to take to bed?

He knew what he was going to do before he took one step into her room. He didn't give a damn about the repercussions. He barely made a sound as he walked to her bed, placed his gun and holster on the side table, and sat next to her.

Jordan glanced over and smiled. He looked relaxed in his worn-out Levi's and pale gray T-shirt. She watched him get settled. He put both pillows behind his neck and gave them a couple of whacks to get them just so. Yawning loudly, he stacked his hands on his chest and closed his eyes.

"Comfy?" she asked.

He didn't open his eyes. "Read me a bedtime story."

"This story is pretty brutal."

"I like brutal."

"No surprise there," she teased. "The date's iffy, but this war supposedly took place sometime between 1300 and 1340. The MacKenna laird claimed the Buchanans had stolen another treasure from them. This treasure was a piece of land near the MacKenna holding that the laird believed should have been given to him."

"Who gave the land to the Buchanans?"

Jordan shook her head. "It doesn't say. The MacKenna laird stewed about this atrocity for months and months. Then, one afternoon in the early fall, a young Buchanan was captured on their land.

"The MacKenna laird decided to hold the boy for ransom. If the Buchanans gave up the slice of land, he'd return the boy. That was the plan, anyway, until some of the MacKenna warriors, in their enthusiasm, accidentally killed the boy. That's how it was written," she said. "They meant to torture him, but had wanted to keep him alive."

"Did the Buchanans agree to give the land back before the boy was killed?"

"They didn't have time to agree or disagree. When they heard one of their young was murdered, they gathered their forces and went to war. They were always fighting with the MacKennas, but this was different. The MacKenna laird knew he was in for it, and he called up all of his allies. It doesn't give the number of clans, but three are named."

"What about the Buchanans?"

She scanned down the page in front of her. "They called up one ally. I'm not sure if it was because they only had one ally or because they only needed the one. The MacHughs. The name alone sent terror through the MacKenna clan. The MacHughs were thought to be inhuman and indestructible. They were much more ruthless than the Buchanans, or so it says.

"The battle took place on a field near Hunter Point. The Buchanans and the MacHughs were hopelessly outnumbered, and the MacKennas foolishly believed they would make quick work of slaughtering the entire two clans."

Jordan's back ached. She fell back and rested on Noah's shoulder. She held the paper up and continued on.

"The MacKennas and their allies were sadly mistaken about the odds being in their favor. The MacHugh clan didn't believe in showing any mercy. After all, the MacKennas had butchered a child. Nor did the Buchanans show mercy," she added. "When it was finished, there were body parts strewn over the field; the ground itself was covered in blood. To this day, the area is called Blood Field."

"What happened to the MacKennas then?" he asked.

"What was left of the clan fled," she said. "They returned to the field the next day to collect their dead and give them a proper warrior's burial, but there weren't any bodies to collect. They were all gone. And therefore there could be no sacred warrior burial ceremony."

"Did they ever find them?"

"No," she replied. She leaned up on an elbow and looked into his eyes. "And back then, if a warrior wasn't given a proper send-off, he couldn't go to the hereafter. He would be condemned to roam in the 'other world' for eternity, forever alone and forgotten."

"How many were killed? Does it say?"

"No," she answered. "But if any of this story is true, can you imagine what it would have been like to walk around the field . . . a field soaked with blood, picking up body parts? An arm here, a leg there . . ."

"A head . . ."

She grimaced. "I'm glad I didn't live back then."

"I don't know," he said. "There could be a couple of benefits. No reading scumbags their Miranda rights or having to watch a judge let them go on a technicality. Back then, if you knew someone was guilty, you got rid of them. Simple as that. You know what else? If the story has a thread of truth in it, I don't care how many warriors were killed on that battlefield. There isn't a number high enough to justify killing one child."

His eyes were still closed, so it was okay for her to stare at him. He wouldn't notice. He was so sexy, so rugged. She forced herself to look away. This could go nowhere, she told herself. But she wanted him. He'd break her heart and leave her devastated, she warned. No thank you.

She was no groupie. No, she absolutely was not. Truth was, she'd gone way past that stage. She was falling in love.

Suddenly in a panic, she quickly swung her legs over the side of the bed, gathered up the papers, and took them to the table. She stacked them next to her satchel and then walked back to the bed. "Noah?" she whispered as she poked him in the shoulder. "Don't you fall asleep on me." He didn't respond. She poked him again. "I want to go to bed."

She was about to give him a harder poke when he reached up and grabbed her wrist. Before she could respond, he pulled her down on top of him. He wrapped his arms around her and rolled her onto her back. His knee nudged her legs apart, and he stretched out between her thighs, bracing himself on his elbows as he looked down at her flushed face.

Her heart raced. She went completely still and waited to see what he'd do. Don't let go, she frantically thought. "Don't let go."

"I won't, Sugar."

She squeezed her eyes shut and groaned. "I said that out loud, didn't I?"

He gently removed her glasses, and his hard chest rubbed against her breasts as he leaned over to put them on the table next to his gun. When he began to nuzzle the side of her neck, shivers cascaded down her arms and legs. His breath was sweet and warm against her skin, and when he tugged on her earlobe, she felt a jolt of longing all the way down to her toes.

"This is a bad idea," she whispered as she tilted her head so he could have better access. She reached up, caressed the back of his neck, and tugged on his hair. She wanted him to kiss her on her mouth.

He lifted up. "Want me to stop?"

She pretended to give the matter her utmost attention. "No." Jordan reached up and kissed his chin. "I was just saying it's a bad idea."

She was sorry she'd said anything because now she worried he would come to his senses and stop touching her. She desperately wanted and needed him to hold her and make love to her.

"Jordan?" His voice was a rough whisper.

Oh, God, he was going to stop. She swallowed. "Yes?"

"Open your mouth for me."

He didn't move. He waited for her to make up her mind.

Any guilt or worry about the consequences of her actions flew from her thoughts. There was only room for Noah. She stared into his beautiful blue eyes and slowly pulled him toward her.

It was all the encouragement he needed. His mouth settled on hers in a kiss that was warm and soft and undemanding. And wonderful. But soon it wasn't enough for him. One taste of her sweet mouth made him crave more. His tongue swept inside and rubbed against hers. He took his time leisurely exploring her mouth until even that wasn't enough. He tightened his hold on her and the kiss deepened.

He was voracious, and he believed he was the aggressor until he felt her pulling on his T-shirt. Did she want him to stop? With a groan he lifted his head. "Tell me what you want." His voice was raspy.

"Everything," she whispered. "Off. Everything off."

The warm glint in his eyes made her shiver. His thumb swept across her lower lip. "You taste good, you know that?"

"Like sugar?"

"Even better," he growled.

He tugged her shirt up over her breasts and pulled his own T-shirt at the same time, but elbows and hands got in the way. He was suddenly eager and hot, as though it were his first time. He knew how to please a woman—God knows he'd perfected his technique over the years—but this was different. Jordan was different. The need to be with her made him ache. He'd never felt this way before.

His shirt came off first, but hers quickly followed. She wasn't shy with him or hesitant. She stroked his back, his shoulders, his arms. He could feel her heart pounding, and when he touched her breast, she arched against him and moaned softly.

Her legs moved restlessly against his. He kissed the side of her neck and slowly moved lower, taking his time, teasing, tormenting. His tongue gently tickled her collarbone, and when at last he reached her breast, he felt her tighten around him.

He began to slowly drive her out of her mind. She had no idea her breasts were so sensitive, but with each stroke of his tongue, she lost a bit more control.

He was losing his control as well. He took a deep, shuddering breath and passionately kissed her. His hands actually trembled. He kissed her again—hard, quick—and then pulled away.

"Be right back . . ." A quick kiss, and he rolled over. "I want to protect you."

Her heart was racing now. As soon as he got up, she wrapped the pillow in her arms and hugged it to her chest. One kiss, she thought, and she had melted. She sighed. Noah certainly knew how to kiss. No other man had ever made her feel the way he did.

The bed sagged when he returned to her. He tugged the pillow away, and she didn't resist. She rolled onto her back, her gaze locked on his. His hands moved to her waist and slowly pushed her shorts down. He threw them off the bed. He'd already removed his pants, and as he moved between her thighs and stretched on top of her, the feel of him made her forget to breathe.

Her hands caressed his back, her touch feather light, until his mouth settled on hers again. Her touch quickly became more frantic. She clutched his shoulders, demanding that he stop tormenting her.

"Noah." She didn't know if she'd shouted his name or sighed it. His hand had moved between her thighs, and he was driving her out of her mind. He knew just where to touch, exactly how much pressure to exert. She writhed in his arms, pleading with him to come to her.

She was desperate to feel every inch of him, to wrap herself in his warmth. His breathing became more labored, and that excited her even more. She would die if he continued to torment her.

Noah delayed as long as he could, to give her as much pleasure as she was giving him. Her response made it impossible to wait any longer. He knew she was ready. Her nails scored his shoulders, and she arched against him. His mouth covered hers and he moved between her thighs and slowly sank into her liquid heat. She was so tight, so hot, he groaned from the sheer bliss. He stayed completely still inside her, panting as he whispered her name.

When he came to her, she cried out. The ecstasy was overwhelming.

"Ah, Jordan." He breathed her name. "Damn."

She wasn't content to let him catch his breath. Every nerve in her body was clambering for release. She lifted her knees to take him deeper and began to move.

Oh, how she wanted to please him, to make him as crazed as she was. She bit his shoulder, kissed him on the mouth, and moved to his neck. She was panting now. He pulled back and thrust deep again, and tears came to her eyes, she was staggered by the intensity of the feelings gathering inside her. His movements became more powerful, more all-consuming, more demanding. It was exquisite.

Even in the throes of raw passion Noah had always been able to control his reactions, to set his pace. But he couldn't control what was happening to him now. He thrust into her again and again, powerless to slow down.

She was every bit as passionate as he. Tension built within her, ready to burst with the need for release.

Wave after wave of sensation poured over her. She'd never experienced anything like it. She let it sweep her away, like a roller coaster plunging to the ground and jolting every nerve, the waves of pleasure coursing through her.

Noah kissed her, then buried his face in the crook of her neck, slow to recover. "Damn," he whispered again.

A curse word . . . and yet, she felt as though she'd just been caressed.

He was panting against her ear. Or was that her panting? She was so shaken, she couldn't hold a thought. The man had turned her into a blithering idiot.

Jordan didn't want to let go of him. Not ever.

He rolled to his side and pulled her against him. Noah held her and stroked her, his touch tender now. Neither spoke, both content for the moment. The minutes ticked away, and she fell asleep in his arms.

In the middle of the night, she awoke. He was still there.

Chapter Twenty-four

A BOOMING CRASH AWAKENED JORDAN FROM A DEEP SLEEP. She bolted upright in bed fearing the motel room had just been split in half. It was pitch-black. Groggy and disoriented, she couldn't make sense of anything.

A thunderbolt shook the ceiling and actually made the bed shudder. She jumped up, then relaxed. It was just a storm. A flash of lightning lit up the window and another sonic boom followed. The clock radio on the bedside table indicated it was five o'clock. Too early to get up.

The storm was a worry. It seemed to be increasingly violent. The rain beat against the window like a stranger's frantic knocking, and the wind picked up and began to howl.

Was a tornado coming? She'd never been in one, but she'd seen several on the weather channel. Would a siren alert them? Did Serenity even have a siren? She pushed a clump of hair out of her eyes and tried to think about it.

Thunder exploded again, the sound ricocheting around the room. Even storms were bigger in Texas, she thought.

"It's okay," Noah whispered. "Go back to sleep." He gently pulled her down next to him, put his arm around her waist, and dragged her up against him until her back was pressed snugly against his chest.

Go back to sleep? Impossible. She was stark naked and in bed with Noah. Sleep was the last thing on her mind. The memory of their lovemaking filled her thoughts. My God, she'd had sex with Noah . . . over and over again. She sighed softly. It had been amazing . . . and astonishing . . . and perfect, but there had also been a stunning discovery. Who knew that sex could be so wonderful? She certainly hadn't known until Noah. Just thinking about the way he had touched her made her whole body shiver . . . and crave more.

It had seemed the most natural thing in the world to fall asleep in his arms. She'd felt so safe and protected. And loved, she admitted. She'd felt loved. If being loved by Noah, even for one night, was a fantasy, she wanted to indulge. What was the harm? She was a big girl. She could protect herself.

She remembered all the wonderful things they had done, the different ways they had made love, and her heart raced. He was a voracious lover. There wasn't anything he wouldn't do or coax her into doing. He wasn't the least bit shy with her and had proved it again and again. Around two he'd nudged her awake . . . or had she awakened him? She didn't think there was an inch of her body that he hadn't kissed or touched.

Apparently she was also insatiable. She had become a wild woman in his arms, and knowing Noah, Jordan would never be able to live it down.

She rolled over and kissed the base of his neck, her mouth lingering on the pulse. She loved his scent—so sexy, so male—and the taste of his warm skin. She kissed him again, but that didn't seem to get much of a reaction until she began to caress him. Her mouth and her fingertips trailed down his chest, circled his navel, and moved lower.

He groaned. "You're killing me, Sugar."

Did that mean he wanted her to stop? She pulled back. "Do you want . . ."

"Oh, yeah, I want."

He pushed her onto her back and covered her with his body. He kissed her hungrily and showed her just how much he wanted her. Their lovemaking was as fierce as the storm raging around them.

Thoroughly sated, she collapsed on top of him and fell asleep.

It was nine o'clock in the morning when he shook her awake. She rolled over to kiss him, opened her eyes, and saw him walk away. He was fully dressed.

"Get moving, Jordan," he called. "We've got to go."

No kiss. No words of endearment. Not even a "good morning." She watched him disappear into his room and then rolled onto her back and stared at the ceiling. Why hadn't he kissed her?

Don't go there, she told herself. Don't let what happened last night become part of something much bigger . . . like falling hopelessly in love with a man who never, ever would commit to a lasting relationship. Last night had been earthshaking, but things had a way of changing in the bright light of day.

She groaned loudly as she stretched and forced herself to get up and stagger into her bathroom.

Halfway through her shower, her mind cleared. Noah had certainly been blasé. In fact, his attitude had bordered on indifferent. She thought about it while drying her hair. He had told her to get moving, but that was it. He hadn't even said where they were going. Were they leaving town? She slipped into a skirt and a fitted pale blue blouse. She hoped they were leaving town. She needed to get out of Serenity and away from this man before she became so emotionally attached that she turned into what she most despised, an NCG, a clinger. She would never let that happen. By the time she'd applied sunscreen and a little makeup and lip gloss, her resolve was firmly in place. She grabbed her lens case and went back into the bedroom. Noah was on the phone.

She waited in the doorway until he finished the call. "Where are we going? Should I pack and check out?"

He shook his head and didn't look up as he secured his gun and holster. "We're to meet Sheriff Randy at ten," he said. "We'll check out when we get back."

"Just let me grab my key and my glasses."

"They're still on the nightstand," he remarked.

And that comment was as close to an acknowledgment that he had been in her bed as she was going to get.

"You ready?" he said. He grabbed his room key and headed for the door.

She picked up her purse and shoved her things inside. How could he be so unemotional about last night? And how come she was so frickin' emotional? She could feel her heart beginning to sink, but she braced herself and followed after him.

She knew what Kate would say. Her friend would tell her it was simply the difference between men and women. And maybe she would be right. But that didn't matter. Noah's behavior still stung, and his attitude was not only insensitive but also downright mean. The big jerk. Okay, now she felt better. She had placed the blame where it belonged. Noah was the one with a problem, not her. She frowned at him as she walked out the door. He didn't seem to notice she wasn't in the best of moods, or if he did, he didn't mention it.

They broke protocol and ate breakfast at a run-down diner on the east side of town. Everything looked greasy, even the orange juice. Jordan settled on a slice of toast and hot tea. Noah, on the other hand, had a Texas-sized breakfast.

She nibbled on her toast and stared at him from across the table.

"Something bothering you?" he asked.

She slowly nodded.

He smiled. "Are you gonna tell me what it is, or am I supposed to guess?"

"We had sex last night. Lots and lots of sex."

Unfortunately, she'd made the emphatic statement just as the waitress was placing the bill on the table. The older woman with big hair giggled like a young teenager. Jordan was mortified and could feel her face heating. Noah's smile turned into a broad grin, and there was a sparkle in his eyes. He was getting a real kick out of her discomfort. As soon as the waitress walked away, no doubt to tell the other employees about the slut at table three, Noah said, "Yes, we did."

She sat back. "Okay then."

"Okay then?" he repeated.

She nodded. "That's all I wanted. An acknowledgment."

As far as she was concerned, the subject was closed. She folded her napkin and placed it on the table, checked the time, and said, "We'd better hurry. It's almost ten."

The cook was staring at her through the order window, as were the two waitresses huddled together behind the counter. Jordan kept her head high as she walked out.

She knew that Noah didn't understand why she needed an acknowledgment, but that didn't matter to her. From this moment on, they were going to go back to the way things used to be. He would be her brother's friend and partner, and she would be a boring but decidedly happy woman who lived in a safe comfort zone.

Noah had just slid in behind the steering wheel when he noticed her scowl. "What's going on with you?"

"I just had a revelation," she said.

"Yeah? What's that?"

"I was thinking about comfort zones . . . my comfort zone. You know, that place you said was so boring and safe?"

"It is boring and safe. I remember what I said."

"And I was wondering—what was missing from my dull, boring life?"

"Sex."

Okay, that too, she admitted to herself. "Besides sex," she said, disgruntled.

"Fun? Laughter? Hot sex?"

He was maddening. "You already said sex," she reminded him. "My mistake," he replied.

Ignoring his sarcasm, she continued. "I'll tell you what was missing. Dead bodies, Noah. There were never any dead bodies in my comfort zone."

Chapter Twenty-five

J.D. USED TO BRAG TO HIS BROTHER THAT IF HE DIDN'T WANT to be found, he wouldn't be found. He knew all the best hiding places in and around Serenity.

Randy knew about some of J.D's hidey-holes, but he didn't know about all of them. For example, J.D. had never told Randy about the abandoned mine he'd accidentally found last year when cutting across Eli Whitaker's land. He'd known he was trespassing, but since Eli hadn't yet put up a fence, J.D. figured it was all right, especially if he didn't tell anyone.

The mine had become his own private getaway. When he was there, he was pulling one over on Eli, and that made J.D. feel good. It wasn't right the way Eli gobbled up all the prime land and had all that money.

J.D.'s second home wasn't much to look at, but he liked it just fine. He'd put down a couple of old sleeping bags and brought in a cooler he'd periodically fill with ice and beer. His only other accessories were two flashlights and extra batteries. He didn't want to run out of light at night when he was reading his girly magazines.

He was proud to admit he didn't read the articles. Looking at the nudie girls was all he wanted or needed.

He even entertained the notion of bringing a couple of the girls from The Lux out for a little howdy-do. He didn't though. He liked having a secret place only he knew about.

The location was perfect. The mine was just far enough outside of Serenity to be forgotten, but close enough to keep a signal on his cell phone. The last couple of days he'd had to be on twenty-four-hour call in case his employer needed something.

He considered calling Randy several times to find out if there was a warrant out for him, but every time he'd start to punch in the numbers, he'd change his mind. He just didn't want to listen to another long lecture. Besides, the boss would find out if there was a warrant out for J.D. or not. He had connections all over town, and at most it would only take a couple of phone calls to find out if that Buchanan bitch had decided to go after him.

Fortunately the disposable phone he'd stolen from Professor MacKenna's house had the number taped on the back. The boss was the only person who knew it.

J.D. was getting anxious waiting to hear from him. Not only would he find out if he was wanted by the police but also today was payday, and he sure could use the cash.

He practically jumped on the phone when it rang.

"Yes, sir."

"I'm on my way," the boss said.

"To the house?" J.D. asked.

There was a long pause. "Yes. That's where we agreed to meet."

"Yes, sir. I'll leave right now."

"Remember to park at least three blocks away and walk over."

"I will," J.D. promised. "Did you remember today is payday?"

"Of course I did. We have a lot of loose ends to tie up before nightfall."

"I know," J.D. said. "Did you find out anything about a warrant?"

"Not yet."

"The new chief isn't going to let two murders go unsolved. I was thinking we ought to come up with a couple of names. If there was a way to pin those murders—"

"I've already got someone in mind to take the fall, but to pull it off I'll need your help. We should be able to wrap it up within a week."

"I knew you'd figure something out. You're so smart about stuff like this."

"I've had practice. Now, hurry up. We've got work to do."

Chapter Twenty-six

WHEN JORDAN AND NOAH WALKED INTO THE POLICE station, Sheriff Randy was in Chief Davis's office trying to pace in front of the desk. Since the office was so small, he could only take two steps forward and two back.

Noah made her stay behind him as he entered. She knew Noah didn't want to give J.D. another opportunity to punch her.

But J.D. was nowhere in sight. Joe spotted them and waved. "Come on in," he called out.

Noah didn't waste time on introductions. "Where's your brother?"

"I don't know where he is," Randy said. "I swear to you I've looked high and low for him, and I've left at least five messages on his home phone and twice that many on his cell phone telling him to come in, and that it was going to be okay because Miss Buchanan agreed not to press charges . . ." He tried to see around Noah. "I was right, wasn't I, Miss Buchanan? Joe told me you weren't going to press charges."

Although Noah took up most of the doorway, she was able to squeeze in next to him. "Yes, that's right."

"Thank you," he said. "I'm trying my best to help J.D. make some good decisions, but it's an uphill battle."

He sounded sincere and contrite, and Jordan suddenly felt sorry for him. It must be awful trying to keep his punch-happy brother in line.

Randy once again addressed Noah. "I know he messed up, but he's my brother, and the only family I have. I really am trying to help him move forward and stay out of trouble. I thought he was on the right path. He was closing down The Lux, and that's a real positive step."

Noah didn't care about that. "How did he know there was a body in Jordan's car trunk?"

"J.D. told me he got a tip on his cell phone."

"I want to know exactly what J.D. told you."

"We were supposed to go fishing, and I went by his place to pick him up. He came tearing out of his house and told me about the tip."

"Who called him?" Noah asked. "Did he tell you who the tip was from?"

"A woman," Randy answered. "It took a long while for me to get that much out of him. He wouldn't tell me her name though. J.D. said he had to protect her, that he'd promised. To be honest, I don't know if he was telling the truth or not." He added fervently, "I hope to God he was."

Looking defeated now, Randy leaned back against the desk. "J.D. is always looking for the big score. He has this pipe dream to buy a ranch. He doesn't know the first thing about ranching, but that don't matter to him. He thinks he's clever, but he isn't, and that's why he gets into trouble. He's done some real stupid things, and he's got a temper, that's for sure, but he wouldn't kill anyone."

"He went to prison because he killed someone," Joe pointed out.

"It was a bar fight J.D. didn't start. That was bad luck all around."

"Bad luck seems to chase J.D., doesn't it?" Joe remarked. "I've got the sheriff's deputies combing the county looking for him," he told Noah. He suddenly noticed Jordan. "Where are my manners? Jordan, come on in here and have a seat."

"I'm fine where I am," she replied.

"All right then. Noah, I've been thinking about the woman J.D. said called him. Now that's something Maggie Haden would do. I wouldn't put it past her."

"I thought of her," Randy said. "She hooked up with J.D. right after I got married. She got real hateful."

"She was always hateful, Randy," Joe said. "You just didn't see it."

Randy shrugged. "I've been looking for her too. Her cell phone goes directly to voice mail, and she doesn't have an answering machine at home."

"Why were you wanting to get hold of her?" Joe asked.

Randy looked over his shoulder at the chief. "Why do you think? She might know where J.D. is. That's the only reason I'd ever call her again." Randy stood. "I've got to head back to my office. I'll keep looking for J.D., but if you and Joe find him, call me right away. I'm worried about him."

Noah got out of the way so Randy could get past him.

The sheriff walked to the door, hesitated a second or two, then turned around and looked at Noah. "Could I have a word with you in private?"

"Sure," Noah said.

He followed Randy out to his car, and the two men stood there talking for several minutes.

Joe took a phone call while Jordan waited for Noah's return. "Where's Carrie?" she asked when he hung up the receiver. "Taking a break?"

"No, she's back in prison," Joe said. "They're supposed to send me a replacement tomorrow, but until then the calls I don't catch get forwarded to Bourbon."

Since his office was not big enough to accommodate a second chair, Jordan leaned against the door frame. "Why is she back in prison? She was part of a work release program, wasn't she?"

"That's right, she was," he said. He moved some papers out of his way and rested his elbows on the desktop. "As one of Maggie's last vengeful acts, she called the prison and gave Carrie a terrible evaluation. Said she was incompetent."

"Did you think she was?"

He shook his head. "She had trouble learning the computer, but she was good enough with the phones and taking messages."

"Then why don't you get her back?"

"Maggie also accused her of stealing supplies, but I don't believe that."

"Joe, you have to do something."

"I'm trying," he said.

Not good enough, Jordan thought.

The minute Noah came into the station, she told him about Carrie. She didn't have to ask him to do something about it because she knew he would.

"There isn't anything more we can do here," Noah said. "So we're going to check out of the motel and get on the road. I want to get Jordan to the airport and back to Boston. If you need anything . . ."

"You'll come back, right?"

"Agents Chaddick and Street will come in on this if you need them to. All you have to do is ask."

Shaking Noah's hand, Joe said, "I wish you could stay around, but I understand you wanting to leave and get back to your life and your job." He turned to Jordan. "Eventually there'll be a trial. You'll have to come back for that."

"I will," she promised.

Relief washed over Jordan when they walked out of the station. She was finally going to leave Serenity.

It didn't take either of them long to pack up their things. Noah planned to put the bags in the car and then check out with Amelia Ann. A phone call changed the plan.

"Noah, it's Joe. The MacKenna house is on fire."

Chapter Twenty-seven

"WHAT IN GOD'S NAME IS GOING ON?" JOE'S VOICE SHOOK when he asked the question. He stood with Jordan and Noah on the sidewalk across the street from MacKenna's tiny rental house, watching the roaring fire consume it.

He shoved his hands in his pockets. "We had a good long rain last night. It should have soaked that roof and kept it wet, but it sure didn't. Look at it burn." He shook his head. "I've never seen a fire eat up a house this quick."

They could use another storm right now, Jordan thought. She shielded her eyes with her hands and looked up at the sky. Not a cloud in sight. The sun was bright and beating down on them mercilessly. As usual, the desert sun was hot and unforgiving.

"No, sir," Joe muttered. "I've never seen anything like this."

Although there wasn't any doubt in his mind that the fire had been set, he still wanted and needed confirmation.

"Look at the way it's going, all four sides of the house burning straight up like that. It's like it was napalmed." Joe pulled his attention away from the fire and looked up at Noah. "I know the fire chief will have to make the call, but I'm betting he'll say it's arson. Don't you agree?"

"Looks that way," Noah said without hesitation. "And I'd say a very powerful accelerator was used to get it started and keep it going."

"Never seen a house burn so quick," Joe repeated, clearly impressed. "I don't get it though. Why burn it down? The detectives and the crime scene crew from Bourbon went through the house from top to bottom, and any evidence they found they bagged and took to their lab. You were in there too. You saw what was left. Just old papers and used-up furniture. Did you see anything worth burning? I sure didn't."

Joe moved so he could see Jordan, who was standing on the other side of Noah. "Sorry about those boxes of papers. I know you were hoping you could have them."

She didn't correct his misconception. Joe had obviously forgotten that she'd made copies. Either that, or he thought she still had more copies to make, but it no longer mattered. The hard copies of his research would have gone into the professor's estate, and she no longer needed them.

"I don't think anyone would go to this much trouble burning a house to get rid of some old history papers," Joe concluded.

Jordan watched the volunteer firemen. They'd given up trying to save the professor's house and were frantically working to keep the house next door from catching fire. If the wind picked up, the entire block could go up in flames.

"Did you make sure all the neighbors got out?" she asked.

Joe nodded. "Old lady Scott was the only one who gave me any trouble. She wouldn't let me get near her to help her down the steps. One of the firemen carried her out kicking and screaming. You know what I heard her say? She didn't want to miss her stories on the television."

"Why won't she let you near her?"

"She doesn't think anyone does enough for her. She's a real pain in the neck. She calls Sheriff Randy one day, me the next

complaining about something or other. Doesn't care whose jurisdiction it is. Anyone walks through her yard, front or back, and she
has a fit. Calls it trespassing. She called me the other day about kids
trampling on her flowers by the front porch." He pointed to the
right. "Her house is two down from MacKenna's. Now I ask you,
would you call those weeds flowers?"

Noah wanted to get him back on track. "Did you talk to the
neighbors? Ask them if they saw anyone hanging around MacKenna's
house?"

"I haven't interviewed all of them yet," he admitted. "I only just
got here a few minutes before you, and I was busy getting everyone out of their houses. I'll start asking questions now. Would you
mind helping me with that?" He walked toward the group of people clustered together at the corner and then stopped. "I'm in over
my head here," he said. "I just don't have the experience, and I can't
be everywhere at the same time. I think maybe I could use some
help from your FBI friends. Why don't you go ahead and call
them?"

It's about damned time, Noah thought. "Be happy to," he said
instead. He made the call immediately, before Joe could have second thoughts. He got Chaddick's voice mail and left a message for
him to call.

As they walked toward the neighbors, Jordan asked, "Where are
the deputies? I know the Grady sheriff is in Hawaii, but didn't you
ask his deputies to lend a hand?"

"They're helping," he said. "Right now they're combing two
counties looking for J.D. He could be hiding in one of about a
thousand places, but they'll keep at it until they find him and bring
him in for questioning."

MacKenna's neighbors were eager to tell what they knew, but
unfortunately none had seen anything out of the ordinary. One
woman had noticed a carpet cleaning van drive down the street,
but she was pretty sure it had driven on to the next block.

Mrs. Scott had information, but every time Joe tried to talk to
her, she turned her back on him and looked up at the sky. It was left

to Noah to charm her, and that only took a couple of smiles and a look of sympathy when she went into a rant about her flowers.

"As a matter of fact, I did see someone," she said. "I saw that no-good Dickey boy cut through my backyard today. I saw him as clear as he could be. I was standing at my kitchen sink making my cherry Kool-Aid drink because I like to have my Kool-Aid while I watch my programs." She paused to glare at Joe before continuing. "Then I saw the Dickey boy sneak past. He was carrying something that had a big handle, like a gas can. I was all set to open my back door and yell at him to get off my property, but he was moving so fast, he was gone before I could get my second dead bolt undone. Not five minutes later I hear shouting about a fire, and people start banging on my front door, so I got out of my La-Z-Boy and turned up the volume on my television so I could hear my programs." Once again, she shot Joe a glare.

"You're certain it was J.D.?" Joe asked.

"I'm certain I'm not talking to you," she snapped. "Now if this nice gentleman were to ask, I'd say, yes, it was Julius Dickey. That ten-pound belt buckle he always wears was plain to see. It was him."

Joe and Noah thanked the various neighbors and headed down the street. Jordan stayed behind, talking to a few of the women. Noticing she wasn't with him Noah turned around and saw Mrs. Scott wagging her finger in Jordan's face. He backtracked to tell her it was time to leave.

"Are we leaving the street or leaving Serenity?" Jordan asked after saying her good-byes to the neighbors.

He honestly didn't know. Though he was anxious to get her out of town and on a flight back to Boston, Jordan was at the center of this craziness, and until Noah understood why the killer was hell-bent on implicating her and keeping her in Serenity, he wasn't going to leave her alone for a second. The thought popped into his mind that he never wanted to leave her.

He shook his head, trying to clear it.

"Do you know what Mrs. Scott called me?" Jordan asked.

He slowed down. "What?"

"'You there.'"

He smiled. "So?"

"So she wanted to know why 'you there'—that would be me—came to Serenity."

"And what did you say?"

"To wreak havoc."

"Good answer."

"'Serenity,' she said, 'used to be a peaceful place.'"

"Until you came to town."

"She would also like to know when I'm leaving. I believe she plans to stay inside and keep her doors locked until I do."

He laughed. "Soon," he promised. "We'll be on the road in a couple of hours. Joe asked me to wait until Chaddick and Street get here. He's nervous. It's a big case, and he doesn't want to mess up. I know you're ready to take off . . ."

"I'm . . . conflicted," she said with some hesitation.

"Yeah? How come?"

"I want to leave, but I also want to find out who, what, and why. And I have a funny feeling the answer's right in front of me."

"You can read all about it in the papers when it's over."

The comment about the papers triggered something in Jordan's memory, but it was too elusive to catch hold.

"After you drop me at the airport, are you going to come back?"

"Sugar, I'm not dropping you anywhere."

He pulled her toward the car. She glanced over her shoulder and saw Joe standing in the middle of the street, talking to a fireman.

"Then what's the plan?" she asked.

"I'm going with you all the way to Boston, so no, as much as I would like to help, I won't be coming back. This isn't my area of expertise anyway. Chaddick's the man in charge now—or will be as soon as he returns my call—and he knows what he's doing. He's been at it awhile, and he's got a lot of experience."

He handed her the keys when they reached their car. "Why

don't you turn the motor on and get the air conditioner going? I'll be right back."

Jordan got behind the wheel, started the engine, and adjusted the air-conditioner dial. She watched Noah in the side mirror. Now he and Joe spoke to the fireman. Then Joe pulled out his cell phone and made a call as Noah headed back to the car. Shaking his head, he looked frustrated. He walked to the passenger side, but she climbed over the console and motioned for him to drive. Sweat trickled down his neck, so she turned up the fan and adjusted a vent to blow directly on him.

"How come you don't want to drive?" he asked.

"Traffic," she said. "I hate driving in traffic."

It took a second to realize what she'd said. He laughed. "What constitutes traffic in Serenity? Three, four cars in front of you?"

"Okay, I just hate to drive." Before he could comment, she asked, "What happened with Joe?"

"He's getting a warrant to go into J.D.'s house. He's talking to a judge in Bourbon now."

"I'm going in there with you," she said. "Because I bet I'll find my laptop. And if I do . . ."

"What? What will you do?"

"Something," she said. "All my files are on it, all my accounts . . ."

"Are you worried someone can get private information?"

"No," she said. "It's encrypted. No one could get into my files."

"Then what are you so worried about?"

"I just know that with all the right information and data, I can figure all of this out."

He was looking out the window. "I wonder how long it's going to take Joe to get in his damn car and drive to J.D.'s house."

"I'd say about five seconds." The calculated guess was based on the fact that Joe was sprinting toward them.

"It's signed," he shouted at Noah. "But we could go in anyway. A neighbor just called in. J.D.'s front door's wide open."

A moment later, they were on their way.

"Shouldn't someone call Sheriff Randy?"

He shrugged. "I'll leave that up to Joe."

She shifted in her seat. "The sheriff did a complete turnaround. He was almost . . . humble at the police station, but back when he drove into the lot with his brother and saw J.D. hit me, he was pretty obnoxious."

"He's doing a fast dance trying to keep his brother out of trouble. He knows . . ."

"Knows what?"

"J.D.'s a lost cause. I understand his loyalty though. It's his brother."

"Does J.D. have that kind of loyalty? I bet not. Sheriff Randy would be better off with J.D. back in prison." She rubbed her arms as though to ward off a sudden chill. "If J.D. happens to be inside his house, you be careful. There was something crazy in his eyes. I don't know how to explain it. He was hateful . . . and creepy."

"I can't wait to meet him. I can be pretty damned hateful too."

"Remember, he's innocent until proven guilty."

"He hit you. That's what I remember."

Joe pulled into J.D.'s driveway. Noah pulled in behind him. "You wait here. Keep the doors locked," he told her.

He moved fast. Pulling the gun from his holster, he held it to his side and met Joe at the front door. "We go in, you head left, I'll go right."

Jordan's heart skipped a beat as Noah, gun in hand, rushed into the house. She told herself that everything would be fine. He was a federal agent, trained to protect himself. She'd heard stories about some of the harrowing situations he'd been in, and he had the scars to prove it. He knew what he was doing. He'd be fine. She nodded to reinforce the thought. Still, freak accidents happened, and sometimes there were unexpected surprises . . . some not the good kind.

She was working herself into a state, as her mother would say.

Then Noah walked outside and everything really was fine. J.D's house was so small, it had only taken a few minutes to make certain no one was there.

She unlocked the car door for him. He pulled it open and said, "It looks like J.D. left in a hurry, and the door didn't catch. Wait until you see—"

Joe interrupted, running from the house into the yard shouting, "They found J.D.!"

Chapter Twenty-eight

AND THEN THERE WERE THREE.

J.D. Dickey was found in the ashes. The firemen discovered what was left of him underneath a pile of still-smoldering rubble near what used to be the back door of the professor's house. They were soaking the last embers when they spotted his remains. The only reason they knew for sure that it was J.D. was the gaudy belt buckle. Its edges were melted and blackened, but the rhinestone initials were still legible.

Jordan sat in the car in front of the smoldering ruins of the collapsed house and watched Noah. He was standing in the front yard talking to Agent Chaddick and Joe while they waited for the FBI's crime scene crew to arrive. He looked over at Jordan every once in a while to make sure she was okay.

Three corpses in one week. Professor MacKenna. Lloyd. And now J.D. Dickey. The boast that Serenity was a safe and peaceful place to live had just been shot to hell. And the town blamed Jordan Buchanan. After all, she was the only connection between the murders and the fire. She wouldn't be surprised if the residents showed up at her motel room with pitchforks and torches to run her out of town.

She could still hear Old Lady Scott's accusations. Never had a murder before she came to town . . . never had a fire like the one that consumed the MacKenna house. Oh, and they never had car trunks full of dead people—before Jordan came to town.

Statistics don't lie. This was more than a run of bad luck. It was a curse of biblical proportions. Even *she* wanted to get away from herself. Jordan knew such superstition wasn't logical, but nothing about this situation was logical. Just one thing was certain: Since Jordan had met the professor, she had become a one-woman plague.

It was impossible to predict what would happen next, but while she waited for Noah, Jordan tried to do just that. It was a frustrating exercise because she didn't have sufficient data, and the horrifying images from the last few days kept breaking into her thoughts. To think clearly again, she needed to erase these pictures from her mind. She reached into the backseat for a folder from MacKenna's research and began reading.

Noah glanced at her and saw her head down, poring over a paper. He had told her to stay in the car, that he didn't want her to see J.D.'s incinerated remains. He didn't think he would ever forget her reaction. She'd looked stunned and then had very quietly asked, "Why in God's name would you think I would want to see a charred body?"

Why indeed? It was a gruesome sight. And while neither Noah nor Chaddick were the least affected by the scene, Joe was having difficulty keeping it together. His face was a shade of gray that Noah had never before seen, and he kept making gagging sounds.

Noah took pity on him. "Joe, you'll feel better if you don't look at him."

"Yeah, but it's like a car wreck. I don't want to look, but I do anyway."

Chaddick was exasperated. "You're a cop," he reminded him. "You come up on a wreck, you're supposed to look, aren't you?"

"You know what I mean."

One of the volunteer firemen motioned them over from the front yard. His name was Miguel Moreno, and he was a retired fireman from Houston who decided late in life to own a ranch. He'd trained the volunteers, which was why they were so well organized, quick to respond, and efficient. Since he'd taken charge, none of his firemen had sustained a single injury. He'd already walked through the rubble several times and was ready to tell Noah what he thought.

"There ain't any doubt that J.D. set the fire, but I'm willing to bet he didn't know his way around such a volatile accelerator. If he did, he sure wouldn't have ignited it while he was still inside the house."

Joe stepped away from the body. "J.D. could have accidentally started the fire too early," he suggested. "The way I see it—he gets inside and he soaks everything down real good, and then he's thinking he'll go out the same way he came in, through the back door. Once he's outside, he'd toss something in to get the fire going, like maybe a rag dipped in kerosene or maybe some rolled-up paper he was gonna light up."

Moreno nodded. "It's possible," he said. "Just needed one spark to get a flash."

"Anything could cause a spark," Joe said, now eager to share his theories. "Maybe when he opened the door to leave, the friction from the metal threshold against his boots made a spark . . . that would have done it."

"Only an arson expert can say for sure what happened," Moreno said. "You have any of those coming to Serenity, Agent Chaddick?"

"I sure do," he replied. "Joe, you think you can handle this with Moreno? Keep the area sealed until my crew gets here? I want to head over to Dickey's house with Noah."

"I can handle it," Joe assured him. "Has Agent Street found anything interesting?"

"I'll know as soon as I get over there."

Joe followed Noah. "Noah, you have a second?"

Noah turned back. "Yes?"

"Do you think the agents will want me to step back now that they've taken over?" he asked in a low voice. "I don't want to get in their way, but . . ." He ended the sentence with a shrug.

Noah motioned to Chaddick. "Why don't we find out right now?"

Joe looked embarrassed when he put the question to the agent. Chaddick, the more diplomatic of the two agents, glanced at Noah before answering. "I know you have heard stories about how we're bullies and roll over the locals when we take charge, and most of those stories are probably true," he added with a grin. "We don't like local interference, but Noah told me this is a different situation. You and Street and I will work this together."

Joe quickly nodded. "I sure appreciate it," he said. "This is a great opportunity to learn from the experts."

That settled, Noah headed back to his car. The windows were down, and he could see Jordan reading some papers while she sipped from a bottle of what was no doubt lukewarm water. Poor Jordan had been waiting a hell of a long time for him to finish up, but she hadn't complained or tried to hurry him along.

Jordan saw him coming and quickly gathered up the papers she'd spread over the seat. She was so hot, she thought she was going to have a heatstroke any second now. She hadn't wanted to keep the engine idling with the air on for such a long time, and so she had turned the motor off and prayed for a little wind to push the heat around.

Earlier, despite Noah's orders, she had momentarily slipped out of the car to sit under the shade of a walnut tree, but the stares from the crowd that had gathered across the street made her uneasy. Whispering to one another, they never took their eyes off her. Who knew what they could be saying? Probably something about tar and feathering or burning at the stake.

When she and Noah had driven from J.D.'s over to the professor's house, she'd offered to return to the motel and wait for him. All he had to do was call her and she'd drive back, but he wouldn't hear of it. He didn't want her out of his sight, and from the steel in his voice, she knew it would be pointless to argue.

Noah got behind the wheel, started the engine, and flipped on the air. Then he turned to her. Her face was flushed. She'd pinned her hair up, but the tendrils at the back of her neck were damp. Her clothes stuck to the curves of her body, and her skin glistened. She looked both utterly beautiful and wilted. It made him feel guilty for what he was about to do.

"How are you holding up?" he asked.

"Good," she answered. "I'm good."

"I hate to ask this of you, but I really need to get back over to Dickey's house. I want to go through it—"

She interrupted. "It's okay. You don't have to explain. You need to do this, and I'm fine, really."

She didn't push him to take her back to the motel because she knew he'd again refuse. He'd insisted that she stay with him, and if that helped him get the job done, she'd cooperate.

Noah didn't notice the time until he was pulling up to J.D.'s house. The day was getting away from him. He couldn't believe how long they'd been at MacKenna's house, and he knew he'd spend as much time if not more going through J.D.'s place.

He parked behind Chaddick's car and said, "We may have to stay another night."

"I know."

"You're okay with that?"

"Yes," she assured him. "We can leave first thing in the morning." How many times had she thought that?

Already inside, Chaddick came to the front door and called out, "You're gonna love this."

Noah nodded back to him before speaking to Jordan. "If you want, you can come inside," he said, "but don't touch anything."

Chapter Twenty-nine

NOAH HADN'T SEEN THIS MUCH SURVEILLANCE EQUIPMENT since he had been at Quantico.

Agent Street was in awe. "From what I'd heard about this guy, I had him pegged as an idiot, you know? But now . . ." His eyes swept the room with all the spying tools lying about. "Some of this stuff is pretty sophisticated and complicated to use. By the look of things, I'd say he knew what he was doing."

"And what exactly was he doing?" Jordan stood just inside the door, surveying the gadgets Chaddick had pulled out of a box and placed on the floor.

Street tossed Noah a pair of gloves as he answered Jordan's question. He pointed to what looked like a tiny satellite dish. "That's a parabolic microphone. Lets you hear conversations at least three hundred yards away."

Noah walked over to get a closer look. "It's got a built-in tape recorder and an output jack," he said.

"I wonder how many private conversations he listened to," Jordan said.

"He wasn't just listening in," Street said. "Wait until you see his video collection. He had cameras set up in a room in that sleazy motel he ran and filmed customers with his girls. We'll probably find the cameras in the smoke detectors or the ceiling lights."

Chaddick nodded. "Did you look at any of the videos?"

"Just one," he answered. "Good quality. Film wasn't grainy at all." He sounded clinical about it. "Graphic stuff."

"Lovely," Jordan whispered. Just being inside J.D.'s house made her feel like she could catch something.

"Check out these binoculars." Noah picked up a pair and examined them. "There's an amplifier attached. Pretty high-tech."

"Yes," Chaddick agreed. "J.D. could watch and listen at the same time."

"And record," Street added. "Some of this stuff is brand-new. Batteries aren't unwrapped yet. I'd say he was setting up to do some real serious business. It's a given he was into blackmail. And with all this equipment, he had to have a list of his clients, right? How else could he keep track of who paid what, when?"

"Maybe," Chaddick surmised. "Did you find any notebooks or papers?"

He shook his head. "I'm guessing he stored everything in his computer."

Chaddick looked surprised. "He's got a computer? Where is it?"

"In the den behind the kitchen. You didn't notice it?"

"I haven't gotten past all these gadgets."

Jordan wasn't paying much attention to the conversation. She was thinking about the cash deposits J.D. had made into his own bank account. The professor was putting large amounts of cash into his account, but J.D. never deposited any more than $1,000 at a time. Had he just started his venture? And where did he get the money to buy this kind of equipment? It had to be expensive.

She walked to the window and looked out at the street while she tried to figure out the relationship between the professor and J.D.

After Noah had gone through the last box, he stood and asked Street if he'd had time to get into the computer.

"I got it up and running, but I can't get into any of the files. He's blocked access. We'll have to take it with us and get one of our techs to work on it. That will take a big chunk of time."

Noah smiled. "Maybe not." He turned toward the window. "Jordan, would you mind breaking into a computer for us?"

She looked over her shoulder. "Be happy to," she said, thankful she could be of use. "It wouldn't happen to be a laptop, would it?" she couldn't resist asking.

"Sugar, didn't we talk about letting that go?"

She smiled. "Just asking."

"You really think you can do it?" Street asked.

"I really do."

She followed Noah into the den. The computer was a new model, and Jordan was impressed. Carrie had told her the prison had offered her computer classes, but she hadn't been interested. Maybe J.D.'s place of incarceration had offered him the same training. And if it had, it looked like he had paid attention.

Noah pulled a chair up to the keyboard for her. "Go to it."

It only took a second for her to pull up J.D.'s files. Opening them would take longer.

"Call me when you're in," Noah said.

He went back into the living room with Chaddick. Street stayed behind and watched Jordan's fingers fly over the keys. Symbols and numbers filled up the screen. He didn't know what she was doing, but she did, and that was all that mattered.

Jordan lost track of time as she concentrated on the computer screen and the task at hand. Finally, she broke through.

"I'm in!" she called out.

A folder opened just as Noah put his hands on her shoulders. "What have you got?"

"A list," she answered. She leaned closer to the screen. "He kept records."

Standing, Jordan moved out of the way so that Street could sit. Her back was stiff, and she noticed it was getting dark outside. How long had she been sitting there? She arched backward to stretch.

Chaddick leaned against the side of the desk. "Does it tell us anything?"

"I'd say so," Street replied. "I've got first names only, no dates but days of the week, offenses, payoffs, and some locations." He began to laugh. "I'm telling you, if all these people live in Serenity, this town's a real hotbed of activity."

"Who's on the list?" Noah asked.

"I've got a Charlene paying four hundred dollars on a Friday at an insurance office."

"Charlene? Why did she pay J.D. four hundred dollars?" Jordan asked.

Street grinned. "He had a video of her shacking up."

"With her fiancé?"

All three agents looked at her, and she realized how stupid her question was. If Charlene had been sleeping with her fiancé, J.D. wouldn't have been blackmailing her.

"Okay, I'm tired," she said. "She was cheating on her fiancé." Suddenly Jordan was full of outrage. "I gave that woman china! Vera Wang!"

Chaddick looked back at the screen. "She's been paying for a while."

"She's been shacking up for a while," Street added. "Guess she didn't mind paying."

"Who was she sleeping with?" Jordan asked. "No, don't tell me. I don't want to know. Yes, I do. Who was it?"

"A guy named Kyle—"

Her hand flew to her throat. "Not Kyle Heffermint!"

Noah thought Jordan's reaction was hilarious. He went to her and put his arm around her. "He's the name-dropper, isn't he? And he was hitting on you."

"He's the one," she affirmed.

"There's a Steve N. here," Street continued.

"Could be Steve Nelson," Noah said. "I met him at the restaurant. He runs the insurance agency."

"He's Charlene's boss," Jordan told him.

Street grinned. "That's not all he is."

"Oh, dear God, she wasn't sleeping with Steve too, was she? No, I don't believe it."

"Want to watch the video?"

"Oh, my God, she was. And Steve's married."

"Yes," Noah said drily, "which is why he'd pay blackmail to keep his affair secret."

"I'm printing this out," Street said, moving the mouse on the pad. "I'll make two copies. You take one, Noah."

"I'll tell you this. Before I leave Serenity, I want to meet this Charlene," Chaddick said.

Noah heard a car pull up outside. He went to the living room and looked out the front window. "Tech crew's here now."

"Good," Street said. "They can box all this stuff up." He went to the printer, sorted the copies, and handed a set to Noah.

"We're taking off early in the morning," Noah told him. "If you need anything, just let me know. And please keep me apprised."

Jordan was more than ready to leave J.D. Dickey's house. Once they were on the road, she said, "You think you know someone, and then you find out she's a sex maniac."

"But you didn't really know Charlene, did you? You'd only just met her," Noah countered.

"That's true. But it's still disheartening."

"Unless you can think of another restaurant, I guess we're going back to Jaffee's. Okay with you?"

"Depends," she said. "Is he on the list?"

He laughed. "You want to look?"

"You do it."

Noah pulled over to the curb, put the car in park and quickly went through the list. He saw Amelia Ann's name and wondered how Jordan would react if she knew.

"No Jaffee," he said.

She sighed. "Good."

Noah thought about the long day he'd put her through. "You're a real trouper, you know that?" He looked at her for a long second, then reached over and cupped the back of her neck with his hand, and pulled her toward him.

"What . . . ?" she began.

His mouth settled firmly on hers. She hadn't expected his kiss, yet she instinctively parted her lips for his tongue. He took full advantage, and the kiss deepened. Noah didn't do anything half measure. The kiss didn't last long, but it was thorough. When he sat back, her heart was pounding. Falling against the seat, she tried to catch her breath.

Noah didn't look like he was having any trouble catching his breath. He put the car in drive and continued on.

"I'm in the mood for fish," he said. "And a cold beer."

No mention about the kiss, no thank-you or even a "wasn't that nice?" comment.

Noah glanced over. "Something wrong?" he asked, knowing full well there was. She glared at him. "You look a little irritated."

Ya think? "No, nothing's wrong."

"Okay then."

"I was just wondering how you can be so laid-back . . . you know, blasé."

"Laid-back and blasé are two different things."

"Then you're both. You just kissed me." There, she'd said it, and it was out there for discussion.

"Mmm, sure did."

"That's it? 'Sure did'?"

She'd sounded so furious, he smiled. Jordan was something when she was wound up.

"What did you want me to say?"

He had to be kidding. He knew exactly what she wanted him to say. That the kiss meant something. It was a big deal. But apparently it wasn't. He'd kissed a lot of women. What was this to him: same old, same old?

She thought about reminding him of the wild time they'd had the night before. She could also point out that this morning he had acted as though nothing out of the ordinary had occurred. She knew that if he responded by asking her what she wanted him to say, she might very well pull a J.D. and punch him senseless.

She bet he'd remember that.

Even though, at the moment, it was a lovely fantasy, violence was never the answer.

They stopped at a red light and Noah looked over. "Now what are you thinking about, Sugar? You've got a perplexed look on your face."

"Violence," she immediately answered. "I was thinking about violence."

He swore he never knew what she was going to say. "What about it?"

"It's never the answer. That's what my father and mother taught Sidney and me."

"And your brothers?"

"They were usually trying to pummel one another into the ground. I think that's why they all did so well in sports. They got to pound other teams."

"So how did you get rid of your aggressive tendencies?" he asked, genuinely curious.

"I broke things."

"Oh yeah?"

"It wasn't vandalism," she explained. "I broke things so I could put them back together. It was a . . . learning experience."

"You must have driven your parents nuts."

"Probably," she agreed. "They were patient with me though, and after a while they got used to it."

"What are some of the things you broke?"

"You have to remember, I was a kid, so of course I started small. A toaster, an old fan, a lawn mower . . ."

"Lawn mower?"

She smiled. "That's still a sore subject with my father. He came home from work early one afternoon and found all the parts of his lawn mower, down to the nuts and bolts, spread out on the drive. He wasn't happy."

Noah was having a hard time picturing her with grease on her face and hands, screwing things together. Jordan was so feminine now. He couldn't imagine it.

"Did you get the lawn mower back together?"

"With my brothers' help, which, by the way, I didn't need. The next week my father brought home an old, broken computer. He told me I could have it, but I had to promise I wouldn't touch any more appliances, lawn mowers, or cars."

"Cars?"

"I never worked on one of those. Not interested. And once I got a computer . . ."

"You found your calling."

"I guess I did. What about you? What were you like as a little boy? Were you packing a gun back then?"

"Ornery," he answered. "I got into my share of fights, I suppose, but we lived in Texas," he reminded her, "and that meant playing football in high school. I did all right and ended up getting an athletic scholarship to college. All through school I was always a model student." Even he couldn't say the lie with a straight face. "I didn't like rules back then."

"And you don't like rules now."

"I guess I don't."

"You're a rebel," she said.

"That's what Doctor Morganstern calls me."

"May I ask you something?"

He pulled the car into the parking lot behind the Home Away from Home Motel's courtyard. "Sure. What do you want to know?"

"Have you ever been in a relationship that lasted more than a week or two? Have you really ever committed to one woman, even for a little while?"

He didn't waste a second thinking over his response. "No."

If the abruptness in his answer and his emphatic tone were an attempt to get her to drop the subject, he was mistaken.

"Goodness. Aren't you Mister Sensitive."

He parked and opened the door. "Sugar, there's not a sensitive bone in my body."

He was wrong about that, but she wasn't going to argue.

"What about you?" he asked. "You ever been in a long relationship?"

Before she could answer, he came around and opened her door. Taking Jordan's hand, Noah walked toward the street. The lot was dimly lit by a lamp at the far end, and the only sound was the night settling in around them.

He stopped for a moment and stared into her eyes. "I know what you're all about, Jordan Buchanan."

"And would you care to explain it all to me?"

"No."

And the subject was closed.

Chapter Thirty

"I'M TELLING YOU RIGHT NOW, IF JAFFEE'S BISTRO IS CROWDED, I'M going in the back door and eating in the kitchen."

Noah asked the obvious question. "Why?"

Jordan looked at him as if the answer should be obvious. "I don't want to go through another inquisition. And I certainly don't want people glaring at me while I eat. It's bad for the digestion."

"People are curious, that's all," he reasoned. "Face it, Sugar. You're news."

"Oh, I'm news all right," she said. "Since I arrived here three people have died. If you consider the number of times I've been here, the number of residents, and the number of unexpected deaths, and then leave room for a statistical anomaly . . ."

"Which I'm guessing would be you."

"That's right. I'm the deviation in my calculations."

"Of course you are," he said drily.

"You can, therefore, draw one conclusion."

"Which is?"

"I've started an epidemic."

He put his arm around her and pulled her toward him. "That's my girl," he drawled.

"This isn't funny."

"Sugar, it kinda is."

She sighed. She couldn't believe how quickly she became rattled these days. "Okay, maybe I'm being a little unreasonable, which, by the way, is totally not me. I'm always reasonable. But here . . . I can't seem to think straight." Especially when I'm around you, she silently added.

They walked around a corner and crossed the street. Jaffee's was directly ahead of them, and Jordan could see a few customers inside, but most of the tables were empty.

"We get in, we eat, we get out. Agreed?"

"That sounds like a wonderful dining experience. Can we sit at a table, or must we stand while we eat?" he asked as he swung the door open.

Angela looked happy to see them. "Hey, Jordan," she called out.

"Hey, Angela. You remember Noah."

"I sure do," she said, smiling. "Your table's waiting for you. With all the big doings today, you must be hungry as all get out." She took their drink orders and said, "You two got in just under the wire. I was about to take off the tablecloths."

"Slow night?" Jordan asked.

"Always is on poker night," she said. "We shut down an hour early so Jaffee can get the kitchen cleaned up. He hates to be late for poker."

Noah went to the men's room to wash up, and when he returned, the drinks were already on the table, and Angela was waiting.

"I hate to hurry you along," she said. "And I promise you can take your time once I get your dinner orders in, but Jaffee would really like to get started fixing your meals."

She made a few recommendations, and as soon as they ordered, she hurried back into the kitchen.

Jordan relaxed. The last table had cleared, and she and Noah were the only customers in the restaurant. Neither Angela nor Jaffee interrupted them.

Noah raised his bottle of beer. "To our last night in Serenity."

She hesitantly lifted her glass of ice water. "*Hopefully,* our last night in Serenity."

He took a long drink. "Any more murders, they'll have to change the name of the town."

She smiled. "I guess I overreacted, didn't I? I was certain we'd be surrounded by a crowd again, asking all sorts of questions about the fire and about J.D. But look at us. We have the entire restaurant to ourselves, and we'll get to eat dinner in peace. That's a nice bit of luck, isn't it?"

Noah smiled back, but didn't comment. Angela was busy folding tablecloths, but he noticed the tray that she had just placed on one of the tables was stacked with decks of cards. Jaffee obviously hosted poker night at the restaurant. Noah wondered how long it would take Jordan to catch on.

Jordan wasn't paying Angela any attention. She was busy thinking about the list Agent Street had compiled.

"What will happen to those tapes J.D. made?" she asked in a whisper. "Will they be made public?"

"Probably not."

"You know what I don't understand? Everyone seems to know everyone else's business, so how was Charlene able to hide her little . . . hobby?"

He laughed. "Hobby? Never heard it called that before."

"How were any of those people on the list able to hide their extracurricular activities?" she asked.

He shrugged. "You want something bad enough, you figure out a way to get it."

She tilted her head and looked at him inquisitively. "Have you ever wanted something so badly that you would risk everything?"

Noah stared at her for a long moment. "Yeah, I guess I have," he said quietly.

Their conversation ended when Angela returned to carry their empty dishes back to the kitchen. Jaffee came out to say hello, and also to ask Jordan if she would mind taking a quick look at Dora.

Noah stood when she did. "Who's Dora?" he asked.

"Computer," said Jordan. "I'll be right back. Finish your drink."

"I'll keep him company," Angela promised. "You want another beer?"

"No, I'm good," he said. "When does poker start?"

"In about fifteen minutes. The men ought to be drifting in pretty soon. Well, look there. Dave Trumbo's getting out of his Suburban, and he's got Eli Whitaker with him. They're always the first to arrive. They're best friends," she added. "Eli's the richest man in Serenity. Some say he could be the richest man in all of Texas."

She jutted her hip out and put her hand on her waist. "I bet you're wondering where he came by all that money. No one knows for sure, but we all like to speculate. I think maybe he inherited it. None of us would dare ask him though. He doesn't come to town much. He likes to stay to himself. He's real shy, and Dave's the opposite. Never met anyone he didn't like, he says."

"Don't any of the women play poker?"

"Sure we do," she said. "But we don't like to play with the men. They're too competitive, and they don't like to visit the way we do. We have our own poker night. Now here comes Steve Nelson. I don't remember if you met him the other night or not. He runs the only insurance agency around."

Jordan sat at Jaffee's computer, unaware that the poker players were arriving. Back at their table, Noah wondered if Jordan could hear the commotion. It didn't take long for the restaurant to fill up.

Jordan quickly solved Jaffee's latest problem. He'd mixed up two different commands. While she heard people talking, she stayed focused on the daunting task of helping Jaffee understand what he had done so he wouldn't repeat the mistake.

"Remember," Jordan told him, "Dora doesn't bite."

Jaffee wiped his hands on a towel and nodded. "But if I get into trouble . . ."

She reassured him. "You can e-mail or call me."

Jordan gave him a few suggestions for troubleshooting, but when she saw the glazed look in his eyes, she knew he didn't understand a single word she was saying. She had a feeling she was going to be getting daily calls from him for a while. That thought made her smile as she headed back to her table. The evening was turning out to be a relaxing one after all. Her biggest dilemma at the moment was dessert. Should she or shouldn't she? Noise intruded into her thoughts, and she came to a dead stop in the doorway when she saw the crowd.

Noah watched her enter the room and thought the look on her face was priceless.

A hush fell over the gathering, and all eyes were on her as she slowly walked over to him. "What's all this?" she whispered.

"Poker night."

"Here? Poker night is here? Why did I think . . . I just assumed . . . Do you think we could just leave now?"

"Doubtful."

"We could sneak out the back . . ."

He shook his head. "Sneaking out isn't an option."

She understood when she turned around. Every man there was standing, and those who had not yet met her were waiting to be introduced.

Jaffee did the honors. There were so many she couldn't remember half their names. Every single one of them said "Hey." After the introductions, they bombarded her with questions.

They didn't just want to know about the fire and J.D.'s terrible death. They also wanted to rehash how she had discovered the professor and then Lloyd in her car. Jordan wouldn't have been surprised if one of them had asked for a reenactment. She answered every question—sometimes twice—in their morbid curiosity. She was able to laugh a few times, and in between the questions, Dave, the natural salesman, tried to sell her a new car.

Noah got his fair share of questions too.

"Does Joe figure it was J.D. who killed those two men?" Jaffee asked.

"He's a smart cookie," Dave said. "I'll bet he does."

"I'd heard J.D. disappeared," a man named Wayne interjected.

"Did Joe have enough to arrest him?" Dave asked.

"Doesn't matter now, does it? The man's dead," Steve Nelson reminded the group. "Say, Agent Clayborne, did you and Joe happen to go through J.D.'s house?"

It was difficult for Noah not to smile. He knew what Steve was fishing for. He wanted to know if J.D. had kept records.

"Yes, we went through it. Everything was packed up by two other FBI agents and taken away. There wasn't much there though."

Steve didn't have much of a poker face. Noah could see the relief in his eyes and understood why. He'd seen Steve's name on the list not only for sleeping with Charlene but for some questionable insurance practices.

"Do you think we'll ever know why J.D. killed those men?" Dave asked.

"Joe will tell us when he knows something," Steve said with assurance.

"My heart goes out to Randy Dickey. He's turned into a decent sheriff. This will be a hard blow for him. I think J.D. was his only family," Dave remarked.

Noah noticed Eli Whitaker standing among the men, listening to the conversation but saying little.

"What do you do for a living, Eli?" Noah asked.

"I raise horses, run some cattle," he answered.

"What breed?"

"The cattle are mostly longhorns," he replied. "They seem to be the hardiest for this part of the country."

Noah followed up with a couple of other questions about Eli's operation, and before long the two were standing apart, having a conversation about ranching.

Dave grinned. "That's the most I've seen Eli talk to a newcomer."

The other men in the group took notice and all nodded in agreement.

Steve turned back to Jordan. "I know you two haven't been

here long, but you don't seem like newcomers to me. You've brought a lot of excitement to our town. When are you and Noah leaving Serenity?"

"Tomorrow," Jordan answered.

"It's been a real pleasure meeting you two," Dave said.

"I think they've had enough questions for one night," Jaffee told everyone. "Why don't you all get drinks from the bar and take your seats?"

While most of the men scattered around the room, Dave and Eli stepped forward with Jaffee to say good-bye to Jordan.

"I'm sure going to miss you," Jaffee said. "And I'm so sorry you lost your research papers. I heard you had to leave them at the professor's house. You go to all the trouble of making copies and then you watch them go up in flames."

"It's a crying shame. Didn't you tell us you came all the way from Boston to get that research?" Dave asked.

"You mean to say it all got burned up?" Eli wondered aloud.

Jordan finally got a word in. "I have the copies. They weren't in the fire, and I had already mailed the bulk of them home before the originals were destroyed. If Joe and the two agents in charge of the investigation now want to see them, I'll have to mail them back."

"That's real good news," Jaffee said. "Your trip wasn't wasted. Dinner's on the house, and don't even think about arguing about that. Dora and I thank you from the bottom of our hearts for all your help. I sure hope you come back here someday to say 'hey.'"

He hugged her good-bye and shook Noah's hand.

"Either one of you need another car, you think of me. I'll drive it to Boston for you," Dave offered.

"He'll do it too," Eli called out as he headed to his table.

Noah left a generous tip for Angela and steered Jordan toward the door amid a chorus of good-byes.

Neither of them said a word until they were a block away. Jordan broke the silence. "Hmm. Poker night. Didn't see that coming."

Noah laughed. "I've never seen that look on your face before . . . when you saw the crowd."

"The evening wasn't too bad. We had a lovely dinner without interruptions, and we met some charming gentlemen," she said. "Charming . . . and interesting," she added with a nod.

"You know what else is interesting?"

"What?"

"Half of those charming men were on the list."

Chapter Thirty-one

JORDAN WAS STANDING IN THE SHOWER RINSING OFF THE HEAT of the day and lathering her hair with apricot-scented soap when the realization hit. She didn't want to go home. She immediately pushed the ridiculous thought aside. Of course she wanted to go home.

She wanted her organized life back, didn't she? When she'd sold her company, she had netted a staggering profit, but now she needed to decide what to do with it. She had toyed with the idea of investing some of the money in developing a new computer processor, one that would be so fast it could handle even the most complicated multimedia software several times over. She had even visualized the design and the prototype. But there was only one problem with her grand scheme to shake up the Silicon Valley giants again. She didn't want to. Let someone else come up with a design that would make the world spin faster and faster.

Not wanting to get into the game again wasn't the only startling revelation. She no longer was in a hurry to run out and buy another laptop and cell phone. In the past they had been her appendages, but she didn't feel laptop dependent anymore, and she was finding it remarkably pleasant not to be answering her cell phone every five minutes. There were definite perks to being unavailable.

"I'm starting to scare myself," she whispered.

What was happening to her? It was as though she were morphing into a completely different person. Maybe sitting in 120-degree heat waiting for Noah to examine the fire wreckage had done something to her brain. Maybe the heat melted it. Or maybe all the showers she'd been taking since she'd arrived in Serenity had washed away her brain cells.

She was dehydrated from exposure to the sun. That's what it was.

She put on her T-shirt and boxer shorts and brushed her teeth. With her toothbrush sticking out of her mouth, she wiped the steam off the mirror and looked at herself. Blotchy skin and freckles. What a prize she was, especially wearing her unisex pajamas.

Jordan put the toothbrush down, reached for a jar of Kate's special body lotion, and opened the door. She'd never worried about how she looked, but now everything was upside down.

Jordan knew what the real problem was. Until this moment, she had refused to admit it. Noah. Oh, yes, he was the problem. He had changed everything, and she didn't know what she could do about it.

Worrying wouldn't improve her situation. A smart woman would run as fast as she could in the opposite direction, but she guessed she wasn't smart because, at the moment, all she could think about was going to bed with him again.

She needed a distraction to take her mind off sex. She decided she would curl up in bed with the professor's research papers and read another grisly tale about bloodshed, decapitation, mutilation, and superstition. That ought to do the trick and take her mind off Noah.

Where were her glasses? She thought she'd left them by her contact lens case in the bathroom, but they weren't there. She crossed the bedroom to the desk and stubbed her toe on the leg of a chair. Groaning, she hopped on one foot while she dug through her satchel.

"Noah," she asked, "have you seen—"

"On the table," he called through the open door between their rooms.

How did he know what she wanted? Was he a mind reader? Her glasses were right where he'd told her they were. "How did you know—"

"You're squinting," he answered before she could finish her sentence. "And you just ran into a chair."

"I wasn't watching where I was going."

He laughed. "You couldn't *see* where you were going."

Jordan noticed water spots on her lenses and went back into the bathroom. She thought she heard someone knocking on her door and called out, "Noah, could you get that?"

A few seconds later she heard a woman's voice coming from Noah's room. The knocking had been at his door, not hers. Curious, she hurriedly cleaned her glasses, slipped them on, and went into the bedroom. Oh, great. Noah was getting personalized turn-down service, and Amelia Ann was doing the honors. Noah leaned against the door frame watching her, but when he heard Jordan, he glanced over his shoulder and winked at her.

He was getting a kick out of the preferential treatment. Jordan wasn't. She couldn't stop staring at Amelia Ann through the doorway. The woman was dressed like a cocktail waitress in a seedy bar. She had on short-shorts; red, open-toed, stiletto heels; and a low-cut blouse she'd apparently forgotten to button. She was definitely advertising. The way she bent over the bed when she smoothed the sheets was comical, but Jordan wasn't laughing. Amelia Ann's behavior was disgraceful.

Muttering to herself, Jordan spun around and pulled off her own bedspread. She put it in the corner, then dumped a stack of papers in the middle of the bed, grabbed a bottle of water, and sat down to read.

The room phone rang. It was her sister, Sidney, calling. "You'll never guess where I am."

"I don't want to guess. Tell me," Jordan said.

"You don't have caller ID?"

"You called my motel room, Sidney. You should know I don't have caller ID."

"I'm in Los Angeles, and I'm surrounded by boxes. Since I can't check into my dorm for another week and a half, I'm stuck in a hotel. Actually, it's a very nice hotel," she admitted. "The bellman carried up all my stuff."

"I thought Mother was going out there with you next week. Why are you there so early?"

"Everything suddenly changed," she said. "I spent the other night with my friend Christy, and when I got home the next morning, Mom had my flight all set up. It was like she couldn't wait another minute to get rid of me. I think I was driving her crazy worrying out loud about Dad."

"So you're on your own now."

"And loving it," she said. "I'm going overboard with room service, but since I can't get into my dorm, what else can I do? I hope Dad doesn't have a fit when he gets the bill on his credit card."

"How's Dad doing?"

"Okay, I guess. You know Dad. Death threats don't seem to faze him. Mother's another story though. She's a wreck, but trying not to let it show. Everyone is so stressed out over this trial."

"Any updates on when it will be over?" Jordan asked.

"No," Sidney answered. "Dad's bodyguards are becoming permanent fixtures on Nathan's Bay. Everywhere I looked, there they were: constant reminders that someone wants our father dead."

"The threats will stop as soon as there's a verdict."

"How can you know that for certain? That's what everyone keeps saying, but come on, Jordan, this is a racketeering case. It's . . . major."

Jordan heard the anxiety in Sidney's voice. "I know."

"And if that horrible man is convicted, won't his family and his business associates still come after Dad? And if he's not convicted, won't the other side—?"

Jordan cut her off. "You'll drive yourself nuts thinking about all of this. You have to hope for the best."

"Easier said than done," she replied. "I am glad I came out here early. I was making it worse on Mom. Now she's got Laurant to worry about . . . and Nick's freaking out . . ."

"Wait a minute. What did you say? What's wrong with Nick and Laurant?"

"Nothing's wrong with Nick. His wife is the worry. I thought you knew . . ."

"Knew what?" she asked impatiently.

"Laurant started having labor pains, really bad labor pains, and the doctor put her in the hospital. She can't have the baby yet. She's only six months along."

"When did this happen?"

"Nick took her to the hospital yesterday. I was already on my way to L.A."

Had Jordan talked to her brother since then? She couldn't remember.

"It's a good thing Nick came back home early and Noah stayed with you, isn't it? It would be awful if he was that far away when Laurant started having problems."

"Poor Laurant. What's the doctor saying?"

"I don't know," Sidney answered. "Mom told me she's hooked up to an IV. They've slowed down the contractions, but they haven't stopped them completely. Listen, when will you get home? Mom sure could use your support now. You're always so cool and calm about everything. Nothing rattles you."

Not anymore, Jordan thought. Thanks to Noah, everything rattled her.

From the corner of her eye, Jordan saw Noah walking toward her, and she promptly lost her train of thought. He wore jeans and a clean T-shirt. He put his gun and holster on the nightstand and stretched out next to her on the bed.

"Jordan? Didn't you hear me? I asked when you were leaving."

"What . . . uh . . . I . . ." Oh sure, she never got rattled. "Tomorrow," she stammered. Noah had reached up and was pulling her down next to him. "Early. We're leaving early. We have a long drive to the Austin airport." She pushed Noah's hand away and turned around. Frowning at him, she wagged her finger in his face and whispered, "Stop it."

"Stop what?" Sidney asked.

"Nothing. I should go."

"Wait. Do you think I should fly back home?" asked Sidney. "I could maybe help out—"

"No, no, you should stay where you are. There's nothing you could do back home. I'll call you as soon as I get back."

"Don't hang up. I didn't ask you how you're doing."

Noah was tickling her neck, causing shivers. "Fine. I'm doing fine," she blurted.

"Did they find the degenerate who was stuffing those bodies in your car?"

"Yes, they did. Talk to you tomorrow. 'Bye now. Keep safe."

She hung up before Sidney could stop her. Then she turned to confront Noah.

"Trying to distract . . ." That was as far as she got before she again lost her train of thought. Noah was pulling off his T-shirt. He had an amazing body. His upper arms were so muscular, and his abs . . .

She mentally shook herself out of her stupor. "What are you doing?"

"Getting comfortable."

She grabbed his hands when he tried to take his jeans off. "For the love of . . . Unless you plan to get under the covers, I suggest you keep your pants on."

"Are you embarrassed?" He seemed puzzled by the possibility. "Sugar, you've seen and touched every—"

"I remember very clearly what I did," she interrupted. She suddenly laughed. "You don't have any inhibitions, do you? I'll bet you could walk down Newbury Street in Boston stark naked and not be fazed."

He grinned. "Depends."

"On what?"

"Whether it's summer or winter."

She rolled her eyes. "It's presumptuous to think you can waltz in here and sleep with me."

He adjusted the pillows behind his head. "I don't waltz anywhere, and I don't plan to sleep, at least not for a very long while. So, do you want me to leave?"

That question was a no-brainer. "No."

She leaned over him, planted her hands on his warm chest, and kissed him. Then she pinched his shoulder and sat up.

"I know you've talked to Nick," she said accusingly. "Why didn't you tell me what was going on?"

He looked surprised. "Sidney told you? I didn't think she knew. Your mother got her out of Boston early so she wouldn't find out."

"Nick should have called me."

"Nick didn't want you to worry, and he knew that you would hear about it when you got back to Boston."

She sat back on her heels. "Find out what?"

He frowned. "Hold on. What exactly did Sidney tell you?"

"No. I want to hear your version."

"Someone broke into your parents' house and left a note for your father in his library. It was stuck to a wall with a knife."

"When did he find it?"

Noah hated to tell her. "He didn't. Your mother did." He sighed and added, "Whoever it was got in sometime during the night. She found it the next morning before your father came down."

Jordan pictured some maniac with a knife creeping through the house and starting up the stairs. She shivered. "They were asleep? Where were the bodyguards?"

"Good question," he said. "There were two of them. One outside and one in. Neither one heard or saw a thing."

She felt sick to her stomach. "He could have gone into their bedroom. And Sidney . . ."

"She wasn't there," Noah said. "She was at a friend's house."

Jordan nodded. "They can get to my father anytime they want, can't they?"

"No. Your brothers are in this now and have beefed up security. No one's going to get that close again."

She didn't believe him. "What did the note say?"

"I'm not sure I remember . . ."

"Tell me," she insisted.

"Jordan, it was just a scare tactic."

"I want to know what that note said, Noah. Tell me."

"Okay . . . ," he answered reluctantly. "The note said, 'We're watching.'"

Chapter Thirty-two

JORDAN'S ANXIETY ABOUT HER FAMILY WOULDN'T EASE UP. She kept thinking about her mother and father asleep in their bed while a cold-blooded killer roamed their house. What made the situation even more chilling was the fact that there were two professional bodyguards on duty, and the intruder had been able to get past them.

Holding her in his arms, Noah listened as she played out every possible scenario: what could have happened, what didn't happen, and what might possibly happen in the future. He'd heard it all before from Nick, who had gone into a rage when he'd found out about the break-in.

"You knew about Laurant too, didn't you?" Jordan asked. Noah didn't answer fast enough to suit her. "Didn't you?"

"Ouch! Stop pinching me. And yes, I knew about Laurant."

"So why didn't you tell me?"

He grabbed her hand before she could pinch him again. "Nick didn't want me to."

"Let me guess. He didn't want me to worry."

"That's right."

She jerked her hand back, rolled away from him, and sat up. "My father and Laurant . . . what other secrets are out there?"

"None that I know about," he said. "And it's not going to do you any good to get all worked up about it."

His calm attitude didn't sit well with her. "Well, I am already worked up about it."

"Don't be so hard on your brother. Nick was only trying to protect you."

"Don't defend him."

"I'm only saying that Nick thought you had plenty to worry about. He was planning to fill you in on everything when you got back to Boston. And Laurant's doing okay."

"She's in the hospital. That isn't 'doing okay.'"

"She's getting the care she needs."

Jordan shook her head. "If you were my brother and I kept something like this from you, how would you feel?"

He gave her a sideways glance. "Sugar, if I were your brother, we'd have a much bigger problem to worry about."

To make his point, his hand slipped under her T-shirt and tugged on the waistband of her shorts.

"Okay, that was a bad example." She gathered up the papers. "I just hate secrets," she muttered.

"Is that so? You're pretty damned good at keeping secrets yourself."

He sounded angry. Surprised by his sudden mood swing, she asked, "What's that supposed to mean? I don't keep secrets."

"Want to tell me about that little scar on the side of your right breast?"

Pretending that she didn't know what he was talking about probably wouldn't work. Knowing Noah, he'd pull off her T-shirt and point to it.

"What about it?"

"I seem to remember hearing about your surgery."

"That was . . . a while ago," she said, trying to think of a way to get out of the corner she'd trapped herself in. "It wasn't a big deal."

"Here's my question," he said. "Didn't you find a lump in your breast—"

"It was just a little bump."

Ignoring her interruption, he continued, "And didn't you check yourself into the hospital and have the surgery without telling anyone in your family?"

She took a breath. "Yes, but it was a procedure . . . a biopsy . . ."

"Doesn't matter. You didn't want anyone to worry, did you? What if something had gone wrong? What if the procedure had turned into major surgery?"

"Kate drove me to the hospital. She would have called every-one."

"And you think that's okay?"

"No," Jordan admitted. "It was wrong. But I was scared. And telling everyone made it more real."

Strangely enough, he understood. He took her hand and squeezed it. "I'll tell you what. You ever pull a stunt like that on me, and there'll be hell to pay." Just thinking about the possibility of her keeping something that serious from him made him angry.

"No more secrets," she promised.

"Damn right."

She tried to get up.

"What are you doing?" he asked.

"I was going to read, but I'm not in the mood to think about old feuds."

He pulled her back. "Read something to me. Maybe a battle," he suggested. "That will relax you."

"Only a man could think that hearing about a bloody battle would be relaxing."

She decided to humor him. She scooted closer, leaned against his chest, and dropped the stack of papers in her lap.

He looked over her shoulder. "How far back have you gotten?"

"I'm not sure. I've been randomly pulling out a story or two from every other century. When I get home I'll make myself read all of it."

"What do you mean, make yourself? If you don't think any of it is accurate . . ."

"Okay, I *want* to read all of it. And then I'm going to do my own research. I want to find the truth." She added, "I'm sure there are *threads* of truth in some of the stories. For the most part, they've been handed down from father to son." She gave him the stack. "You choose one."

She watched him flip through the pages. "Wait," she said as she snatched one of the papers. "I just saw . . . There it is again."

She pulled out the page and held it up. "See? In the margin. The professor wrote the date 1284 again. I've seen it on two other pages in the margins. And what's that? A crown? A castle? 1284 has to be when he thought the feud started. Don't you think?"

"Maybe," he allowed. "The numbers are thick, like he was going over them again and again so he wouldn't forget."

"Oh, no, he wouldn't need to write the date more than once. If what he told me about his memory was true, he didn't need to write anything down. He'd remember. I think he must have been absentmindedly scribbling while he thought about something else."

"Hold on. What did he tell you about his memory?"

"He was boasting," she said. "He said he had an extraordinary memory. He never forgot a face or a name no matter how much time had passed. He recorded these tales to organize them for other people to read someday, but he had committed every detail to memory. He claimed he was a voracious reader. What newspapers he couldn't get his hands on, he read on the Internet."

Noah remembered all the newspapers littering the professor's living room floor. "Look through the rest of the pages," he suggested. "See if he did any sketches or wrote any other dates."

She didn't find any in her stack, but he found a couple in the bottom half of his.

"What does that look like to you?" He pointed to something sketched in the margin at the top of the page.

"Maybe a dog or a cat . . . with that long mane, a lion. I'll bet it's a lion."

The last drawing he found was easier to figure out. Another crown. A very poor drawing of a lopsided crown.

"You know what I think?" he said. "Professor MacKenna was crazy."

"I'll admit he was strange, and he was obsessed with his work."

"I think he made it all up."

She shook her head. "I don't. Maybe *I'm* crazy, but I think there really is a hidden treasure."

Noah continued to flip through the pages. "Some of these aren't dated."

"It can be a guessing game. Maybe the name of a king is mentioned . . . or a new weapon, like a crossbow. That would give us an approximate time period, but the rest are just guesses."

"Read this one." He handed her the papers and leaned back.

As if it were the most natural thing in the world, he pulled her closer and put his arm around her.

She began reading in a soft clear voice.

Our beloved king is dead, and in this time of our terrible grieving, the clans have been embroiled in battle after battle to gain power and control over the others. We have a pretender who demands to be king and struggles to rule, and there is now constant political turmoil.

Greed has taken root in the hearts of our leaders. We do not know how this will end, and we fear for our children. There is no unbloodied ground to walk upon, no cave in which to find sanctuary for our old and our young. The road is desolate. We have witnessed murder and infidelity. And now betrayal.

The MacDonalds are warring with the MacDougals, and the western coast is their battleground. In the south the Campbells fight the Fergusons, and the MacKeyes and the Sinclairs spill their blood in the east. There is no refuge.

But it is the treachery in the north that we now most fear. The MacKennas have new allies from the other end of the world to help them destroy their enemy, the Buchanans.

The MacKenna laird shows no interest in stealing the Buchanans' land and forcing the warriors under his rule, though we know such a thing could never be accomplished. Nae, perhaps in the past, that was the MacKenna's intent, but no longer. He wants to destroy all of them, every man, every woman, every child. His anger is fierce.

Though we must never openly speak of this, even in whispers, we believe the MacKenna laird has made an evil pact with the King of England. The king sent his emissary, a young prince who came to the court from a distant domain that is now ruled by the king. A witness observed this secret meeting, one of our own, and we believe his words to be true, for he is a man of God.

The king wants a foothold in the north, and his eyes are on the Buchanan land for its position in the highlands. Once the land is conquered, his soldiers will advance toward the south and the east. He will conquer Scotland, one clan at a time, and when they are under his rule, he will gather a massive force and go north into the land of the giants.

The prince has told the laird that the king has heard of the animosity between the Buchanans and the MacKennas, and even though he believes destroying the Buchanans with his help should be reward enough, he will sweeten his pact by giving the laird a title and a silver treasure. The treasure alone would elevate the laird above all other clans, for there is a mystical power to the treasure. Aye, with this treasure, the laird would become invincible. He would have the power he longed for, and he would have his revenge against the Buchanans.

Greed overtook the laird, and he could not say no to the devil's bargain. He called up his allies, but he did not tell them about his meeting with the emissary or the pact he had struck. He concocted a story of infidelity and murder, and demanded they follow him into war.

We too fear the Buchanans' wrath, but we cannot allow this slaughter, and we have determined that one of us will go to their laird and tell him of this plot. We do not believe the King of England should have power in our land. The MacKenna laird may wish to sell his soul, but he will not.

With great trepidation, our courageous friend Harold went alone to speak to the Buchanan laird. When he did not return, we believed the Buchanans had killed him. But Harold was not harmed. He returned to us, and his body was sound, but terror had overtaken his mind, for he declared to us that he had seen him. Harold had seen the ghost. He had seen the lion in the mist.

Noah interrupted Jordan. "He saw what?"

"Harold had seen the ghost. He had seen the lion in the mist," Jordan repeated.

Noah smiled. "A lion in Scotland?"

"Maybe it's a figurative lion," she suggested. "After all, there was Richard the Lionhearted."

"Keep reading," he coaxed.

"Has the Buchanan laird gathered his allies?" we asked.

"Nae," came his reply. "He sent messengers to the north to call forth one warrior. That is all."

"Then they will all die."

"Yes, they will die" another said. "The English king is so sure of victory he has sent a legion of soldiers

Noah interrupted again. "A legion? Come on. Do you know how many that would be?"

"Noah, I've already read about a ghost and a lion in the mist. What's the big deal about a legion?"

He laughed. "You're right."

"Do you want me to continue or not?"

"Go on," he said. "I promise not to interrupt again."

"Where was I? Oh, yes, the legion." She found her place and resumed reading.

"The English king is so sure of victory he has sent a legion of soldiers with the treasure to Laird MacKenna. He has also ordered these soldiers to join the MacKennas in their battle against the Buchanans. The MacKenna laird has only just been given this news. He cannot stop the advance, and he knows that his allies will turn against him when they discover he has a pact with the king. They will not fight by the side of an English soldier."

Jordan dropped the paper. "He did it on purpose."

"Who did what?" Noah asked.

"The king. He sent soldiers knowing the MacKenna allies would turn against the laird. He also knew they would find out about the pact. The clans would know that MacKenna joined forces with the king. For silver. Talk about betrayal."

"And they all end up killing each other."

"Yes," Jordan said. "Which is exactly what the king wanted. How could the MacKenna laird believe the King of England would keep his word?"

"Greed. He was blinded by greed. Did he get the treasure?" he asked.

She picked up the paper again. "The victory belonged to the Buchanans."

"I was rooting for them," Noah drawled. "They were the underdogs. Besides, I'm in bed with a Buchanan. I should be loyal."

She didn't comment. She read on, then stopped. "Oh, no, I'm not reading these descriptions of the actual battle. Suffice it to say, there were a lot of severed body parts and heads gone missing. The few English soldiers who survived returned to England. I wish I knew what king it was," she said.

"What happened to the MacKenna laird?"

She skimmed another page before answering."Ah, here it is.'The MacKenna laird lost his treasure and the king's promise of a title.'"

"What title specifically?"

"I don't know. But he lost it. He lived the rest of his days in disgrace. And get this—his clan blamed the Buchanans. I'll bet Professor MacKenna found a way to twist this so he could blame the Buchanans too."

"For what?"

"I guess everything. The English soldiers, the treasure—"

"The laird must have put quite a spin on the facts to get his clan to believe him."

She agreed."This legend has everything. Greed, betrayal, secret meetings, murders, and no doubt, infidelity. There was infidelity in the story, but I skimmed over it."

"Nothing much has changed over the centuries. You know that blackmail list of J.D.'s that Street printed out? It's the same old story. Infidelity, greed, betrayal. You name the vice, it's on the list."

"I hope that's an exaggeration. I know Charlene's been cheating on her fiancé, but there's always one who doesn't conform. Could I see the list?"

He started to get out of bed. She pushed him back. "Never mind. I don't need to see it. Just tell me. Is Amelia Ann on the list?"

"Yes, she is. Nothing illegal though. She got treated for an STD, and J.D. knew about it. She paid him a hundred dollars so he wouldn't tell her daughter."

"A hundred dollars was probably a lot of money for her to scrape together. She wouldn't want her daughter to be disappointed in her. It could be worse."

"It gets worse. Remember the videos that Street found at J.D.'s house?"

"Yes."

"His victims weren't the only ones he taped. Evidently he liked to watch some of his own sexual escapades too. And one of the tapes was labeled 'Amelia Ann.'"

Jordan's mouth dropped open. "Are you serious? Amelia Ann and J.D.?" She gave the news a moment to sink in and then said, "That would mean that J.D. could have given her the sexually transmitted disease, wouldn't it?"

"It's possible," said Noah.

"I hope Candy never finds out. What's wrong with the people in this town? Haven't they ever heard of cable?"

"Sweetheart, sex trumps cable any time of the day or night."

She shook her head. "This is just wrong. All wrong."

She had heard enough about the secret, sordid lives of the locals. She gathered the papers, dumped them into her bag, and got back in bed.

Noah's eyes were closed.

"Noah?"

"Hmmm?"

"Are you attracted to women who wear short-shorts and stiletto heels?"

He leaned up on his elbow to look at her. "Where did that question come from? Who wears short-shorts and stilettos?" he asked.

"Amelia Ann."

"Yeah?"

"Oh, please. Don't tell me you didn't notice."

"She's not my type."

She smiled and reached across his chest to turn off the light. "Good answer."

Chapter Thirty-three

"I CAN'T BELIEVE I'M ADMITTING THIS TO YOU, BUT I'M GOING TO miss Serenity."

Noah and Jordan were driving past Jaffee's Bistro when she made the comment. A hint of morning lit the sky, and a soft, golden glow surrounded them. It was dark inside the restaurant. Jaffee wouldn't be opening up for hours.

"What exactly are you going to miss?" he asked.

"I had a life-changing experience here."

He couldn't resist. "Sex was that good, huh?"

Exasperated, she shook her head at him. "That isn't what I was talking about. But speaking of sex . . ."

"It was pretty damned good last night, wasn't it? You wore me out."

It wasn't just good, she thought. It was amazing and incredible and wonderful, but if she told him so, Noah's arrogance would get completely out of hand.

"Stop trying to embarrass me. It won't work," she warned.

He didn't contradict her. She was wrong though. It was working: She was blushing.

"What was your life-changing experience?" he asked.

"I guess it was more of a life-changing decision. I've realized that I've been a slave to technology, and that's going to change. There's more to life than building computers and designing bigger and better and faster . . ." Her sigh was long and drawn out. "I want more out of life."

He flashed a smile. "Good to know."

"The first thing I'm going to do when I get home is make a list of all the things I want to do. Cooking is number one," she said, nodding. "I'm going to take a cooking class. No more take-out."

"A list, huh?"

"That's right."

The drive to the Austin airport was a long one and it gave them time to talk about a variety of topics. One was the differences in their upbringing. Noah was an only child, whereas Jordan came from a gaggle of siblings, as she referred to her brothers and sister. Noah didn't realize the importance of having his own space because he'd always had it. Jordan told him how she had longed to have a little privacy. Her biggest complaint, however, was being constantly teased by her brothers. Noah laughed as she recounted some of the pranks they had played on her and her sister when they were young. He thought growing up in such a big family was a blessing—a constant party.

Occasionally there were pauses in the conversation, but Jordan felt so comfortable with him, she didn't need to fill the silences with small talk. They had been in the car a couple of hours before she finally got up the nerve to ask him to explain an earlier remark he'd made that had bothered her.

"Do you remember telling me you knew what I was all about? What did you mean by that?"

He glanced over at her. "You sure you want to know?"

How bad could it be? "I'm sure."

"I've known you for a long time, and I know how your mind

works, especially where men are concerned. You like control. You'd like to control everyone and everything."

"That's not true."

He ignored her denial. "You especially like to control the men you date. I've met some of them, Sugar, and I know what I'm talking about. You go for the weak ones. But then if you can walk all over them, you don't want them. I'll bet you haven't slept with any of them. Maybe that's why you choose that type, so you won't get involved. I'm right, aren't I?"

"No, you're wrong," she insisted. "I like sensitive men."

"But you went to bed with me. And I sure as certain am not sensitive."

"You make me sound terrible," she said.

"You're not terrible, you're a sweetheart. A *bossy* sweetheart," he added with a grin.

"And I do not want to control anyone," she said vehemently.

"I'm not worried. You'll never control me."

She folded her arms. "Why do you think I would want to? And don't you dare tell me I can't stop myself."

"You're getting upset."

Duh. "And about sex . . ." she began.

"What about it?"

"Are you familiar with the expression 'What happens in Vegas stays in Vegas'?"

"Yes," he replied. "I've seen the commercials."

"All right," she said. "I'm proposing that what happened between us in Serenity stays in Serenity. We're bound to run into each other sometime or other on Nathan's Bay. You'll be fishing with one of my brothers and I'll be checking in with the family and I don't want you to feel awkward . . ." She stopped when she realized what she was saying. "Okay, you wouldn't feel awkward, but I don't want you to worry about me feeling awkward." She was making a mess of her speech. "Do you understand what I'm trying to say?"

"Yes," he replied. "Why are you worried about—?"

"I just am," she interrupted. "My question is: Do we have a deal?"

"If it will make you happy . . ."

"Do we have a deal?"

"Yes."

She thought it might be pushing the matter to suggest that they shake hands, but she was happy to have it settled. It shouldn't be too difficult to pretend that nothing extraordinary had happened. She was a pro at pretending. She could even pretend she hadn't fallen in love with him . . . couldn't she?

Chapter Thirty-four

BY THE TIME JORDAN ARRIVED HOME, IT WAS WELL AFTER midnight. Noah carried her bags up to her brownstone apartment, checked each room just to make sure everything was as it should be, then kissed her good-bye and left without a backward glance.

He was already moving on, she thought. And she needed to do the very same thing.

When she fell into bed, she immediately crashed, and slept hard. In the morning, she opened her eyes and instinctively reached for Noah, but he wasn't there. Feeling groggy and disoriented, she threw off the covers, put on her favorite ratty old robe, and padded into the kitchen. She pushed the play button on her answering machine as she walked past, and while she made herself a cup of hot tea, she listened to her messages. All forty-nine of them.

Three of the messages were from Jaffee. He wanted to know just how serious the delete button was because he had accidentally hit it when he was trying to save all his recipes and had lost them. He hoped he could get them back. Would she send him an e-mail telling him what to do, if indeed anything could be done?

"My computer mail is working fine," he explained. "I haven't messed that up, so I'll get your reply. I've already left you two phone messages, and this is the third, and I'm guessing you aren't even home yet. Please check your messages on your computer when you get in."

How serious was the delete button? Jordan smiled. She guessed there really were people who needed extensive training on computers. Jaffee, was one of them. She would phone him later. After she listened to and erased the rest of the messages, she carried her cup of tea across the living room, curled up in the window seat that overlooked the Charles River, and stared out the window at nothing in particular.

Love wasn't all it was cracked up to be. How long was she going to be miserable? Since she'd never really loved anyone the way she loved Noah, she didn't have a timeline. She hoped that phase one of getting over him was feeling sorry for herself, because she was now wallowing in self-pity.

In no hurry to get dressed, she stayed in her pajamas until the middle of the afternoon. Around three p.m. she got a glimpse of herself in the mirror and cringed. So she took a shower and got dressed.

Nick called just after she'd put in her contacts.

"I was just about to call you," she said. "How's Laurant? I don't want to phone the hospital and disturb her if she's sleeping. Can she have visitors?"

"She's okay," he said. "The doctor wants to keep her another day at least, and I'm keeping the visitors to a minimum so she'll rest."

"I won't come today," Jordan said. "Give her a kiss for me and tell her I'll be by tomorrow."

"Be ready to answer a lot of questions," Nick said.

Oh, God, what did Laurant know? "Why?" she asked nervously. "What questions? Why would Laurant want to ask me questions?" Could Jordan have sounded any guiltier? Did Nick notice?

"Jordan, what's the matter with you?"

Of course he'd noticed. "What's the matter?" she replied. "Nothing's the matter. I was just wondering why your wife would want to question me."

"Oh, I don't know. Maybe she wants to ask you about those bodies you found," he said sarcastically.

"Oh, yes. The bodies. The dead bodies." She could not believe she'd forgotten about them. "Okay, then. I'll answer her questions."

"Are you angry with me? Is that why you're acting so squirrelly?"

So much for her brother's hotshot detective skills. "Um, that's right, I am."

"Tell me why."

"You know why," she stalled.

"It's because I left you in Serenity, isn't it? You were in good hands with Noah, but I'm your brother, and I should have stayed. I'm right, aren't I? That's why you're angry."

She was going to burn in purgatory for this lie alone. "Yes. That's exactly why."

"Doctor Morganstern ordered me back to Boston, and I don't feel guilty about doing my job, Jordan. Besides, I was here when Laurant started having contractions. I needed to be here."

"Okay then. Well, I forgive you."

"That was quick."

"You did what you had to do," she blurted. "I've got to go now. Someone's at the door. 'Bye."

There really was someone at her door. UPS was delivering the research boxes she'd sent one-day air. After she brought them in and stacked them inside the front door by the coat closet, she went to her computer and turned it on. She wanted to get through her e-mails before she sent a message out to all of her addressees explaining that she was shutting down the computer for a while. She wouldn't say for how long.

It took the rest of the afternoon and evening to get through all her cybermail. She still hadn't called Jaffee back, and she made a mental note to do that first thing in the morning.

A bag of microwave popcorn was Jordan's dinner. She stretched out on her sofa and channel-surfed while trying to keep Noah out of her thoughts. But he kept intruding. What had he done all day today? What was Noah doing now?

"Oh, this has to stop!"

Determined to think about something besides Noah, Jordan thought back over other aspects of her eventful journey to Texas. An innocent trip had become a firestorm leaving three men dead and a little town dazed. Had she been told beforehand what she was heading into, she never would have believed it. There were still so many unanswered questions, and she hoped that Agents Chaddick and Street would be able to get to the bottom of it all and wrap up the investigation quickly. All the intrigue and the deceptions were enough to make one's mind spin, so Jordan concentrated on sorting it all out, starting with Professor MacKenna.

His story about the inheritance had been a lie. He'd obviously moved to Serenity because of the money he was getting. But where did he get those cash deposits? Were he and J.D. working together? Did J.D. kill the professor because he learned he was holding out on him? The professor was making five-thousand-dollar deposits while J.D. was collecting nickels and dimes. With his hair-trigger temper, J.D. could have easily killed him. And then J.D. himself went up in a blaze while trying to stir up even more trouble.

If they were working together. That would certainly solve part of the mystery, but what Jordan couldn't work out was their association. The professor was a strange duck, a loner. He didn't play well with others. So why'd he hook up with J.D.?

It didn't add up.

She considered a second possibility. Sneaky blackmailer J.D. had found out about the money the professor was getting from a third party, and then tried to blackmail him. But the nutty professor couldn't be blackmailed. If MacKenna had threatened to go to the police, J.D. knew he'd be sent back to prison. He couldn't risk that, so he killed the professor to shut him up.

But something about that didn't sit right either. Jordan thought it was a good bet the professor was involved in something illegal too.

Where was Professor MacKenna getting the money? That was the million-dollar question.

Sometimes you need to *stop* thinking about a problem for the solution to present itself. Jordan fell asleep waiting for that to happen. She was still waiting the next morning when she woke up. And by noon, she gave up. Jordan was unaccustomed to any sort of problem-solving failure. Obviously, this was a whole new can of worms.

Car keys in hand, she was walking out the door on her way to visit Laurant when her phone rang.

"Jordan, Agent Chaddick here. I've got some interesting news. We found your laptop."

"You did? Where did you find it?"

"On eBay."

"Excuse me?"

"Maggie Haden had it. She was trying to sell it on eBay. I guess she can kiss any hope of resuming her career good-bye."

Jordan hadn't time to absorb the news before Chaddick said, "I've got to take this call. I'll get back to you."

Jordan dropped into a chair. Maggie Haden. The gall . . . the unmitigated . . .

Her phone rang again.

"Jordan, Agent Chaddick again. Listen, I've got some other news. Not so good."

"Yes?" she asked hesitantly.

"We just received a preliminary autopsy report on J.D. Dickey. It's a homicide."

All of Jordan's earlier conjectures disappeared. She faced a new, more troubling scenario: The killer was still out there.

Chapter Thirty-five

PAUL NEWTON PRUITT WASN'T GOING TO LET ANYONE DESTROY his new life. He had worked hard to get where he was, and he wasn't going to run and hide and then start all over again. Not this time.

He had come a long way. Murder didn't faze him these days. First there was the Scottish pip-squeak; then Lloyd, the lumbering idiot; and finally his eager but stupidly greedy little helper, J.D.

He hadn't been at all squeamish about killing any one of them. Hadn't had any remorse either. Pruitt had killed once before and had learned a valuable lesson. He would do anything to protect himself.

He'd thought he'd found the perfect patsy in J.D. And placing the bodies in Jordan Buchanan's cars had bought him more time. Then, getting rid of J.D. would take care of the last link to Pruitt.

Or so he thought.

He'd been one of the first to hear the results of J.D.'s autopsy.

There shouldn't have been anything left of him to examine, but there was. The cracked skull had given him away, and J.D.'s accidental death was now listed as a murder.

Getting his hands on the copies of Professor MacKenna's papers was becoming critical.

Chapter Thirty-six

NOAH HAD BEEN STUCK IN SEMINARS WITH DR. MORGANSTERN for the past two days, and he hated every minute of it. He wasn't a seminar kind of agent, which he mentioned several times, but his complaints didn't matter to the doctor.

Morganstern wanted a bigger budget. The lost-and-found program he'd created several years ago had been immensely successful, and with their impressive records, Noah and Nick were the doctor's best advertisement for expanding the program.

Each interminable seminar ended with a question and answer period. In Nick's absence, all of the questions were directed at Noah. Had Nick been there, he would have stepped in and taken over that portion of the program. He was far more diplomatic and polished. But because his wife, Laurant, was in the hospital, Nick got a pass on attending the conference.

The lucky bastard.

By the end of the second day Noah could barely be civil to the other attendees. Sitting at a table with the doctor at the end of a long corridor, he waited for the next seminar to begin. Morganstern, Noah noticed, looked completely relaxed, but then Noah had learned that nothing ever got to him.

The venerable Dr. Peter Morganstern encouraged Nick and Noah to call him by his first name, but they would do so only when alone with him.

Noah whispered, "Hey, Pete, I want to ask you something. You think you'll still get your bigger budget when I start shooting people? Because if I have to listen to one more long-winded lecture from another boring speaker, honest to God, I'm gonna shoot somebody . . . and then myself. And I just might take you with me for making me wear a suit and tie."

"As a psychiatrist, I've been trained to pick up on subtle hints, and I should probably be alarmed—"

"*Subtle* hints?" Noah began to laugh.

Pete smiled. "However, since I feel the same way about the speakers, I won't be too concerned, even though some of your comments during our last chat did make me wonder."

Noah knew that "chat" was Morganstern's code word for their private conferences. As a psychiatrist, Pete's goal was to get inside Noah's head and make sure he wasn't about to go postal. The good doctor always found a way to accomplish it.

"Are you worried about me?" Noah asked him.

"Not in the least. How was your trip to Texas?"

Noah shrugged. "I kept her alive. That's about it. I trust you heard what went on?"

"Yes, I did."

"Agents Chaddick and Street took over the investigation."

"Which is as it should be," Pete said. "That's their area."

"I hated giving it up," he admitted.

"What about Jordan?"

"What about her?" he asked sharply.

Pete raised an eyebrow. "I was wondering how she handled the stress."

"Okay. She did okay." There was a note of pride in his answer.

"Jordan has always had a special spot in my heart. My wife and

I don't ever play favorites, but if we did . . ." He added, "She has a wonderful heart, doesn't she?"

"Yeah, she does," Noah said softly.

"Have you spoken to her since you've been back?"

"No."

The abrupt response didn't go unnoticed. Pete didn't say a word. He picked up a pencil and twirled it between his fingers while he waited for his subordinate agent to talk to him. It didn't take long.

"What do you want from me?" Noah demanded.

And still Pete didn't speak. Frustrated, Noah asked, "What are you fishing for?"

"I've noticed you've been on edge since you've been back," Pete said. "I'm curious to know why."

"I thought I made that perfectly clear. I hate seminars."

"But that isn't the reason for your anxiety, is it?"

"Ah hell, Pete. Anxiety? Are you kidding me?"

Pete smiled again. "When you're ready to discuss whatever is going on with you, Noah, let's talk."

He was letting him off the hook. Noah could have gotten up and walked away, but he didn't. He leaned back in the cushioned chair and, blankly staring as Pete sketched on his notepad, thought about how edgy he'd been lately.

"What are you drawing?" Noah asked after a minute.

Pete's mind was somewhere else too. He looked at his sketch for a few seconds. "I'm not sure. It might be a calendar." He nodded. "My subconscious must be trying to help me remember a date."

"You guys believe those chicken scratches mean something, don't you?"

"I don't," he said. "But a persistent, recurring sketch or doodle . . . yes, I'd look at that closely." He checked his watch. "I don't believe we need to attend this last meeting."

Noah felt as though he'd just been given a last-minute reprieve from the governor. He walked with Pete to the parking garage.

When they reached the third level, Pete headed in one direction and Noah in the other.

Pete had his keys in his hand and was opening his car door when he heard Noah call to him.

Pete looked over the top of the car. "Yes?"

"What made you decide to leave me in Serenity and bring Nick back? Was there a meeting or a review Nick needed to attend? Or was it something else?"

"What do you think?" Pete grinned as he slid into the driver's seat and pulled the car door closed.

Noah stood in the corner of the garage and watched Pete drive away. The truth almost knocked him off his feet. He'd been played . . . and he was supposed to be a highly trained, astute, pick-up-on-all-the-signals agent. So much for his razor-sharp skills.

"Son of a bitch," he whispered.

Pete had blindsided him. Noah had never considered the possibility that the psychiatrist might have had an ulterior motive. Unbelievable. When he'd been apprised of Jordan's situation in Serenity, Pete had decided then and there to be clever. He'd leave Noah and bring Nick home.

"Son of a bitch," Noah whispered again. Pete had been matchmaking.

Noah called Nick from the car. When his partner answered, Noah could hear Nick's two-year-old, Samantha, laughing in the background.

"I'm heading over to the hospital to hit on your wife," he told Nick.

"Pick me up on your way," Nick said. "Sam, put that down." Noah heard a crash, then Nick's sigh. "I swear to God, I don't know how Laurant does it. Hostage negotiations are a piece of cake compared to bargaining with a two-year-old."

Traffic was a bear, but that was the norm for Boston. Noah thought about Serenity. No traffic there. Just murder and mayhem.

Nick waited on his front porch holding pretty little Sam. A

stunning brunette took the baby when Noah pulled into the drive.

"Is that a new babysitter?" Noah asked. "I haven't seen her before."

"She's our backup sitter," Nick explained.

"Sam like her?"

"Yeah, she does." Nick waited a minute and then, puzzled, asked, "Aren't you going to ask if she's married? She's not. Want her phone number?"

Noah shook his head. "Not my type."

Nick, though happily married and faithful to the love of his life, had certainly noticed how attractive the babysitter was. "How can *she* not be your type?"

"She just isn't," Noah said. "Nick, you look like you haven't gotten any sleep in a month. Is Sam keeping you up?"

"No, I read her a story and she's out for the night. I'm the one having the trouble. It's odd. When I'm out of town on a case, I sleep just fine, but when I'm home, I need Laurant to be next to me. But she isn't now, and I'm not sleeping."

Noah understood. He hadn't been sleeping much either since he'd been home.

"Got any suggestions?" Nick asked.

"Yeah. Stop acting like a girl."

Nothing Noah said ever bothered Nick, probably because their senses of humor and personalities were so much alike.

"How was the conference?" Nick asked with a straight face. He knew how much Noah detested anything that remotely hinted of bureaucracy. "I was really sorry I had to miss it."

"Very funny."

Nick had a good laugh. Then he asked, "How come you haven't commented on the verdict in my father's court case?"

"What? The verdict's in?"

"It's been all over the news channels. Guilty on all counts."

"I've been locked up in meetings and didn't hear. Your father must be relieved. How long was the deliberation?"

"Just a couple of hours. That's not the only good news. One of the detectives called to tell me they were looking at the guy's cousin for the break-in on Nathan's Bay."

"How sure are they?"

"Sure enough to pick him up."

They were still talking about the case when Nick parked the car in the underground garage at the hospital.

"Your father will be happy to get rid of those bodyguards. I know they were driving him crazy by following him everywhere he went," Noah said.

"I'll bet he's already dismissed them."

Noah removed his suit jacket and tie and left them in the car. He rolled up his sleeves as he walked.

A tall, leggy blonde strolled toward them. She slowed down, as if waiting for a reaction, smiled at Noah, glanced at the gun at his side, and kept going.

Nick noticed that Noah hadn't noticed. He didn't even break his stride.

"Is something wrong with you?" Nick asked.

"I saw her." Noah shrugged. "Again, she's not my type."

The elevator was directly across from the emergency room station. Nick pushed the button.

Noah's phone rang. He saw the caller ID. "That's Chaddick," he said as he flipped the phone open. A nurse and a security guard frowned at him. The nurse pointed to the wall and shook her head. The sign on the tile next to the elevator buttons said no cell phones were allowed. There was also an outline of a phone with a red X through it.

"Yes?" Noah said into his phone.

The federal agent got right to the point. "Noah? Chaddick here. J.D. Dickey's death has been ruled a homicide."

Noah cursed loudly. The security guard started toward him, so he pulled out his FBI badge and held it up as he listened to Chaddick's explanation. The guard backed away.

Noah snapped the phone shut as the elevator doors opened. His mind was racing. There were dozens of suspects on J.D.'s blackmail list, and Serenity was a thousand miles away. Still, Noah had learned to pay attention to his instincts, and he suddenly felt very uneasy.

With a killer on the loose, where was Jordan?

Chapter Thirty-seven

JORDAN BROKE DOWN AND PURCHASED ANOTHER CELL PHONE identical to the one J.D. Dickey had smashed before he'd decked her. She could have gotten a newer model, she supposed, but she already had an extra battery in a charger sitting on her desk and a cord for her car that was specifically designed for her old phone.

She told herself she wasn't slipping back into her old tech ways. She was just being smart. A cell phone was a safety tool, especially when Jordan was jogging by herself or driving on the highway. If anything happened, help was just a phone call away—providing, of course, she could get a signal.

She kept the same phone number, and when she returned home after making her purchase, she immediately plugged the unit into her computer to program it. By the time she'd changed her clothes, brushed her hair, and applied a little makeup, the new phone was ready to go.

Visiting hours at the hospital would be over in an hour and a half. To avoid the rush-hour traffic on her way there, Jordan took as many side streets as possible. Unfortunately, a lot of other drivers did the same thing.

She pulled her car into a spot in an underground parking garage adjacent to the emergency room entrance. It was well lit, and there were people coming and going. The ambulance bay was next to the automatic doors.

Just outside the entrance, eating a chocolate bar, a nurse sat on a bench. Chocolate reminded Jordan of Jaffee's chocolate cake. She still hadn't called him. How long had he been waiting to hear from her? She pulled out her phone and saw that she had a signal. She could call him now. But maybe later was better. If Jaffee had a lot of computer questions for her she'd be on the phone for a good, long while, and visiting hours would soon be over. Jordan couldn't miss visiting Laurant. No matter what, she vowed, as soon as she came out of the hospital, she'd call Jaffee.

Entering Laurant's private room on the fifth floor, Jordan was surprised to find herself walking into a small crowd. Her father had just arrived and the judge was kissing his daughter-in-law Laurant on the cheek. Nick was there, too, sprawled in a chair half-asleep.

And there was Noah, leaning against the window ledge, waiting to talk to Judge Buchanan, who had just turned in his direction. Noah's arms were crossed and he looked perfectly relaxed. Jordan had wondered how she would feel when she saw him again, and it was exactly as she had thought: A stabbing pain shot through her heart.

So relieved to see her, Noah got angry. *Where the hell had she been?* Nick had told Noah that Jordan was on her way to the hospital, but she'd sure taken her own sweet time getting there. Did she come by way of New Hampshire?

The wait had been agonizing. He'd called her home phone and only reached her answering machine. If she had a damned cell phone, he could have been able to get hold of her while she was en route and would have known she was safe. It was the not knowing that had been tearing Noah up inside.

Jordan hugged her father and squeezed Laurant's hand. Since Nick looked like he was asleep, she didn't bother with him. Not sure of what she was going to say to Noah, Jordan finally looked over at him and managed a smile.

"Hi." Not so very imaginative, but it was all she could come up with. It's nice to see you again had been her second choice. Thank God she hadn't said that.

He straightened. "We need to talk."

His greeting wasn't so hot either. He sounded like a drill sergeant. Grabbing her hand, Noah headed for the door.

"Be right back," she called over her shoulder.

He pulled her halfway down the hall before stopping and facing her.

"Listen . . ."

"Yes?" Jordan kept her voice as low as his.

"Are you okay?"

She didn't know how to answer. The truth was out of the question. She wondered how he would react if she told him, no, she wasn't okay, she was miserable—thanks to him.

"Oh, you know . . ." she stalled.

He frowned, waited.

"What did you want to talk to me about?" Jordan asked.

"I talked to Chaddick."

Suddenly Jordan was past her awkwardness with Noah. "I did too. Can you believe it? Were you as stunned as I was?"

"Well, I was surprised," he said.

"The gall," Jordan huffed.

"The what?"

"The sheer gall of that Haden woman. On eBay no less! How could she possibly think she wouldn't be caught?"

"Jordan, what are you talking about?"

"My laptop. Maggie Haden was trying to sell it on eBay."

Noah lowered his head. "Sugar, you need to focus on the bigger picture here. Didn't you hear? J.D. Dickey's death was declared a homicide."

"Yes, I know. And you're right. That's the bigger picture. I've been thinking about it a lot, but it always seems I end up with more questions than answers. Who do you think is behind it?"

"I don't know," he admitted. "There's no shortage of suspects, thanks to J.D.'s list. But I'll tell you one thing: I'm not going to stop worrying about you until this case is closed and the killer is behind bars."

"Serenity's a long way from here, Noah. You don't need to worry about me. Down in Texas, I was simply in the wrong place at the wrong time."

"Humor me," Noah said. "Just be careful, okay?"

"Yes, okay."

"And get a damned cell phone."

Where had that come from? "You're such a charmer," Jordan whispered, following him back into the hospital room.

Her father was telling Nick and Laurant a funny story about one of his "shadows," the name he'd given to the contingent of bodyguards who had been constantly at the judge's side for the last few months. Jordan was happy to see her father laughing again. The lines in his face had diminished, and he looked as though a great burden had been lifted from his shoulders.

When Nick raised a question about the lapse in security at Nathan's Bay, the judge downplayed it, praising the agents for their dedication and professionalism. He admitted, however, that he was glad to be rid of them.

The conversation was interrupted when Laurant's doctor arrived on his evening rounds. Everyone in the room was glad to hear the doctor say how pleased he was with the results of the medication and the tests. Laurant's contractions had stopped, and if all stayed calm through the night, she could go home as early as tomorrow morning. After promising to stop by their house tomorrow to help with Sam, Jordan left a few minutes before visiting hours were over.

Noah followed her into the hallway. From behind, he called out, "Wait for me. I'll walk you to your car."

"I have to make a phone call that I've been putting off," Jordan said, pulling out her cell phone. She held it up. "And as you can see, I already purchased a 'damned cell phone.'"

Noah grinned. "Okay then. Go make your call, but wait for me downstairs, inside by the emergency room entrance."

"Fine," she agreed.

"Your father's leaving soon. I'll come down with him," he said.

She stepped inside the elevator, then turned around. Noah watched as the doors closed between them.

OUTSIDE, PAUL PRUITT PATIENTLY WAITED FOR JORDAN. SLUMPED down behind the steering wheel, certain no one would notice him, he figured he'd found the perfect spot. His rental car was tucked neatly in between two sedans. He'd backed the car in to ensure he could quickly get away.

It wouldn't be much longer. On the seat beside him, ready to fire, was the gun.

The entire day had been a waiting game. Most of the afternoon, he'd been parked down the street from Jordan's apartment. Earlier he had identified her car parked in front of her building, so he'd known she was inside. His plan was to wait until she left the area, and then Pruitt would break into her apartment and get what he needed. He didn't care how long it would take. He could wait one hour or twelve. Didn't matter to him.

He'd carefully mapped out his strategy. Once he'd broken into her apartment, he'd pack up all the copies of MacKenna's papers she had shipped from Serenity. He'd brought along a bunch of big cardboard boxes for just this purpose. After he had all the documents, he'd disappear, and any and all evidence implicating Paul Pruitt would be gone.

He had thought about tearing up her apartment so it would look like a simple break-in, but he'd realized how foolish that plan was. Why would a thief steal research papers?

Let Jordan wonder why they were taken. Without the

copies, she'd never figure it out. And Pruitt could keep his nice new life.

Unfortunately, his plan got a little more complicated once Pruitt had actually gotten inside Jordan's apartment. He had been walking across her living room when her phone rang. The answering machine quickly picked up. Jordan's father was calling to tell her that he would meet her at St. James Hospital, and to remind her that Laurant's room number was 538.

Good, he had thought. She was on her way to St. James Hospital. He didn't know who this Laurant was and didn't care. He planned to be long gone before Jordan returned home and discovered the theft.

It had been a piece of luck that Pruitt had noticed the notepad on the coffee table. Seeing what was written on it, he'd stopped cold. There, in the center of the page, pulsating like a neon beacon, were the numbers: 1284. And surrounding the numbers were a bunch of question marks.

She'd gotten too close. He tore the sheet of paper from the notepad, staring at it as his mind raced. Once again, everything had changed. But yet again, he knew what had to be done.

Her father . . . yes, her father, Judge Buchanan, was at the hospital. A perfect opportunity. Paul had done enough research on Jordan Buchanan to know who her father was, and he had immediately recognized the name when he recently heard it on the news. It was impossible to miss. The media were saturating the airwaves with reports about the major court case verdict and the judge who had presided over it. The news reports also mentioned the death threats the judge had received. So if he timed it just right, Pruitt could make it look like Judge Buchanan was the target, not his daughter Jordan.

And here he sat, in an outside parking lot with a good view of the hospital doors. If luck were truly on his side, any minute now the judge would walk through those hospital doors with his daughter.

Suddenly, Paul sat up. Was that her? Yes . . . Jordan Buchanan was coming through the doors.

Pruitt reached for his gun, waiting for just the right moment.

STEPPING OUTSIDE THE EMERGENCY ROOM DOORS INTO THE PARK-ing garage, Jordan turned on her cell phone and called information for Jaffee's phone number. Checking her watch and subtracting an hour, she was sure Jaffee would be at the restaurant.

Jordan knew the operator would connect the call for her, but she wanted to write down the number in case she had to call Jaffee back. She dug through her purse for a scrap of paper and a pen. Holding her phone to her ear with her shoulder, she waited, pen poised to hear the phone number. There were two benches, one on each side of a concrete pillar. Both were empty. She started toward the one farther away from the entrance. The bright fluorescent lights above the sliding glass doors bothered her eyes, and one of the tubes was flickering annoyingly and making a low buzzing sound.

As the operator recited Jaffee's number, two orderlies walked out, loudly talking to an ambulance driver, so Jordan needed to ask the operator to repeat the number. She quickly wrote it down.

She settled on the bench as the call went through.

"Hello." It was Angela on the other end. Jordan held her hand over her other ear to block out the background noise.

"Hello, Angela."

"Jordan? Hey, Jordan! How are you doing? Jaffee's sure going to be happy to hear from you. He's really been fretting over Dora."

"Is this a busy time at the restaurant? Should I call back?"

"We're closed. We had bankers' hours today. Jaffee made a triple-sized chocolate sheet cake and drove it over to Trumbo's house in Bourbon. His wife, Suzanne, is having her monthly bridge club."

"I'm sorry I missed Jaffee. Please tell him I'll call tomorrow."

"Oh, no, don't wait till tomorrow. You can catch him over at the Trumbo house. Jaffee's wife is one of the bridge players in the club, so Jaffee drives her to Bourbon and waits to bring her back home. It's the same every month. He takes a big old chocolate sheet cake for Suzanne to serve and a bottle of Bailey's Irish whiskey for Dave to lace his coffee with. Since he has to drive back home, Jaffee says he only drinks his coffee straight. No lacing for him. He'll be sitting there in Dave Trumbo's kitchen, so you can call him on the Trumbo's house phone. I know he'd be upset if you didn't call tonight."

Jordan promised she'd call Jaffee right away. She tried to hang up, but Angela wasn't quite ready to say good-bye.

"Did you hear? They say J.D. Dickey got murdered?"

"Yes, I heard that," said Jordan.

"I can't say I'm too sorry about it. Folks sure have been acting strange since we heard though. Usually when news this big hits this town, our restaurant gets jam-packed. Everyone wants to come in and jabber on about it . . . like they did after you found that professor man and Lloyd, remember? The restaurant drew real crowds then. But no one's come in to talk about J.D. It's like they're all hiding in their houses."

"I'm sure they must be frightened. Until an arrest is made . . ."

"I know what you're saying. Until then, we've got some crazy murderer running around town, so of course everyone's scared witless. Still, there's something else going on."

"I'm not sure what you mean."

"Suddenly, no one looks me in the eye. It's like they're embarrassed or something. I was in the grocery story getting some more half-and-half for the restaurant and I saw Charlene doing her shopping. I went over to say hey to her—I know she saw me—but what does Charlene do? She leaves a cart full of groceries in the middle of the aisle and speed-walks out of the store. Her face was flaming red too. Then I hear from Mrs. Scott. A similar thing happened to her over at the hardware store—only with her it was Kyle

Heffermint not looking *her* in the eye and hightailing it out of the store. I sure wish I knew what was going on." Angela sighed.

The tapes were what was going on, Jordan knew. Charlene and the others on the list obviously weren't yet sure if anyone else in town had heard about their transgressions. Oh, no doubt, they were in a panic now.

"That all sounds very strange," Jordan said.

"That's what I thought," said Angela. "Now you hang up and call Jaffee . . . Oh, but before you do, I was just wondering . . ."

"Yes?"

"I was thinking about you and Noah, and how perfect you two look together, and I wondered if you've decided to stay with him."

The question caught Jordan entirely off guard. "I . . . I don't know."

"Noah's sure a catch. But then so are you, and don't you forget it. Jaffee says he's sure he's seen your picture in one of those outdoor magazines."

Was that supposed to be a compliment? An outdoor magazine? Had Jaffee thought she'd made the cover of *Lumberjack Weekly*?

Jordan laughed. "Are you sure Jaffee didn't think he saw me in *Glamour*?"

She was teasing, but Angela was serious. "You're the Ralph Lauren type, you know?"

"Thank you, but—"

Angela interrupted. "I'm just stating the truth. Just don't make the same mistake I made, Jordan. Don't wait eighteen years for any man. And if he doesn't realize what he's got right in front of him, he's never going to know."

With that as the final word, Angela finally hung up. Jordan found another blank scrap of paper in her purse and again called information. She thought about Angela's comments while waiting for the operator to key in her request for Dave Trumbo's phone number.

Behind her, the glass doors opened. A woman walked out carrying a basket of wilted flowers. Jordan looked around and spotted her father stepping out of the elevator at the end of the hall. Behind him was Noah.

"I have two listings for a Dave Trumbo," the operator said. "A Dave Trumbo Motors at 9818 Frontage Road and a Dave Trumbo at 1284 Royal Street."

"I want the home . . . Wait. Will you repeat that second address on Royal please? Did you say 1284?"

"Yes, 1284 Royal. That number is . . ."

Jordan was so stunned she dropped her phone in her lap. Dave "I'll-make-you-a-deal" Trumbo lived at 1284 Royal.

Wait until Noah heard this! Jordan grabbed her phone and shoved it into her purse, then jumped to her feet. A car backfired, the sound huge and piercing. A nearby chunk of concrete from the pillar suddenly exploded. She instinctively pivoted to get away from the flying fragments. The car backfired again, and Jordan felt a tremendous jolt from behind. Tires screeched, and a car sped past her in a blur. She caught a glimpse of the driver out of the corner of her eye, just as her legs gave out.

Everything happened in slow motion: Noah pushing her father, running toward her, shouting, pulling his gun from his holster.

Jordan's eyes closed as she slammed into the pavement.

Chapter Thirty-eight

THE HOSPITAL WAS IN LOCKDOWN. NO ONE WAS GETTING IN OR out until the all clear was sounded. Policemen blocked every entrance, and emergencies were temporarily being shuffled to other medical centers. The police also were doing a thorough search of the garage and a floor-by-floor search of the hospital to make certain there weren't any other shooters hiding inside.

The attempted murder of a federal judge was big news, and there were television crews set up on all sides of the hospital. They were all competing to get an interview with anyone who might be able to tell them what had happened.

Judge Buchanan's daughter was reported to be in critical condition. One reporter speculated—on the air no less—that if Jordan hadn't been within seconds of emergency personnel, she would have bled to death.

That was something the Buchanan family didn't need to hear. They were gathered in the surgical waiting room, talking in whispers and pacing while they waited for Jordan to emerge from surgery.

Two policemen stood guard outside the door and had made it perfectly clear that they weren't going to let Judge Buchanan out of their sight until his bodyguards took over. Two of them were on their way to the hospital now.

Judge Buchanan had aged twenty years since he'd watched his daughter crumble to the ground. Noah had thrown him into a wall to get him out of the line of fire. The judge had heard him yell, "Down! Get Down!" as he raced toward Jordan. He'd never forget the look on Noah's face when he'd knelt beside Jordan. He looked destroyed.

Jordan's mother sat beside her husband, gripping his hand. Tears streaked down her face.

"Someone needs to call Sidney," she said. "I don't want her to hear it on the news. Has anyone called Alec? Dylan? Where's Father Tom?"

"He's on his way back to Holy Oaks," the judge told her.

"Someone needs to call him. He'll want to know. And we need a priest here now."

"She's not going to die," Zachary, the youngest, shouted angrily.

Noah had separated himself from the family. He didn't want to talk to anyone. He couldn't talk now. Standing in front of a window across the room from the others, he stared blankly out into the night. It was difficult to breathe, impossible to think. He was in a cold rage. Blood . . . there had been so much blood. He had felt Jordan slipping away from him.

This waiting was horrific. He'd been shot before, and he remembered it had hurt like hell, but that pain was nothing compared to what Noah was feeling now. If he lost her . . . Oh God . . . he couldn't lose her . . . couldn't live without her . . .

Nick had taken the elevator down to Laurant's room to tell her what had happened. His wife was sound asleep, and so he decided not to wake her. He pulled the plug on the television set on his way out the door and told the nurse on duty not to mention the shooting. Tomorrow would be soon enough to hear such bad news.

When Nick returned to the surgical floor, he spotted Noah standing alone. He went to stand beside him.

And the wait continued.

Twenty minutes later, the surgeon, Dr. Emmett, walked into the room. He was smiling as he pulled off his cap. Judge Buchanan rushed to meet him.

"Jordan did just fine," the doctor said. "The bullet went through her rib cage, and she lost some blood, but I expect a full recovery."

The judge shook the doctor's hand and thanked him profusely.

"How soon can we see her?" he asked.

"She's in recovery now, and she's already coming out of the anesthesia. I'll let one of you go in, but only for a minute. She needs to rest." The surgeon started for the door. "If you'll follow me."

The judge didn't move. "Noah?"

"Sir?"

"If she's awake, give her our love."

Nick had to give him a shove to get him moving. The news that Jordan was going to be okay had made Noah weak with relief. He followed the doctor down the hall.

"Just one minute," Dr. Emmett instructed. "I want her to sleep."

Jordan was the only patient in the recovery room. A nurse was checking her IV, and when she saw Noah, she stepped out of the way.

Jordan's eyes were closed.

"Is she in pain?" he asked.

"No," said the nurse. "She's coming in and out of consciousness."

Noah stood beside her bed, content to watch her sleep. His hand rested on top of hers, and he could feel the warmth. The color was returning to her face.

He leaned down and kissed her forehead and then whispered into her ear, "I love you, Jordan. You hear me? I love you, and I'm never letting you go."

"Noah . . ." Her voice was a hoarse whisper. She didn't open her eyes as she said his name.

He wasn't sure she had heard him, and so he tried to soothe her. "I love you. You're going to be okay. The surgery is over, and you're in recovery. You need to rest now. Sleep, Sugar."

She tried to raise her hand, and her brow wrinkled into a frown.

"Sleep now," he whispered, gently stroking her hair.

"He shot me." Though weak, her voice was surprisingly clear.

"Yes, you were shot, but you're going to be fine."

She struggled to open her eyes, but her eyelids were too heavy. "I saw him."

She drifted off again. Noah waited. She saw him? She saw the shooter? Did she know what she was saying?

She whispered the words again. "I saw him."

Her voice faded. He leaned over her with his ear close to her lips. Her words were faint but slow and measured. "He tried to kill me . . . Dave . . . Trumbo."

She fell back into a deep sleep.

Chapter Thirty-nine

DID JORDAN UNDERSTAND WHAT SHE HAD TOLD HIM? OR was she hallucinating from the drugs that were still in her system? Noah had to make sure. He waited by the side of her bed, and each time she awoke he asked her again to tell him what she had seen.

The answer was always the same. Dave Trumbo.

Her eyes were open now, and he could see that she was in pain.

"You have to let her sleep," the nurse told him. "You've been in here fifteen minutes, and that's enough time."

"She's hurting," he said anxiously.

"Yes," she said. "I was just about to give her something. It's important to keep ahead of the pain. She'll sleep until tomorrow. She'll be moved to ICU by then."

The nurse injected morphine into the IV. He waited until she had finished and then asked, "Does she know what she's saying?"

"I doubt it," she answered. "Most of my patients don't make much sense at all. And she won't remember anything she said by tomorrow."

Noah kissed Jordan again and went out into the hallway. Nick leaned against the wall, waiting for him.

"I don't know what to do," Noah said. "I can't think . . ."

"Jordan's going to be okay. Take a breath, Noah. It'll be all right."

He didn't understand. "Yeah, I know she's going to be okay. That's not the problem now. She told me something, and I don't know if I should believe her or not."

"What'd she tell you?"

"She saw the shooter," he said. "She's pretty out of it," he admitted, "but she kept saying the same thing. Her voice was getting stronger, and she seemed more alert. I tell you, I think she did see the bastard. I heard the car tearing out of the parking lot, but I got outside too late to see it."

"I don't know if you can believe anything she said. She's drugged . . ."

Noah threaded his fingers through his hair in agitation. "The nurse told me she hears some crazy things, but still . . ."

"You gotta wait until Jordan really wakes up. She's going to be in so much pain they'll keep her sedated for at least twenty-four hours. It will be a while before she's lucid."

Noah shook his head. "She saw him, and she told me who he was. Dave Trumbo. He's the guy who sells cars in Bourbon. A big shot around Serenity. I don't think you met him."

"Why would a car salesman come all the way to Boston to kill Jordan?"

"I don't know, but ten to one he wouldn't come here unless he thought she could connect him to the three murders in Serenity. I'm not going to wait around until she's clear of the pain medication."

"You can't put his name out there yet. What if it's all in Jordan's head? You have to have more before you go after him."

Noah nodded. "It's Trumbo."

"Easy way to find out. Call him at home. If he answers the phone, you'll know Jordan dreamed it up."

Nick got the number from information. He made sure he'd blocked the caller ID and handed the phone to Noah.

Trumbo's wife answered.

Noah's voice was syrupy sweet. "Hi, there. This is Bob. I'm really sorry I'm callin' so late."

"Oh, it isn't late," she said.

"Could I speak to Dave? He told me to call him if I had a question about my car, and darned if I can't figure out this remote alarm thing."

"I'm so sorry, Bob, but Dave's not here. He's in Atlanta at a big auto show. May I take your number and have him call you?"

"I'm in a real fix. Don't know if you can hear it, but the car's alarm is blarin' away outside and is wakin' up all the neighbors. Do you happen to know where he's stayin' in Atlanta?"

"No, I don't. What a shame. He just called me a few minutes ago. But he was in such a hurry, we didn't have long to talk, so I didn't get the name of his hotel. He was planning on coming home tomorrow but said something's come up and he may have to stay in Atlanta longer. What about the service manager? I'm sure he'd be happy to help you. I could give you that number."

"I really appreciate it, but I think I should be able to work this out myself. Hope Dave's havin' a good time in Atlanta. 'Bye now."

Noah disconnected the call, looked at Nick, and said, "That son of a bitch is here. She said he's at an auto show in Atlanta, but he's here, Nick."

They headed down the hall toward the waiting room.

"What do you know about this Dave Trumbo?" Nick asked.

"He's a car dealer. That's about it, except for two other things. He isn't home, and he hasn't told his wife where he's staying in Atlanta."

"We need more than that to go after him. He could be taking a vacation with his mistress or maybe he really is at a car show. I'll get some agents to look for him in Atlanta. They can check the show as soon as it opens tomorrow morning."

Noah nodded. Nick was calming him down. "Okay, good," said

Noah. "We've got to see what we can find out about Trumbo. Call Chaddick and tell him what happened. See if he can get any leads to locate him. And tell him he's got to figure out a way . . . a quiet way . . . to get Trumbo's fingerprints."

"You think he's in the system?"

"That's what we need to find out. I want to know everything there is to know about him."

Nick nodded. "I'll run his name and see what I can come up with. One phone call and we can get his history."

"Is your father still here?" Noah asked.

"Yeah, why?"

"I want to put a twenty-four-hour guard on Jordan, and I want her to stay in critical condition. Your father needs to know that the party line is that Jordan's still critical."

"Okay, what else?"

"Find Trumbo. If Jordan knows something that connects him to the murders, he's going to come after her again."

Chapter Forty

NICK HAD TAKEN OVER ONE OF THE HOSPITAL'S WAITING rooms and was using it as a command post as he called in every possible favor. He got Pete Morganstern out of bed to make calls because he knew the eminent doctor could get the information much quicker than either he or Noah could.

Noah was also on the phone to Texas, Chaddick had really come through for him. Noah didn't know how the agent had accomplished it, but he had gotten into Trumbo's office and had taken several items he was certain had Trumbo's fingerprints on them. One of those items was a coffee mug with the imprint "Best Dad in the World."

Chaddick gave Noah an update while on his way to the lab. "Should have something in a couple of hours . . . *hopefully* a couple of hours," he qualified. "How is Jordan doing?"

"Okay," Noah said. "She's sleeping."

"It's a hell of a situation we've got here," Chaddick said. "Street is on his way to the office. He'll run a computer search on Trumbo and see what he can find."

There were now at least four agents searching through the FBI's voluminous computer files, but Dr. Morganstern was the first to break the strange news to Noah.

"Dave Trumbo's life started fifteen years ago. According to the records, he didn't exist before then. New social security number, new name, new everything."

"Witness protection?"

"Maybe," Morganstern agreed. "I'm waiting to hear something more. Fingerprints would certainly save us some time. Any possibility . . ."

Noah told him about Chaddick. "As soon as he knows something, he'll call. I'm betting his prints are in the system."

Noah found Nick and explained what Morganstern had found out. Nick wasn't surprised. He'd heard the same information from another source a short while ago.

Every few minutes Noah would look in on Jordan to assure himself that she was sleeping soundly. He was becoming so familiar with the monitoring devices, he didn't need to ask how her body was responding to trauma. Her pulse and blood pressure were both steady. The rhythmic beeping sound of her heart was a comfort to him.

He didn't sleep at all through the night, and when he had gone in to check on Jordan around seven, they were in the process of moving her to a private room.

"It's a step down from ICU," the nurse said. "She's doing just great. Once we get her settled, you can sit in the room with her."

It was great news. He was walking out of the unit when the nurse caught up with him.

"Excuse me . . . Agent Clayborne?"

"Yes?"

"Is the patient still supposed to be listed as critical?"

"That's right," he said.

She looked worried. "I'm afraid word will get out. Someone will leak it to the media. They always do."

He agreed. "I'm just trying to buy us a little more time." He was desperate to find out who Trumbo was before that news was also leaked to the press.

Nick had done a complete turnaround from the night before. He now wanted to plaster Trumbo's face and name everywhere.

Noah held him off. "Obviously fifteen years ago he changed his identity. He can do it again," he pointed out. "And we would never know if and when he might come after Jordan again. We have to wait until we hear from Chaddick. We both know the guy's been hiding from something, so his fingerprints are bound to turn up on a file."

Noah paced for a while and then went into Jordan's new sterile, white room. He stood at the foot of the bed watching her, his hands shoved in his pockets.

Nick entered a minute later. "Man, you look worse than she does," he whispered.

They both noticed her smile. It was fleeting, but it was there. "You hear us, Jordan?" Noah asked.

She smiled again. And then she fell back asleep.

Judge Buchanan stood at the door. "How is she?" he asked.

Noah beckoned to him. "She's good."

"I'll sit with her for a while," the judge said. He quietly pulled the chair close to the bed. "Go get some rest," he ordered both of them, knowing full well neither would. Nick turned to follow Noah out the door when his father called his name.

"Nicholas."

"Sir?"

The judge got up and walked into the hallway so he wouldn't disturb his daughter.

"Your wife would like to have a word with you."

"She's awake?" he asked, surprised. He quickly looked at the time. "It's already past seven? I thought it was . . ." He shook his head. "I've lost about four hours. Does Laurant know about Jordan?"

"Yes, she does. She was watching the news when your mother and I walked in."

"I unplugged the television . . ."

"Apparently, someone plugged it back in. Your mother's sitting with her, and both of them want an update on Jordan's condition. I'll switch places with your mother in a little while. She'll want to be with Jordan."

Nick took the stairs to get to Laurant while Noah went back into the waiting room to call Chaddick. He'd been checking in with him every half hour. He was probably driving the agent nuts, but Noah didn't care. He'd stop harassing him when he got the information he needed.

Dr. Morganstern appeared in the doorway. Noah raised his index finger to ask him to wait while he answered Chaddick.

"Okay, I've got his name," Chaddick blurted.

"Who is he?"

"Paul Newton Pruitt."

Noah repeated the name for Morganstern.

"Have you ever heard of him?" Chaddick asked.

"No. Tell me," he ordered.

"For openers, he's been dead for fifteen years. Yeah, I know, he isn't dead," he rushed on. "I'm just telling you what I read. Pruitt was connected. He testified against a mob-connected guy named Chernoff. Ray Chernoff. No doubt you've heard of Chernoff. Pruitt's testimony sent him away for a couple of life sentences. Pruitt was supposed to stay in protective custody and testify at two other trials, and then they were going to put him in witness protection."

"So what happened?" he asked as he rubbed the back of his neck to ease his tension.

"Pruitt vanished," Chaddick continued. "That's what happened. The agents in charge found blood in his apartment. A lot of blood, and all of it was his. No body though. After a lengthy investigation, they concluded he was killed by one of Chernoff's associates. They also concluded that they'd never find his body."

"He staged his own death and started over."

"And he did a fine job of it until now," Chaddick added.

"Was Chernoff's trial high-profile?" asked Noah.

"It sure was."

"Lots of camera time?"

"As I recall, not a lot," said Chaddick. "They tried to keep it out of the press to protect their witnesses, but you know how that goes. Why?"

"Jordan told me that Professor MacKenna had bragged to her that he never forgot a face. I'll just bet the professor saw Pruitt and recognized him. That's it!" said Noah.

"The cash deposits. MacKenna was blackmailing him. Nasty," Chaddick muttered. "It seems to me, half of Serenity was being blackmailed by J.D. I couldn't figure the professor's angle, but it looks like he had a rather lucrative sideline as well."

Noah dropped down on the sofa and hunched forward into the phone. "So now we know."

"I'm telling you, everyone under the sun is going to go after this guy. You're going to get flooded with agents wanting in on this. And if Chernoff's gang hears that Pruitt's surfaced, they're going to be on the lookout for him too. I just hope he hasn't already gone to ground."

"No," Noah said. "He's still here."

"You're sure?" Chaddick didn't wait for confirmation. "I'm getting on the next plane to Boston. I want to be in on this too. I talked to Trumbo. I mean Pruitt. Hell, I shook his hand."

"You're serious? You're coming here?"

"Damn right. Wait to kill him, okay?"

It was funny really—Chaddick assuming Noah would find Pruitt and also assuming he'd kill him. But in fact that was exactly what Noah planned to do.

Chapter Forty-one

HAD HE GOTTEN THE JOB DONE OR NOT? WAS JORDAN Buchanan going to live or die? Ironically, Pruitt's life hung in the balance as well. If she survived, he'd have to go back and finish the job, but if she died, he could return to his family and his work.

She was still listed in critical condition. Pruitt had called the hospital twice during the night for an update. He'd gotten through to ICU with his second call and had been informed by an efficient but harried nurse that Jordan Buchanan had not regained consciousness.

He had checked into a run-down motel close to the airport to wait it out. He'd snatched only a couple of hours' sleep, staying glued to the television news station. The early-morning news on Channel 7 ran a story on Judge Buchanan and his impressive career on the bench. On another local channel there was a taped interview with a matronly woman with bleached straw hair and painted-on eyebrows who swore she had witnessed the shooting. She was quite animated as she described what had happened. She had just walked out of the hospital when gunfire erupted. She insisted that, had she been one minute later, she would have been the innocent victim instead of the poor federal judge's daughter. She told the interviewer she was cutting behind an ambulance to get to her car when the gunfire started blazing.

Her account of the shooting was all wrong. She claimed to have seen two men firing at the judge, one hanging out the passenger window of a late-model Chevy sedan. As the car careened around the corner, both the driver and the other man opened fire. Logistically, what she claimed was impossible. If there had been two men and both had been firing their weapons, then one of the gunmen would have been shooting into parked cars.

The TV reporter doing the interview didn't catch the inconsistency. His voice reeked of false sympathy. "That must have been terrifying. Did you see Judge Buchanan's daughter fall? Can you remember how many shots were fired? Did you see them? And could you identify them?"

"No," she'd answered. That was the only time during the interview the woman seemed nervous. No, she couldn't possibly identify either one of them. Their faces had been covered, and they were wearing hoodies.

And on it went. The more sympathy and interest the newscaster showed, the bigger and more outrageous the story became. The pathetic woman was making the most of her moment of fame. Eager to please and impress, she smiled into the camera and continued to embellish her account.

The good news for Pruitt was that every news bulletin update began with the same lead-in, the attempted murder of a federal judge.

It was an automatic assumption, and there weren't any questions raised. Why would there be? There had been death threats against the judge. Of course he was the target, and his daughter was just an innocent bystander.

But Pruitt still needed to destroy the copies of the research. He was going to buy a paper shredder from an office supply store. He'd already searched through the phone book and found several that were at least twenty miles away from the hospital. He then planned to return to the motel and spend the afternoon shredding and stuffing plastic bags with the confetti paper. When he was finished, he would drop the bags into the Dumpster behind the motel and be done with that problem.

That stupid little man had almost destroyed his life. Pruitt didn't feel an ounce of remorse for killing him. The bastard had been blackmailing him and deserved to die. The fool obviously had not guessed the lengths Pruitt would go to to protect himself.

A stupid twist of fate, Pruitt thought. That's what it was. Someone had walked into his showroom to look around while his car was being repaired in the service department. He'd seen Pruitt then, and as he had explained later over the phone in a disguised voice, he had recognized him from the Chernoff trial coverage. The man bragged that he'd never forgotten a face, and Pruitt's face was especially memorable. At one point, Pruitt had been led into a courthouse to testify against the patriarch of the Chernoff family. He had tried to cover his head as he was rushed into the building, but despite the law's attempt to keep his picture out of the media, the cameras had gotten a couple of good shots.

By testifying and telling family secrets, Pruitt had been breaking the code, but he'd been promised amnesty, and his freedom was worth any price he had to pay. He'd worked as an enforcer and a collector for the Chernoff family, and he'd given the prosecutor names. He also swore under oath that he had witnessed his employer, Ray Chernoff, murder his own wife, Marie Chernoff. Pruitt's details about the crime were so accurate, the jury believed him. When that crime was added to a myriad of others, Chernoff received three consecutive life sentences.

Most of what Pruitt had told the jury was true. He was quite specific about the killings ordered by the boss when a "client" refused to cooperate. He'd only tweaked a few important facts. He lied when he said that he himself had never killed anyone. He also lied when he said that he had witnessed Ray brutally stabbing his wife to death. In reality, it was Paul Pruitt who had killed Marie Chernoff. The opportunity had presented itself, and Pruitt pinned the murder on Ray Chernoff.

After the verdict, Ray was dragged out of the courtroom screaming at Pruitt, swearing revenge.

Killing Marie was the most difficult thing Pruitt had ever done, and to this day he thought about her. Oh, how he had loved her.

He had been quite the womanizer before he had met her at a Christmas party. The second he laid eyes on her, he had fallen in love with her. They started their affair that very night, and he pledged his undying love to her at each of their clandestine meetings from then on.

But sweet Marie became consumed with guilt. She would meet him and spread her legs for him, and then she would get dressed and go to church to light a candle for her sin of adultery. After a while, even that wasn't enough. She told Pruitt she wanted to end their affair, that she would confess her sins to her husband and beg forgiveness. Pruitt remembered picking up the knife and walking toward her. He hadn't meant to kill her. He just wanted to scare her a little, make her see that both of their lives would be over if she told. But Marie got hysterical and he couldn't stop. He'd cried as he stabbed her.

He justified his actions by telling himself there hadn't been any other way. Ray might have forgiven Marie for her infidelity, but he certainly wouldn't have forgiven Pruitt. In the end, didn't it come down to kill or be killed?

Once Ray Chernoff was put away, Pruitt thought he might have a chance. But things didn't work out. Though Chernoff was behind bars, he still had plenty of connections on the outside, and the government's promise of protection was a joke. Even if they relocated Pruitt, he'd be watched. No, he had to take care of himself. For several weeks he lived the life of a paranoid, and then, finally, one day he arrived home to see a shadow on the stairwell. There was no mistaking the fact that the man hiding one flight above him was pointing a gun and lying in wait for him. Pruitt took off and hid in a bar down the street until the coast was clear. Then he cautiously returned to his apartment and did what he had to do. As far as anyone knew, Paul Pruitt died that day.

For the last fifteen years he'd lived a lie. He'd been so careful. After the first ten years, he began to relax. He had moved as far away from his home as he could imagine, settling in a small town in Texas. He got a job selling cars in Bourbon and eventually worked his way into owning the dealership. He'd even managed to find a wife who wouldn't ask too many questions. When people suggested that he do more advertising, he declined. He never wanted a camera near him. He was content right where he was. He had enough money to feel important. Maybe his ego got the better of him a time or two. He did like it when people looked up to him. He had earned some respect as Dave Trumbo in his part of the world, and he liked the fact that they were glad to see him when he came around.

The call from an anonymous man who had recognized him threatened to take everything away. After that first message, he'd tried to track down the caller. Every time he put the cash in the manila envelope and mailed it to another post office box, he'd try to find out who the blackmailer was, but each time the mystery man called, he'd give Pruitt a different address. Pruitt had even hidden and waited by one of the post offices to see who would carry out the package, the one he had marked with a fluorescent yellow pen. He'd put in two long days and nights sitting in a car on a street in Austin, binoculars in his lap, hoping to catch a glimpse of the bastard. When no one picked up the money in that time, he had returned to Bourbon. As the demands for money increased over the next month, Pruitt grew more panicky.

J.D. Dickey put an end to all of that. Pruitt had never met the man, but he'd heard about him. He knew he'd been in prison and also knew his brother was the sheriff of Jessup County. He had to give it to J.D. for having the balls to walk into his office, shut the door, and calmly tell him he could help him solve his little problem.

And what would that problem be? Pruitt remembered asking.

J.D. had laid it all out on the table. He explained he'd gotten into a new line of work that he found quite lucrative. He was now into blackmail. Before Pruitt could react to his confession, J.D. put his hands up and assured him that he hadn't blackmailed him, and he had no plans to do so in the future.

He wanted to work for him. Pruitt remembered the conversation almost word for word. J.D. had told him how he would spend his days and evenings cruising neighborhoods and listening in on conversations with his surveillance equipment. If he heard something interesting, like a man cheating on his wife, well then, he'd make a note of it. Sometimes he'd even get into a room and set up a microphone or a camera. He found that videotaping sex brought him a lot of money. Some Serenity residents had some peculiar sexual habits. J.D. then gave Pruitt several examples.

It took J.D. a while to get back to Pruitt's problem, but Pruitt didn't mind. He was fascinated by what he was hearing. J.D. finally came around to the subject of Pruitt's blackmailer. He explained that he had been parked up the street from the man's house and had listened in as he talked to Pruitt on one of his cell phones. He didn't know what Pruitt had done but assumed that he was probably having an affair or maybe something more serious, like skimming money off his profits at the dealership and not reporting it to the IRS. J.D. said he didn't care what he had done, but he could help him get rid of his blackmailer. He could chase him out of town. And he would do it free of charge if Paul would put him on his payroll for future problems. Maybe he could be like a lawyer and be on retainer, J.D. suggested.

Pruitt quickly agreed. Relieved that J.D. didn't have a clue about his real identity, he made the decision then and there to force J.D. to help him get rid of the blackmailer. Then Pruitt would get rid of J.D.

When J.D. gave up the professor's name, he didn't have any notion that he was signing MacKenna's death warrant. Pruitt told J.D. that he wanted to talk to MacKenna before J.D. scared the professor into leaving town. He asked J.D. to meet him at MacKenna's house, though J.D. hadn't known the professor was going to die.

Pruitt now remembered how he had had a good laugh as he told J.D. that he was now an accomplice to murder, and right then he was going to get rid of the professor's body for Pruitt.

J.D. was terrified. Pruitt didn't care. He told him to follow his orders and everything would be just fine. The first priority was to get rid of the body.

In retrospect, Pruitt realized he should have been more specific. He also should have realized how stupid J.D. was. He shook his head as he thought about it. J.D. believed he was so clever, dumping the professor's body in Jordan Buchanan's car because she was a stranger in town. He thought he could place the blame on her, and he had it all set up. Or so he thought.

But J.D. hadn't expected Lloyd to witness him stuffing the professor's body in the trunk. And J.D. hadn't expected that Pruitt—or Dave, as he knew him—would do whatever it took to keep Lloyd's fat mouth shut. In fact, he hadn't thought much of anything through. J.D. certainly hadn't thought that Dave Trumbo would kill him.

Paul Pruitt stacked his hands on his chest and leaned back. It would have been so much simpler for all involved if J.D. had taken the professor's body out into the desert and buried it, but he had to go and try to be clever instead.

Pruitt fell asleep wondering if he'd killed J.D. outright when he'd clobbered him from behind. Or had J.D. simply been stunned, and had he felt the fire eating his flesh?

Chapter Forty-two

PILLOWS TUCKED ALL AROUND HER, JORDAN WAS SITTING UP in bed—with medical assistance—when Noah checked on her later in the afternoon.

She looked pale again, which Noah mentioned to the nurse after the woman finished checking Jordan's temperature.

"Well, she's been up and has walked a few steps today," she said cheerfully. "She's worn out."

Jordan was more clearheaded each time he saw her. She took this opportunity to plead her case again. "May I have some water *please*?" she asked.

The nurse briskly shook her head. "Absolutely not. Nothing at all by mouth yet. I'll get you a cold washcloth and maybe a few ice chips."

What was she supposed to do with a washcloth? Noah waited until the nurse left, then came around to the side of the bed and gently touched Jordan's hand. "How are you feeling?"

"Like I've been shot." She sounded disgruntled.

"Yeah, well, that's what happened, Sugar."

So much for sympathy. Her mother had sat at her bedside most of the morning, and each time Jordan opened her eyes, her mother was dabbing the tears on her cheeks, asking what she could do to make Jordan feel better. She also kept calling Jordan "you poor darling." Noah, on the other hand, went the opposite route, acting like getting shot wasn't any big deal. Jordan much preferred his approach.

"I'll bet you're anxious to get back to your life," she told him.

She sounded pitiful. Her eyes closed for a second, and she didn't see his exasperated expression.

"Don't go to sleep just yet," he said.

"That's a change. Everyone else who comes in here insists again and again that I sleep."

"Do you remember what you told me in recovery?"

She eyed him suspiciously. "Was I talking a lot?"

"Not too much," Noah said with a laugh. "But you did say something about the shooting."

Her eyes widened with the returning memory. "Yes . . . Dave Trumbo tried to kill me." Then, as though what she had said finally penetrated, she continued. "Why did he shoot me? What did I ever do to him?" She thought for a minute and said sarcastically, "I guess maybe I should have bought a car from him."

She closed her eyes and tried to think. She knew she wanted to tell Noah something else, but she couldn't remember what it was.

"You didn't do anything to him," he assured her. "You can sleep now. We'll talk later."

Noah moved the chair close to Jordan and sat. He was so weary. If he could rest for just a minute . . .

"Did you figure it out yet? I did." Her voice interrupted his dreams.

He looked over at her and saw a smile. "What did you figure out?"

"The date—1284. And the crown."

"What are you talking about?"

"MacKenna's research papers, remember?"

"Yes, I remember."

"The date isn't a date."

Did Jordan know she wasn't making any sense? "Okay," he agreed, tentatively.

"It's Trumbo's address. 1284 Royal Street. That's where he lives. So why don't you go there and get him so I can have a little chat with him?"

Noah smiled. The old Jordan was coming back full force.

"I can't believe I didn't figure it out earlier. In my defense," she continued, "I was reading historical research. But you know what else?"

"Tell me."

"Trumbo saw it. It's the only way he could have known."

"What did he see?"

"When he first met me, I was in Jaffee's restaurant, and I had a lot of the research spread out on the table. He called it homework. He had to have seen it."

Her mouth was dry and her throat was sore. She swallowed and said, "Trumbo saw the date, 1284, and a crown. What he saw was his address in MacKenna's papers, but we didn't know what it was. The boxes I mailed . . . they're inside my apartment. There might be more incriminating information about him in those pages. You should send someone over. It's evidence now."

Noah made the call to Nick then and there. "We've got people on their way," he assured her.

"They'll need my key."

"No they won't. They can get in. You can rest now."

"So you didn't catch him yet?"

"Not yet. But I will."

Jordan's eyelids drooped, and he waited until she'd drifted off before he closed his own eyes.

An hour later, Nick shook him awake. "They're waiting for us."

Noah sat up with a start. His hand automatically went for the snap on his holster. "What the . . ."

"Wake up. They're waiting," Nick repeated.

"Lower your voice. You'll wake Jordan."

Nick laughed. "She's already awake. You were out. We've been carrying on a conversation for a couple of minutes now."

It wasn't until Noah stood up that he realized that Judge Buchanan and Jordan's youngest brother, Zachary, were in the room with them. Nick motioned for Noah to follow him out to the hallway. Noah caught himself before he ordered a federal judge not to wear out his own daughter.

Nick walked toward the elevators. "I've got some bad news," he said. "Pruitt broke into Jordan's apartment. He took the copies."

"Ah, hell." Noah cursed his stupidity. "Why didn't I send someone over there sooner?"

"Jordan got shot. She's been your priority . . . and mine."

Noah issued a deep sigh. He couldn't let his guard down. He needed to be on his game now more than ever before. For Jordan's sake. "I need caffeine."

"Pete's waiting for us in the cafeteria. Food's bad, but you should eat something. I did, and it was god-awful."

"Good advertisement. I can't wait!"

The elevator was taking too long, so they took the stairs. Dr. Morganstern was sitting alone at a corner table. Noah grabbed a soda and went over to join him.

There was an untouched dinner salad in front of Pete. He saw Noah looking at it. "Reminds me of my days in medical school," Pete said with a disgusted scowl, pushing the plate away. "Let's get down to business," he said. "There are several agents eager to take this case. They're anxious to get Pruitt, and they want him alive."

"Hold on," Nick said. "Are they thinking they'll give him another pass if he'll testify against some more of Chernoff's associates?"

"To be honest, I don't know. They're being evasive."

"Pruitt killed three people in Serenity and was trying for four with Jordan. No way is this lowlife gonna get a pass," Nick countered.

"That is not our decision . . ."

"Yes, it is." Noah was emphatic.

Nick backed him up. "Damn right."

Dr. Morganstern didn't pull rank on them. "I happen to agree with you," he said.

"Where are these agents?" Nick asked.

"Across town, waiting for the okay."

"Okay for what?"

He sighed. "To go public with our search for Pruitt."

"That's crazy," Noah protested. "He'll vanish."

"And what do you propose?" Pete asked.

"They're playing this all wrong," said Noah.

"I'm listening."

"Pruitt thinks he's safe for now. But he doesn't know what's in those papers, and whether we have any more information about him."

"But how can you be sure that's what he thinks?"

"Because he's here. Everyone's on the lookout for him, and he hasn't surfaced. Pruitt's cautious. Jordan told me that she had the research papers spread out in front of him with his street number right there plain as day. He might suspect there's other incriminating information in the professor's research."

"He thinks he can still fix this," Nick added.

"Yes, and he's halfway there," Noah concurred. "He broke into Jordan's apartment and got the copies."

"Now what?" Pete asked.

"Jordan," Noah answered. "Pruitt's waiting to hear if she makes it or not."

The doctor drummed his fingers on the table. "If we put Pruitt's name out there, we'll lose him."

"Exactly," Noah said. Nick nodded.

"We can't let that happen. You have a plan?" said Pete.

Noah was glad he asked. "Yes, sir, I do. We're setting a trap for this rat."

"Where?" Nick asked.

Noah said, "I'm going to lure Pruitt back to Jordan's apartment, but we'll have to move fast to set it up."

Nick smiled, but Pete frowned, saying, "And how are you going to accomplish that?"

"Just one phone call," Noah answered. "That's all it will take."

Chapter Forty-three

"ANGELA. THIS IS NOAH CLAYBORNE."

"Oh, my goodness. Noah!" On the other end of the phone, Angela was clearly surprised at his call. He heard a small crash and wondered if the waitress had just dropped some of Jaffee's dishes. "You poor thing. How are you doing? We were devastated to hear about Jordan. It's been all the talk around Serenity. How is she? We heard she was listed critical."

"Yes," he said. "I'm trying to stay . . . hopeful, you know? It's hard."

"Oh, I know how it is. We're all praying for her. And you too."

"She hasn't regained consciousness," he said.

He looked down at his notepad and drew a line through the first of several pieces of information he wanted to give her.

"She hasn't? I'm so sorry. I sure wish there was something I could do."

"The reason I'm calling . . ."

"Yes?" Angela said eagerly.

"They gave me her things . . . you know. And I was going

through her purse to get her phone so I could turn it off, and I saw a note she had written to herself to call Jaffee at the restaurant. I don't know . . . I was just wondering if she did call him. If so, Jaffee was probably the last person . . ." Noah paused as his voice broke.

He crossed off the second line. Was he overdoing it? Angela seemed to be buying it.

"No, Jordan didn't talk to him. She talked to me." Angela gasped. "I was probably the last person she spoke to. She seemed happy and cheerful. She told me she was going to call Jaffee, but he never did hear from her."

"Yes," Noah said. "That must have been when it happened. The gunman was trying to shoot her father, but Jordan got in his way. I blame myself," he added sadly.

"Why on earth would you blame yourself?" Angela asked.

"Jordan was waiting for me to join her, but I ran into some people I knew, and I lost track of the time. We were going to go back to her apartment. She was so excited to show me . . ." His voice broke again.

"Show you what?" Angela urged.

"You know all those research papers she made copies of?"

"Yes. She told me they were historical papers."

"That's right. But she told me that when she checked some info on her computer, she spotted something she really wanted me to see, something that didn't have anything to do with history, but she wouldn't tell me what it was."

He drew a line through another subject and continued. "I thought maybe she might have told Jaffee, but since she didn't talk to him, I'll have to get over there sometime and look myself. But not now. I'm not leaving the hospital. I wasn't by her side when she got shot, but I'm going to be there when she wakes up, no matter how long it takes. We can look at the information on her computer together when she's better. Whatever Jordan found will have to wait."

When their conversation ended, Noah hung up the phone and turned to Nick. "The word's out."

"How long will it take to reach Pruitt?"

"Hour, maybe two, tops."

THE NET WAS IN PLACE. TWO AGENTS WATCHED THE ENTRANCE TO Jordan's apartment building and two more watched the back door. All four were well hidden. Pruitt could walk past any one of them and take no notice.

Noah and Nick were parked at one end of the block in Nick's car, and two other agents were also monitoring from their parked car at the block's opposite end. A third vehicle with two more feds in it was parked in a driveway between buildings. Once Pruitt started down the street, they'd have him hemmed in.

If he came down the street.

They had been waiting for over two hours. Nick was lobbying to change locations and wait inside Jordan's apartment. "We could trap him by the computer. We could have it all set up and spring on him. Wouldn't you like a couple of minutes alone with him? I sure as hell would."

Noah rejected his plan. "It's a bad idea."

"Okay then. We could spring on him as soon as he opens the apartment door."

"That wouldn't work. It's a bad idea too."

Nick sighed. "Why? I'm telling you we could spring—"

Noah began to laugh. "What is it with you and springing?"

"An element of surprise," Nick explained with a deadpan expression.

"Okay. So, as much as I understand your need to *spring* on Pruitt, I'm not gonna let you lie in wait up there."

Nick pulled an apple from his pocket. He wiped it on his sleeve and took a big bite.

"Did I tell you about the fire at MacKenna's house?" Noah asked.

Nick took another bite before replying with his mouth full. "You said it burned down."

"It didn't just burn, Nick. That fire was nuclear. You should have seen it. It's like it imploded. The place was incinerated in a couple of minutes. Smoldered for a long time though."

"Sorry I missed it."

"Pruitt set that fire. He knows his way around chemicals."

"You did evacuate Jordan's neighbors, didn't you?"

"Yes," Noah answered.

Several minutes passed in silence. The only sound was Nick chomping on his apple. "Too bad we can't spring," he said.

"Someone's coming." Noah and Nick heard an agent's excited whisper in their earpieces.

"I see him. That's him," another said.

"You sure it's him?" the first asked.

"Black jogging suit with the hood up . . . in August. That's him. He's sure walking slow."

The figure came around the corner and into Noah's view. He leaned over the steering wheel to get a good look at him.

"Is he carrying something? Yeah, he is. What is that?" Nick asked. He looked at Noah. "Could he be cooking up another fire?"

The man turned and walked up the steps of Jordan's apartment building.

"We can't let him get inside. We have to take him down in the street," the agent closest to the man said. "Go!" he yelled.

"Wait," Noah ordered, but it was too late. Three overzealous agents swarmed into the street, guns drawn. Two pointed their guns in the man's face while the third grabbed the box the man was dropping.

Noah and Nick rushed forward.

"That's not him," Noah yelled angrily.

"What are you doing? I didn't do anything wrong," the man stammered. Barely more than a teenager, he was unshaven, and his hair looked like it hadn't seen shampoo in a month. "Be careful with that box. It's delicate. I'm not supposed to shake it." The punk was so scared, he could barely get the words out.

"What's in the box?" one of the agents barked at him.

"I don't know. A guy gave me a hundred bucks to deliver it to his girlfriend. I'm supposed to leave it at her door. Look, honest. I didn't do anything wrong."

Noah turned and sprinted back to his car. Nick was right on his heels, shouting back to the agents, "Get the bomb squad over here." He pointed to one of them, "You got this?"

"Yes, sir."

Nick dove into the car as Noah started the engine.

"Call the hospital and check on Jordan," Noah shouted. "Just to be sure."

He took the corner on two wheels. Slamming his foot on the accelerator, Noah hit the siren.

"Do you think Pruitt's onto us?" Nick asked as they raced through Boston's streets.

"No way of knowing. Pruitt could have set this kid up to do his dirty work and be on his way back to Texas, or he could have something else up his sleeve. Whatever his plan, we've got to make sure Jordan isn't a part of it."

Chapter Forty-four

HE NEEDED TO TIME IT JUST RIGHT. ANY MINUTE NOW, THE messenger Pruitt had hired would be placing the gift-wrapped box outside of Jordan's door. Liquid fire, that's how he thought of his special brew. It had worked so beautifully on MacKenna's house. And it would work beautifully again. There were enough chemicals inside that box to blow the top floor of the apartment building into the stratosphere and burn what was left to the ground. Probably overkill, he thought, but he wouldn't have to worry that Jordan Buchanan's computer might somehow still be operable.

He'd set the timer and had exactly one hour before the explosion. He needed to get to Jordan before then. Once her apartment went up, the police and the FBI would be on her at the hospital like ants on a picnic. They would then know that Jordan had been the intended target of the shooting. But if Pruitt could get to her today, no one would ever know why.

Thank God for small-town gossip. Pruitt had just arrived back at the motel, shredder in hand, when he'd gotten the phone call from his wife, Suzanne. She had just heard from Jaffee's wife, Lily, who had heard from Jaffee, who had heard from Angela that Jordan Buchanan was hanging on to life by a thread. It was just so sad that something this tragic had to happen to someone so young—and so nice. What was the world coming to? Three people killed in Serenity, and then this lovely young woman, who had been traumatized enough, goes home to Boston and gets shot down by some maniac who's out for revenge against her father? And that handsome FBI agent, Noah Clayborne, who was with her in Serenity turned out to be more than just a friend. He had called Angela and could barely talk, he was so brokenhearted. Angela had told him that Jordan's last phone call, right before she was shot, was to her. Angela said poor Noah Clayborne sounded absolutely lost. It didn't look like poor Jordan was going to make it but he was searching for a ray of hope. He was trying to think positive thoughts, planning Jordan's return home from the hospital. The last thing Jordan had said to him was something about those research papers she had come to Serenity to get. She was so excited for him to see some surprising information she'd stored on her computer—something she'd learned from the papers that the dead professor had given her. She was some sort of computer genius, everybody says. But now Noah may never know what Jordan wanted to tell him. It was all just so very sad. . . .

Suzanne cackled on, but Pruitt's mind had strayed. What other information had Jordan found in Professor MacKenna's notes? What was on her computer? Maybe she had already figured everything out.

He walked into the hospital without anyone noticing. He looked down at his feet in case security cameras were pointed his way. He wasn't worried he would be recognized. The police were looking for gangsters related to Judge Buchanan's racketeering case, right? And even if Jordan could identify Dave Trumbo, she wouldn't see him closely, not until it was too late.

The security personnel didn't pay much attention to him either. No reason to. He'd stopped at a big supermart where you could buy anything from toothpaste, to automotive parts, to professional uniforms. He'd picked up a pair of surgical scrubs. The hospital was a huge medical complex and there were so many physicians and nurses bustling about, no one paid Pruitt any attention.

The elevator opened as soon as he pushed the button, and he rode alone up to the fifth floor, mentally practicing what he would say if he was stopped by a nurse. The second he stepped off the elevator he scanned the numbers beside the doors, looking for the one he'd been given when he'd called the information desk. An arrow indicated Jordan Buchanan's room was around the corner on the right. He turned the corner and stopped. A uniformed police guard stood outside her door. Pruitt changed direction, and he had to change his plan as well.

He hadn't anticipated a guard, but that was an oversight. Of course her father would want to beef up security.

Back in the elevator, he looked at the hospital directory printed on the wall. Pushing the button for the second floor, he headed down to radiology. No one was in sight when he walked out into the empty corridor. It took only a couple of calls on his cell phone to get the name of her surgeon and her internist. Then he called the fifth floor and told the nurse that Dr. Emmett had ordered more X-rays for Jordan Buchanan.

From the sound of her voice, the nurse was young and inexperienced. She didn't ask questions. She simply hung up the phone, then promptly called radiology and gave them the doctor's verbal orders.

Pruitt heard the orderly take the call. Fortunately, it was a slow evening, and radiology was empty. Nevertheless, Pruitt had to wait ten minutes before the slow-moving blond orderly came through the doors and got on the elevator to retrieve Jordan. With an iPod in his shirt pocket and tiny earphone wires hanging from his ears, he hummed to an unrecognizable song.

Pruitt liked the isolation of his hiding place. There were dark rooms, darker corridors, and empty reception desks. The chances of anyone interrupting were not a concern.

He looked around the radiology floor and found a perfect spot in a cubicle just inside the swinging doors to the X-ray room.

Would the guard accompany Jordan to radiology? Most likely. Pruitt would have to take him first. Come up behind him and hit him hard. And while he was going down, Pruitt would grab his gun. Unless the iPod orderly hung around. Pruitt was hoping he would park an unconscious Jordan and then go to get the X-ray tech. If that didn't happen, Pruitt would have to deal with him too. That wouldn't be difficult, and he wouldn't make a sound. Pruitt's techniques for keeping his former clients quiet were all there. Funny how you didn't forget such things.

Beyond the swinging doors were several changing cubicles, where patients changed into gowns before their scans. Each had doors that clicked shut. There were clean gowns stacked on the shelves inside each cubicle, and lo and behold, a metal rod with plastic hangers.

He had thought he would have to break into the supply closet to find something he could use as a club to hit the guard, but the metal clothes rod would do just fine. It took Pruitt a few minutes to get the screws loose using a dime. About ten or twelve inches long, the rod was the perfect weight for the job. It fit nicely in his hand.

He pulled the door of the cubicle toward him, leaving it open a crack so he could see Jordan being wheeled by. He'd get a warning. He had noticed that when the button for the swinging doors was pushed on the other side, lights would come on in here.

His eyes adjusted to the dark. He wasn't sure how much time passed before he heard voices. A minute later, the lights blinked on, and he heard the whoosh of the doors slowly opening inward.

Not too eager, he calmed himself. Timing had to be perfect.

Then there they were. First he saw Jordan, then the orderly pushing her wheelchair. The guard trailed behind. That was a nice piece of luck. The guard was last, but he would be the first to be taken down.

Gripping the bar, Pruitt slowly pushed open the door and stepped out. The guard didn't hear him coming. Pruitt struck him hard at the base of the neck, reaching for the guard's gun as the man crumpled to the floor.

The orderly managed to hear the noise over his music and whirled around, confusion in his eyes. "Hey . . . what . . .?"

Down he went. The rod caught him on the side of his face just above his ear. It happened so fast he didn't have time to duck. The orderly crashed into Jordan, knocking her from the wheelchair to the floor.

Pruitt kicked the chair out of his path and picked up the gun. His eyes were cold and fiendish. Jordan wondered if that was the last sight she would see before she died. She screamed and doubled over, trying to protect herself.

Suddenly Noah crashed through the doors. Pruitt barely had time to turn his head before a bullet from Noah's gun cut through his shoulder. He swung around to reach for Jordan, but Noah shot him in the chest, and Pruitt fell to the floor with a shocked look on his dying face. He struggled to raise his gun, but Noah shot again. The explosion was deafening and reverberated down the empty corridor.

Jordan faded into its echo.

Chapter Forty-five

JORDAN WAS CURLED UP ON THE SOFA IN THE SUNROOM, PRE-tending to be asleep so her mother would stop fussing over her. She'd already covered Jordan with one afghan and was threatening to get a heavier blankct.

The windows were open and a lovely cool breeze freshened the air. She could hear the ocean waves rolling onto shore. Her parents' home on Nathan's Bay was surrounded on three sides by water. In the winter, the glass windows would be covered with a layer of ice. In the summer, a cool breeze came off the water, a welcome relief on the rare humid or hot days.

It was a lovely place to visit, but Jordan was ready to go home. She felt like she was a constant worry to her mother. And she missed her own bed. She missed her window seat.

And most of all she missed Noah. Since that terrible night in the hospital when he'd picked her up in his arms and carried her to her room, she'd missed him.

He and Nick were on an assignment. Laurant told Jordan that Nick checked in with her every night that he was away. He'd been gone four days now, but Laurant expected Nick home tomorrow. Jordan didn't ask her about Noah. That was over, and he had returned to his life. What happened in Serenity . . .

She sighed. If she didn't get up and try to be productive, she'd start crying. That's all her mother would need to hear. Then she'd have Jordan in bed with a nurse standing over her around the clock.

Her ribs were still sore, and she winced when she stood up. The housekeeper, Leah, was stacking dishes in the kitchen.

"I'll do that," Jordan offered.

"No, no, you rest."

"Leah, I know you mean well, but I am sick and tired of being told to rest."

"You lost a lot of blood. Mrs. Buchanan said you should not overtire yourself."

Jordan noticed the number of plates and followed Leah into the dining room. The oblong table took up most of the space with six chairs on each side and two at each end.

"Let's see. Laurant and Nick will be here." Leah counted. "With baby Sam," she added. "I'll bring the high chair in after I give it a good scrubbing. And Michael will be home. And Zachary of course. Alec and Regan will be here next weekend."

"So it's just family?" said Jordan.

"With Zachary always bringing home strays from college, I've gotten into the habit of setting extra places."

Jordan asked again what she could do to help, and when Leah shooed her away, she went upstairs to her old bedroom. Her parents used the room for guests these days.

She'd heard from Kate and Dylan. They were back in South Carolina, and Kate wanted Jordan to come down and recuperate there. Jordan hadn't yet made up her mind whether or not to go. She felt so restless and out of sorts.

What remained of the afternoon Jordan spent in her old room reading. Thankfully, the police had found her copied pages from

Professor MacKenna's research undamaged in the back of Pruitt's rental car. And now that she had access to research sources, she could check out the validity of the professor's stories.

At sunset, Michael came upstairs to get her. He actually suggested that he carry her down the stairs.

"My recovery period is officially over," she announced during dinner. "And I don't want any more pampering."

"That's nice, dear," her mother crooned. "Did you get enough to eat?"

Jordan laughed. "Yes, thank you."

"Nick's in the sunroom. Why don't you go say hello?"

She headed in that direction, stopping when she heard laughter. She knew that laugh. Noah was with her brother.

She backed up, stopped, thought about it, and backed up another step. She suddenly noticed how quiet it had become in the dining room. No wonder. When she looked back, she saw her family members all leaning forward, intently watching her. Now she had to go into the sunroom to say hello. Jordan took a deep breath.

Nick was sprawled on the sofa. Noah sat in an easy chair. Both were drinking beer.

"Hey, Nick. Hey, Noah."

They both laughed. "Well hello to you," Nick said.

"Hey back at you. Jordan, you're not in Serenity now," Noah interjected. "How are you doing?"

"Fine. I'm fine. I guess I'll see you later." She turned around to walk away.

"Jordan?" said Noah.

She turned back. Noah set his beer on the end table. "Yes?"

He stood and started toward her. "You remember our deal?"

"Yes, of course."

"What deal?" Nick asked.

"Never mind," Jordan said. "What about the deal?" she asked Noah.

"What deal?" Nick asked again.

"When we left Serenity, Jordan and I agreed to go our separate ways," Noah answered.

"Did you have to tell him?" she said, disgruntled.

"Yeah, well, he asked."

"If you'll excuse me," Jordan said, beginning to pivot again.

"Jordan?" said Noah.

She stopped once more. "Yes?"

He was slowly advancing. "Like I was saying . . . about that deal we made . . ." He stopped in front of her. "It's just not gonna happen."

She opened her mouth to argue, but didn't know what to say. "What do you mean?"

"Deal's off, that's what I mean. We're not going our separate ways."

"I'll give you two a little privacy," Nick said, rolling off the sofa.

"We don't need privacy," Jordan insisted.

"Yes, we do," Noah countered.

"Why?"

"Because I want to be alone with you to tell you how much I love you."

Jordan felt as though the wind had just been knocked out of her. "You do . . . No, wait. You love all women, don't you?"

Nick pulled the door shut behind him.

Noah wrapped Jordan in his arms and whispered all the words he'd been storing in his heart. He nudged her chin up and kissed her. "And you love me, don't you, Sugar?"

All her defenses melted. "Yes, I do."

"Marry me."

"And if I do?"

"You'll make me the happiest man in the world."

"Noah, if we were to get married, you couldn't date anymore."

"There you go. Always giving me attitude. I don't want any other women. Just you. Only you."

"I may be cutting back some, but I'm not giving up on computers," Jordan warned.

"Why would you think I would want you to?"

"My comfort zone? Remember that little speech?"

"Yeah, I know. It got you out of your apartment, didn't it?"

"And into your bed," she added. "You know what I've decided? I'm going to write a program that a four-year-old would understand. Then I'm going to figure out a way to get computers in schools and community centers that can't afford to buy them. You get a child started early, she'll become a natural. Technology is here, and I want to use it to write the future with."

He nodded. "That's a good start. A simple program. I'm sure Jaffee will be happy to hear about that."

"Speaking of Jaffee, I talked to Angela yesterday. She says the restaurant has been packed ever since they heard about Trumbo. The whole town is reeling from the news."

"They've had a lot to deal with lately. Chaddick tells me this bombshell has overshadowed J.D.'s list. He and Street are about to wrap things up."

Jordan shared a couple of other ideas with Noah and then listened to him talk about his work. His job was so stressful, but he made such a difference when he succeeded. The failures were devastating to him. He wanted and needed to come home to her.

He sat down on the sofa and pulled her onto his lap. "Do I need to get down on one knee?"

She smiled. "Loving you isn't easy."

"Marry me."

"You're arrogant and egotistical . . ." she paused, " . . . and sweet and loving and funny and charming . . ."

"Will you marry me?"

"Yes, I'll marry you."

Noah kissed her passionately, and when he realized how much he didn't want to stop, he pulled back. "I guess you'll want a ring," he said.

"Yep."

"What about a honeymoon?" he asked.

She nuzzled his neck. "You mean before or after the wedding?"

"After."

"Scotland. We have to go to Scotland for our honeymoon. We could stay at the Gleneagles, and then we could drive up into the Highlands."

"And look for your treasure?"

"I don't need to look. I know where it is."

"Yeah? You figured that whole feud thing out?"

"I did," Jordan boasted.

"Tell me," said Noah.

"It all started with a lie . . ." she began.

About the Author

JULIE GARWOOD is the author of numerous *New York Times* bestsellers, including *Slow Burn, Murder List, Killjoy, Mercy, Heartbreaker, Ransom,* and *Come the Spring.* There are more than thirty-two million copies of her books in print.

About the Type

This book was set in Bembo, a typeface based on an old-style Roman face that was used for Cardinal Bembo's tract *De Aetna* in 1495. Bembo was cut by Francisco Griffo in the early sixteenth century. The Lanston Monotype Company of Philadelphia brought the well-proportioned letterforms of Bembo to the United States in the 1930s.